The Kings of Ayutthaya

T0327221

THE KINGS OF
AYUTTHAYA

A Creative Retelling of Siamese History

ROBERT SMITH

 Silkworm Books

ISBN: 978-616-215-134-7

First published in 2017 by
Silkworm Books
104/5 M. 7, Chiang Mai–Hot Road, T. Suthep, Chiang Mai 50200, Thailand
P.O. Box 296, Phra Singh Post Office, Chiang Mai 50205, Thailand
info@silkwormbooks.com
http://www.silkwormbooks.com

Cover: Detail of mural in Wat Chong Nonsi, Bangkok
Photograph by Radklao Charoenrat © 2017 by Silkworm Books

Typeset in Minion Pro Regular 11 pt. by Silk Type

Printed and bound in Thailand by O. S. Printing House, Bangkok

5 4 3 2 1

CONTENTS

AUTHOR'S NOTE

The Kings of Ayutthaya is a chronological account of the development of Ayutthaya, the root of modern Thailand. It is an interpretation of the historical record, stretching from the birth of the kingdom of Sukhothai to the destruction of Ayutthaya and spanning a period of over five hundred years. The chapters are in a creative nonfiction format for each of the kings. I have adopted this approach as it allows me to impart some of the flavor of the period into each of the reigns, which builds into a picture of how the city and the nation evolved. While most of the characters in this book are historical figures, those who do not appear in the historical record are fictitious, and any resemblance to real persons, living or dead, is purely coincidental.

This book was inspired by my earlier novel *King Naresuan the Great,* which details the life of Thailand's national hero. I must confess to having included some of the text from that book in the chapters covering his reign and in the preceding chapters. Its relevance remains.

I hope this book serves as meaningful introduction or adjunct to Thai history. It is an exceptional story.

My thanks go to Bill Smart (W. D. Smart, author) and Alessandra D'Angelo for their help and support.

On a personal note, this book is an attempt to give back to the people of Thailand who have wecolmed me so readily. My hope is that this text honors their story.

Before Ayutthaya:
Sukhothai Kingdom

1

KING SI INTHRATHIT

1238–C. 1270

IT WAS A TIME OF CHANGE. The land of Lavo, with its capital at Angkor, was in decline. In the Khmer capital the drought of many years continued, refugees fleeing southward from the wars in China destabilized the existing order, and religious change caused uncertainty. The Khmer had dominated the land, including most of modern-day Thailand, for centuries. The gradual southward movement of the Tai people from the south of China into Lan Na, Sukhothai, and the Chao Phraya basin saw the region change in character and grow in confidence.

"The messenger says that General Khomsabad Khlonlampong is leaving Si Satchanalai and moving his army eastward to join up with the army of Khlon Lampong the Bold coming from Angkor. They plan to meet at Mueang Rat," said Pho Khun Bang Klang Hao, prince of Bang Yang.

"Then we must leave immediately. Our combined forces will meet General Khlonlampong before he has a chance to unite the Khmer forces. This information may prove invaluable," said Pho Khun Pha Mueang, the lord of Mueang Rat.

"It is the greed and oppression of our people that has driven us to take this action. Let him pay for his excess."

"General Khlonlampong has driven our people to near starvation. They will fight well to see him gone," said Pho Khun Pha Mueang. "If we can stop the two armies uniting, then victory will be ours."

"The general travels in great pageantry and state, with his war elephants dressed as if for show. He will move slowly."

"His arrogance may be his undoing. The Khmer are under attack from many directions, particularly from the Viet and from Lopburi to our south. I am surprised that they are mounting such a campaign. To them we are only an outpost at the western edge of their empire."

"To them it is all the same. The Khmer do not intend to surrender their empire weakly. Be assured of that."

"And I for one have no wish to live under them any longer. We do battle," said Pho Khun Bang Klang Hao, as he put his arm around his comrade. Together they left their war tent, signaling war to their troops waiting expectantly outside.

The army of General Khlonlampong was caught unawares and routed. Over one hundred elephants were captured and over one thousand impressed soldiers joined the ranks of the army of Sukhothai.

The second battle, outside the town of Mueang Rat, was a victory for the combined troops of Sukhothai. Khlon Lampong the Bold saw his troops run. He and the Khmer turned away, never to return.

The two victorious generals sat astride their horses overlooking the detritus of the battlefield and watched as those who had died were being removed from the battlefield.

"Two victors, one king," said Pho Khun Bang Klang Hao. "Only one of us can take the crown."

"You are to enter Sukhothai alone," replied Pho Khun Pha Mueang. "It is your destiny to be king. If you agree, I will be honored to serve as your general," said his elder comrade. "The Khmer are in full retreat. Lopburi and Suphanburi are distracted fighting them. Now is the time to take territory. It is my destiny to make war, now is the time to carve out the kingdom of Sukhothai with you as king."

"Sukhothai is your city. You will withdraw your troops?" asked Pho Khun Bang Klang Hao.

"I will not dispute the kingship with you, my lord. My wife is Khmer and that would count against me with the people, but it is your leadership that united and inspired us. I remain your ally and will attend your coronation, but the people need to see an undisputed leader enter the city, and that is you," said Pho Khun Pha Mueang with sincerity.

"Then I give you Si Satchanalai in return, and ask you to consecrate me at my coronation. Strengthen the walls of Si Satchanalai, as I will strengthen Sukhothai."

The clasped hands cementing their agreement. So it was that Pho Khun Bang Klang Hao entered Sukhothai alone to be crowned king:

> Afterwards Pho Khun Pha Mu'ang consecrated . . . Pho Khun Bang Klang [Hao] as Chao Mu'ang Sukhothai, and conferred his own name on his ally, that is to say the name of Sri Indrapatindraditya.

Under a white canopy fringed in gold sat the new king, surrounded by his subjects. One by one, representing their town or village they came forward to offer their suzerainty. With his war elephants in full regalia, their tusks sheathed in gold, King Si Inthrathit received the sword of Jaiyasri from Pho Khun Pha Mueang. Buddhist monks chanted as the crown was placed on his head, their presence indicating that the kingdom of Sukhothai was to be devoutly Buddhist. The kingdom of Sukhothai was born and was ruled by the first member of the Phra Ruang dynasty.

King Si Inthrathit then set out to establish his kingdom. He ruled as a village headman would, as a father figure. This was the model of kingship that would define the Phra Ruang dynasty. He was accessible to his people; he forbade slavery and did not levy taxes on the people. When he was secure the king set out to enlarge his domain, to expand the borders of Sukhothai, and to make the Theravada Buddhist faith the central tenet of his growing kingdom.

On a cool January day the new king walked with his wife, Queen Sueng, to the gleaming white Khmer Lankan-style temple of Wat Chedi Si Hong. On this still day they looked at the figure of the golden *singha* (mythical lion) sitting astride the elephants, flanked by divinities holding vases of flowers. They sat on a simple rattan mat placed there by their retainers, with a selection of local fruit in dark brown glazed bowls by their side.

"The old religion is no more," said King Si Inthrathit, as he moved his hand across the panorama of forest that lay to his south and east.

"We will build over there by that stand of trees, leaving the old intact. I will command the monks to levy the people to help them build. Sukhothai will be a center of learning and a center of our religious faith. He looked at his wife's belly. She was carrying the first of what would be their five children—three boys and two girls. One of the boys would die young, but the others would secure the dynasty.

Work progressed on strengthening the walls of the twin cities of Sukhothai and Si Satchanalai. To the south, the city of Kamphaeng Phet came to King Si Inthrathit to declare its acceptance of his suzerainty and its desire for the protection of the king of Sukhothai. The city was the first of many. As the Khmer withdrew from their western provinces a power vacuum developed; warlords arose and border disputes became rampant. Gifts were exchanged, marriages arranged, and military support provided as the kingdom of Sukhothai expanded its domain.

In 1258, twenty years into the reign of King Si Inthrathit, a further influx of refugees fleeing the Mongol conquest of southern China started to pour into the kingdoms of Bagan (central Burma) and Sukhothai and into the wider Chao Phraya basin (central Thailand) as the armies of Kublai Khan finally subdued the independent kingdom of Nanchao. As refugees flooded into the city, an exquisite golden palanquin carried by four slaves approached Sukhothai with a troop of fifty mounted soldiers. It did not take long for the refugees to identify them as the emissary and soldiers of the great khan.

"My lord and master Kublai Khan, emperor of China, son of heaven, great lord of the Mongols, and khan of the Golden Horde, sends his greetings and affection to his brother to the south," said the emissary fluently in the Tai language.

King Si Inthrathit bade the emissary sit. Tea was served, and all except the king and the Mongol emissary left the room.

"What is it you seek?" opened King Si Inthrathit.

"I have observed on my travels through your lands that you are a Buddhist people. The great lord welcomes all religions and looks favorably on your faith and on your kingdom. The great lord instructs me to ask that you accept his suzerainty and pay homage to him," said the emissary.

"The great lord honors me with his request. What is it you ask of me?" asked King Si Inthrathit.

"We ask only that you accept the great lord as your master, and pay an annual tribute of three hundred catties of silver to him as a sign of your submission," asked the emissary, clearly enjoying the moment.

"That is indeed a great sum."

"The great lord has been generous in his demands as you are of Buddhist faith. Be assured others do not receive such a generous offer."

"My kingdom is willing to accept the suzerainty of the great lord, but the amount is greater than the income of the state."

"You do not levy taxes on your people, and merchants passing through pay little tax."

"It is the way of my kingdom. We benefit in other ways, as does the emperor of China as we provide safe and unfettered access to the merchants who travel from the west."

"Your acceptance of the great lord's suzerainty is acknowledged, and the son of heaven will be pleased. You will agree to two hundred catties, then?" asked the emissary.

"It will be my honor to do so," responded King Si Inthrathit.

"Excellent, King Si Inthrathit, we will arrange details. You will send an embassy each year, and for our part we will arrange for trade between us and will, how do you say it, encourage traders to pass through your territory."

"My eldest son, Ban Mueang, is to inherit the throne. I will send my youngest son, Prince Khamhaeng, to the great khan with our tribute."

"The great khan will welcome your second son. He will see many wonderful things. An alliance with us brings many benefits," said the emissary.

When the Chinese emissary had left Sukhothai, King Si Inthrathit sat with his old comrade-in-arms, now well into his seventies, Pho Khun Pha Mueang.

"Two hundred catties. That is a sizable sum," remarked Pho Khun Pha Mueang.

"Better than the three hundred that he first demanded," replied the king. "People are flooding into the kingdom. We can produce more rice and sell the excess—other fruits as well. Some of those coming will join your army. We need to further expand our borders. We cannot go west beyond Tak and into the land of Bagan as the Chinese are to offer them terms, but we can look to the heartland, toward Song Khwae and Phrae to the north."

"My king, I am an old man now, but my sons are willing and able."

"Good, come to me with a plan. We need to expand the kingdom. We need to secure the income. We need to meet the Chinese demands," said the king.

The following year the young Prince Khamhaeng made ready for his journey to the court of the great khan. The emissary had long departed but had left two of his men to accompany the prince and the tribute. It was to be a long and arduous journey through mountains, sacred landscapes, hilltop villages, and cities—the likes of which the young Prince Khamhaeng could never have imagined.

At sixteen years of age, already well schooled in the city of Lopburi and highly trained as a warrior, the journey held no fear for the prince. He was at ease, confident with people and enthralled by the adventure. New sights, new smells—and the people, so many people! As he neared the court of the great khan he entered city upon city. Each city was protected by sturdy walls and behind them low-lying buildings with golden roofs, interspersed with red and gold temples standing proudly on the high ground. Between them stretched farmland as far as the prince could see. It was a land of rice paddies, some on the flatlands and some carved into the mountainside. There were long, straight roads, farmers moving their goods to market, women bent over as they carried loads on their backs, and soldiers riding, mindless of others, through the endless melee.

It was two weeks before the mission would arrive in the city of the great khan when the party from Sukhothai stopped at a wayside inn in the city of Jingdezhen. As usual the welcome was warm and genuine, the young prince drawing the attention of many of the serving girls. But this time Prince Khamhaeng's attention didn't go to the serving girls but to the pottery that the area was famous for. Still struggling with the language, the prince, accompanied by one of the emissary's guides, discussed the design, process, and materials with local artisans. He could envisage the same being made in Sukhothai.

The party made their way to the capital of the great khan in the newly completed summer capital of Shangdu. The prince marveled at the city, a city surrounded by a high, square, brick defensive wall and festooned with flags. As they entered the outer gate their credentials were meticulously checked by fierce-looking mustachioed soldiers before the party was taken to their accommodation.

As they passed through the streets the young prince could not help but notice the buildings, their walls of white and silver. They were decorated with magnificent paintings of beautiful women, courageous knights, winged dragons, and animals beyond the prince's imagination.

The prince looked up in awe at the house where they were to stay. It was as large as his father's palace in Sukhothai.

If this is where we are to stay then what will the palace of the great khan be like? Prince Khamhaeng thought to himself.

It would be a week until he found out. The prince from Sukhothai was schooled in how to behave in the presence of the great khan. Breaches in protocol could mean death. The young prince listened intently. He spent his spare time that week wandering around the city. The people seemed happy, and they were intrigued by this young prince from a foreign land far to the south. As he mingled and ate in their company, Prince Khamhaeng began to understand the China of the great khan.

On the evening prior to his audience with the great khan, Prince Khamhaeng attended a banquet in a majestically decorated hall where two thousand people were seated at tables. The great khan sat at the far end of the hall surrounded by wives, children, and grandchildren. The prince watched as those who approached the great khan made nine bows, as he had been taught to do. Many were rewarded with precious gems or items of jewelry that sat in an open casket next to the great khan.

After the feast, which offered so many of the most delicious foods, the entertainment began. Jugglers, magicians, dancing girls, acrobats; the parade seemed endless. Finally the great khan rose, and as he did so all in the great hall rose with him, although some needed to be supported. When he and his family left, the festivities ended and an endless procession of gilded palanquins returned the guests from whence they came.

The following day was the day of his audience, and wearing his best clothes brought with him from Sukhothai, the prince, sitting in a palanquin, passed through the Mingde gate and entered the royal palace complex. It had been dark the previous evening, so the prince had not seen the vista that now opened up before him. Inside the palace outer walls lay a landscaped paradise with lakes, bridges, mature trees, and animals, many of which were unknown to the young prince.

A giraffe came alongside the palanquin; it bowed low and its long tongue licked the prince's outstretched hand. Long-legged birds of all colors, ostriches, cranes, white deer, roe deer, deer with twisted horns, and monkeys of many different types roamed the park. He had his bearers stop, and the young prince stared amazed at the hippopotamus grazing languidly by a nearby pool.

The white and gold royal mansion of Muqingge lay in the center of a lake, as if it was the center of a wheel with four spokes emanating outward. The spoke the palanquin took headed directly north along a tree-lined, white causeway. Flocks of birds rose as they passed, and the young prince could see a plentiful supply of golden carp swarming in the waters beneath him as if in anticipation of food. Finally the palanquin arrived and Prince Khamhaeng exited. Behind him servants carried away the boxes containing the tribute, no doubt to be shown to the emperor, or to his exchequer. The prince carried in his right hand a boxed golden Buddha, a gift from his father to the emperor.

He marveled again. This munificence was beyond his comprehension. As his party entered the reception area he noticed first the delicate, decorated pots that sat along the wall. Then he noticed the finer pots and vases on display. He picked one up. It was decorated with blue birds looking down upon two lovers as they crossed a bridge. The vase was so light, yet strong. As he carefully put the vase back he could sense the relief of those around him. He reminded himself to be more circumspect in the future.

He was ushered into a room where about twenty people were waiting to pay homage to the great khan. As the prince looked around he saw races unknown to him. Arabs he had met as they traversed Sukhothai on their way to China, but here were so many other people, their origin unknown to him.

A tall man with olive skin and dark hair approached. As they struggled to communicate they both finally understood that the tall man came from a city called Fiorenza, and the prince from Sukhothai. Neither were any the wiser. Finally they entered the royal chamber and sat cross-legged on the floor to the right of the golden royal throne. To their side sat an ornate golden table and from it a fountain rose into the air leaving the soothing sound of running water as it trickled away.

When the great khan entered they all supplicated themselves before him, and waited patiently as the court went through its many rituals before the audience commenced. They were called one by one, and each bowed nine times before the feet of the great khan. Prince Khamhaeng followed the tall man from Fiorenza. The prince had been schooled in how to behave when meeting the great khan and was meticulous in his duty. He indicated he wished to present a gift and a retainer came and took it on behalf of the khan. The golden statue sat in a box of highly polished teak. The retainer removed the outer seal and the great khan slowly opened the box to see what was inside. His face beamed as he saw the golden Buddha, its captured light reflecting back on his face. He was a man interested in religion, and he held Buddhism in high regard. The statue was in a style new to him, and Prince Khamhaeng could see he was enthralled by the gift.

After the audience had been concluded Prince Khamhaeng was surprised to be summoned into the presence of the great khan.

"Welcome, Prince Khamhaeng of Sukhothai," said the great khan through his interpreter.

The great khan was a large man, mustachioed in the manner of his soldiers, and with piercing eyes that seemed to stare intensely at the prince.

"Thank you for the image of the Buddha. It is my understanding that the Buddha traversed your lands before his death. You must feel greatly honored?"

"Very much so. His teachings form the basis of our society. We try to act as the Lord Buddha would want at all times."

"It is good to hear that such a place exists. In times of war, the teachings of one so wise are increasingly important. I understand you have shown an interest in the pottery made here?" he added knowingly. "I have ordered that twenty of our artisans and their families travel with you when you return. They are to teach your people."

"You have my gratitude and that of my people," replied Prince Khamhaeng.

"Now, young prince, come and walk with me."

Prince Khamhaeng returned from his journey far more knowledgeable and aware than when he left. He would make the journey again upon the death of the great khan.

It was over two years later, when Prince Khamhaeng was nineteen, that Lord Sam Chon, ruler of Mueang Chot, attacked the city of Tak, at the western border of the territory of Sukhothai.

My father went to fight Lord Sam Chon on the left. Lord Sam Chon drove forward on the right. Khun Sam Chon attacked in force, and my father's men fled in confusion. I did not flee. I mounted my elephant, opened (a way through) the soldiers and pushed him in front of my father. I fought an elephant duel with Lord Sam Chon. I fought Lord Sam Chon's elephant, who was called Mas Mueang, and beat him. Lord Sam Chom fled. Then my father named me Phra Ram Khamhaeng [Rama the Brave] because I fought Sam Chon's elephant.

King Si Inthrathit died in 1270. His first son had died young, but he left two sons and two daughters. The kingship fell to the eldest son, Ban Mueang, who reigned for ten years. He continued his father's support for the Theravada Buddhist faith and his expansion of the kingdom, although the establishment of a new kingdom to the north caused ongoing problems throughout his reign.

To the north of Sukhothai, a prince from a collection of Thai settlements on the banks of the Mekong River moved south and established the new kingdom of Lan Na, centered in the city of Chiang Mai, which he founded in 1296. In doing so he assimilated all the surrounding principalities into his realm. Prince Mangrai conquered Mueang Lai, Chiang Kham, and Chiang Khong, putting himself on the border of the Sukhothai kingdom. Following the death of King Si Inthrathit an uneasy truce existed between Sukhothai and Lan Na. Borders were fluid and ill-defined, but frontier skirmishes throughout the reign of King Ban Mueang were commonplace. Sukhothai instead looked to the south to expand and tolerated its new northern neighbor.

King Ban Mueang placed his brother in charge of the town of Si Satchanalai. The artisans and their families that accompanied Prince Khamhaeng on his return from Shangdu were settled there and supported by the prince. A large kiln was constructed to produce the high-quality ceramics so admired by the prince on his journey to China. Sawankhalok ware was in time sold both locally and internationally. The revenue it brought helped to support the Sukhothai kingdom for many years.

Si Satchanalai was now a city governed by Sukhothai. This change sent out an unmistakable message to its northern neighbor: No further!

2

KING RAM KHAMHAENG THE GREAT
1275–1317

There is fish in the water and rice in the fields. The lord of the realm does not levy toll on his subjects for traveling the roads; they lead their cattle to trade or ride their horses to sell; whoever wants to trade in elephants, does so; whoever wants to trade in horses, does so. . . . When he sees someone's rice he does not covet it, when he sees someone's wealth he does not get angry.

Ram Khamhaeng Inscription

THE YEAR 1277 SAW the peaceful accession to the throne of King Ram Khamhaeng of Sukhothai, the second son of King Si Inthrathit.

The concept of kingship in Sukhothai was based on two overriding influences. The first was the Hindu-based caste system of the Khmer, the previous rulers of the land. The second was the Theravada Buddhist concept of the *dhammaraja*, a king who rules his people in accordance with dharma, the teachings of the Buddha. Ram Khamhaeng supplemented these ideals by instituting a model of paternal rule over his subjects, as expressed in the appellation of the king: Pho Khun Ram Khamhaeng (*pho* is Thai for father).

The rainy season was drawing to a close. It was time for the Buddhist festival of *kathin*, celebrated by the ruler, the noblemen and noblewomen, and the young men and women of rank, down to the humblest in the kingdom. The month-long ceremony saw flowers woven into pillows and displays, cowrie shells hung outside people's homes, minstrels playing, magicians performing, and areca nuts gathered in great abundance to be distributed throughout the kingdom. On the final night a torchlight procession took place, wending its way through the hills and trails to the forest monastery. The single-file procession retraced its steps to the square outside the palace where the people of Sukhothai would come together to watch their king light candles in honor of the Lord Buddha, set off fireworks, and hand out alms. Rice wine was given freely, and none were expected to work the following day. It was a time of plenty, and the new king devoted himself to his kingdom. The Ram Khamhaeng Inscription encapsulates the feeling of the time. It is said that King Ram Khamhaeng hung a bell at the entrance to his palace. Those with a grievance would ring the bell, and when the king heard the call he would come and question the person, examine the case, and decide the outcome.

The king, recently married and with a baby daughter, invited the abbot of Sukhothai to rule alongside him. Bhikkhu Somdet Phra Phray and his monks would ensure that Buddhism remained central to the kingdom and that work would continue on the temple complex commenced in the time of King Si Inthrathit. Free men and women were levied to provide labor as the temple complexes of Sukhothai were planned and built.

"This place is to be a center for religion, for learning, and for art," said the king as he surveyed the cleared land interspersed with new, gleaming temples that King Si Inthrathit had designated when he accompanied his wife Queen Sueng all those years before.

It was during the start of his reign that King Ram Kamhaeng invited the leader of the Sri Lankan monks from the southern city of Nakhon Si Thammarat to preach Sri Lankan Theravada Buddhism in Sukhothai. Their message was embraced and quickly merged with the existing religion, a religion that also embraced pagan, animist, and Hindu beliefs. Their message helped to frame religious thinking in Sukhothai.

"The city of Sukhothai will be a holy place—one that provides enlightenment and direction in these trying times," said the bhikkhu.

"We must not fall into the trap that has snared the Khmer with Angkor Wat. We must not place all our effort on building and neglect other areas of our nation. We can expand our control to the south and the southeast. We can go no further west than Tak at present without raising the ire of the great khan," said the king.

"You will need to conclude the treaty we have discussed with Lan Na and Phayao. With our northern frontier secure we can expand elsewhere as King Si Inthrathit intended."

"The reign of my brother was constrained by the threat from our neighbors to the north. If we can conclude the peace then the Chao Phraya basin, and even the disputed Mon lands to the south, lay open. I know both King Mangrai and King Ngam Mueang well from our days being schooled in Lopburi. Together we are in a position to work out a truce. We know each other like brothers."

"Conquest will bring the riches and the labor we need to build our city and provide an excess of rice. You will lead our troops and I will ensure our plans for the building of Sukhothai and the development of our schools move forward," replied the bhikkhu.

"We are of one mind. Our first move is to meet with King Mangrai, and King Ngam Mueang of Phayao, in Chiang Mai at the next full moon and conclude our treaty," said the king.

Clouds were on the horizon. Despite King Ram Khamhaeng's closeness to China there was a justifiable fear of Mongol invasion coming south from the conquered lands farther north. King Mangrai of Lan Na and King Ngam Mueang of Phayao, together with King Ram Khamhaeng, met at a summit where the three kings made a pact that they would support each other if attacked and respect one another's borders.

The young King Ram Khamhaeng almost caused the treaty to collapse within a matter of months. Summoned back to the burgeoning city of Chiang Mai by King Mangrai, and accompanied by Bhikkhu Somdet Phra Phray, the king of Sukhothai faced the first major crisis of his reign.

"My wife has confessed that you seduced her during our treaty negotiations. She could hardly say otherwise!" fumed King Ngam Mueang, looking at his wife's belly. "What have you to say for yourself?"

King Ram Khamhaeng rose slowly, walked across to King Ngam Mueang, and supplicated himself at the feet of his accuser, acknowledging his wrongdoing in the most public way possible. He rose slowly, head down, bowed and backed away from the king of Phayao.

He is showing a wisdom and humility beyond his years, thought King Mangrai, who would tell this to King Ram Khamhaeng in private afterward.

"The fault was mine, and mine alone. I accept that and hope you will forgive the Lady Suroya."

The king of Phayao was pleased that King Ram Khamhaeng had acknowledged his wrong for all to see and issued his direct apology. His anger slowly dissipated.

"You have both agreed that my word is final on this matter," said King Mangrai. "King Ram Khamhaeng, you will pay restitution to King Ngam Mueang. That, and your public display of humility, is, I consider, adequate. The matter is closed. The treaty between us remains in place."

It was a very contrite King Ram Khamhaeng who attended the evening banquet. He had been forced to humiliate himself in public. He had learned his lesson and was genuine in his remorse.

With the pact still in place, the king called his two leading generals. General Kalavarnadit and General Jiang were both of the family of Pho Khun Pha Mueang, the general who had stood aside as King Si Inthrathit founded the kingdom of Sukhothai. The families were closely connected both by marriage and by history. Their loyalty was guaranteed.

"General Kalavarnadit and General Jiang, I bid you welcome," said the king.

"We are honored," replied General Kalavarnadit.

"It is time to fulfill the wishes of my father King Si Inthrathit. He envisaged a kingdom that stretched to the south and to the east. It falls to us to make that kingdom a reality."

"Saengcharao stands ready," said General Jiang, commander of the garrison town now known as Kamphaeng Phet. "The city is protected by moats, walls, fortresses, and watchtowers. The city is impenetrable. Our troops are well drilled and well equipped. They thirst for war—they thirst for victory."

"General Kalavarnadit, as you know we have concluded a treaty with Lan Na and Phayao. They will not attack us."

"Are you sure you can trust them?" questioned the general.

"They have both sworn a solemn oath, as have I. I feel certain they will not renege on the oath. However, Si Satchanalai is now your town, and its safety is in your hands."

"I understand," said General Kalavarnadit. "I will leave a holding force, but the remainder of my men will be placed under your command."

"We start by taking the center, the town of Song Khwae," said the king, speaking of the town that would come to be called Phitsanulok. "From there we can strike toward the south toward Phetchaburi and Nakhon Si Thammarat and then into the lands of the Mon. Phetchaburi is a seat of Buddhist learning, and to unite our kingdoms would ensure that our faith spreads throughout Southeast Asia. My spies in Phetchaburi and Nakhon Si Thammarat tell me there is growing unrest as king after king fights for the crown. The entire area seems to be run by petty warlords who claim to be kings, still trying to fill the void left when the Khmer withdrew. They are not united, and that is a division we can exploit."

"A noble undertaking," said General Jiang. "What of the kingdoms of Lopburi and Suphanburi?" the general asked.

"Lopburi and Suphanburi present a different face. Lopburi has only just rid itself of the Khmer. It remains weak, but Suphanburi has not taken advantage of that weakness. It was the armies of Suphanburi that were instrumental in driving the last of the Khmer from Lopburi. Since then they have withdrawn their forces. I understand that Suphanburi respects the status of Lopburi as a Buddhist center and a place of learning. They have made an alliance that ensures the independence of both states. They will soon be looking toward the Chao Phraya basin. No doubt we will meet them in time, but not now. We need Song Khwae to define our kingdom's eastern extent," said the king.

"We will ready our men and head toward Song Khwae. We battle only where diplomacy fails," added the king firmly. "The size and readiness of our army should mean we avoid many potential battles.

I learned much from visiting the great khan, particularly when we talked of war as we walked around his garden outside the royal palace of Muqingge, and you have passed my knowledge on to your troops. Soon our men will fall from the sky and defeat the opposition. The bhikkhu has ordained the day of our departure. We have thirty days to prepare," concluded the king.

In the following days the king and Bhikkhu Somdet Phra Phray discussed the nation and the future.

"When I was in China I saw how records were kept and information stored and communicated. The Chinese use a system of writing similar to the Arab traders that traverse our lands. Our writing system is poor. You and your monks are to set your minds to devising a script. It is my wish to write down the laws that will govern my kingdom, as I have seen the Chinese do. I have a great wish to complete the many challenges I have set for myself while I am king. You are to help me. You will rule as I campaign," said King Ram Khamhaeng.

Bhikkhu Somdet Phra Phray bowed his head, acknowledging the tasks, and left the royal chamber.

The formidable army gathered at Kamphaeng Phet. The people of the town supplicated themselves, their foreheads pressed to the ground as the army of King Ram Khamhaeng accompanied by his two generals commenced their first campaign. Song Khwae, strategically placed on the banks of the Nan River, was the first target.

The governor of the city looked out as thirty thousand soldiers gathered outside the walls of his city. The city-state owed no allegiance and had been independent since the Khmer withdrew nearly forty years previously. The governor realized that its independence was about to end.

A rider came forward, into arrow range, and neared the gate.

"King Ram Khamhaeng of Sukhothai wishes to meet in his tent at noon tomorrow. You will be afforded safe passage," he shouted from his horse. "I leave your terms of surrender here, in the dust," he added, symbolically throwing the document at the feet of a soldier who had emerged from behind the barred gates.

The following day at noon Governor Srihawong of Song Khwae rode resplendently on his war elephant into the camp of King Ram

Khamhaeng. With four fighters positioned at the feet and a lead fighter to the fore, the small procession made itself known in the camp of the king of Sukhothai. Twenty accompanying soldiers formed a guard around Governor Srihawong as they were guided into the war tent of King Ram Khamhaeng.

"Your war elephant is a magnificent animal," opened the king.

"The forests that border our rivers are plentiful with elephants. We are fortunate to have many Mon families in Song Khwae. As you know they are masters in the training of elephants."

"We are related through the sister of my father."

"She is my second wife. My first wife died in childbirth many years ago."

"I have not seen my aunt for many years. It would be good to do so."

"That can be arranged."

"You have seen my terms?"

"They are acceptable. I will not negotiate. It would sully our future relationship," said the bulky Governor Srihawong. "I have had no illusions that Song Khwae can remain independent indefinitely. That is one reason I adopted the title governor and not king. I humbly accept your overlordship and do so willingly."

"I learned much from visiting the great khan. The suzerainty of Sukhothai brings with it benefits in trade and security. I have given this visit much thought. A road will be built connecting your city with both Sukhothai and Kamphaeng Phet. This will encourage trade and allow for the quick movement of troops between our cities in the spirit of mutual defense."

A battle had been avoided. Governor Srihawong remained as governor of Song Khwae, and his soldiers swelled the ranks of the army of Sukhothai. Three days later their joint troops left, heading toward Sa Luang (Phichit) where the cavalry of King Ram Khamhaeng would first see action as they "fell from the sky" upon the unprepared defenders. As news passed, many towns and villages sought out the army of Sukhothai to pledge their allegiance. The vacuum left by the Khmer withdrawal was being filled. The days of the petty warlords were slowly drawing to a close, and the kingdom of Sukhothai grew.

The army was built upon the wishes of the king, who wanted to win the people to his cause. Where their leaders submitted willingly they would remain in place, with their advisers. The king of Sukhothai left monks behind to ensure correct governance and extract tribute, but at the same time he worked to build communication and trade. There were to be no massacres and no looting of those defeated. To build a kingdom required support from those within its borders.

Three years passed before King Ram Khamhaeng would return to Sukhothai. The king entered the newly completed Wat Mahathat and supplicated himself in front of the seated image of the Buddha

"As you see we have now completed the golden Buddha housed within the temple," said Bhikkhu Somdet Phra Phray with the modesty only a monk could offer.

"The statue is magnificent—so serene," said the king, as he and the bhikkhu left the temple. They walked around the temple complex. A lotus-bud-shaped *chedi* faced them as they left the hall of the Buddha; four corner stupas and four *prang*, reminiscent in style of those built by the Khmer, sat in the cardinal positions at the corners of the chedi. To the north and south were two standing images of the Buddha.

They walked along the path; canals gilded with water lilies ran on both sides with fish bubbling in the water as they passed. Together they entered the ordination hall to be greeted by a seated image of the Buddha in the attitude of subduing Mara. In the Buddhist faith Mara and his retinue are the personification of ignorance, obstructing the Bodhisattva (the Buddha-to-be) from attaining enlightenment. The Bodhisattva pointed his finger to the ground to call upon the goddess of the earth as witness that he had acquired enough merit to attain enlightenment in his lifetime.

"You have carried out my wishes not only in building this temple, which honors the Buddha perfectly, but in running the kingdom in my absence," said the king.

The bhikkhu bowed his head, acknowledging the compliment from his king. Together they walked into the city and to the temple halls of the serene walking Buddha—the style of which would become a hallmark of Sukhothai art. There the king gave alms to the waiting senior monks and to the sages who studied the *Tripitaka* and who had traveled to the city from Nakhon Si Thammarat.

The king remained in Sukhothai for three months. He planned new buildings, started new road-building projects, had pottery kilns built in Sukhothai, and worked with the bhikkhu on the new writing system, discussing and detailing laws he wanted written down. He had little need for sleep and would work relentlessly to build his city, its temples and schools, and his kingdom.

This period was short-lived. General Kalavarnadit arrived unannounced at the head of a battalion of his troops.

"My king, I bring dire news," he said.

The king and the bhikkhu sat down opposite the clearly fraught general.

"Tell the story as it happened," the king began.

"We were pushing south in accordance with your orders. We were advancing on Ratchaburi, my troops approaching from the west and the army of General Jiang from the north. The local warlord, General Arun, would not submit to our demands, and we readied for battle. My advance was held up by a torrential rainstorm, and by the time my troops arrived the city had fallen to General Jiang. His troops had looted the city, against your explicit orders. I was angry and confronted my cousin. He laughed and claimed this was his city. He drew his sword, and we fought. He died by my hand," said General Kalavarnadit.

"I cannot believe this of General Jiang," murmured the king, shocked.

"After his death his troops looked to me to lead them. I ordered that all the spoils of the battle be returned, and that we should make recompense to the city. I told his troops that they could join my army if they wished, but only if they built a new temple on the site of our battle—a temple to signify new beginnings and to act as an apology to the city. I commanded my men to look on but not to assist. This is a task that only the soldiers of General Jiang are to accomplish."

"You appear to have handled a potentially dangerous situation well and at a deep personal cost to yourself. I will ride with you back to Ratchaburi and show remorse for what has happened."

"I will accompany you," said the bhikkhu. "Has the site of the new temple been consecrated by the local monks?" asked the bhikkhu of General Kalavarnadit.

"Yes. Both they and my men, under the orders of Commander Makoto, watch over the soldiers of my now dead cousin as they labor at the task."

"General you have much to explain to your family. Go to them. I thank you for what you have done. This situation could have escalated and damaged the reputation of the kingdom of Sukhothai. It is your prompt action that seems to have averted a crisis. You have the personal thanks of your king. We will ride south at the full moon."

The new temple at Ratchaburi was complete. The king, General Kalavarnadit, and the bhikkhu stood alongside the monks of Ratchaburi as their new temple was consecrated. Restitution had been made, and the confidence and trust of the people had been regained.

The great khan looked on the states to his south with concern. Sukhothai had pledged allegiance and remained in favor, but the kingdom of Bagan that lay far to the west in modern-day Burma had paid no tribute despite requests made in the years 1271 and 1273. The great khan made forays over the years and finally ordered his troops to attack Bagan in 1273. The Mongols quickly gained victory and organized the Shan states in northern Burma as the province of Zhengmian, finally forcing King Narathihapate of Bagan to accept the suzerainty of the Chinese empire in 1276. In 1277, King Narathihapate was assassinated, and the commitments he had made to the great khan were not honored. The great khan subsequently ordered his troops southward into the heartland of Hanthawaddy (Burma), where they wreaked havoc, destabilizing the country for centuries to come.

෴

His Mon name was Magadu, but he was known in Sukhothai as Makoto. He came from the Shan states that lay to the west of Sukhothai. He had proved himself as a soldier and a commander as he fought alongside King Ram Khamhaeng and General Kalavarnadit in battle. The king, impressed by his service, awarded him the title

Phra Chao Fa Rua, meaning "heaven leaking," and made him captain of the palace guards.

"You are my one true love," declared Makoto.

"And you are mine," said Lady Soidao, daughter of King Ram Khamhaeng.

"It is you I want to marry, it is you I want to spend my life with," he breathed as he held her close.

She put her arm out and pulled him closer.

"My father will never allow it. Like my sisters he wants to arrange a diplomatically advantageous marriage for me. It is his way. It is how he expands the kingdom," she whispered as they lay together.

"No, that I cannot allow. I want you to be with me and no other," he said. "Come with me, away from here. Return with me to Pegu, to my family."

"Yes," said Lady Soidao finally.

☙

"What do you mean she has gone?" asked the king.

"Her bedchamber was not slept in last night and her horse and some clothing are missing."

"The captain Makoto is also nowhere to be found."

"Check the stables. See if his horse is still here."

"We checked immediately. His horse has gone also."

"Turn out the guard—we ride west after them. He must have returned to his Shan homeland or his family," said the king. "I will kill him for this!" he vowed. It would be many years until they were found.

Makoto and Lady Soidao made their way to Pegu, a city to the south of Hanthawaddy. There they met with Makoto's family and were married. Makoto had learned much while serving King Ram Khamhaeng, a king who ran his kingdom as if he were the father and his people were sons, and who used every tactic, be it arranged marriages, military might, or assassination, to expand it.

They moved to the Mon city of Martaban, where Makoto, now called Wareru, his Shan title, plotted to gain the governorship of the city. He asked his beautiful sister Hnin U Yaing to choose her bathing place in a spot by the river where the incumbent Bagan governor Aleimma would see her. The governor duly fell in love, and asked Hnin U Yaing to marry him. At the wedding ceremony, Wareru had the Bagan-appointed governor killed, and became the lord of Martaban.

The Bagan empire was fading under the onslaught of the Mongols, and King Wareru secured first the city before carving out the beginnings of the new kingdom of Pegu. He formed an alliance with Tarabya, the governor of Pegu, each marrying the other's daughter, and together they fought successfully against the Shan northern forces, thus securing the new kingdom. Tarabya then fell afoul of King Wareru, who had him captured and executed. The kingdom of Pegu that Wareru founded would survive for over two hundred and fifty years.

☙

It was a still, baking hot summer day. The sea in the distance glistened as the two kings, their armies at their backs, faced each other astride their war elephants.

"Do we battle on elephant-back? Do we fight the honorable *yuddhahatthi*?" asked King Ram Khamhaeng.

King Wareru had his elephant kneel and dismounted. He supplicated himself in front of his reluctant father-in-law, King Ram Khamhaeng, and accepted the suzerainty of the kingdom of Sukhothai. He swore to King Ram Khamhaeng the oath of allegiance invoking the god Indra, the god considered a leading supporter of Buddhism and the supernatural power that had helped the Lord Buddha to attain enlightenment.

Sukhothai in the reign of King Ram Khamhaeng, by a blend of careful diplomacy, shrewd alliances, military campaigns, and a commitment to his Buddhist faith, had extended its power and influence. Boundaries were fluid and alliances loose and personal, based on relationships between the king and those who accepted suzerainty. As would happen often in the history of Southeast Asia of the period, the death of a king would often cause those who had accepted overlordship to reassess their arrangement. Sukhothai drew inspiration from many neighbors. The Khmer legacy is evident in its architecture and its influence on government. Theravada Buddhism came to dominate the culture of the Sukhothai period. King Ram Khamhaeng, in continuity with the indigenous traditions of worshiping spirits, continued to make offerings to a local guardian spirit deity even after adopting Theravada Buddhism. Thus the two religious traditions were merged.

King Ram Khamhaeng's city of Sukhothai was abundant with Theravada Buddhist temples and many types and styles of Buddha images, and the kingdom reached its political zenith under his guidance. He reinvented the Thai writing system, introducing the *lai sue Thai,* or the Thai alphabet, adapting it from the ancient Khmer, Mon, and Burmese alphabets for easier reading. He introduced a system of laws that favored neither rich nor poor, and left a secure kingdom that is regarded as the forerunner to the modern kingdom of Thailand. Upon his death the kingdom would decline militarily and soon the kingdom of Ayutthaya would rise, but its dedication to the Theravada Buddhist religion would continue to flourish for centuries.

Following King Ram Khamhaeng's death many of the vassal kingdoms of Sukhothai liberated themselves. The kingdom of Uttaradit to the north declared independence, followed by the Lao kingdoms of Luang Prabang and Vientiane in the east. In 1319, the Mon state to the southwest broke away, and in 1321 the kingdom of Lan Na took over parts of Sukhothai's territory. To the south the powerful city of Suphanburi, which had fallen to King Ram Khamhaeng, broke free during the reign of his successor, King Loethai. The decline was slow, but soon Sukhothai found itself threatened by a new, developing kingdom: Ayutthaya. The legendary Phra Ruang dynasty would gradually fade from power.

The Legend of Phra Ruang—The Epic Hero of Si Satchanalai and Sukhothai

According to the legend Phra Ruang was a son of the ruler of Hariphunchai and a female Naga, a creature of the underworld.

The rumors of his super-human acts came to the ears of the Khmer state ruler who held supreme power over the small towns of the Thai. He ordered a tax collector to arrest Phra Ruang. His man pursued Phra Ruang to a Wat in Sukhothai where he had become an ordained monk. Phra Ruang said the words, "Stay here, don't move," to the tax collector, whose body then gradually transformed into a rock-like solid mass on the ground.

When the ruler of Sukhothai passed away Phra Ruang was voted the ruler of the town. Phra Ruang was a son-in-law of a ruler of Si Satchanalai and became his successor. He ordered his men to construct many temples in the town. After making Si Satchanalai into a flourishing town, he and his brother, Phra Lue, traveled to China for Chinese ceramic technology. They introduced this knowledge into their homeland.

One day Phra Ruang bathed in the main river of the town. He was below the rapids and never came back. This is the end of his story.

U-Thong Dynasty
(First Reign)

3

KING RAMATHIBODI

1351–69

WITHIN A SHORT PERIOD after the death of King Ram Khamhaeng the alliances that marked the kingdom of Sukhothai began to unravel. Suphanburi and Nakhon Si Thammarat to the south declared independence, and the vacuum left in this region by the retrenchment of the Khmer made itself felt again. The period was marked by the renewed rise of the towns of Suphanburi and Lopburi, located west and east, respectively, of the Chao Phraya River.

The kingdom of Sukhothai did little to protect its far-off interests. The kingdom moved in another direction. Its army became a primarily defensive force as King Loethai inherited the throne upon the death of his father.

The new king absorbed himself in the religion of his nation and is credited with the writing of the *Traiphum Phra Ruang* (*Three Worlds according to King Ruang*—Ruang being the dynastic name). The text describes the worlds of Buddhist cosmology and is rich in meaning. The king earned the sobriquet King Loethai the Pious. Prince Lithai, the son of King Loethai and a grandson of King Ram Khamhaeng, became king upon the death of his father, taking the title of King Maha Thammaracha.

While Sukhothai flowered, the line of "-varman" kings that had ruled the magnificent Khmer empire for over five hundred years was no more. Pressures of refugees from the collapsing Nanchao kingdom and its neighbors in the south of China, the impact of Theravada Buddhism on a previously Hindu society, an obsession with building, and an ongoing drought had all contributed to its downfall. The rebellion of the slaves in 1336 saw blood spilled in a conflict that would echo through the coming centuries.

The city of Angkor was heavily reliant on slaves and had seen many slave uprisings over the centuries. The Chinese merchant Zhou Daguan wrote in 1296, only forty years before the bloodiest uprising of all, that

> Most families have a hundred or more [slaves]; a few have ten or twenty; only the very poorest have none at all.

The bloody rebellion changed the face of Angkor. As resources became increasingly stretched it was the slaves that had suffered the most. It started with a small uprising but spread throughout the city. Slaves fought with whatever they could find, while the Khmer army was ruthless in trying to put down the revolt. Thousands died, often executed after they surrendered. Atrocities of a like rarely seen before were carried out by both sides. Finally the slaves broke free of the city and fled, mainly into the area of the Chao Phraya basin, or toward the Dai Viet in the east.

Many of Tai origin fled toward their kinfolk to the west. At a time of ongoing labor shortages, they were made welcome. Their harrowing stories were passed throughout the country. U-thong, the future King Ramathibodi, heard the tales as he grew. The glory days of the Khmer were gone, but this memory imprinted itself in the mind of the future king.

King Trosek Pream (which in Khmer means "sweet melon") seized the throne and faced the task of rebuilding the shattered kingdom. The city of Angkor was renamed Siem Reap, meaning "the leveling of the Siamese," a name which reflected back on the events that so changed the country.

The chronicles of the time tell the following story of King Sweet Melon:

> He was formerly a farmer in the royal palace. He grew such a sweet melon that the king gave him a sacred spear in order to fend off thieves who might come to steal the precious melon.

One night, the king had been so craving the melon that he walked onto the melon field to pick one for himself. [The farmer] mistook the king for a thief and speared him to death. After that, he took the princess as his wife and ascended the throne.

Whatever the truth, the old order was gone and a new king, King Lamphongsaraja now ruled. He looked to rebuild his kingdom.

Kamboja Pradesa, the king of Suphanburi, passed away suddenly in his sleep, leaving no heir.

Phraya Choduk Setthi, with the title Krom Tha Sai, (Department of the Left Port—left being for commerce from the east; right from the west) was the leader of the Chinese in Suphanburi, and a very cunning and ambitious man. His life was now dedicated to his son and to the advancement of his family.

The Chinese held a unique place in the developing Thai culture. Many started life in the burgeoning commerce that existed between the two countries, and it was here that Phraya Choduk Setthi's son U-thong made his fortune. Over the years he had been schooled by a series of tutors in the type of education that would make him more acceptable among the ranks of the Thai elite. He was rewarded when at the age of thirty-one he married Princess Kitiyakara, the first daughter of the prince of Lopburi. He was now connected by marriage to one of the most important ruling houses in the Chao Phraya basin.

The death of the king unlocked a door that just needed a push to open. U-thong required no further bidding. He had discussed the impending situation with his father on many occasions, and they moved quickly. Continuity, particularly when it comes to the royal succession, is paramount.

Within three days it was agreed. U-thong, acceptable to all parties, was king. In the prime of his life and with royal connections, his accession to the throne sealed an alliance between two major cities: Suphanburi and Lopburi. To U-thong it was his right. He felt he was born to be king, and now he had to prove that he was worthy of it.

The Sukhothai kingdom to the north was fading as a military force as king after king immersed himself in the Buddhism that was central to the beliefs of the kingdom. Lopburi and the kingdoms to the south followed a different model of kingship than that of Sukhothai, one reminiscent of the Khmer period. The king was an absolute monarch, assuming the title of *devaraja,* or "god-king," as opposed to the *dhammaraja* of the Sukhothai period. It was the Khmer influence that underpinned the traditions and social structure of those kingdoms and states lying to the south.

King U-thong was, like his father, a clever man. During his first two years King U-thong had his father by his side to advise him. He formed closer military and economic alliances with Phetchaburi and Lopburi and strengthened his army at a time when others were weak. He launched attacks on Sukhothai to the north, gaining considerable territory but meeting stubborn resistance as he neared Kamphaeng Phet and Sukhothai itself. To King U-thong, Sukhothai was just another dominion to conquer. It would only be in later years and after many intermarriages that the true influence of the Sukhothai concept of kingship would be felt. His kingdom, the kingdom of Suphanburi, was in the ascendant.

Sukhothai's domain had shrunk, but its army remained strong. There were many bloody battles until a truce was reached. King U-thong took another wife, Mae Luang, a daughter of King Maha Thammaracha I, and the marriage helped encourage peace between the two kingdoms. As a sign of good faith King U-thong returned the captured city of Chainat, thereby sealing the peace.

The king's father was one of the first to die when the smallpox epidemic swept through the cities of the Chao Phraya basin. Suphanburi suffered greatly, and the people looked to their king for guidance.

"The illness spreads throughout the city," reported General Thaodi. "We have followed your orders and burned down the old quarter, but there is no sign of the sickness lessening."

"Then we must leave," said the king.

"You mean we are to abandon the city?" asked the general.

"I see no option. We must move all east, away from the contamination coming from the sea."

"Many will die."

"So be it. It is the weak and sick that will die first. I look to establish a new city inland from the sea. One that will rule for a thousand years. Some good may yet come out of this pestilence."

Leaving some of his troops in charge of the city, the king ordered that his city be evacuated and the people relocated. To where, he had no idea. All he had to follow were the tales told by the old ones.

King U-thong rode at the head of his troops. Those who followed his orders, willingly or unwillingly, straggled behind carrying their meager possessions. As the line of refugees from this, the most deadly of diseases, headed east, possessions were abandoned and the weak and sick left behind by the roadside.

"We must find shelter for the night," said the king.

"There are only small villages that I know of," replied General Thaodi. "If we head south we will find only swamp and forest until we near the sea. We need to head east, toward the great rivers, but for tonight I fear our people will be sleeping in the open."

"Then that is what they will do. Tomorrow morning and every morning you will send men to scout ahead. We are looking for good land near water. We will walk until we find a suitable site. The weak and the sick will perish, but we will not stop until we find a site worthy of establishing a new beginning. The old ones tell of a turning in the river, a sacred plain. Perhaps there is truth in what they say," responded the king.

The procession trudged onward for seven more days and nights until they came to a broad bend in the river cradling a rectangular piece of land, smooth, level, and seemingly uninhabited.

"This land is almost surrounded by the Lopburi River—almost an island," said General Thaodi scanning the landscape with his hand. "We are fortunate that some from our city and those from the coast know the area. They say the area has been peopled over time, but the annual floods, although they don't engulf the whole plain, make it unsustainable."

"Unsustainable as a village, perhaps, but as a city that is a different matter. I see something more. I see a place protected by a mighty river, a river that provides fertility to the land. Maybe the old ones were right," said the king, spurring his horse forward along the bank of the river.

"The waters are plentiful in fish," observed the general as they crossed the causeway and arrived on the ground that was destined to become Ayutthaya. Ten mounted soldiers followed behind.

"Look around. See if there are people here," commanded the general to his troops. A small village of no more than twenty people lay on the far side of the rectangular plain. The people were fishermen and understood the ways of the river. The ruins of three temples and a faded golden Buddha that lay captured in a stand of trees looked out over the fast-flowing Lopburi River.

Arun claimed he was a *ruesi,* (a hermit-sage) and stated that he had been in this place since the time of the journey of the Buddha many centuries before. The ruesi said that the Buddha had come to this place and prophesied that a great city would one day be built here. He added that Buddha had left him to pass on these words, and he described their meeting for the newcomers:

> Meanwhile, he received information about the island where the city of Ayutthaya is built, and appeared surprised that such a beautiful site was not inhabited nor built upon.. But he met a hermit (called rishi by the Siamese) who informed him that previously there was a city there called Ayutthaya. But how it declined he had no knowledge and added that no other city could be rebuilt there. The reason was that at a palace Wo Talenkang, now in the middle of the city, there was a pool in which there was a voracious dragon, called Nagaraja by the Siamese, who on being disturbed blew poisonous saliva from his mouth. This brought about such an epidemic that everybody around there died of the stench. Thao U Thong asked the rishi whether the dragon could not be killed and the marsh filled in. The rishi answered that this would not be a remedy, but that a rishi (like him in every respect) should be thrown in. Thus Thao U Thong

had the whole country searched to find such a person. The rishi further declared that Thao U Thong, after killing the dragon and filling in the marsh, should do three things if he wanted to live in that place in health: shoot an arrow and catch it again in his quiver; smear his body daily with cow dung; and blow on a horn every day, just as Brahman priests do when they go to their temples or places of devotion.

Thao U Thong said that he knew how to fulfill these conditions and went with a perahu to the middle of the river, shot an arrow upstream, and as the arrow came down the quiver went to the water and received the arrow. In place of cow dung he covered his body with rice meal every day mixed with a little serujis, saying that the rice would not grow unless the land had been fertilized. By this he meant that the cow dung is also part of the rice. With regards to the blowing of the horn, he had sirib leaves rolled close together and ate it as pinang, which had some similarities with the blowing of horns. The rishi replied. 'Since thou hast made the arrow return to thee, thy people shall be united with each other and thy kingdom freed from internal wars. Secondly, because thou so cunningly applied the cow dung, thou and thy people shall suffer little from smallpox. Thirdly and finally, because thou has rolled the sirib which had a likeness horn, the gods shall have great love for you and bring you great fortune.'

In the meantime, the messengers sent out returned to Thao U Thong the tidings that a rishi like that they were ordered to look for could not be found. Thao U Thong kept this message secret, went to speak the rishi at the mouth of the marsh where the dragon was, and without warning threw him in and filled in the marsh. Sine then the dragon has never again appeared, and the land has been free from epidemics.

"Bring the people here and set about clearing the land," said the king. "We have found the site for our new city—one that will look both to the land and to the sea."

The land was cleared, and a defensive wall, albeit only a mound with wooden stakes, was built. Behind it homes took root. King

U-thong ordered the construction of three temples in an area named Bueng Phra Ram by the ruesi Arun. It was the area where the original temples had stood.

As the land was cleared and trees removed, a huge Buddha image was revealed, covered in flaking gold leaf. It stood nineteen meters high and twenty-two meters wide and was exposed to the daylight after many years of seclusion. Fallen and crumbled walls surrounded it. The ruesi had gone, but the story of the Buddha was ingrained in the minds of the local villagers.

According to their story the image was housed in Wat Phanan Choeng, the original *wat* (temple) in the area, and was built in the year 1326. According to the locals, it was the result of a tragic love story, built when a visiting princess from China killed herself over a perceived slight from the local king. The ruler was overcome with remorse and built the temple as penance. The king was long gone and only the story, passed down from generation to generation, remained.

King U-thong ordered the Buddha statue cleaned and made ready for worship. He neither strengthened the walls nor built a temple around it. This was seen as a sign of respect to those who had lived on the plain in the past. Upon completion King U-thong established Ayutthaya—a name that means "undefeatable"— as his capital.

In 712, a Year of the Tiger, second of the decade, on Friday, the sixth day of the waxing moon of the fifth month [Friday, March 4, 1351] . . . the Capital City of Ayutthaya was first established.

For his coronation King Ramathibodi brought eight Brahmins from the Indian city of Varanasi to officiate. Brahmins were known to have acquired vast knowledge, which was passed down from father to son and kept within the family. These learned Brahmins remained to help the king to establish an efficient administration and to plan for the future. Their very presence attracted court chamberlains, physicians, astrologers, and scribes, many of whom were fluent in Khmer. The city grew quickly, endowed with abundant resources, a growing workforce, and plentiful food.

The king established the four state offices to enable him to manage his kingdom. These were the Ministry of the Interior (Wiang), the Ministry of the Treasury (Khlang), the Ministry of the King's Household (Wang), and the Ministry of Agriculture (Na).

"We plan for the future," said the king.

"Then let us look to the past for lessons," said Brahmin Deshpande. "The legacy of the Khmer is plain. Their monarchy was absolute, as yours shall be. None other than royalty and family are allowed to speak in your presence, unless you invite them to. All land is to be owned by the king. It is only you who grant your subjects the right to live and work on it. Build both palaces and temples—they link the king with the people and demonstrate the importance of Ayutthaya to the outside world. Ayutthaya lies at the center of the kingdom, with the four cardinal points around it—Lopburi to the north, Phra Pradaeng to the south, Nakhon Nayok to the east, and Suphanburi to the west. These strategic cities are to be ruled by your sons or your close family. They protect and enclose your kingdom."

"Lopburi and Suphanburi are my cities now, and my first wife is a princess of Lopburi," said the king. "I will place Prince Phangoa as governor of Suphanburi. He is of the ruling family. I will put my young son Prince Ramesuan in charge of Lopburi. He will have to learn quickly."

"And Nakhon Nayok?"

"Nakhon Nayok will be our first battle. Their king is of Khmer blood. He will resist," replied the king. Changing the subject, he said, "Chinese traders continue to travel into the city."

"They provide you with wealth and stability as your city grows. From here you have access to the sea. Three mighty rivers from the north meet here, providing you with an inland port, accessible by seagoing vessels. Trade needs to be organized. Traders will come."

"Nakhon Si Thammarat to our south should pledge their allegiance."

"In time. First establish your city and ensure support. Then expand. Send missions to Sukhothai and Nakhon Si Thammarat. Make peace, and then you can concentrate on your true enemy," said Brahmin Deshpande.

"The Khmer," said the king. The once-mighty Khmer remained a threat. To ensure the security of his realm the king felt the need to crush them. The tales he had heard when growing up about the massacre of the slaves had left an indelible mark on him.

"The Khmer," echoed his Brahmin counselor.

King Ramathibodi was the first king of Ayutthaya. He was empowered by his relatives in the city states of Suphanburi, Lopburi, and Sanburi. Ayutthaya was ruled by the king as an absolute monarch. The structure and hierarchy established in the early years would play an important role throughout the entire period of the kingdom. The king charged relatives and high-ranking aristocrats with looking after the provincial towns that were close to Ayutthaya. Other cities, those being governed by their own rulers, swore their fealty to Ayutthaya. Their integration into Ayutthaya would be gradual, but as the city grew so did Ayutthaya's dominion and its importance.

It was five years after the founding of Ayutthaya that King Ramathibodi welcomed his first visit from Persian merchants with a special banquet. It was a sign of the growing recognition of the city and the first tangible result of improving relations with Sukhothai, whose emissary was also in attendance at the banquet.

To the king's left sat his second queen, the Khmer Queen Veasna, heavily pregnant with their third child, and in the place of honor, at the king's other hand, sat Sheik Sa-id. It was a night of music. The jugglers left the room, and a troop of Persian musicians entered. Both the king and queen sat spellbound as the music played. It was unlike any music they had heard before, so different from the Chinese and Khmer music that had reigned for so long.

"Magnificent," said the king as the musicians left the chamber.

"I am pleased you like our music," said Sheik Sa-id. "It is the music that has been played in our royal court for many generations."

The sheik whispered to an aide, and three musicians reentered the room, bowed low, and presented their instruments for the king and queen to appraise.

"They are unlike ours," remarked the queen.

"When you next visit you must bring us some," said the king.

"That I shall certainly do, but in the meantime let our musicians explain to your artisans how they are made," said Sheik Sa-id. "They can also instruct your musicians about how our music is played."

"Thank you for your kindness," said the queen.

As the evening drew to a close Sheik Sa-id presented both the king and queen with the most exquisite of clothing from the Persian court.

"This is a *khil'a*," said Sheikh Sa-id to the king. It is a gift from our caliph. The gift of a *khil'a* can only be made by a caliph, and I have the honor of presenting this gift on his behalf."

The king and the queen examined the garment and looked closely at its intricate weave. They were impressed by the craftsmanship, and the king considered having his weavers produce a similar material. The evening wound down. Gifts had been exchanged and agreements made.

King Ramathibodi, from his position at the top of the social hierarchy, prudently chose the best from the Lopburi and Suphanburi elite and defined the style of government for Ayutthaya, adopting the elaborate rituals from Angkor and refining them to suit his new city. Unlike the openness displayed by the kings of Sukhothai, however, he remained aloof from the common people, who had to be silent in his presence and were forbidden to even look at him when he passed.

King Ramathibodi made Theravada Buddhism the official state religion and invited monks from Sri Lanka to reinforce the faith in his kingdom. He also established laws for his new kingdom and had them written down in Pali, an Indo-Aryan language favored by Theravada Buddhism.

Monks of the Pa Kaeo sect also went to Sri Lanka, and King Ramathibodi had a temple built to mark the pilgrimage. The monastery took its name from the order of monks: Wat Pa Kaeo. In time the head of the sect was raised by King Ramathibodi to the position of patriarch, and the temple became known as the temple of the supreme patriarch. Over the centuries it would become known as Wat Yai Chai Mongkhon.

The temple was marked by a stupa that lay in ornate gardens populated by tropical birds, water lilies, and white stone Buddhas. Around the central stupa the Buddhas fanned out into long rows of near-identical figures, although closer inspection revealed subtle variations in facial expression and posture.

☙

Nakhon Nayok had fallen, its pro-Khmer king dying in battle. The city now paid homage to Ayutthaya. With the fall of Nakhon Nayok and other smaller cities recognizing the growing power of Ayutthaya, the kingdom that had begun as a patchwork of semiautonomous states slowly coalesced. Those owing fealty would provide men for war or for labor in return for the protection and benefits of a closer relationship with Ayutthaya. They were soon called on to provide troops for war.

The cities of Suphanburi and Lopburi had given King Ramathibodi their support as he built his new capital of Ayutthaya. There were, however, a number of issues between the two cities that could cause conflict. The choice of U-thong, an outsider with a foot in both camps, was an attempt to find an amicable middle ground. Tensions first surfaced over the expansion of Ayutthaya.

Suphanburi looked toward expansion to the north and the south—in particular north to the kingdom of Sukhothai. Their earlier defeat to King Ram Khamhaeng and their enforced subservience were considered a shame on their city. It was a shame they wanted to avenge. King Ramathibodi, in agreeing to a truce and marrying Princess Mae Luang, had ended any plans to move his kingdom northward. With the founding of Ayutthaya he looked east toward Angkor. The city had long been the focus of Lopburi, who had been under the Khmer yoke for many years. Tales that accompanied the influx of the slaves all those years before had left their mark. They wanted Angkor gone. Having made peace with Sukhothai, King Ramathibodi looked to the golden city of the Khmer.

During the 1350s and early 1360s King U-thong had ridden against the Khmer, getting as far as Angkor but never being able to enter. Time had not been kind to the old king. His body ached with arthritis as he planned his next campaign. It was his wish to see the end of the Khmer, and that was to be his legacy. In 1367 he gathered the largest army from all corners of his domain, but when the time came he was unable to travel. The army left with his son Prince Ramesuan at its head.

The prince became separated from the main Siamese army and was attacked by the Khmer and captured. On hearing the news, King Ramathibodi requested the aid of Prince Phangua, the young governor of Suphanburi, to secure the release of his son and to take command of the army.

The Khmer held out for nearly a year before Angkor fell. The Angkorian king, Lamphongsaraja, died late in the siege, and in his place the Siamese installed the crown prince, Phasat, as a vassal of Siam. The old kingdom was transformed into an absolute monarchy owing tribute to Ayutthaya, slavery was revived, and a tax and levy system was introduced and enforced in the spirit of the king of Ayutthaya. Ten thousand captives, including craftsmen, artisans, and farmers, were taken back to Ayutthaya to serve their new masters. Prince Ramesuan was released, and he returned home, shamed by his capture.

In 1369, the year of King Ramathibodi's death, the kingdom he founded was recognized by the new Ming dynasty as the chief power in the region. Ayutthaya was already regarded as the strongest kingdom in mainland Southeast Asia but lacked the manpower to dominate the region. The king's body was embalmed, as was the tradition at the time, and his son Prince Ramesuan took the throne. His succession, as with many that followed, was to be disputed.

One of King Ramathibodi's most outstanding legacies was to leave a permanent mark on the personality of the Thai: his belief in the dharma. Buddhism was a common heritage among the fragmented kingdoms of India. Together with the kings of Sukhothai, Burma, and Cambodia, the rulers of Siam observed Theravada Buddhist religious precepts. King Ramathibodi introduced Buddhist doctrines into the law governing royalty and government officials, as well as in civil and criminal law. This new basis for legislation was taken largely from the Khmer royal court as it had functioned during the golden age of Khmer power. It was to shape future generations of Siamese who would come to identify their ethnicity and nationalism with Buddhism.

The reign of King Ramathibodi had set a new style of politics in the Chao Phraya basin. Over his reign he provided common ground where local-level leaders came together to see the advantages of collaborating. His legacy lies in the fact that when he died his kingdom remained intact. The local leaders did not fragment, as was often the case, but remained committed to Ayutthaya.

Suphannaphum Dynasty
(First Reign)

4

KING BOROMMARACHA I
1370–88

KING RAMATHIBODI DIED on his way back from an unsuccessful attack of the walled Sukhothai garrison town of Kamphaeng Phet. His later years had seen his body racked with pain. His death was imminent. It was a time when kings would nominate their successor. It was also a time when the succession could be—and frequently was—disputed.

Prince Ramesuan had faced his father's wrath on his return from his unsuccessful role in the capture of Angkor Wat. King Ramathibodi had to call on his cousin Prince Phangua, the governor of Suphanburi, to rescue his captured son and take the city. Prince Ramesuan had returned home in disgrace. His failure was recognized throughout the kingdom.

His son had no intention of letting his failure at Angkor stand in his way to the throne. As the messenger rode directly from the camp of King Ramathibodi to inform the prince of his father's death, his well-rehearsed plan took shape. His men surreptitiously took over all the roles of soldiers defending the city and by morning the new king had masterminded a bloodless coup. He had, however, misjudged the feeling against him following the debacle in Angkor.

"The ingrate has seized the throne," fumed Prince Phangua. "The throne that we helped his father win."

"And the families of Lopburi stand behind him," replied his mother, Prasuja Akara Devi, the aged queen of Suphanburi.

"This I will not allow. I saved him from the Khmer. He is seen as weak and will struggle to retain the obedience of others."

"We cannot allow the house of U-thong to control Ayutthaya. The city would be nothing without the support of Suphanburi."

"I will raise my troops and attack him in Ayutthaya."

"You will do no such thing," said the fearsome queen to her fifth son. "That would lead to a civil war between Suphanburi and Lopburi, and that we must avoid at all costs. If we fight among ourselves then our enemies outside will benefit. No, you will prepare your troops and keep them close to hand. Our conquest of Sukhothai must be put on hold. You will allow me the time to play the politics I enjoy so much. I will attend the funeral of the late king on behalf of our family. You will stay away as a sign of our displeasure. I will then visit with our cousins in Lopburi. Allow me to plant the seeds of discontent and then give a dose of fear to our upstart king. You will ensure that your army and that of your cousin Nakhon In are ready when I call. His support and loyalty can be counted upon."

With the city secured Prince Ramesuan's mind shifted to his father's interment. It was only after that was completed that he could be crowned king. The body of the king was embalmed, and in the following days mourners arrived from around the kingdom. They followed the royal procession of elephants cloaked in the red of Ayutthaya, professional mourners who wailed and screamed their lament against a background of discordant instruments, and the generals of the king to the chosen site where his father's body would be interred inside a walled crypt.

King Ramesuan ordered that work be started on a new temple at the site, Wat Phra Ram. The temple and surrounding houses would each have a large prang with chedis positioned at the four cardinal points. The prang would have four images of the mythical Garuda, a favorite of his father. The temple was sited behind the large pond created when two neighboring temples were constructed. The new king may have been vain and self-serving, but he understood the need to show respect and ensure continuity.

Prasuja Akara Devi of Suphanburi arrived in Ayutthaya with all the pomp that her many years deserved. Her soldiers, resplendent in the blue of Suphanburi, a full retinue of her officials and ministers, and, perhaps more telling, a white elephant arrived with her.

"You have seized the throne."

"I am my father's son. The throne is mine by right."

"So I have heard you say."

"I have moved quickly in order to ensure my father receives his full burial rites as a king."

"You have moved very quickly. Some would say you have moved with undue haste."

"Continuity is important, is it not?"

"As is protocol, is it not?"

A moment's silence reigned between King Ramesuan and the elderly queen.

"I have brought a white elephant with me. You are to look after him on my behalf."

"Of course, Aunt," replied the king, realizing that he now had an obligation to the queen and, by extension, to the house of Suphanburi.

"After the funeral I will visit your family in Lopburi. We have much to discuss," she said.

℘

"I have visited my cousins in Lopburi," said the aging queen to Prince Phangua on her return to Suphanburi. "They have come to understand my wishes in this matter. The white elephant I left in the care of the usurper is ailing. It will be seen as a sign that his reign will be cursed with misfortune. You are to send Nakhon In and his troops to Ayutthaya, where the upstart king will surrender and abdicate in your favor. The outgoing king will assume the governorship of Lopburi in return for his abdication, and you will leave him unharmed throughout your reign. When Nakhon In indicates all is in order, you will enter the city to be crowned king. You will take the name Somdet Phra Borommarachathirat, King Borommaracha."

"You have averted a civil war," remarked the future King Borommaracha.

"And I very much enjoyed doing it," said his mother. "But watch Lopburi. They are of Mon descent, as we are of Tai—they were not best pleased to acquiesce.

"You are to complete Wat Phra Ram, where his father's remains will lie," she added. "I will rest now. The kingdom is in your hands from this moment." The year was 1370.

At the age of sixty-three the new king brought a maturity to the throne.

> [The] king was wise, eloquent, devout, religious, liberal toward
> the ecclesiastics and the poor. By nature a war-minded ruler,
> a lover of weapons, he took great care of his soldiers and the
> community."

Among his first actions was ordering the completion of Wat Phra Ram, and in order to seek legitimacy for his reign and his city he sent an embassy to Emperor Hongwou, first emperor of the Ming dynasty, thereby ensuring cordial relations throughout his reign. Four missions were sent to China in the year 1373 alone: two from the king and two from U-thong's widow and the mother of the deposed King Ramesuan; the latter two were rejected by the Chinese.

"The war with Angkor is finished. Now is the time to look northward," said the king.

"To Sukhothai?" said Nakhon In.

"The capture of Sukhothai opens the entire north to us,"

"By virtue of its position Phitsanulok controls traffic from the north. In many ways it is now more strategically important than Sukhothai."

"The city remains loyal to Sukhothai, but you are right. We will campaign against Sukhothai—all of Suphanburi wants redress from the wrongs they have committed against us over the generations—but Phitsanulok gives us control of the Nan River and the trade that goes with it."

"What of Lopburi?"

"The son of King Ramathibodi harbors aspirations to the throne. He is not a good leader and does not engender the support of those outside Lopburi. My mother demonstrated clearly to me the power of diplomacy in these matters. I will seek her guidance. I know she already has her spies in his camp. I think it is only the intrigue that keeps her alive," said the king, smiling at the memories of his mother's wiles and machinations.

"We leave a holding force here. The rainy season is nearing its end. We move on Sukhothai," he added.

The kingdom of Sukhothai had regained many of its former dependencies under the reign of King Maha Thammaracha. Constant forays into the north from Suphanburi had led to a resurgence of the Sukhothai military. With their style of government and their strengthened military, King Borommaracha saw a kingdom that was a threat on two fronts.

As his army gathered the king heard the news of the death of King Maha Thammaracha of Sukhothai.

"They will be in disarray. Now is the time to attack," said Nakhon In.

"His son will inherit the throne. I understand he is a religious man, not a warrior,"

"Then all the more reason to attack,"

"We wait while they honor their king. I do not want to be seen as a conqueror who took advantage of this situation. Let them do right by their king, then we attack."

"You have learned a great deal at the feet of your mother," said his commander Nakhon In.

In 1371, the cities of Nakhon Phangka and Phichit fell to the army of Ayutthaya. By 1373, King Borommaracha and his commander Nakhon In sat outside the seemingly impregnable walls of Kamphaeng Phet. The army of Sukhothai retreated behind the walls. Despite numerous attempts King Borommaracha could not find a way past Kamphaeng Phet's formidable defenses and returned to Ayutthaya to regroup and refocus.

News of the death of his mother, the Suphanburi queen Prasuja Akara Devi, reached King Borommaracha just as he returned to Ayutthaya. He immediately left to attend her funeral. On his return he ordered the building of Wat Maha That, the Temple of the Great Relic, directly opposite the royal palace. The Venerable Thammakanlayan, the supreme patriarch of the city-dwelling sect, was to have his seat there, a relic of Buddha was to be enshrined, and a green-jeweled statue of the Buddha was commissioned. The temple was also to house the bones of his mother.

"Lopburi has been quiet. I had the opportunity to talk with my mother's friends at her cremation. The consensus is that they are biding their time. Waiting for my time to pass," said the king.

"You have a son now. They must realize you will nominate him as your successor?"

"The would-be King Ramesuan is, I am sure, watching events very closely."

"My troops are ready to attack Sukhothai," said Nakhon In.

"We will leave soon. I have spoken with Lady Mae Luang. She, like me, realizes it is only a matter of time until Sukhothai falls. She has agreed to my request that she visit her relatives in Sukhothai, particularly her younger cousin, the king. I am agreeable to an amicable settlement if they accept our suzerainty. We will wait and see. We will not attack Sukhothai directly, but while my wife is talking with her family we will launch an offensive against Phitsanulok. It sits nominally under the kingdom of Sukhothai but remains largely independent. It would allow us to set up camp close to Sukhothai, and that would worry them," said the king.

The city of Phitsanulok, the gateway to the north, fell after three weeks of fighting. Terms were agreed upon and the governor, Khun Sam Kaeo, remained in power, although now owing allegiance to Ayutthaya, not Sukhothai.

"I embrace the culture and religion of Sukhothai," said the governor of Phitsanulok to King Borommaracha as the king of Ayutthaya paid his first visit to his new northern city. "But I also understand the realities of the situation. It is only a matter of time until Sukhothai falls."

"Show me to Wat Phra Si Rattana Mahathat. I have never seen the temple," said the king.

"It was built in the reign of King Maha Thammaracha, in the year 1357. He also built Wat Phra Phuttha Chinnarat and Wat Phra Si Satsadaram," said Khun Sam Kaeo with pride, as he and King Borommaracha sauntered under royal umbrellas toward the temple as the sunshine beat down. Their entourage paced themselves carefully in the background.

"The king built this temple on the east side of the Nan River with a stupa in the center, *wihans* in the four corners, and two terraces to our left. When the king ordered the casting of the templ's main Buddha image, he was dissatisfied with the results. He ordered a second made but was still not happy. Then an old white-robed ruesi came forward and said that he could make it right. When this third Buddha image was finished the king was spellbound," said the governor.

The sight of the red glazed image of Phra Buddha Chinnarat, cast in the attitude of subduing evil, caused the king of Ayutthaya to fall to his knees in supplication.

"It is more magnificent than they say," said the king. "I am beginning to realize that the kingdom of Sukhothai is different in so many ways."

"And so similar in many others," said the governor.

The king left, taking with him ten thousand people as agreed in the settlement. Land was aplenty, but people to farm it were scarce. The taking of people was a theme that would echo through the coming centuries. In a time of constant wars between Thai, Khmer, Burmese, Lao, and others, gaining new subjects to replace those killed in battle, to build, or to farm became an objective of war.

The following year, 1376, saw King Borommaracha again try to take Kamphaeng Phet. It appeared that the embassy of Lady Mae Luang had met with no success as the city, reinforced by a Lao army sent from the emerging kingdom of Nan, stood its ground behind the walls. It was late in the campaign when the joint forces of Sukhothai and Nan emerged to give fight to the Ayutthayan army. It was an inconclusive battle and resulted in the capture by Ayutthaya of five thousand Nan troops and, more importantly in the long term, the return of the troops of Nan northward to their home. The walls of Kamphaeng Phet, however, stood firm.

It was not until 1378 that King Borommaracha returned to lay siege to the city again. King Maha Thammaracha II led his troops out of the fortress town and against the Ayutthayan forces led by King Borommaracha and Nakhon In. The ensuing battle resulted in a victory for the Ayutthayan troops, with the soldiers of Sukhothai retreating behind the safety of the walls of Kampang Phet.

"There is an emissary from the king of Sukhothai at the camp gates," said the captain of the guard. "King Maha Thammaracha II wants to talk."

"He was a fool to come out and give us battle. He was safe behind his walls. Let us see if he accepts the inevitable," said King Borommaracha.

The reluctant king of Sukhothai was forced to take the oath of allegiance and from that time on was to rule his kingdom as a vassal of Ayutthaya. In order to maintain hegemony over Sukhothai, King Borommaracha attempted to weaken Sukhothai by dividing it into an eastern part and a western part. The western part kept its capital in Sukhothai, while the eastern kingdom, with its capital in Phitsanulok, was given to a prince of Sukhothai who became the adopted son of the Ayutthayan king. Both were considered independent states by their new rulers. A policy of divide and rule had been put in place by King Borommaracha. It had taken him six invasions over a period of eight years to conquer Sukhothai. The route further north now lay open for Ayutthaya to extend its influence into the kingdom of Lan Na.

Now into his seventies, King Borommaracha visited the city of Sawankhalok, which lay on the northern edge of his kingdom of Sukhothai. He received a visitor from Ayutthaya. He was a young man, no more than nineteen, but one well practiced in his craft since childhood. He was Surathin, the first son of Phatcharaphon, spymaster to the late queen Prasuja Akara Devi.

"I am sorry to hear of the death of your father," said the king. "He was of great service to my mother over many years."

"It falls to me to carry on his mantle," said Surathin. "You have a task for me?"

"I need you and your family to go into the neighboring kingdom of Lan Na. I need to understand what they are thinking and what they are planning. They are Tai people like ourselves—you should fit in easily."

"My family is skilled in many aspects of running a royal household. We will get into positions that enable us to learn what you ask and report back."

"Your father has taught you well. I will leave men here. You will communicate with me through them."

Surathin bowed to his king and left the room.

"Now for our next guest," said the king to his commander, the young Prince Nakhon In of the house of Suphanburi.

They mounted their horses and rode to a stand of trees where they dismounted and waited. Soon over the crest of a small rise a solitary figure rode into view. Prince Maha Phrom, the younger brother of King Kue Na of Lan Na, and the ruler of Chiang Saen, dismounted and greeted the king of Ayutthaya as an equal.

"My brother is ill and not long for this world. He has nominated his young son as inheritor to the throne. The throne is mine by right and I seek your support," opened Prince Maha Phrom.

After a lengthy discussion, King Borommaracha concluded, "So it is agreed. I will hold my army in Ayutthaya and await your call. You are to prepare your army and together we will launch an attack on Lan Na. Once your brother the king is toppled, you will acknowledge Ayutthaya as your overlord. The throne in Chiang Mai will be yours."

"Time to return to Ayutthaya. It has been three long years. It is too long to leave a city, even if it is in good hands," said the aging king, turning to Prince Nakhon In. "I have been away too long."

"Prince Ramesuan has been quiet, which I don't think is a good thing. He has a well-trained army and has launched a few minor forays as bandits on the coast become troublesome or when the Khmer encroach, but other than that he has remained distant," said his minister of the interior upon the king's return.

"He is not a man to be trusted. Tonight, I will announce my son Prince Thong Lan as my successor. This news will not be well received by the house of Lopburi. I want you to ensure that your spies in his camp keep us well informed as to his intent. He is a cunning and ambitious man, one waiting for my imminent death. I am an old man now. How my continuing to live must annoy him," said the king, smiling at his own observation.

News arrived from Surathin, the king's spy in the court of King Kue Na of Lan Na, of a serious dispute between the king and Prince Maha Phrom. Following the argument the young prince had left Chiang Mai and headed south. On hearing this the king of Ayutthaya placed his army on alert anticipating being called on in the imminent future. When the sixth king of Lan Na, King Kue Na, died in 1385, his nominated successor was his young son Prince Saen Mueang Ma. Prince Maha Phrom launched an attack on Chiang Mai but failed in his attempt to breach the city walls. Defeated but undeterred, Prince Maha Phrom retreated to Sawankhalok, inside Ayutthayan territory, where he called on the king of Ayutthaya to support his claim.

King Borommaracha was ready for war when the message from Prince Maha Phrom duly arrived. The army of Ayutthaya marched north. The attack of Prince Maha Phrom on Chiang Mai had, in many ways, been a ruse. The prince knew he could not take the city alone, but his attack showed intent. His army and that of King Borommaracha met outside the city of Lampang with the intention of taking that city and advancing to Chiang Mai from there.

Prince Saen Mueang Ma had preempted the move and had arranged for a large force to be stationed in Lampang. He too had his spies.

A series of bloody battles took place before the king of Ayutthaya and Prince Maha Phrom withdrew. Failing to take Lampang, they advanced on Chiang Mai where they were defeated, retreating south through Mueang Li. The first advance by Ayutthaya into the kingdom of Lan Na had failed. Many more attempts were to follow.

Prince Maha Phrom retreated to Kamphaeng Phet with his army. Thinking they were dealing with an ally, the gates were opened and the defeated army of the ruler of Chiang Saen entered the city. In an act of duplicity the army of the prince then staged a coup within the city, claiming it for their own. A short time after, hearing of the news of his former ally seizing the city, King Borommaracha returned with his army to Kamphaeng Phet.

The king of Ayutthaya, his army three times the size of the army of Chiang Saen, stared over the walls and into the city.

"We have been here before," he said to Prince Nakhon In.

"It will be a long and costly siege, as we know to our cost," replied the prince.

"The prince of Chiang Saen is a man of little honor. I was wrong to trust him. He gives us many reasons to war with Lan Na, and that will cost him his kingdom, whether I am king or my son is."

"Do we offer him a way out?"

"Kamphaeng Phet is our city and is almost impregnable. I would sit here and starve him out but many of our soldiers and citizens are inside. As much as I now detest this man I fear we must talk," said the king.

Prince Maha Phrom had also realized his error in taking Kamphaeng Phet, but he needed to find a way to extricate himself from the situation that allowed him to return to Chiang Saen, even if it was to serve King Saen Mueang Ma. He went out to speak to King Borommaracha.

"So it was decided," said the king to Nakhon In after the meeting. "He will leave the city, taking with him Phra Sihing, the Buddha image that he will offer to King Saen Mueang Ma in conciliation. His troops will not be harmed, but he is never to enter the territory of Ayutthaya again."

It was the king's final act. The following morning he died. His son Prince Thong Lan, cousin to Prince Nakhon In, was to inherit the throne.

U-thong Dynasty
(Second Reign)

5

KING RAMESUAN

1369–70
1388–95

THE YEARS HAD CHANGED PRINCE RAMESUAN, son of U-thong.
The obsequious, self-serving prince had been replaced with a more
modest, merciful, and forgiving man. The city of Lopburi had
prospered under his rule, and he had established a reputation for
his ability on both elephant and horse. His devotion to the Buddha
was demonstrated in his building and repair of temples and his giving
of alms, making him much loved by his people.

He had grown up, but he had not abandoned what he considered
his right—to be crowned king.

On the death of King Borommaracha his son Prince Thong Lan
succeeded to the throne at the age of fifteen. King Thong Lan reigned
for only seven days, the time needed for the former King Ramesuan,
son of King Ramathibodi, to gather his army and to come from
Lopburi. Prince Ramesuan had long planned for this day, as King
Borommaracha had suspected.

As messengers rode hastily to Ayutthaya and Lopburi with
the news of the death of the king, both plans sprang into action.
In Ayutthaya the city was placed on alert, and the defensive wall,
slowly reinforced during King Borommaracha's reign, was secured
and troops positioned as if expecting an attack. Arrangements were
made for the coronation of the new king. It would take some time for
the body of King Borommaracha to be returned to Ayutthaya. It was
customary that the crowning of the new king would follow the new
practice of the cremation of the old king, but King Borommaracha

had left clear instructions that his son was to be crowned immediately after the news of his imminent death was received in Ayutthaya.

Prince Ramesuan had been plotting for this moment for many years. When he had seized the throne in 1369 it was achieved by force, and he guessed—correctly—that King Borommaracha would have anticipated the same strategy. This time his strategy was stealth, not force.

Under the cover of darkness, dressed in black and with their faces masked, the best of Prince Ramesuan's men slid through the opened side gate and into the city. Each had his task. Those who ran the Ministry of the Interior and the Ministry of the King's Household were marked for death. Those running the Ministry of the Treasury and the Ministry of Agriculture were to be captured and held.

The most important task was to capture the young king. Quietly they neared his chamber. Two guards fell to the ground as their throats were cut from behind, their assassins holding their hands over the mouths to stop the gurgling sound as they died. With their eyes now fully accustomed to the dark they entered the king's chamber. His concubine rolled over in her sleep as they neared the king. She was grabbed by one of the assassins and a knife slowly run across her throat. The king awoke to find two men holding their knives close. They indicated that he was not to make a sound. Their orders were perfectly clear. They knew what had to be done.

As the soldiers of Prince Ramesuan's army stealthily made their way through the open gate, the young king, hands tied, was bundled into a crimson velvet sack and taken to Wat Khok Phraya, the place designated by Prince Ramesuan for his execution. The crimson velvet sack ensured that his royal body would not be touched by a commoner and that the blood spilled would not show. The king was beaten to death with a club of sandalwood; blows fell on his head and upper body. Death in this manner was seen as a mark of respect. Afterward the body was thrown in a pit near the place of execution.

The following day Prince Ramesuan entered Ayutthaya to be crowned king. Overnight many of King Borommaracha's closest allies had vanished. The new king arrived with new ministers and court officials. It was clear to all that this coup had been meticulously planned and executed. The Lopburi faction had returned to power, at the expense of those from Suphanburi.

King Ramesuan immediately set to work. Royal protocol, fast developing in Ayutthaya, was rigorously enforced. Those who remained in positions of power soon learned to show due respect to their new king. Within a month the city was secure and running as the new king had envisaged. Suphanburi, its position lost, could only look on and accept the crumbs from the table, as those from the city of Lopburi ruled the kingdom.

"You acted with speed and forethought," said Prince Nakhon In, commander to the late King Borommaracha and of the house of Suphanburi.

"My accession was many years in the planning," said King Ramesuan. "I thank you for coming."

"If my king calls then I come."

"Again I thank you. You command the army and they would fight at your behest."

"To what end? We would end up with an endless round of succession disputes that could destroy the kingdom that both your father and my uncle have built."

"Then we may have common ground on which to build. Accept that the focus of Lopburi has always been to control the Khmer. That has not changed. Your uncle achieved much in subduing Sukhothai. You and I know that a change of ruler encourages vassal states to question their loyalty, and I anticipate Sukhothai will be among those. I will fight the Khmer. They are growing strong as the next generation arrives. It is a fight that I and the soldiers from Lopburi will undertake. You are to look to our northern frontier, if that is acceptable to you. I need your support, and the support of the house of Suphanburi. Making you my commander of the northern frontier should allay some of their concerns. Will you give your support?" asked the king.

"You killed my cousin, the young prince, but with honor, and for that I thank you. I offer my support, but my house will be watching," said Prince Nakhon In.

"I ask you to undertake a further task for me," said the king. "You are to travel to China as my ambassador and to inform the court of

the emperor of the change that has taken place here. A junk crewed by
Chinese and Thai sailors sits at anchor in Phra Pradaeng ready to take
you. Many gifts and trade goods are now being taken aboard. I have
not wasted my time idly while waiting to become king. My subjects
to the south have learned much about the sea from the Chinese. It is
something I have encouraged."

They spoke in the developing language used by royalty, ministers,
and courtiers. As the king was held to be divine, the language needed
to talk to him and about him needed to be different from that used
by the commoners. U-thong spoke Thai as his first language. The
language of the Khmer, however, heavily influenced the Thai court,
as did their protocol and royal traditions. The vocabulary of the court
known as *kham rachasap* not only took from the Thai and Khmer
languages but over time integrated words from Sanskrit and Chinese
as well. Initially, the royal vocabulary was meant for the aristocrats
and commoners to use when talking about the kings. In later years, as
Ayutthaya grew in importance and sophistication, an entire language
developed within the court.

King Maha Thammaracha II of Sukhothai had only been able to
look on at the events that surrounded the capture of Kamphaeng
Phet by the prince of Chiang Saen and the subsequent removal of
the city's prized Buddha image. His kingdom was divided and weak.
However, Ayutthaya was in a state of flux following the death of King
Borommaracha and the accession to the throne of King Ramesuan.
The king of Sukhothai looked toward King Saen Mueang Ma of Lan
Na to help free his kingdom from Ayutthaya.

"Prince Nakhon In," said the king. "I have been informed by King
Borommaracha's spies in Chiang Mai that King Maha Thammaracha
II has requested the assistance of King Saen Mueang Ma in order to
free his kingdom from our overlordship."

"The last act of King Borommaracha was to allow Prince Maha
Phrom to return to Lan Na with Phra Sihing, our most revered image
of the Buddha. The kings and people of Sukhothai are devout and

caring. The removal of an image so loved would have pained them deeply," replied Prince Nakhon In.

"As we discussed earlier I wish only peace with Sukhothai, but this I cannot allow. Ready your troops. We leave for Sukhothai tomorrow!" said King Ramesuan. "Your visit to China will have to wait!"

The soldiers of King Saen Mueang Ma were caught unawares as the army of Ayutthaya ambushed and routed them. Determined to ensure that this event could not recur, King Ramesuan pursued the retreating army back to Chiang Mai, where he laid siege to the city.

King Ramesuan erected a stockade away from the Chiang Mai city moat and established camp, effectively surrounding the city. He had with him a new weapon, manned by Persian mercenaries: the cannon. Such a weapon had never been used in Southeast Asia; the city walls were for defense against men and quickly crumbled under the bombardment.

King Saen Mueang Ma, holding a fan, went up to look at the ramparts. He had a soldier attach a written message to an arrow and shoot it down.

The message said, "I ask the king to pause his attack for seven days so that I might send out presents to the king and thus repair the breach in our royal friendship."

"What if the king of Chiang Mai is trying to play a trick on us?" King Ramesuan asked his commanders and ministers. Answering his own question, he continued, "Nonetheless, we will abide by his request. He is a great king, so we will do what is honorable."

The army of Ayutthaya stood by as the week passed. Within Chiang Mai fences of split bamboo were woven and set in place where the cannon bombardment had demolished the existing wall. Seven days passed and the king of Chiang Mai did not come out to offer the promised presents. The army officers and soldiers complained that rice had risen in price and that no place could be found to buy it. They asked permission to attack immediately.

The king was angered and directed an assault to be launched. Operations were abandoned on one side of the city and a bombardment of cannon was timed to fire simultaneously. The king of Chiang Mai fled and King Ramesuan entered the city on his royal elephant.

Nak Sang, a son of the departed king of Chiang Mai, was captured and brought before the king.

"The king of Chiang Mai, your father, has played us false. We had taken him at his word that he would come out and deal honestly with us. We were even prepared to uphold him on the royal throne, but now it cannot be so," the king said.

King Ramesuan placed Nak Sang on the throne in place of his father after he had sworn an oath of allegiance in front of the ministers and commanders of the courts of Ayutthaya and Chiang Mai. The king allowed a certain number of people to remain in the city before forcibly removing the remainder south to help populate the cities of Phatthalung, Songkhla, Nakhon Si Thammarat, and Chanthabun. King Nak Sang traveled south with King Ramesuan to the mueang of Sawangburi. On his way back to Chiang Mai he passed the long row of his people being taken south.

Mae Luang, widow of the late King Ramathibodi, had traveled, even at her late age, to meet with her nephew Lue Thai, King Maha Thammaracha II.

"You are not a warrior, you are a monk," she said to her nephew.

"The theft of Phra Sihing was the breaking point for my people. We stood firm for many years only to see our kingdom split in two by King Borommaracha. He divides our people to help him rule his kingdom and then permits the prince of Chiang Saen to take our most revered image of the Buddha as an offering to his king," replied King Maha Thammaracha II.

"He agreed to this only to stop bloodshed. He did not understand how your people felt."

"My people would have preferred death to seeing the image removed. Your late king did not understand my people," said the king, adding, "He died the following day. Was that not a sign?"

"We have a new king now—my stepson. A king from my house, the house of Lopburi, the house of U-thong. I have spoken at length with him. He wants peace with Sukhothai. He is not of the house of Suphanburi. It is they who urge war against you. Our new king wants peace."

"You are of Sukhothai and you speak from your heart. I will meet with your king in the spirit of conciliation," said the devout Buddhist king.

A pact of friendship was agreed between Ayutthaya and Sukhothai, marriages were arranged, and peace reigned between the two nations for many years.

On his return from concluding the pact in Sukhothai, King Ramesuan ordered the building of Wat Mahathat in Ayutthaya.

> Then the King went out to observe the precepts at Mangkhalaphisek Hall. At ten thum he looked toward the east and saw a Great Holy Relic of the Lord Buddha performing a miracle. Calling the palace deputies to bring his royal palanquin, he rode forth. He had stakes brought and pounded into the ground to mark the spot. The great holy reliquary which he built there was nineteen wa high, with a nine-branched finial three wa high, and named the Maha That Monastery. Then the King had the Royal Rite of Entering the Capital performed and festivities were held in the royal residence.

In 1393 the resurgent Khmer under King Kodom Bong attacked the nearby provinces of Chonburi and Chantabun and took thousands of prisoners back to Angkor. King Ramesuan acted quickly; an opportunity to demonstrate Ayutthaya's superiority to the Khmer was not one to be dismissed. The Ayutthayan forces were led by General Phraya Chai Narong. The two armies met at Yaek Bridge on the main road to Angkor in a bloody battle in which both sides fought valiantly. The Khmer had stockades built from which to defend, and the death toll in taking them was high, but it was the forces of General Phraya Chai Narong who in the end proved victorious after three long days of fighting.

The Khmer king fled by boat. General Phraya Chai Narong descended from his war elephant and had hand cannon fired down on the boats. Some gunpowder exploded, but the king of the Khmer got away. The crown prince, a grandson of King Kodom Bong, was captured, and a vassal king was placed under the watchful eye of Phraya Chai Narong. His occupying soldiers were eventually chased out, but the city was mortally wounded after the 1393 invasion.

Some ninety thousand prisoners were taken back to Ayutthaya, decimating the remaining population of Angkor. Among this vast number of prisoners were a considerable number of scholars, artisans, and builders whose skills could be put to good use as Ayutthaya continued to flourish.

Wat Phukhao Thong, the Monastery of the Golden Mount, had just been completed on King Ramesuan's orders. The monastery had been built on the site of a shrine to the guardian spirit of Ayutthaya.

> One evening the King walked to Mangkhalaphisek Hall; and Thao Mon, who had died earlier, came and sat blocking the path where the king was walking.

The king and the spirit looked directly at each other. As the king approached the spirit vanished, leaving the king dumbfounded. In the days that followed the king quickly sickened and died, leaving his son, Prince Ram, as his heir.

6

KING RAMARACHA

1395–1409

THE SUCCESSION WAS NOT DISPUTED, and the twenty-one-year-old son of King Ramesuan became the fifth king of Ayutthaya. His father had left him a legacy of peace with Sukhothai and the Khmer no longer a threat. Prince Ram had been born, brought up, and schooled in Ayutthaya. He was of royal blood and would be treated in the manner his position demanded.

The new king knew little outside Ayutthaya. In his twenty one years he had rarely left the city. He was a product of his upbringing and in many ways ignorant of the world that lay outside.

"Prince Nakhon In," King Ramaracha commenced. "You have served my father well. Your loyalty is to be rewarded.

"Your Majesty," replied the prince.

"You remain in command of the western army, but in addition you will be granted the governorship of Suphanburi.

"You have my thanks," replied Prince Nakhon In.

Prince Nakhon In rode from Ayutthaya side by side with his most trusted friend and confidant, Okya Mahasena, tutor to the new king, and also of the house of Suphanburi.

"One of the first acts of the new king was to give you Suphanburi. That is a surprising move on his part," said Okya Mahasena.

"He feels that my loyal service deserves reward."

"Does he not know his history? Does he not understand the conflict between the house of Lopburi and the house of Suphanburi? Does he not remember how his father killed your cousin, the young prince Thong Lan? His father was wise enough to place governors from

Lopburi to rule over Suphanburi. They were unpopular, yes, but they contained any excesses that we felt. To put a prince of Suphanburi in the governor's role is either a very clever move by our new king, or a very stupid one."

"I feel our new king has been too cloistered. He enjoys the pageantry of being king. Time will tell if he can be king," said Prince Nakhon In, the new governor of Suphanburi.

The small kingdom of Nan, far to the north, sent no embassy to the enthronement of King Ramaracha. This was taken as an insult by the new king who set out to right the wrong that had been committed on the throne of Ayutthaya and to him personally.

"They insult me. They must be made an example of!" raged the king.

"They have no understanding with us and regard themselves as an independent kingdom," replied Okya Mahasena, just returned from Suphanburi.

"Then they must be taught otherwise."

"They have close ties with both Lan Na and Sukhothai."

"Both vassal states of Ayutthaya. It is time for them to understand they exist only at our behest. People say my father left a settled and prosperous kingdom. It will not remain so if I allow insults to go unavenged. I will war with Nan and give my people a famous victory," trumpeted the king.

"I am your adviser and I ask you not to undertake this retribution. The kingdom of Nan owes us no allegiance. To send an embassy to your coronation could be seen as acceptance of Ayutthaya's suzerainty over them. I beg you to understand their position."

"I will not be seen as a weak king. Those who wrong me will be punished."

"They wrong you, but this wrong can be righted without bloodshed. It is the mark of a good monarch to use diplomacy in the first instance, as I have taught you."

"I need a victory to show my strength to the kingdom."

"Victory, yes, but victory is not always gained through war."

"What do you suggest?" asked a mellower king.

"I suggest that we send an embassy to Nan. A substantial embassy with elephants and soldiers. One bearing gifts of friendship and one that makes it clear to their ruler, Chao Khamtan, that you are displeased and that your displeasure will only be sated when he accepts the suzerainty of King Ramaracha and the kingdom of Ayutthaya."

"And this will be my idea?"

"Of course, my king."

"Then so be it. You will head the embassy," said the king. "A king that leads by diplomacy. I like that," he mused.

The embassy caused consternation in the small northern kingdom. Proud of its independence, Chao Khamtan was careful not to agree to the demands, however well phrased by Okya Mahasena. He thanked the king of Ayutthaya for the honor of his request, but he asked for time to consult with his ministers and his people. Okya Mahasena left; this was followed closely by the departure of Chao Khamtan, two of his ministers, and his personal bodyguard. They headed not south to Ayutthaya but southwest to Sukhothai.

Chao Khamtan entered the legendary city of Sukhothai to meet with his cousin Sai Lue Thai, the effective ruler of Sukhothai and the son of the monk-king Maha Thammaracha II. Nan had been a vassal state of the kingdom of Sukhothai, and intermarriages over the generations closely linked the two kingdoms.

"Cousin, I have been offered the chance to accept the suzerainty of Ayutthaya or be conquered and made a vassal state," said Chao Khamtan directly.

"That is not a choice I would like to make," replied Sai Lue Thai.

"It is a choice that I seek your help in making. Your father is a wise man. His devotion is respected throughout the kingdom, but I know that in his heart he yearns for Sukhothai to be free."

"As do I."

"I seek a pact, a pact between Sukhothai and Nan as we have had in the past. One where we will come to the aid of each other if attacked."

"The mere existence of this pact may deter the young king of Ayutthaya from attacking so far north. It may also demonstrate to him that Sukhothai, although a vassal state of Ayutthaya, does not accept that status willingly. I will follow my father as king, and I wish that the kingdom of Sukhothai be returned to its former glory. Our army is being strengthened and trained as we speak. Your proposal fits in well with my intentions," said Sai Lue Thai.

"Then you will agree?"

"My father is honor-bound to Ayutthaya. He will not break his oath. It is I who will sign. The agreement will come into force upon the death of my father, although if the opportunity offers itself, I will fulfill it earlier," said Sai Lue Thai, the future King Maha Thammaracha III.

King Ramaracha's intentions on Nan were put to one side as a number of issues and disputes with Sukhothai took hold. It was nothing major—the querying of taxes, disputes over the honesty of appointed officials, and reports of increased banditry, among other complaints. Now two years into his reign the king embarked on ensuring the loyalty of Sukhothai.

"We will promulgate our laws on Sukhothai. They are a vassal state. With our laws in place they can deal with these disputes in a manner acceptable to us," said the king confidently.

"They have their own laws, decreed under King Ram Khamhaeng. They form the foundation of their kingdom," said Okya Mahasena.

"Then it is time for them to change," blazed a petulant King Ramaracha. "This you will not talk me out of. I will work with the Brahmin on ensuring our laws are clear to them. I will travel personally to Sukhothai when they are ready. You will not accompany me."

In the year 1397, King Ramaracha set out on a state visit to his vassal kingdom of Sukhothai. He traveled in great state with royal elephants resplendent in the red of Ayutthaya at the fore and drummers beating out a steady rhythm. The royal procession, accompanied by a substantial army of five thousand fully armed and battle-ready soldiers under the command of Prince Nakhon In, entered Sukhothai, and the city fell to the ground as the king passed by.

The procession slowly made its way through the streets before the royal elephant dropped to its knees to allow the king to dismount. The royal palace, with intricate wood carvings, stood next to the famed temple of Wat Mahathat in the walled central zone. The soldiers under the command of Prince Nakhon In lined up behind the king, presenting the monk-king Maha Thammaracha II, dressed only in the plain saffron robes of a monk, with a formidable sight.

"Your kingdom presents me with many issues," said the king of Ayutthaya when they were alone.

"We have many pressing issues, that is true," replied the king of Sukhothai.

"Today we solve them. Today your kingdom will adopt the laws and organization of Ayutthaya. You will be fully integrated into our kingdom. You are the first of our vassal states to receive this honor," said the king of Ayutthaya, as he had been schooled to do.

"By saying this you leave them no choice," said his Brahmin before he left Ayutthaya. "By taking Prince Nakhon In to protect you, you demonstrate that you trust Suphanburi, and that you take their concerns about Sukhothai seriously. You will leave three of my Brahmin brothers in Sukhothai to oversee the implementation, together with ten monks chosen from among the forest-dwelling Buddhist sect in this city. We will have with us a number of retainers and messengers who, it must be stressed during any talks, should be allowed free and unfettered movement both inside and outside the city at all times. By doing this you make clear to Sukhothai that they are no longer an independent kingdom, and in doing so you crush any aspirations they have."

With Sukhothai secure Prince Nakon In returned to Suphanburi and embarked on his second visit to China at the behest of the king. He would return to find Ayutthaya in chaos.

"I have heard nothing from the petty state of Nan," said King Ramaracha. "Did your mission achieve nothing?" he asked of Okya Mahasena. "I will deal with Nan. You are dismissed."

His old tutor inwardly balked at the way the king, his pupil for many years, now spoke to him. He was the king's adviser, but often his advice was dismissed. The king sought the counsel of the Brahmins and the monks, embracing the religion and the ritual. He was becoming distant from the reasoned voice of Okya Mahasena, and this did not augur well for the future.

The king's spies in Chiang Mai sent news to Ayutthaya that the vassal kingdom of Lan Na was dissatisfied with its relationship, and that there was open talk in the court of freeing themselves from their vassalage to Ayutthaya. Added to that, the Khmer had not paid their due tribute. An embassy was sent by the king of Angkor. The Khmer explained that their kingdom was under attack from the Dai Viet to the east and the resources could not be found to make the payment. The king raged, cursing everyone. He was finally taken to his chambers, where he stayed for four days.

He emerged and called his minister of the interior. It was evident he was still in a foul mood.

"You are to send a mission to Nan," he started without preamble. "Nan will submit to Ayutthaya. Tell them if they do not then we will war against them and their kingdom will be reduced to dust. Make no pretense. No gifts will be given. They have had more than enough time."

He then called General Ket Kaeo, one of his generals from Lopburi.

"An embassy from the Khmer has arrived and they have not paid their tribute. You are to return, carrying the heads of their embassy in a sack with you, and make them pay. Make them understand that the king of Ayutthaya is not to be trifled with."

Unknown to the king, King Maha Thammaracha II of Sukhothai had died the previous day. His son, Sai Lue Thai, was made King Maha Thammaracha III. Also unknown to King Ramaracha was the existence of the mutual defense pact between Sukhothai and Nan.

King Maha Thammaracha III had long planned for this day. Over the past few years he had readied his army. When news reached him of King Ramaracha's demands on Nan, he invoked the pact and in the year 1400 proclaimed independence from Ayutthaya. His troops quickly captured the town of Nakhon Sawan, an important northern gateway at the confluence of the Ping and Nan Rivers.

King Ramaracha was no war general. He relied on others to do the fighting. Prince Nakhon In was in China, so he was having to rely on generals from Suphanburi who were proving reluctant to fight, making excuse after excuse.

"We are torn," mused Okya Mahasena. "Does Suphanburi support the king against our hated enemy Sukhothai, or is this war to our advantage? The king is proving himself unable to organize his army.

His rages are legendary and those around him are increasingly concerned. We wait for the return of Prince Nakhon In."

The prince returned after his three-year sojourn in the storied land to the north to find the kingdom in crisis. He was summoned immediately by the king but first met with Okya Mahasena outside the city walls of Ayutthaya.

"I fear the king is proving unfit to govern. The troops of Sukhothai have regained much of their old territory. Our generals have been biding their time waiting for your arrival. Only you can lead our troops and regain Sukhothai for Ayutthaya, but consider the implications of succeeding. You will be the most powerful man in the kingdom, more powerful than the king. This he will not allow. You will face two options—either that the king will exile or kill you, or that you seize the crown for yourself, for Suphanburi, and for the good of Ayutthaya."

It took four long years before Prince Nakhon In led his troops triumphantly into Sukhothai. In Suphanburi, Prince Nakhon In received a hero's welcome. The old enemy had been defeated, but the words of Okya Mahasena still echoed in his head.

In Ayutthaya, King Ramaracha fluctuated between days of clarity and days where he saw nothing but ghosts and demons as the forces of Suphanburi plotted against him. His kingdom was secure, but it was not he who had secured it. Had he allowed Prince Nakhon In too much? Was the prince after his crown? These and many other thoughts ran through his head. Finally he summoned his old tutor Okya Mahasena to him.

"Suphanburi plots against me. Prince Nakhon In desires my throne," raged the king, pacing up and down incessantly.

"Prince Nakhon In has served at your behest and secured Sukhothai for Ayutthaya."

"He has secured Sukhothai for Suphanburi. The house of Lopburi sees that clearly. Does he want the throne? Answer me or I will throw you into the dungeons where you will rot and wither away."

"I am not privy to the thoughts of Prince Nakhon In. My life is in Ayutthaya serving you," implored Okya Mahasena.

"Get out of my sight, and leave Ayutthaya. You are no longer allowed to serve me," said the king dismissing his long-serving tutor with a wave of his hand.

It was with a big sigh of relief that Okya Mahasena looked back on Ayutthaya as he left. As he did so one of his old servants rode to his side.

"The king has ordered your arrest," he said. "Quick, follow me."

They headed off the main track and made their way across the river to the village of the Cham. Okya Mahasena sent a message to Prince Nakhon In advising him of what had happened, and waited. Within the week Prince Nakhon In and his army arrived in the village.

"You are to lead the army and take Ayutthaya. You were right in what you said many years ago. He wants me dead. He cannot allow me to live," said Prince Nakhon In to Okya Mahasena.

"I have planned for this day. There are many sympathizers within the city. At the sight of the army they will fulfill their allotted roles. If my plan succeeds, there will be turmoil and panic in the city, making its defense more difficult."

"You are to lead the army. I cannot be seen to be part of this. When the city is secure I will be waiting here," said Prince Nakhon In. The capital fell as the prince's army appeared. King Ramaracha was captured, and the future King Intharacha entered the city. The old king was exiled, and the house of Suphanburi reigned again.

Suphannaphum Dynasty
(Second Reign)

7

KING INTHARACHA

1409–24

KING INTHARACHA MOVED QUICKLY to secure his position. King Ramaracha was forced to abdicate, clearing the way for his successor. With the abdication settled the old king was exiled to a village to the south of Ayutthaya, where he was kept under guard until his eventual death. Following his coronation the new king placed Lopburi, the native city of the old king, under the direct administrative control of Ayutthaya.

In King Intharacha's mind the long-standing feud between Suphanburi and the U-thong clan in Lopburi was over.

The king honored his lifetime friend and confidant Chao Phraya Okya Mahasena in a lavish ceremony.

"I thank you for your kindness," said Okya Mahasena.

"Your steadfastness and honesty over these long years have made this day possible," replied the king. "I ask you to continue to serve me in Ayutthaya."

"I am deeply honored."

"I still have to ensure the conquest of Sukhothai and will return there shortly. When I am absent from the city, Ayutthaya is in your hands. Of particular import to me is establishing cordial relations with Emperor Yongle of the Ming dynasty. We will send an embassy informing the emperor of the changes that have occurred and emphasize our loyalty and our wish to both honor him and trade with him. I met with his envoy, the eunuch Khang Yuan, in secret and his fleet admiral Zheng He when I landed from China. I have cordial relations with the Chinese and will try to maintain them."

"Yes, I knew of your meeting with the Chinese, although I am not sure the former king did," said Okya Mahasena with a smile.

In 1411, two years after King Intharacha's accession to the throne, King Saen Mueang Ma of Lan Na, who had regained the throne shortly after King Intharacha had left for Ayutthaya, died, resulting in a succession dispute between his two sons, Prince Yi Kumkam and Prince Sam Fang Kaen. Prince Yi Kumkam, the ruler of Chiang Saen, appealed for help in averting a state of civil war after his army was defeated in a battle with Prince Sam Fang Kaen.

King Intharacha sensed an opportunity to test the loyalty of King Maha Thammaracha III of Sukhothai. He commanded him to raise an army and send them north to support Prince Yi Kumkam. Their combined armies first attacked Phayao but were unsuccessful. Although the defenders of Phayao did not have cannon of their own they melted down brass tiles and used the cannon they forged to demolish the earthen fort built by the besieging army.

The armies of Prince Yi Kumkam and King Maha Thammaracha III consolidated their forces at Chiang Rai and then moved on to Chiang Mai. The strengthened walls stood firm against cannon fire, and a stalemate developed between the forces outside supporting the claim of Prince Yi Kumkam and those inside the city supporting the claim of Prince Sam Fang Kaen.

Prince Sam Fang Kaen offered that rather than having a prolonged siege with many deaths, the outcome should be settled by a single battle between his brother and himself.

The two combatants faced each other across the featureless plain alongside the Ping River. The soldiers of both armies gathered on the opposite riverbank, some climbing trees for a clearer view.

Armed equally with a long, sharpened sword called a *krabi*, a curved sword, and a knife, both brothers looked over the flat, baked clay battleground at each other. Prince Sam Fang Kaen raised his hand to salute his brother and Prince Yi Kumkam saluted back. For a brief moment they realized they were brothers, but the die was cast. Today they were warriors engaging in single combat to the death. At the signal both advanced cautiously in the manner of their fights when growing up together. Both knew each other's strengths and weaknesses well.

Initially the pace was furious, with blows checked or avoided. Gradually the pace slowed. The fight turned when Prince Sam Fang Kaen used his *krabi* to impale the foot of his brother. For a brief moment Prince Yi Kumkam could not move. That was all it took for Prince Sam Fang Kaen to slice his curved sword into his brother's neck. His brother fell to the ground, blood pouring from his wound, and died, his eyes looking directly into the eyes of his brother.

The generals and soldiers of Prince Yi Kumkam would now join the army of the new king, King Sam Fang Kaen, and the army of Sukhothai turned from the battlefield. Undeterred by the defeat, the king of Sukhothai took advantage of the situation by marching his troops to Chiang Rai and capturing the now poorly defended city, looting it, and taking seven thousand people back to Sukhothai.

On hearing the news of the defeat of his candidate for the throne and of King Maha Thammaracha III's sacking of Chiang Rai, the king of Ayutthaya gathered his troops and rode to confront the Sukhothai king.

"The fight was fair and honorable," said King Maha Thammaracha III, but his eyes showed fear.

"You were to install Prince Yi Kumkam on the throne. Those were your instructions."

"Both sides were equally matched. We could not find an entry to Chiang Mai. Their walls had been strengthened and our cannon made little impact on them."

"Then you tunnel, then you poison their water, or then you starve them out!"

"But King Sam Fang Kaen offered the duel. It was only right to honor his request."

"Honor his request! This is war, not a game of chess. You accepted his offer as it was the easy way out. I am your king, and I paid you the compliment of demonstrating my trust in you, even after our previous history. I knew from our battles you were weak, unable to make the telling thrust, and again you demonstrate this to me. From this day on you are king in name only.

I will leave General Wangnuan as chief resident. You will do as your father did and enter the monastery, where you will be monitored. I will ensure the general runs Sukhothai as I want," said King Intharacha, holding the actions of the king of Sukhothai in disdain.

King Intharacha took the captives with him, placing most in Nakhon Si Thammarat on the Malay Peninsula. The city was still trying to recover from the cholera outbreak of over fifty years previously. Despite the building of temples and roads the city still struggled to survive. King Intharacha knew the importance of the city as both a port and a buffer to the Malays establishing themselves with their new religion of Islam in Malacca to the south of the peninsula.

When King Intharacha returned to Ayutthaya he was met by Okya Mahasena, who looked concerned.

"An envoy from China has arrived. He holds a letter from the emperor to be delivered only to you. He requests an immediate audience."

"I will refresh myself after the journey. Tell the envoy that I would not insult the emperor by not being properly attired before reading his letter."

The envoy, dressed in blue silk and wearing the tasseled, coronet-shaped hat favored by the Ming dynasty, bowed. Unlike others he regarded himself as an equal to a foreign king. As a representative of the emperor a small bow would suffice. King Intharacha, who had visited China on two occasions, understood both their manner and their language. As King Ram Khamhaeng had all those centuries before, he had witnessed the glories and military might of China and had learned to respect it.

The envoy handed the scroll to the king who accepted it with both hands, lowering his head as a sign of respect. He then turned and left the room leaving King Intharacha to read the letter. The king examined the emperor's seal.

I reverently took on the mandate of Heaven and I rule the Chinese and the yi. In my rule, I embody Heaven and Earth's love and concern for the welfare of all things and look on all equally, without distinguishing between one and the other. You,

king, have been able to respect Heaven and serve the superior
and have fulfilled your tribute duties. I have been greatly pleased
by this for a long time. Recently Yi-si-han-da-er Sha, the king of
the country of Melaka, inherited the throne. He has been able to
carry on his father's will and has personally brought his wife and
children to the Court to offer tribute. This loyalty in serving the
superior is no different from yours. However, I have learned that,
without reason, you have intended to send troops against him.
With the dangerous weapons troops carry, when two sides meet
in combat, it is inevitable that there will be great injuries on both
sides. Thus, those who are fond of employing troops do not have
virtuous hearts. The king of the country of Melaka has already
become part of "the within", and he is a minister of the Court.
If he has committed an offense, you should report details to the
Court. You must not rashly send troops on this account. If you
do so, is it not the same as having no Court? Such actions will
certainly not be your wishes. Perhaps it is your ministers using
your name in despatching troops to pursue private quarrels. You
should consider such matters deeply and not allow yourself to
be deceived. If you develop good relations with neighbouring
countries and do not engage in mutual aggression, the prosperity
which will result will be limitless. You, king, should bear this
in mind!

"What do you make of it?" asked Okya Mahasena of the king.

"The emperor wants us to take no further action against Malacca.
They have clearly reached an agreement either for trade or as a
military port."

"But we are taking no action."

"We are not, but the pirates of Lopburi are. We must write to the
emperor ensuring him that we will deal with these incidents and stop
them recurring. We must make it clear that these incidents happened
under the previous dynasty, and we will not permit such actions to
affect our relationship with him."

"So you think the Chinese are using Malacca as a staging port?

"I think it likely. The Chinese are looking to expand southward by sea. It would make sense for them to have such a well-positioned port."

"Then let us hope they use the port for trade and not as a port to attack us."

"We have little to offer them but wood and rice. There are better targets than us. However, we must redouble our efforts to trade with them. They need to see us as a worthwhile ally. Let us look at enlarging the Chinese compound as a first step," said the king.

"Now to the serious business," said Okya Mahasena. "Asayuth."

"How could I forget? The city buzzes with excitement. By next week the city will be full of visitors. And the royal barge?"

"It is finished and awaiting your royal approval."

"Then let our craftsmen wait no longer!"

The royal palanquin arrived outside the palace with the mounted honor-guard to the fore and rear. The king, excited, sat opposite Okya Mahasena as the palanquin sped through the streets of Ayutthaya. The king could see out, but he could not be seen from the outside. The palanquin passed buildings, many painted in white, some decorated with murals depicting ghosts, past loves, or heroic battle scenes. Temples gleamed in white with gold and red roofs glinting in the afternoon sun. They seemed to stop and look as the king passed by. People supplicated themselves, falling to the ground, their heads pressed firmly downward as the king passed. Finally, they came to the vast workshop on an offshoot of the Pa Sak River.

The craftsmen had little time to prepare for the royal visit and scrambled down from where they were working to supplicate themselves just in time as the king and Okya Mahasena entered. They would remain silent and in that position until the king left.

The royal barge, which had taken three long years to build, had yet to be lowered into the water. But it was finished.

Its keel had been carved from one giant teak tree trunk, over forty meters in length and weighing over fifteen tons. The king stood mesmerized.

"It looks magnificent," said the king, viewing the golden, two-tiered ship. "It will sit well in the water."

He moved nearer, running his hands along the ornate carving—the *suea* or tiger barge, with the body and the black stripes of the tiger running the length of the vessel. As the king approached the prow of the ship the eyes of the tiger seemed to stare directly at the king as its head jutted proudly forward.

The minister of the navy hurriedly entered and supplicated himself before his king.

"Rise, Chao Kamchang," said the king.

"I apologize for not informing you of my visit, but when Okya Mahasena reminded me of the festival of Asayuth I could not wait to view the new royal barge. Accompany me to the deck if you would?" requested the king, honoring his minister of the navy.

The deck was smooth—polished, but not slippery. The royal cabin, carved in teak wood high in the center of the vessel, was red and black and highly lacquered. When the king was aboard, it would be draped in curtains to ensure that none of his subjects could look upon his divine personage. It was enough that they knew their king was inside. The king strode the deck looking in minute detail at his barge as Okya Mahasena and Chao Kamchang waited. As he came back a broad smile crossed his face.

"When can I see it in the water?" he asked impatiently.

The ceremony of Asayuth had its roots going back to the reign of King Ram Khamhaeng of Sukhothai. He ensured that his navy was ready for battle by making his boat crews compete against each other. The boats were now exquisitely decorated for Asayuth and the crews would be dressed in their finest clothes, but underneath and when the festivities had finished, the boats were still weapons of war.

King Borommaracha had instituted the ceremony called Asayuth, which included a race between the king's barge and the queen's barge. The queen's barge was usually allowed to win as it was believed to foretell a coming year of plenty.

Prior to the race of the royal barges, a series of boat races were held where each town or city throughout Ayutthaya would race their war boats against each other. The boats, approximately twenty feet in length, were rowed with oarsmen alternating on each side and would sprint along a straight course measuring about a kilometer. The finishing line was the royal pavilion opposite the royal throne, where the king would judge the winner. Finally, only two boats would remain for the grand finale. Victory was a great honor bringing considerable prestige to the town or city that was declared by the king to be the winner.

The following day the new royal barge entered the water. The king looked on as the monks blessed the vessel and performed the ritual wai to the female spirit that was thought to be aboard every vessel. A garland of flowers was placed over the prow to ensure good fortune, and the king watched as the crew, drawn from the craftsmen who had built the boat, rowed the vessel out into the Pa Sak River. The royal barge was named *Suea Kamron Sin* in tribute to the tiger staring from its prow.

Emissaries from Japan, Persia, and Aceh looked on as a procession of vessels passed by. Headed by the king's and queen's royal barges and followed in turn by the barges of the royal families and ministers, the procession made its way downriver before turning. The royal barge procession itself consisted of eight barges including those of former kings, although those vessels were difficult to keep seaworthy because of their great age.

The emissaries and the people of Ayutthaya looked on as over five hundred boats passed by. Some were gilded, some were decorated with garlands of flowers, and the working barges gleamed after being heavily lacquered in preparation for the day and for the working year that lay ahead. As the king arrived in the royal pavilion the racing boats from the towns and cities of his kingdom saluted as they passed by in battle formation. They would head downriver and race against one another and the prevailing flow of the river.

The river, a muddy brown, flowed listlessly in the hot sun as the racing commenced. Finally two teams emerged. The final would be between Nakhon Si Thammarat and Sukhothai. The king leaned to Okya Mahasena.

"Following our recent troubles with Sukhothai it would be good if they didn't win," he said, rubbing his chin gently.

The crowd roared as they passed by. Sukhothai won comfortably.

The king, as was the tradition started by King Borommaracha, allowed the winning team to stand in his presence with their eyes downcast. He placed a garland of flowers over each of their heads. Afterward he was rowed in a smaller royal barge to be transferred to the royal barge, *Suea Kamron Sin*. His new royal barge was duly defeated by the queen's barge, thereby ensuring fertility and abundance in the coming year. As the sun set, the golden royal barge shimmered against the river.

King Intharacha, despite his displeasure with King Maha Thammaracha III, gradually allowed his general to loosen his control over the king of Sukhothai. The king wanted to try an approach that did not rely on military strength. There was already a history of political marriages between the two kingdoms, and King Intharacha, with three sons and four daughters, looked to tighten the relationship between the two kingdoms.

The opportunity came with the death of King Maha Thammaracha III in 1419 as his two sons quarreled over the succession. King Intharacha offered to mediate the dispute and suggested once again that Sukhothai be divided into two parts, to be ruled separately by the two disputing princes, Phaya Ram and Phaya Ban Mueang, who, being the elder son, was given the title King Maha Thammaracha IV. The king exacted a price from Sukhothai for his mediation. Sukhothai was forced to accept vassal status, and the border city of Chainat was to be given permanently to Ayutthaya. The two princes were betrothed to two of King Intharacha's daughters.

Two Ayutthayan princes, Chao Ai Phraya (the first chao phraya) and Chao Yi Phraya (the second chao phraya) were sent to rule the two border cities of Mueang San and Chainat. On the death of their father the king, these two elder sons—Chao Ai Phraya, then in Suphanburi, and Chao Yi Phraya, then in Sanburi—fought each other on elephants as they met on their way into Ayutthaya to claim the throne. But neither was victorious:

One curious tradition is on record, the date of which is at the beginning of the fifteenth century. On the death of King Intharacha, the sixth of the dynasty, his two eldest sons, who were rulers of smaller provinces, hastened, each one from his home, to seize their father's vacant throne. Mounted on elephants they hastened to Ayuthia, and by a strange chance arrived at the same moment at a bridge, crossing in opposite directions. The princes were at no loss to understand the motive each of his brother's journey. A contest ensued upon the bridge—a contest so furious and desperate that both fell, killed by each other's hands. One result of this tragedy was to make easy the way of the youngest and surviving brother, who, coming by an undisputed title to the throne, reigned long and prosperously.

The youngest brother, Chao Sam Phraya (the third chao phraya), living in Chainat, was then proclaimed king with the title of King Borommaracha II. To make merit for his dead brothers the new king had two chedis built on the spot where they had died. The bodies of both brothers were cremated, and on their cremation site he had Wat Ratchaburana built in their memory.

8

KING BOROMMARACHA II
1424–48

"I am unprepared," said the young King Borommaracha II. "I did not expect the throne, particularly in this manner, my brothers killed by each other's hand. You were my father's best friend since childhood and you have been alongside me as I grew from a child. I need your help and your advice. I need you to guide me in these early years."

"I am an old man now, not long for this world. I will stand at your side, but the time for you to govern alone will come sooner than you think. Today the boy is gone. Today you will be crowned king, and the man will emerge," said Okya Mahasena.

Following the coronation, they met again.

"My king, you ask me to advise you. I say always be aware of the house of U-thong. They covet your throne. Do not stand still—expand the kingdom north to Lan Na, east to Angkor or to the sea, and west to Tenasserim or Tavoy. Watch to the south where the Muslims are growing, keep moving onward. Trust only a select few. Ayutthaya holds many secrets and has many spies. Choose those you trust wisely. Choose family first. Others will have to earn your trust.

"Honor your mother and father, and honor your religion. Attend all the festivals and be seen to be caring of your people. That is my advice. The decisions you make are yours—nobody else's—and that is how you will be judged," said Okya Mahasena with a seriousness in his voice.

The new king's first task was to start the construction of Wat Ratchaburana in memory of his brothers. The temple was seen as a celebration of their magnificent death. Ayutthaya was a city renowned for its craftsmanship in gold and silver. King Borommaracha II wanted the temple and crypt to be splendid. It was where his brothers' ashes would be interred.

In 1424, monks from Chiang Mai and from Cambodia returned to Ayutthaya from Sri Lanka, where they had been reordained. These monks returned with two learned Sinhalese monks and a relic of the Buddha. The group reordained an adviser to King Borommaracha's wife, and stayed in Ayutthaya for four years, passing on their knowledge and wisdom.

They were members of a monastic community that flourished in Nakhon Si Thammarat and Phatthalung to the south. The monks who belonged to the sect, known in Ayutthaya as the southern sect, were stricter than the existing Theravada Buddhist monks.

In the same year as King Borommaracha's accession to the throne of Ayutthaya, Emperor Yongle of the Ming dynasty died. His reign was followed by the Emperor Hongxi, who on the day of his accession stopped all overseas voyages. Overseas trade was restricted and the Jingdezhen kilns, seen by King Ram Khamhaeng all those years before, ceased to work privately and now were to produce ceramics only at the emperor's discretion.

The name given to the glazed ceramics produced only in the kilns of Jingdezhen in China, and in the kilns of Sawankhalok and Sukhothai by the Europeans, who would arrive shortly, was celadon, and due largely to the Chinese voyages in the Southeast Asian seas and the Indian Ocean, celadon ware was very popular. At a stroke the supply of celadon from China stopped.

"That leaves us as the only supplier," said the king.

"If the news I have brought you is true—and I do not doubt its authenticity—then the Chinese are withdrawing inside their empire and virtually stopping all trade," said Okya Mahasena. "The new emperor feels that their empire is so great that they have no need to mix with barbarians, as they call all foreigners. Their withdrawal not only provides us with a monopoly on celadon ware but opens up new trading opportunities formerly closed to us by the Chinese blockade of the sea lanes."

"We must increase production in Sawankalok and Sukhothai."

"Yes, but it is not an easy task. It is a skill that requires considerable training. It will take time, but it is an opportunity not to miss."

"We must look for new trading opportunities," mulled the king out loud.

"You are the king. I am only your adviser. If I may suggest, find the best of your people and set to work."

"When we first talked about providing me with help and advice you said that the decisions I make are mine, and mine alone. You were my father's adviser for many years and served him well. I think that the time has come for me to make my own decisions. I thank you for your service on behalf of my father and myself. Go and enjoy the days that remain to you," said the king.

Okya Mahasena supplicated himself on the floor.

"Be gone, my friend," said the king good-naturedly.

The following day King Borommaracha called his ministers and officials and replaced the minister of the interior and the minister for the king's household. The king told of the information he had received regarding China and set his ministers and officials tasks that they were to complete on pain of death. The king could see the benefits that could accrue to the nation, and fully intended to maximize those gains.

The king rode at the head of his troops as they traveled the partially built road that would link Ayutthaya with Phitsanulok. Alongside him was his spirited wife Queen Akara Chaya, who had no intention of being cosseted in a palanquin for the duration of the journey. They were to visit her brother King Maha Thammaracha IV in Sukhothai.

"It will be good to see my brother again. The last time we met was at your coronation."

"I am concerned he may not agree with my proposal to increase the production of celadon."

"As we talked of before we left Ayutthaya, you can leave my brother to me. There is no need for conflict. There has been enough conflict between Sukhothai and Ayutthaya. Leave him to me. A sister knows how arrange these things."

"He will have to agree to me leaving additional troops in Sukhothai under General Phaitrit."

"The general is not a popular man, but we have learned to work with our chief resident."

"He is not in Sukhothai to be popular. He is there to carry out his king's wishes."

"Which he does admirably," said the queen. "But when it comes to convincing my brother, I know how to handle him."

"And Phitsanulok?"

"That will be a more difficult proposition. To leave the ancient capital will tear the heart out of my people."

"To be king in Phitsanulok will enable Sukhothai to thrive. The city controls access to the Nan River, one of the rivers that bring so much trade north and south. Sukhothai sits to one side. It is too far west to have any meaningful influence now. The move will allow the kings of Sukhothai to thrive."

"It will need to be handled delicately, but, as I have said, leave the handling of my brother to me," said the queen spurring her horse into a gallop.

The visit passed smoothly. King Maha Thammaracha IV was of a different ilk from his more warlike father. He understood that the golden days of Sukhothai had passed, but he recognized his role in keeping the heritage and traditions of his kingdom alive.

The kingdom of Ayutthaya thrived. The sales of celadon ware increased substantially, bringing in much-needed revenue to the government. New traders from Southeast Asia and the Middle East found Ayutthaya to be a city that welcomed them. The gold and silver that trade brought made possible new projects. New temples were constructed and roads were built, slowly bringing the kingdom together. The walls of Ayutthaya were strengthened in case of attack. The increased wealth brought new demands on the king, particularly from his generals.

"We have strengthened the army, and our borders are secure," said General Kongtam. "King Maha Thammaracha IV has now moved the capital of Sukhothai to Phitsanulok. He was understandably reluctant to move—it was the city of his forefathers. I think it was the intervention of the queen that finally convinced him. I had never seen Sukhothai before. It is a remarkable city. Never have I seen anywhere with such magnificent tributes to the Buddha. It was a truly holy experience."

"It is a stunning city. The monks will remain, but the kingdom is centered to our north. Phitsanulok will become one of our new cardinal cities. King Maha Thammaracha IV understood why he had to move his capital, and I am pleased that my wife's efforts bore fruit," said the king.

"It is essential that the old cities of Sukhothai and Sawankhalok are firmly under our control. Control over the production of celadon ware is now of crucial importance to our economy.

"I will visit King Maha Thammaracha IV in Phitsanulok shortly, and we will make merit at Wat Phra Phuttha Chinna Si together."

"Your point about the strength of the army is not lost on me," continued the king. "Phitsanulok is strategically placed, both to advance northward and as a bulwark if threats come from that direction. With Phitsanulok we control the Nan River. We control north–south trade."

"I have been conscious that this is the feeling within the court, and from the royal families. I learn from my spies in Lan Na that they remain united under King Sam Fang Kaen, although his tendency toward animist worship is becoming more pronounced. We have no claim on Lan Xang and little to gain from mounting a war against them. General, I have decided that you are to march the army to Angkor and place them under the hegemony of Ayutthaya. There are stories of a resurgence and there are still many riches awaiting us. This conquest will demonstrate to our neighbors that we have designs on expanding our kingdom, and the victory I expect you to bring me will sate the centuries-old desire of the families of Lopburi for the conquest of Angkor, and give me some peace from their constant meddling in affairs of state," concluded the king.

The year was 1217 as King Jayavarman VII of Angkor looked down from Phnom Bakheng over the city of Angkor as the sun set. King Jayavarman—the king who had driven out the Cham, the king who built the city of Angkor Thom, and the king whose building works would be compared to those of Rameses the Great of Egypt. His city of one million people lay before him. As he neared death his kingdom sat at its peak. It extended from the coast of Vietnam to the borders of the Bagan empire in Burma. It reached as far north as the area around Vientiane in Laos and encompassed all of modern-day Thailand and much of Malaysia.

He had ruled for thirty-six years and was now in his nineties. He was a man of contradictions: a fearless warrior, a meditative man, and a thinker. A patron of Mahayana Buddhism, he cast himself as a bodhisattva, one who, motivated by great compassion, has vowed to attain Buddhahood for the benefit of all sentient beings.

His rule had seen the ongoing change of Angkor from a Hindu to a Buddhist kingdom. Under King Jayavarman the city was to see a building frenzy that included the construction of the city of Angkor Thom and the Bayon, the already-famous temple where stone faces depicted two hundred and sixteen faces of Buddhas, gods, and kings. As king he had built over two hundred rest houses and hospitals throughout his reign and built a network of roads to connect all the cities of his empire.

Whatever the reason for the empire's decline over the next two centuries, the end loomed in 1431 as the Thai army under King Borommaracha II and General Kongtam came down from the Chao Phraya River basin, through Phanom Rung and then Aranya Prathet, and stormed into the complex of Angkor.

"The Siamese have breached our defenses to the south and east. They are nearing the Great Wat and will move toward Angkor Thom," said soldier Sing.

"We retreat to the new city. Its defenses are strong," cried General Leng to his men. We will defend the city of generations until our death, an honorable death!"

General Leng, his father, and his grandfather had served the king. Now he looked up at the benevolent face of King Jayavarman VII, carved in stone, staring down on him. He was about to give his life, as many had before him. Soldier Sing retreated with his comrades through the gates of the Bayon temple. The heads of Buddhas, gods, and kings looked down upon him as the wooden gate was barred closed behind him. He could sense his fear. Death was near, an honorable death. One that would see his rebirth. He had nothing to fear.

For some reason walking through the market came into his mind. The girls, bare breasted, with their hair hanging loose, cloth tied from their waists down, their hands and arms covered in rings and ornaments. The sellers, tattooed, sitting cross-legged on their mats with their wares on display. The smell of food wafting by in the still warm air. He thought of the festivals. He thought of his wife. He hoped to meet her again in the next life.

The general shouted. Soldier Sing couldn't hear what was said, but all the soldiers retreated further and took up position on the steps leading up to the statue of the great King Jayavarman VII. The gate was breached and the Siamese surged into the compound. Their eyes were aflame. The world moved slowly. The man beside him died, and he was pushed further up the steps. From the corner of his eye he caught the sight of a Brahmin, tall and wearing gold, fighting. He looked again. The Brahmin had gone.

He was forced back, his sword fighting foe after foe, his senses alert, but irrevocably the tide of the battle was against them. His feet touched the statue of the once great king. To one side his general still fought. Finally, the statue of King Jayavarman VII was left in silence, the dead bodies of his countrymen all that remained. They lay up the steps and at the foot of the ever-watchful statue.

The Siamese army, without command, ran amok through the city while their commanders looked on. Those who had not died were taken as slaves, or worse. As the frenzy ended statues of sacred images, lions, horses, and oxen were loaded on carts to be brought to Ayutthaya. The city of Angkor, once the biggest city of its day, smoldered as it was looted.

The Khmer king had fled. King Borommaracha II put his son Prince Inthaburi on the throne, taking the Khmer princes, together with what remained of their families, back to Ayutthaya. The once-dominant power of Southeast Asia was now a mere vassal state of the expanding Ayutthayan empire. Lopburi was placated.

The city of Ayutthaya turned out in festive mood to greet the returning victors. The Khmer were defeated. The old enemy vanquished. The king ordered that the plunder from Angkor was to be given to temples. The Khmer royalty were well treated and the captured Brahmin given positions within the palace. Their influence and the traditions of the Khmer not only lived on but grew within Ayutthaya.

@w

King Borommaracha II had a second son, Prince Ramesuan. His first son, the young Prince Inthaburi, had been murdered only six months into his tenure as governor of Angkor. His father named Prince Ramesuan *upparat* (heir apparent.)

In 1438 King Maha Thammaracha IV, the king of Sukhothai, died leaving no direct heir. The opportunity this presented was not lost on King Borommaracha II. His own son was of royal Sukhothai blood through his mother. He had contemplated making his wife queen of Sukhothai as she could be considered next in line, but queens had never ruled. So the seven-year-old Prince Ramesuan was duly crowned king of Sukhothai—the first king of Sukhothai to be crowned in Phitsanulok. When he attained fifteen years of age—a man—the heir apparent was sent to rule as upparat of Phitsanulok in a move that would become a pattern among the kings of Ayutthaya and their chosen successors.

The succession settled, King Borommaracha II looked north at the kingdom of Lan Na. In 1442 a dynastic dispute arose, giving King Borommaracha II the opportunity to involve Ayutthaya. King Sam Fang Kaen, who had ascended the throne of Lan Na after defeating his brother in hand-to-hand combat, had repudiated Buddhism and turned away from Buddhism in favor of animism. His people became increasingly concerned, and their concern was championed by his sixth son, who was crowned King Tilokkarat, forcing King Sam Fang Kaen to abdicate. In 1442 there took place a great ordination of five hundred sons of prominent families on the banks of the Ping River. A revival of Pali Buddhism had taken root.

A dynastic war broke out when the tenth son of Sam Fang Kaen, Prince Thao Soi, refused to acknowledge his brother Tilokkarat as king. He took his discredited father to Mueang Fang and from this base began a war against his brother. King Tilokkarat counterattacked, however, and overran Mueang Fang, whereupon Thao Soi abandoned his father and fled to Thoen. Thao Soi persuaded the governor of Thoen to seek military aid from the most powerful of Thai kingdoms, Ayutthaya.

Sensing an opportunity to expand his influence into Lan Na, King Borommaracha II led an army to the assistance of Thao Soi. Before they could reach him, King Tilokkarat ran Thao Soi to the ground and killed him.

King Borommaracha II, undeterred by this setback, continued his advance into Lan Na, taking many captives along the way. However, King Tilokkarat had appointed as his commander the highly capable General Muen Lok Nakhon, who made good use of his spies. They infiltrated King Borommaracha's army and warned of its approach. Knowing where the Ayutthayan army was located, the army of Chiang Mai was able to set a trap and block the advance. As the battle started the infiltrators from Lan Na cut off the tails of the Ayutthayan elephants, causing the animals to stampede within the Ayutthayan lines. Taking advantage of the chaos, the army of the city of Chiang Mai took the offensive and attacked fiercely. The Ayutthayan army broke and ran.

It was an ignominious end to a war between Ayutthaya and Lan Na that would continue, in one form or another, for many centuries. King Borommaracha II returned to Ayutthaya.

෴

The year was 1401 when a fugitive prince from Palembang was driven from his home city of Singapore following a Thai attack and crossed the sea. He was resting under a tree by a river when his dog started to attack a mouse deer, which later pushed the dog into the river. The bravery of the mouse deer impressed him and he set about building a city on the spot. He named it after the *melaka* tree he had rested under.

The growth of Malacca followed the rising power of Ayutthaya to its north. Sultan Megat Iskandar Shah, the ruler at the time of King Intharacha, was increasingly concerned with the threat posed by Ayutthaya. He ordered the construction of a wall surrounding the city with four guarded entrances. Inside the city another fortress was built to store the state's treasury and supplies. In a preemptive move, the king of Malacca traveled to China in 1418, where he raised his concerns about Ayutthaya to the Emperor Yongle, who in turn wrote to King Intharacha.

King Borommaracha II had always remembered the words of Okya Mahasena. He had always looked to expand. When he took this expansion southward into the Malay Peninsula, he ordered an expedition for the invasion of Malacca overland via the city of Pahang. With the Malay Peninsula the kingdom would secure a substantial seacoast and the trading advantages that came with it. The Malay Peninsula beyond the Ayutthayan city of Nakhon Si Thammarat was sparsely populated. Food became scarce, and the Muslim rulers stood firm against their would-be Buddhist conquerors. The sultan gave orders that all men from the cities and the outlying districts be assembled to help defend Malacca.

From ancient times the country of Siam was known as Shahru'n-nuwi, and all princes of these regions below the wind were subject to Siam. . . . And when news reached Siam that Malaka was a great city but not subject to Siam, the [king] sent an envoy to Malaka to demand a letter of 'obeisance': but Sultan Muzzafar Shah refused to owe allegiance to Siam. The Raja of Siam was very angry and ordered an expedition to be made ready for the invasion of Malaka. Awi Chakra was to command the expedition and to take a vast army with him. And word was brought to Sultan Muzaffar Shah that the Raja of Siam had ordered Awi Chakra, his war-chief, to lead an army, in numbers past counting, overland to Ulu Pahang. When Sultan Muzzafar Shah heard this, he gave orders that all men of the outlying districts be assembled and come up river to Malaka. And all the men of the outlying districts foregathered in Malaka. . . .

Meanwhile the men of Siam arrived, and they fought with the men of Malaka. After a long battle, in which many of the soldiers of the Raja of Siam were killed, Malaka still held out and the Siamese withdrew. On their retreat they flung down in Ulu Muar the rattans they had used for tying their baggage. These rattans took root and grew, and they are there to this day, known as the rattans of the Siamese.

After nearly two years of fierce fighting the army of Ayutthaya returned home. They would return in the reign of King Trailok.

☙

In 1448 King Borommaracha II launched a further campaign against Lan Na. Another succession dispute had flared up when King Tilokkarat seized the throne of Lan Na. The country fractured, and the governor of Nan and Phraya Kenyhao sought the support of the king of Ayutthaya in overthrowing the new king. King Borommaracha II, sensing another opportunity, formed his army and marched north. He died on campaign and the Ayutthayan forces returned home leaving King Tilokkarat to secure the throne of Lan Na.

Prince Ramesuan was then made King Borommatrailokkanat, more commonly known as King Trailok.

9
KING TRAILOK (AYUTTHAYA)
1448–88

KING TRAILOK WAS PROCLAIMED upon his coronation a divine being and leader of Buddhism, as was the custom in Ayutthaya. He was a devout king and would be the longest-serving king in the history of Ayutthaya. His reign would do much to influence the future direction of the kingdom. His father was from the house of Suphanburi, while his mother was a princess of Sukhothai who was born in the garrison town of Kamphaeng Phet. Born in Ayutthaya in 1431, when his father was assembling his troops for the onslaught against Angkor, the future king spent much of his early life both in Ayutthaya and with his mother's family in Kamphaeng Phet, Sukhothai, and Phitsanulok.

At the age of fifteen he was appointed upparat of Phitsanulok. It was here that the two sides of his upbringing would first collide. The royal family of Sukhothai had been removed from their ancestral home by King Trailok's father, King Borommaracha II. The enforced move had split the Sukhothai royal family. Some understood the reasons for the move and its strategic advantages, while others longed to return to their city and way of life, a life independent of Ayutthaya.

"Mother, I am now king and as such intend to rule my kingdom justly and with wisdom," said the serious young king. "I have read and reread all the great writings on kingship. I now have to translate those words into action, but I fear my first action will be with our family in Sukhothai," said a concerned young King Trailok.

"My son, you are of the ruling houses of both Sukhothai and Suphanburi. You rule by right. As I did with your father many years ago I will travel, this time with Prince Borommapan and your first wife, to meet with our family. If we can settle any dispute in peace, that will be far more preferable than war," replied Queen Mother Akara Chaya. "I know there are some among our family that are not happy with a king of Ayutthaya as king of Sukhothai, and others who seek to free Sukhothai from us. This cannot be allowed. Too much blood has already been spilled."

"Father talked with me before his final campaign. He felt he still had much to accomplish, and I have made many promises to him that I am duty-bound to keep. The first of these is that this palace is to be handed to the supreme patriarch to be converted into a monastery to be called Wat Si Sanphet. I have decided to have a temple built within the grounds of the royal palace. This will be in keeping with the memory of the kings of Sukhothai, who would often build within their palace compound—and hopefully demonstrate to our family that Sukhothai is still valued. I have already had plans drawn up for a hall with a five-tiered gilded roof. I have selected a new site for the new royal residence just to our north, on the Lopburi River. Already the ground is being cleared for the Bencharat Palace. I spent much of my time as upparat in Phitsanulok designing the building," said the king.

"The handing over of the palace is a tradition that goes back to the time of King Ramathibodi and beyond that to the reigns of the kings of Sukhothai. I can see you have planned well for your accession to the throne," responded the queen mother proudly.

"Which leads to the second promise that I must keep, and it concerns King Ramathibodi. The king's body was preserved in keeping with tradition, but it was the wish of Father that the body of the old king be removed from his crypt and cremated as is now the practice. He told me I should order the construction of Wat Phra Ram on the cremation site and erect a reliquary for the ashes of our founding monarch."

"Yes, I knew that was my husband's wish. He always wanted to be involved personally with the cremation of the old king. Time, more than anything, left his wish unfulfilled. He could never find the time with all the demands placed upon him.

"The festival of *thot kathin* nears as Buddhist lent draws to a close. You will head the procession of royal barges from Wasukri Pier to Wat Arun (Temple of Dawn), where you will present the saffron kathin robes to the monks for the coming year."

"The weavers have finished?"

"They delivered early this year. I used their hand looms as a child while growing up in Kamphaeng Phet. It takes over one month to weave one robe, and that does not include the preparation of the yarn and the dying of the cloth. It requires a patience that I do not possess," said the queen mother.

"You need to take this opportunity to talk with the supreme patriarch. Assure him of your commitment and involve him in your reign. He is a good man. Offer the robes, give the palace to the monks as the tradition of King Ramathibodi demands, and fulfill your father's wishes. Understand that the monks are our communication with the people. They are the sangha and are present in every town and village. They can support your reign in a way that cannot be otherwise achieved," she continued.

"Thank you mother. Your counsel is wise as always. We will deliver the robes, and I will speak with the supreme patriarch."

"Did you make any further promises to your father?"

"Only one—that I would launch a further invasion of Malacca. The retreat hurt him deeply. He remained suspicious of the city following their conversion to Islam and perceived them and their religion as a threat. It was a threat he wanted ended, but the war with Malacca can wait. I have instructed that the fleet be renewed, but that will take time. I intend to attack by sea, not by land this time," concluded the king.

"And I will leave for Phitsanulok. I will stay for a few months. It will be a good opportunity for the young Prince Borommapan to meet his family from Sukhothai, and it will give me the opportunity to assess the strength of feeling among them."

The procession of royal barges, including *Suea Kamron Sin*, the aging but still impressive royal barge of King Intharacha, headed downriver to Wat Arun. King Trailok was conveyed in the royal barge of his father. During his lengthy reign he would have three royal barges built, each more magnificent than the last.

The towering white and gilt prang of Wat Arun stood looking down on the king and the royal procession as they disembarked from the royal barge. The king led, with the supreme patriarch—the seniormost monk in the land—following one step behind as the procession climbed in single file the steep, ascending, curved steps to the chamber that lay over halfway up the prang. Nine monks sat chanting around the edges of the whitewashed chamber, which was pungent with the aroma of incense wafting in the still air. The monks continued to chant as the king, followed by the patriarch, entered. From the center of the prang the king could look down on the earth below. There was palpable concern from the monks as their king peered into the black abyss that ran down the center of the prang.

The king presented the kathin robes to the seniormost monk and to those monks at his side in the prang. By presenting the robes in this way the king was symbolically passing out the robes to all the monks who would receive his gift.

The ceremony drew to a close and the king sat with the seniormost one. Monks lined the room, eating the meal the king had generously provided. The king ate after the monks, as was the tradition.

"Walk with me?" requested the king of the supreme patriarch.

Side-by-side they walked into the cloistered pathway on the north side of the temple. The king looked to ensure they were alone. The only ones watching were the stone Buddha statues, each with its subtly different face, their torsos clad in gold sashes to honor the visit of the king.

"I thank you on behalf of my monks for the gifts you have generously bestowed upon us," said the seniormost monk.

"It is my intention to support the faith in all ways possible," replied the king.

"You favor Sri Lankan Buddhism?" asked the patriarch.

"Its stricter interpretation appeals more to me. I am a man who likes discipline and order, and that is what I seek in my kingdom."

"Then we are of one mind. You have graciously dedicated part of your palace to be the site of a new temple."

"It is my desire to copy the example set by King Ramathibodi in this respect when he turned his residence of Wianglek into Wat Phutthai Sawan, and also to demonstrate my inclusion of the customs of Sukhothai within my kingdom. I intend to follow the example set by their kings and have the temple built within the compound of the palace."

"That is a generous act on your part and one that will be appreciated. You have clearly thought much on this matter."

"As upparat while my father aged, I thought deeply about the kingdom I envisaged. My reign may be fleeting or it may be long-lasting. I intend to use my reign to advance Ayutthaya spiritually, militarily, and administratively. My desire is to leave a strong and well-ordered kingdom when I die."

"You speak wisely for one so young."

"I need your support to achieve my goals. You—the sangha—communicate directly with the people. Your message is important as it will shape the way in which the people view me."

"They will view you favorably, of that I am sure."

"And I also desire that your monks be my eyes and ears, both in the kingdom and beyond our borders."

"I understand," said the seniormost monk.

"I intend to restructure society in Ayutthaya," said the king. "This will have ramifications for the sangha. I would like to take this opportunity given to us by the festival of *thot kathin,* to discuss these matters with you."

"My king, you are a divine monarch. I will honor your orders and your wishes whatever they may be."

"I thank you for your commitment. However, these changes are profound and will affect the sangha greatly. I feel it important that you, and you alone, should be the first to hear them."

_____

King Trailok more than anyone realized his position as king was tenuous, and set out to ensure that he stood at the pinnacle of a rigid structure where all knew their status.

The king quickly started to work with his ministers on the reform to the kingdom's administration. He completely overhauled the government, better defining the roles of the five departments of interior affairs, the capital city, the royal household, the treasury, and agriculture. He ensured they were staffed with appointed and not hereditary officers. In addition the king brought about a separation between the civil and military administrations, areas that had previously been closely interwoven.

The king sat in his private chambers with Kulkhani, his Brahmin adviser of many years. Brahmin Kulkhani was one of the Brahmins captured when Angkor was sacked by the Siamese in his father's reign and had been the king's tutor, mentor, and friend since childhood.

"We have spoken over many years," said the six-foot-tall Brahmin. "We have distilled the essence of the Khmer success and the Khmer fall, and we have extracted from our observations the manner in which your society will be structured. We have looked to India, to China, and far back in history. Now we are nearing our conclusions.

"We are of a single mind. The society we have discussed builds on what already exists. More importantly it places you, my king, at its head. All are beholden to you for their place in society. You have the power to raise an individual, and you have the power to make them fall," continued the Brahmin. "By placing you securely at the top your continuation is assured."

"I have discussed my plans with the seniormost monk as you know. Like you he understands what I am trying to achieve and has pledged his full support," said King Trailok. The structure we have discussed is like a pyramid with me at the top, close royal family within five generations below, followed by seven grades of nobles from *phaya* at the top to the rank of *thanai* at the bottom," said the king.

"Yes. And the system is such that you, and only you, have the ability to raise a person or to withdraw your support. The titles of the nobility remain nonhereditary. They exist at your behest and, as a result of that, you command their loyalty," replied Brahmin Kulkhani.

"And underneath the nobles we formalize ranks for commoners," remarked the king.

"As we have discussed. The scribes are working on our plans now. Each person will be given a rank in *rai*."

"As in the land measurement?" interrupted the king.

"Exactly. Their rank will be commensurate with their job or their value to society," continued the Brahmin.

"But their rank can be changed?" asked the king.

"It was your wish over our months of discussion that people should be able to move up and down the rankings. Men of lower caste can raise their rai through marriage to a noble woman. A father blessed with a beautiful daughter could to try to marry her to someone of high rai and receive an increase in his rank in return, and of course men who prove their worth and ability can be raised at your command."

"The Chinese are exempt?"

"Yes. They have their place in our society as traders and tradesmen. It is a role they fulfill admirably. Both they and women are exempt," replied the Brahmin.

"We are putting in place a bureaucracy capable of managing and enforcing these changes?" asked the king.

"All is in hand. We will hold records on all individuals who have rai status. Changes lower down the order will be managed by those we will place in control. They will report to me, and I in turn will report to you. Civilian matters will fall under the remit of the Mahatthai. Every freeman will have to be registered as a servant—phrai—with the local lord for either military service or corvée labor on public works. He can also meet his labor obligation by paying a tax," added the Brahmin. "Through this bureaucracy we will tighten our control over the structure of society, make it easier to enforce social discipline, and enable the easy mobilization of manpower."

"The ability to call on manpower is one that a king needs," said King Trailok. "But of equal importance in my mind is the ability to structure social order."

"Together we will put in place a system for how people of different status should interact," said the Brahmin.

"Yes. It is important that both nobles and commoners know how to act in one another's presence. It is also important that nobles understand that they will be held to higher levels of account than commoners," said the king.

"The laws, which will soon be published, will be clear on that. I know you feel that often nobles do not act in accordance with their status," said Brahmin Kulkhani.

"With these laws in place I intend to make sure they act appropriately. Be assured of that," said the king firmly.

"We have introduced the Mahatthai to manage civil matters. However, we need to ensure that the Kalahom, who will administer the military, are given enough power and resources. Many will not like the controls we are putting on them," said the Brahmin.

"We need the best. The threat grows every day, particularly from the north. We need an army led by soldiers, not just by the inexperienced sons of nobles. All should undergo military service, but the role of the Kalahom is also to ensure the introduction of more modern weapons and to organize the building of stone fortifications to protect Ayutthaya and other cities throughout the kingdom," said the king. "Our land is sparsely populated. Some regions are only accessible by river. As the kingdom grows we need to exert control over our possessions, reigning in the autonomy of our regional lords and ensuring that all in the kingdom understand their role, their status, and their obligations. We have made decisions that will allow both myself and my heirs to govern with absolute power in a structured society. Soon I will announce my intention to my ministers and the court," continued King Trailok.

"There will be dissent."

"There will be no dissent. I will be patient and explain why and how the changes will affect our society. I will allow those in power to discuss their concerns with me, and I will listen to their views and act accordingly if their arguments have merit. I will allow discussion, but not dissent," said the king. "We will promulgate laws—laws that cannot be disobeyed, laws that will benefit the kingdom.

The new laws, which eventually became known as the *sakdina* system, built on the social and cultural order that had developed at the local level over centuries.

To resolve the question of succession, every member of the royal family was ranked by his relation to the current king; if a family member was removed from royal descent by more than five generations, he was declared a commoner and no longer eligible for the throne. King Trailok also formalized the appointment of the *upparat*, the heir apparent or the second or vice-king, so the people would know who their next king would be long before he actually took the throne.

Over time sakdina slowly pervaded everything.

@www

Queen Mother Akara Chaya, mother of King Trailok, died in 1450. It was her efforts that had held the heirs of Sukhothai together. With her passing the clamor to establish an independent Sukhothai reasserted itself. Prince Yuthisathian, a Sukhothai noble, was now second in line to the throne of Sukhothai following the birth of the ill-fated Prince Borommapan to King Trailok. He was a childhood friend of King Trailok, who had, according to Prince Yuthisathian, promised him the title of upparat of Phitsanulok in their youth. When this honor was not forthcoming, Prince Yuthisathian, governor of Phichit, headed to his family seat in Sawankhalok, returning home to raise an army.

Sawankhalok remained an important city to the north of Sukhothai, bordering the kingdom of Lan Na. To Ayutthaya it was an important garrison town, and more than that its kilns produced some of the nation's finest celadon ware, still heavily in demand. Prince Yuthisathian raised the banner for an independent Sukhothai and called for others loyal to the kingdom of Sukhothai to fight alongside him.

He garnered many supporters but realized he was fighting the kingdom of Ayutthaya and his old childhood friend King Trailok, a man of high ability and integrity who was also a cunning and consummate politician. Even with his supporters, Prince Yuthisathian could see only eventual defeat against the superior numbers of the Ayutthayan army. He looked north to the kingdom of Lan Na for support.

Under King Tilokkarat the kingdom of Lan Na had prospered. The king had quieted his enemies and laid a foundation for a kingdom that could one day emulate or surpass Ayutthaya. Prince Yuthisathian offered the subservience of Sukhothai if King Tilokkarat would help him secure independence from Ayutthaya.

The opportunity was there, and the timing was right. The battle lines were drawn. The king of Lan Na well remembered how the old king of Ayutthaya had supported the usurper against him early in his reign. He was no friend of Ayutthaya.

King Tilokkarat sent his army south for what would be the first of many wars over the next century. In Ayutthaya King Trailok, who had been monitoring events closely, dispatched an army to counter this insurrection. The king of Lan Na sent troops to attack the town of Chaliang (Sawankhalok, or Si Satchanalai), to the north of Sukhothai. The advance army of Lan Na was surprised by a late-night counterattack by the defenders of Chaliang. The king of Lan Na moved to join the fray, but before his forces could strike a blow, word came that Luang Prabang had sent an army to invade the important Lan Na city of Chiang Saen.

King Tilokkarat's army immediately moved to return. With the army of Sukhothai too small to mount a campaign on their own and most of the army of Lan Na heading back to battle their old enemy, King Trailok ordered his troops to press their sudden advantage. In 1452, the army of Ayutthaya captured the Lan Na capital of Chiang Mai. The king of Luang Prabang, King Sai Tia Kaphat, then intervened in the war, forcing the army of Ayutthaya to retreat and the army of Lan Na to defend themselves. A peace was made between King Tilokkarat of Lan Na and King Sai Tia Kaphat of Luang Prabang, and after their forces had regrouped the army of Lan Na again marched southward, briefly holding Kamphaeng Phet before a truce was agreed and hostilities temporarily halted.

This was the only time the two kings would meet face-to-face.

The royal canopy, new and in resplendent blue, was raised outside the "Wall of Diamonds," Kamphaeng Phet. Inside the magnificence was on display for all to see. King Trailok would today meet his father's old enemy, and his own current one. King Tilokkarat arrived on his war elephant with an honor guard of twenty soldiers as agreed. Together they entered the tent.

"You have come to my land uninvited," began King Trailok, staring directly into the eyes of his adversary.

"I was invited by Prince Yuthisathian, the rightful king of Sukhothai," replied King Tilokkarat.

"You have been misinformed. Prince Yuthisathian is but one of a number in line to the throne of Sukhothai. And the kingdom of Sukhothai is but a vassal state of Ayutthaya. I am its rightful king."

"Your internal affairs are no concern of mine. The ancient kingdom looks north to where the three kings met. The union between Sukhothai and Lan Na is one that stretches back far beyond the birth of your kingdom.

"But my kingdom *was* born. You speak of the history, of the three kings. Their time was many years ago. I sit outside my city of Kamphaeng Phet unable to enter. I will enter Kamphaeng Phet. How I enter is up to you."

"You expect me to run like a dog with its tail between its legs. You are an arrogant young puppy if you look to threaten me."

"I merely point out your situation. My army is twice the size of yours. Your supply lines are disrupted. Your defeat is inevitable. I sit on Ayutthayan soil without the fear of insurrection at my back, whereas your kingdom sits surrounded by enemies from both within and without. The longer you stay and fight the more your enemies will be emboldened to take your throne."

"You are not your father. He understood the ways of war. You are cold."

"I am thorough in my planning if that is what you mean. I do not want to lose my men at this time and I offer you and your army retreat to your lands unmolested. You are not welcome here. Prince Yuthisathian will be handed over to me as a sign of your good faith."

"Prince Yuthisathian is in Chiang Mai."

"Then you will send him to me."

"I will send him when we return," said King Tilokkarat, but as he said this his eyes looked away.

The troops of King Tilokkarat left the following morning. The king of Lan Na never sent Prince Yuthisathian to King Trailok.

❦

In 1455, King Trailok sent his well-prepared naval force to Malacca in order to extend his empire and to keep his promise to his late father. The ruler of Malacca readied his navy to meet the attack.

And after a while the Siamese again attacked Malaka, under the command of Awi Dichu. And when news of their coming reached Malaka, Sultan Muzaffar Shah commanded Bendahara Paduka Raja to make ready a fleet to repel the attack. When the fleet was ready, Bendahara Paduku Raja set out to repel the Siamese. The Siamese by this time had almost reached Batu Pahat.

Now the Sri Bija 'diraja had a son named Tun 'Umar who was a great fighter and a man of "reckless bravery." Tun 'Umar was sent by Bendahara Paduka Raja to reconnoitre, and he set forth with a single boat, now edging forward, now coming back. And when he encountered the Siamese fleet, he straightaway attacked and sank two or three Siamese ships, then shot off to their flank. Then he returned and attacked other ships again sinking two or three, after which he withdrew. The Siamese were astounded.

Then when night had fallen Awi Dichu advanced, and Bendahara Paduka Raja ordered firebrands to be fastened to mangrove and other trees growing along the shore. And when the Siamese saw these lights, so many that no man could number them, their war-chiefs said "What a vast fleet these Malays must have, no man can count their ships! If they attack us, how shall we fare? Even one of their ships just now was more than a match for us!" And Awi Dichu replied, "You are right, let us return home!" Whereupon the Siamese returned to their country and the retreating Siamese were pursued by Bendahara Paduku Raja as far as Singapore.

The *Sejarah Melayu* tells of the Siamese preparing for a third invasion. Then the Siamese prince Chao Pandan was killed by "the spiritual prowess of a Sayyid who sent a magic arrow" flying into the body of the young prince. With the death of the prince, Siamese attempts to conquer Malacca were abandoned. Sultan Mansur sent embassies to the Thai court, and gradually good relations were established between the two countries.

The threat to Ayutthaya now came from the north.

10

KING TRAILOK (PHITSANULOK)

1463–88

KING TRAILOK WAS VISIBLY SHAKEN by the outcome of these two wars. "I am concerned. We have a partial victory against the joint armies of King Tilokkarat and Prince Yuthisathian, but the threat has not gone away. I see the threat from the kingdom of Lan Na increasing. They are in the ascendant and seek to enlarge their kingdom," said the king, looking casually out of the window at those plying their trade on the crowded river.

"I share your concern. With Prince Yuthisathian on their side they have a constant reason to war against us. My spies in Chiang Mai tell me that King Tilokkarat looks on Ayutthaya with jealous eyes," replied Brahmin Kulkhani.

"The defeat by the navy of Malacca can be tolerated. It was my father's war, not mine. I have honored my obligation. Let us be done with it. We shall seek peace and trade with them. Lan Na is a far more serious enemy."

Brahmin Kulkhani relaxed into a meditative state as the king looked on. The king knew that the Brahmin was not meditating but thinking. The king, also deep in thought, stared out the window, watching the river traffic. In the distance he could hear chanting as men pulled together to inch their barges forward. The river, wide though it was, appeared crammed with boats of all different types. Sailors shouted and gesticulated, although their voices were lost in the cacophony of noise and activity. Fully five minutes passed before the Brahmin spoke.

"With that established, I look at the situation with the eyes of a trained Brahmin. Our teachings, handed down from father to son, tell of a capital city that is at the center of the kingdom with the four cardinal points to protect it. Ayutthaya has Phitsanulok now to the north, Phra Pradaeng to the south, Nakhon Nayok to the east, and Suphanburi to the west. Your threat now comes from the north. When Ayutthaya was founded its enemies were Angkor and the many disparate states that surrounded it. Your enemy has moved. Your city has not."

"What do you suggest?" asked the king.

"If it is to be war with Lan Na then you must consider that your northern cardinal point, Phitsanulok, becomes your main city. It becomes your base for both attack and defense. Ayutthaya is a defensible city and will serve its purpose well if you are forced to retreat. I have lived here for many years but do not fully understand the geography of your country. What lies between Phitsanulok and Lan Na?"

"The land is sparsely populated, mountainous, and thickly forested. The old Sukhothai garrison town of Kamphaeng Phet lies to the west of Phitsanulok. Sukhothai lies northwest. The ancient capital of Nakhon Thai lies about one hundred fifty kilometers to the north of Phitsanulok and to the east of Sukhothai. Nakhon Thai has been under the remit of both Sukhothai in the past and Phitsanulok in recent years."

"Is it well-defended?"

"No."

"Then we must strengthen it. What routes are open to invading armies from the north?"

"From the north, down the Nan River to Phitsanulok, or by way of Phetchabun in the river valley to the east and then across to Ayutthaya. Phitsanulok is more direct and has the river by which to move troops and supplies. Phetchabun is a long and more mountainous route but is more difficult for us to defend against."

"If you were King Tilokkarat what way would you come?"

"Logic dictates Phitsanulok. Communication between his army and that of Prince Yuthisathian would be quicker and more certain.

There are good roads connecting Phitsanulok to both Sukhothai and Kamphaeng Phet. To attack by Phetchabun would require a two-pronged approach with Prince Yuthisathian attacking from the west and King Tilokkarat from the east. That said, if I were King Tilokkarat I would not fully rely on my allies in Sukhothai. They are unproven."

"I would suggest that Ayutthaya is the wrong base from which to fight this war. You can better coordinate any strategies from Phitsanulok."

"It is not as well-defended as Ayutthaya. It does not have the same natural and man-made defenses."

"Perhaps it is a city to sacrifice if the war goes badly. I am not saying do not strengthen the city's defenses, but if the situation goes against us we make our final stand here, in Ayutthaya."

"I will move the capital. This will demonstrate the seriousness of the threat to the people. I will leave Prince Borommaracha as upparat in Ayutthaya, where he will act as king. Ayutthaya deserves to be ruled by a king. Phitsanulok is suitable in many ways. It houses the Phra Buddha Chinnarat and the city has a commitment to both Ayutthaya and to our faith. It is a city that I enjoy. A city away from the spies and the incessant gossip of the court. The fact that I, the king of Sukhothai, will be seated in the capital of the kingdom of Sukhothai as agreed by King Intharacha and King Maha Thammaracha IV will make a direct point to Prince Yuthisathian. I will not cower before the man. I know him well from childhood. He is weak under pressure, indecisive. I will confront him. I will see him destroyed and his 'kingdom' subdued," said the king forcefully.

"Three years ago I ordered construction of Wat Chula Mani in Phitsanulok. It is now nearing completion and will shortly be dedicated to the Lord Buddha. I will announce my intention on that day," concluded the king. "Now I would speak with my son."

As King Trailok detailed his reasoning to his fifteen-year-old son he could sense the excitement and anticipation of the young prince.

"When the capital is moved to Phitsanulok you will remain here as king—not as upparat, but as king!" declared King Trailok. "Ayutthaya deserves to be ruled by a king. It is important that the people of the south do not feel abandoned by the move of the capital to the north. I count on you to rule in my stead."

"What do you wish of me as king?" asked the young Prince Borommaracha.

"To rule justly and wisely. To act in concert with the sangha and to ensure the sakdina is made part of our society. To support me militarily when I call and to attend the celebrations and honor the festivals. Live as King Borommaracha III. The kingship will be yours when I die."

"The Khmer have moved south to Lovek but still need to be watched."

"Yes, but it is not just the Khmer we need to concern ourselves with. I intend to make peace with Malacca. Together we can both benefit from trade. I need Ayutthaya to be strong in trade. I know you understand this already. Grow this city. It will be yours from this day, and the kingdom will be yours after my death."

"And Lopburi?"

"A wise response. Yes, watch them closely. They still eye the throne."

"The army?"

"I will move most of the army to Phitsanulok. The threats from Lan Na and Sukhothai must be met with force. I will leave a sizable contingent of troops with you. I will, no doubt, call on you in times of need. Be ready."

"I understand the threat from the north, but I look to expand the kingdom."

"What do you have in mind?"

"To our west lie the city states of Tavoy and Tenasserim. They will give us access to the Bay of Bengal and the Indian Ocean."

"They will be difficult targets. The Tenasserim mountains and the dense jungle protect them. Land attack will only be possible in the dry season."

"Yes, I have thought of that. Both cities accepted the suzerainty of King Ram Khamhaeng of Sukhothai. It can be argued they owe the same tribute to us, the successors of Sukhothai. Their conquest is likely to be long and drawn out, but war keeps the minds of the people occupied."

"They would be good additions to our kingdom. You have thought long and hard about this."

"You have taught me well, Father," said Prince Borommaracha.

@/w-

The army of Prince Yuthisathian, supported by troops from Lan Na, had launched two unsuccessful attempts on Phitsanulok in the years 1459 and 1460. In 1461, before the capital city could be moved, news came that a large army from Lan Na had entered the kingdom of Ayutthaya with King Tilokkarat at his head and Prince Yuthisathian, who had been made governor of the town of Phayao by King Tilokkarat, by his side. Their intention, as King Trailok was informed, was to take Sukhothai and then move on Phitsanulok. However, a Chinese attack from Yunnan on Chiang Mai forced King Tilokkarat to withdraw his troops from Ayutthaya again. Although no battle took place the intent was clear.

Phitsanulok had grown from a frontier garrison town into a major urban center, specializing in the manufacture of the celadon porcelain that used to be the preserve of Sawankhalok and Sukhothai, and benefiting from its dominant position at the crossroads of northern Siam. With its grand temples built alongside a major strategic waterway, it was a city where diverse cultures met and exchanged ideas freely.

The king of Ayutthaya did not have to wait long for an invasion. Later that year another invasion was launched by King Tilokkarat of Lan Na. King Trailok and his second son, Prince Intharacha, reacted from Phitsanulok. His eldest son, King Borommaracha III, came from Ayutthaya through Pichit and north to Sukhothai. He caught and routed the army of Lan Na in open battle. The Lan Na army retreated in disarray.

King Borommaracha III, called upon for the first time by his father, pursued the retreating army and fought General Han Nakhon in yuddhahatthi, the elephant battle. His victory in this duel added to his aura as a consummate warrior and ensured the capture of many troops of Lan Na and the withdrawal of the rest.

An Ayutthayan army under the command of King Trailok's son Prince Intharacha, who the previous year had succeeded in reconquering Phrae, clashed with the returning army of Lan Na at the battle of Doi Ba, a farming village on the outskirts of Chiang Mai. The battle was fought in full moonlight. Sitting astride their war elephants, the prince and his officers attacked three of the leading nobles of Lan Na. It was a bold move, but the prince was mortally wounded by an arrow.

The second son of the king was dead. His body, as was common practice in times of war, was cremated, a small chedi left marking the spot. His bones were returned to Phitsanulok to be honored by his father. The loss of life on both sides in this particular battle was considerable.

Despite limited territorial gains Lan Na was weakened by a combination of internal power struggles and the casualties suffered during the war. A stalemate developed between the two warring states and a treaty was agreed in 1464, bringing an end to hostilities.

King Trailok set about renovating old temples and establishing new ones. He was a devout Buddhist, and his support for the sangha was evident throughout his reign. There were practical reasons to support the sangha, but King Trailok demonstrated a commitment that went beyond what would be expected.

In 1465, King Trailok entered the monkhood at the recently completed Wat Chula Mani in Phitsanulok for a period of eight months to make merit. He became the first king of Ayutthaya to be ordained as a Buddhist monk. in choosing Wat Chula Mani rather than the temple of the Phra Buddha Chinnarat, perhaps the king was being careful not to upset his southern subjects by showing a total commitment to the north, or being careful not to cause resentment among the Sukhothai elite by using what was now their spiritual center. The king had five men ordained immediately before him, emulating the Buddha and his five disciples—a grand gesture. An orthodox monk from Sri Lanka officiated at the ceremony, giving the entire event deeper meaning and gravitas in the minds of the people. Neighboring kings sent emissaries together with royal gifts of bowls and robes for the occasion. Even King Tilokkarat of Lan Na sent an ambassador to Phitsanulok for the occasion. The ordination was held at a time of great religious revival throughout Southeast Asia. The interpretation and reorganization of the Buddhist doctrine was discussed, together with a project that had been many years in the making, the translation of the *Maha Chat Kham Luang* from Pali to Thai.

The *Maha Chat Kham Luang* is the story of the Bodhisattva's last existence on earth before being reborn as as the man who would become the Buddha. Its thirteen chapters tell the story of Prince Wetsandon (Thai version of the Pali name Vessantara), a tale that extols the virtue of self-sacrifice. It would be chanted by the monks delivering the story.

The Tale of Prince Wetsandon

The Bodhisattva was born as Prince Wetsandon, the son of King Sanchai and Queen Phutsadi of the kingdom of Siwi. From childhood the young prince proved himself to be very generous and charitable. On the day of his birth a baby white elephant was brought by its mother to the royal stable. At the age of sixteen Prince Wetsandon married Princess Matsi, who bore him two children.

Meanwhile, the neighboring kingdom of Kalinga was suffering drought and famine, despite the ruler's vow to live strictly by the religious precepts. At the suggestion of his people the king of Kalinga sent eight Brahmins to Siwi to ask Prince Wetsandon for the white elephant, which was believed to bring prosperity and plentiful rainfall. When it was learned that Prince Wetsandon had given away his magic white elephant, the people were angered and demanded that Prince Wetsandon be banished from the kingdom. His father, King Sanchai, had no choice but to comply. Before he departed Prince Wetsandon gave away all his valuables and possessions. As a result, he, his wife, and their two children had to start their journey on foot.

They passed through the kingdom of Cheta where the king asked them to rule in his stead, but Prince Wetsandon refused. When they finally reached the mountains the exiled prince led the life of a hermit while Princess Matsi took care of the children. Meanwhile, back in the kingdom of Kalinga, an aged Brahmin mendicant by the name of Chuchok acquired a beautiful young wife named Amittada, who married him to repay her family's debt. Initially she was obedient to her old husband and took good care of him—for example, by fetching water from the well each day. The women of the village disliked her since their husbands were demanding the same service from them. They mocked her and picked quarrels with her and made her miserable. Finally Amittada sent her husband to bring back the children of Prince Wetsandon as slaves so that she wouldn't have to face her antagonizers.

After many adventures Chuchok finally arrived at the home of the banished royal family. He waited until Princess Matsi had departed before approaching Prince Wetsandon. The prince acceded to the Brahmin's request and the two children were led away. At this point, the god Indra assumed the form of a Brahmin and asked Prince Wetsandon for his wife. When the prince willingly gave her away, Indra revealed himself and returned Matsi to him.

Meanwhile Chuchok lost his way and instead of going back to Kalinga found himself and the children in Siwi. King Sanchai saw and recognized his grandchildren and paid Chuchok a great ransom for his grandchildren. Chuchok, however, did not live long to enjoy his great fortune—he died of gluttony shortly afterward. The story ends when King Sanchai and his army invite Prince Wetsandon and Princess Matsi to return and rule over Siwi.

The *Maha Chat Kham Luang* in many ways mirrored the tradition of royally sponsored religious texts such as the *Traiphum Phra Ruang* during the days of the independent kingdom of Sukhothai. The *Maha Chat Kham Luang* would be passed to the sangha, who would in turn spread its stories and its subtleties throughout the cities, towns, and villages of Ayutthaya. The monks would read the words of the king and the people would understand the messages in the stories and in doing so understand the role and status of their king.

King Tilokkarat of Lan Na responded to the ordination of King Trailok by building a series of temples and Buddhist edifices, including the seven-spired Wat Chet Yot, built to host the Eighth World Buddhist Council in 1477. It was a change in approach that marked this period of Southeast Asian history. More was devoted to religious issues than to military matters. All the major powers in the region—Ayutthaya, Lan Na, Lan Xang—sought to unite their people by building new temples and integrating the sangha more deeply into their reigns.

The year 1471 saw the capture of a female white elephant. There was great celebration, and it was written into law that all white elephants in the realm were to be owned by the king. These "white" elephants— actually from a Thai word that means "auspicious elephant"— were often more pink than white and symbolized strength and prestige as well as the king's righteousness and power. After capture, palace experts would examine the elephants and classify them into one of four mythical families. The "white elephant" would go on to play an important role in the history of Ayutthaya during the coming centuries.

@~~

The peace between Lan Na and Ayutthaya did not last. There were no defined borders, and encroachment into what the other side regarded as their territory was commonplace. Then, open war broke out after King Tilokkarat had an entire embassy of Ayutthayan diplomats in his court massacred.

The chief envoy [of the Siamese delegation] was a Brahmin. Some of the actions of this person excited suspicion; he and his party were arrested and, on being flogged, confessed they had buried in various parts of the city seven jars containing . . . magic herbs and talismans. These were burnt, ground to powder, and the powder cast into the river. . . . The Brahmin followed them, with stones tied to [his] feet. The other envoys were dismissed, but had not gone far when they were set upon by troops despatched ahead for the purpose, and massacred to a man.

King Trailok advanced with his army into Lan Na, capturing the city of Chaliang (Si Satchanalai) where he killed the incumbent governor. Subsequently the city changed hands a few times, but in the end King Trailok recaptured Chaliang and renamed it Sawankhalok.

Again a stalemate developed and in 1475, after he had suffered a number of setbacks, King Tilokkarat sued for peace. This time no treaty was agreed. The two kings took each other's word that hostilities were ended, although King Trailok remembered well the duplicity of King Tilokkarat in not delivering Prince Yuthisathian after their agreement outside the walls of Kamphaeng Phet.

The peace between them continued until the end of both their reigns. Despite the peace proving itself King Trailok maintained Phitsanulok as his capital, content to stay away from the petty rivalries and spies that bedeviled court life in Ayutthaya. His son, the upparat but carrying the title King Borommaracha III, ruled in Ayutthaya. Apart from ceremonial visits, King Trailok was satisfied with letting his son learn the arts of kingship in Ayutthaya.

The young ruler of Ayutthaya also had a role in the kingdom's expansion; Tenasserim fell to King Borommaracha III in the 1460s and Tavoy in 1488 before he gained the full kingship of Ayutthaya.

On trade the king exercised a monopoly with the right to be the first buyer of any import and to set the price. Although benefiting the crown, the gradual impact of the many restrictions and the levy on labor or military service weakened Ayutthaya. Many freemen looked elsewhere to make a livelihood. This would leave a manpower shortage that would become evident in later Burmese attacks.

King Trailok's last major religious act took place in 1482 with the restoration of Wat Phra Si Rattana Mahathat in Phitsanulok, which housed the famous Phra Chinnarat Buddha image.

A fifteen-day festival, which also celebrated Phitsanulok being his capital for twenty years, was held. The king gave presents to Brahmins, officials, monks, and the people. King Trailok's youngest son, Prince Chettathirat, and the eldest son of King Borommaracha III were ordained as monks. When they left the priesthood the following year Prince Chettathirat was appointed upparat of Phitsanulok, putting him next in line for the throne after King Borommaracha III in Ayutthaya.

In 1487, King Tilokkarat of Lan Na died at the age of seventy-eight after reigning for forty-four years. The following year, King Trailok died at the age of fifty-seven after reigning for forty years.

His reign was one of the most influential of all the kings of Ayutthaya. He left a legacy of a society structured under the sakdina system, a set of laws that would last beyond the eventual destruction of Ayutthaya, and a reorganized military and social administration that secured the position of the king.

By moving the capital to Phitsanulok, King Trailok convinced those in the north of his kingdom, particularly those of Sukhothai, that he was a fair and just ruler. Religious activities became an area where the two kingdoms, Ayutthaya and Sukhothai, could finally be integrated.

11

KING BOROMMARACHA III
1488–91

AFTER KING TRAILOK MOVED HIS CAPITAL CITY and his government to Phitsanulok in 1463, Ayutthaya was reduced in status to the southern cardinal city, with his young son, King Borommaracha III, as upparat and the ruler of Ayutthaya and the region surrounding it. The young upparat would rule for twenty-five years until the death of King Trailok in 1488, but only three further years as king in his own right.

It was only two weeks into his reign that he faced what would be the first of many decisions he alone would make. The descendants of Sheik Sa-id, who had visited King Ramathibodi over a century before, now lived in a trading enclave within the walls of Ayutthaya. To them Ayutthaya was an entrepôt, a trading city where they had enjoyed a certain status and safety over the years. They had even consulted by King Borommaracha II about their Islamic faith before he launched his failed attack on Malacca. Now they were drawn to the attention of King Borommaracha III, but not for the best of reasons.

Abd Al-Qadir had been summoned before the young king. He was the leader of his community and as such was responsible for their behavior. Three days before, a young Muslim man had been found dead near the city gates, and the king wanted to know what had happened.

"Abd Al-Qadir, your family has been with us for many years," said King Borommaracha III.

"We have been deeply honored to be permitted to settle and trade in your magnificent city," said the fawning Abd Al-Qadir, who lay prostrate on the floor with his eyes cast downward. He spoke using the language of *rachasap,* which his father had schooled him in since childhood. "It is the language of the court," said his father, the previous leader of the *ummah,* as the Muslim merchants called their community. "There will come a time when you will be called on to use the royal language." Now was the time.

"There has been a death. A young man, a Muslim, was found with his throat cut. What do you know of this?" asked the king.

"His death is unfortunate, may God's peace, mercy, and blessing be upon him. The murderer has been found and has been handed to your guards. He has confessed willingly."

"Go on."

"The dead boy is a Sunni Muslim from the west. In recent years the Sunni have arrived in your magnificent city to trade. There is an enmity between us that has festered for many centuries. Both my father before me and I have tried to mediate between us, but in this case I have failed." He pressed his head to the brick floor.

"What is the nature of this enmity?" asked the king.

"Its roots go back far in history, beyond when my people first came to trade in Ayutthaya. Decrees in our sacred texts the Qur'an and Hadith encourage us to travel to spread the holy religion to other lands as a holy pilgrimage. You have welcomed us to your city and allowed us the freedom to build the Kudi Cho Fah mosque, for which we are eternally grateful."

"My grandfather was suspicious of your religion, particularly as it grew so quickly in Malacca, but I am happy that you stay and live in peace."

"For which I and my people thank you. Those of us who settled here many years ago are of the Shiite sect. Those who have arrived over recent years are Sunni Muslims from Malacca and the islands to the south, and from the west. There are many differences between us in our interpretation of our religion, and in our society and our culture. It is these differences I have failed to keep in check."

"And this difference caused the fight?"

"Ultimately, yes," said Abd Al-Qadir.

The king called his first minister to him and they talked earnestly for some time.

"My decision has been made. We cannot tolerate murder within our community. The man who has confessed will be executed. Furthermore only your sect will be allowed to remain within the walls of Ayutthaya. Those you call Sunni will only be permitted to live outside the walls, but they will still be permitted to trade."

"The audience is over," said the minister.

Abd Al-Qadir backed out of the chamber, his eyes remaining downcast.

"My son," he wailed quietly to himself. "They are to execute my son!"

With the war against Lan Na being controlled from Phitsanulok, these years saw a period of peace and prosperity for Ayutthaya. King Borommaracha III looked to the future. A future where he would succeed his father as the full king of the kingdom of Ayutthaya. The young king looked to bolster trade and to increase his possessions. Ayutthaya exported rice to Malacca and in return imported cloth and luxury goods. Tamil traders would carry the cloth from India to Malacca for onward shipment to Ayutthaya. While Ayutthaya was happy to sell rice via Malacca, it did not like the additional cost of importing goods from India via Malacca or its own reliance on a Muslim state that should rightfully be part of Ayutthaya. The kingdom sought alternatives.

Tenasserim beckoned. King Borommaracha III had fought hard on behalf of his father over the previous years to secure the port of Tenasserim for Ayutthaya. It was protected on the landward side by the Tenasserim mountains, a steep and jungle-covered range accessible only during the dry season, and a mixed but united Mon, Bamar, Karen, and Muslim population. King Borommaracha III's army fought to gain the all-important Three Pagodas Pass. In early 1464, just one year after his father had made him king of Ayutthaya, came news of a breakthrough. The Three Pagodas Pass, the gateway to this independent state, had finally fallen.

Tenasserim, its neighbor Tavoy, and the port of Mergui further to the south had enjoyed independence since the fall of the Burmese Bagan empire some two centuries earlier. With the Ayutthayan claim on Tenasserim from the days of King Ram Khamhaeng of Sukhothai, it looked to the west to secure ports bordering the Andaman Sea and into the Indian Ocean. King Borommaracha III led his troops to the walls of the city of Tenasserim.

The city of Tenasserim was well protected on the seaward side but was not as well defended from a landward attack. As the superior numbers of the Ayutthayan troops gathered, the governor of the city surrendered and sought terms. The king, at the head of his troops, entered the city. There were to be no reprisals. Those from Ayutthaya had fought long and hard against a worthy adversary. The city would remain untouched.

Ayutthaya had acquired a foothold on its west coast. It was an area rich in tin and precious stones, but the prize was the port itself. Members of the Ayutthayan treasury arrived to secure the trade in and out of the port. With the access to Ayutthayan imports and exports the port grew in trade, and Ayutthaya benefited from the duties gathered and the greater trading opportunities. To the south lay Tavoy. The fiercely independent state was defended by inland mountains and sturdy walls facing seaward. The city was reluctant to give up its independence. Gradually Ayutthaya exerted its control southward on the Malay Peninsula, and Tavoy also fell under the influence of Ayutthaya.

King Borommaracha III continued to build trade links. Diplomatic exchanges and trade links were established with Korea, Japan, Java (horses being in much demand), and India. In these years the majority of trading was carried out on behalf of the king, princes, and nobles.

In 1488, King Trailok died in Phitsanulok. His body was returned in great solemnity to Ayutthaya, where it would be cremated and his bones interred. His body would lay in state as royalty and nobles would gather for the cremation ceremony.

The death of a king, particularly in a divine monarchy, reveals the king as mortal. The ceremony surrounding his death allows for the king to pass peacefully in the minds of his people, and the subsequent coronation of his successor demonstrates the continuity of the realm. The king is not considered "dead." He is considered to have passed to a higher existence.

King Borommaracha III looked on as the body of his father was ceremonially washed with water and anointed with special oils infused with spices. As the monks continued their preparations the son reflected back over the glorious reign of his father and how he could build on his legacy. He watched as the monks invested the king with monarchical garments and placed a gold coin in his mouth.

The body of the king was placed inside the *phra kot* (urn-shaped coffin), which was decorated with an ornate pattern and the four faces of Brahma; at its base were animals that live at the foot of Mount Meru. The top of the casket was decorated with red paper painted in tiers as naga, garuda, asura, and the gods Indra and Brahma. The inside was painted with a host of silver and gold flowers.

He and the king's close family moved forward and, in accordance with custom, poured scented water over the dead king's hand as a personal tribute. As the king had died, subjects came from throughout the empire to pay their respects. The monks attended to the needs of the dead, chanting, praying, saying mantras, and burning incense.

The king's body was taken on his royal carriage to the funeral pyre, and the royal coffin was placed on a layer of fresh soil that had been added by the late king's close family. The next in line to the throne, King Borommaracha III, lit the flames and was endowed with merit from the previous king.

Professional mourners screamed and wailed to lament the passing of their king. A discordant blend of a brass flageolet, gongs, conch shells, and drums played as the king made his last journey. Waiting at the eleven-tiered pyre, the aged head priest visiting from the island of Munay stood to offer final prayers to the deceased king.

On his ascension to the throne King Borommaracha III moved the capital back to Ayutthaya, making Phitsanulok again one of the secondary cities. In accordance with tradition he placed his brother Prince Chettathirat as upparat, heir apparent in Phitsanulok.

No sooner were his father's funeral rites completed than news came of an uprising in Sukhothai. King Borommaracha III and Prince Chettathirat quickly put the insurrection down. From this point on Sukhothai was fully integrated into the kingdom of Ayutthaya, although the title "king of Sukhothai" continued symbolically.

King Borommaracha III died in 1491, three years into his reign. While serving his father in Ayutthaya, he had expanded the kingdom to the Andaman Sea in the west and developed trade links that would serve the kingdom well in the coming years. Militarily he aided his father when requested, conquered Tenasserim and Tavoy, and kept the slowly resurgent Khmer in check. He was followed on the throne by his brother Prince Chettathirat, who would reign as King Ramathibodi II.

12

KING RAMATHIBODI II

1491–1529

Pra Nakorn Sri Ayutthaya is the capital city in which the king lives, and so do the nobles, officials, and all administrators. The capital city is situated on a small island in [the] Chao Praya River. Its surrounding area is a flat field. The stone wall was constructed to surround the city with 2 Dutch miles circumference. So it is a very big capital city. Its vicinity consists of many immediate Buddhist monasteries. The population is dense in the capital. There are long, wide and straight aligned roads. There are canals that are converted from Chao Praya River to the capital. So it is very convenient for transportation. Besides the roads and canals, there are also small ditches and alleyways. So, in the rainy season, people can easily travel to houses. The houses are built in Indian styles but roofed with tiles. Ayutthaya is therefore a luxurious city packed with over 300 Buddhist monasteries exquisitely built. There are many pagodas, topes, molded figures, and statues that are coated with gold brightening the whole area. The capital city situates on the riverbank and the city plan was orderly planned, so it is a very beautiful city. Its location is good, its population is dense, and it is a good trading area both domestic and foreign trade. As far as I am aware, there has not been any king in this region has ever reigned the beautiful and prosperous city as Ayutthaya. The city is on a very good location, regarding the militarily [sic] strategies, so it is very difficult for the enemy to impregnate because the surrounding area will be flooded for 6 months annually in the rainy season. The enemy cannot stay for a long time, so they will eventually retreat.

José van Santen, Dutch trader in Ayutthaya

WAT PHRA SI SANPHET WAS BUILT during the reign of King Trailok. It sat within the grounds of a vast palace complex that already included the Sanphet Prasat Hall with its five-tiered gold roof that gleamed brightly under the midday sun. It was to be the place of interment of the remains of King Trailok, his father, and King Borommaracha III, his brother. King Ramathibodi II had two large chedis built to the east and center of the palace to house the ashes of his father and elder brother. To the west a third chedi would later be built in 1530 by his son and royal successor, King Borommaracha IV, to hold King Ramathibodi II's remains. From this time on the remains of many royal family members were placed in small chedis built on the site.

A principal hall of worship called the *wihan luang* (royal chapel) was built on the site in 1499, and a year later the king ordered the construction of the Phra Buddha Chai Si Sanphet, a sixteen-meter-tall standing cast Buddha image covered in gold. This statue became the main object of veneration in the royal chapel.

૭৵~

The kingdom that King Ramathibodi II inherited soon found itself threatened not only by Lan Na but also by the sultanate of Malacca to the south. It did not take long for war with Lan Na to erupt again.

Phraya Suriyawong, a son of King Ramathibodi II, was in Chiang Mai as a Buddhist monk. On leaving he took with him a venerated statue, the famed crystal Buddha.

King Yot Chiang Rai, the grandson of King Tilokkarat, ordered his army readied when he heard the news. The king of Chiang Mai sent a formal request to King Ramathibodi II not only that the statue be returned but also that his son face punishment. This King Ramathibodi II could not allow.

The king ordered the chamber cleared except for his son.

"What were you thinking!" exclaimed the king of Ayutthaya, not a man known for his patience.

His son looked at him. The arrogance of royalty had vanished. He may have been a prince, but now he was just a naughty boy.

"You understand that soldiers will die because of your actions. King Yot Chiang Rai is probably leading his troops against us now. We will have to give battle and then sue for peace. We will almost certainly give a town to the king of Lan Na by way of settlement and later return the crystal Buddha," fumed the king. "You will learn from this. If you desire to be king after me you will learn from this!" With that he dismissed his son.

Events followed as the king had told his son, with many men dying needlessly. Within the year King Ramathibodi II was raising another army, this time to quell a series of Khmer raids along Ayutthaya's coastline. Many decades had passed since the sacking of Angkor. The Khmer capital had been moved south to Phnom Penh, but the nation remained disjointed and without leadership. The country was run by a series of warlords, each vying to increase his power.

The Ayutthayan army again marched to its eastern neighbor. The city of Angkor, overgrown and populated only by monks, was passed by. One by one those warlords near the frontier were hunted down or forced to retreat deeper into Khmer territory. The Ayutthayan army stopped outside the capital of Phnom Penh to receive its annual tribute. The point had been made. There were no further encroachments over the coming years.

In 1507, King Kaeo, now king of Lan Na following the death of King Yot Chiang Rai, commenced an offensive into Ayutthayan territory. The smaller country of Lan Na felt that its best interests were served by always being on a war footing against its larger neighbor to the south. As he moved south through Sawankhalok, his forces were met and repulsed in a hard-fought and bloody battle near Sukhothai. The next year Ayutthaya invaded Lan Na, but after taking Phrae the invaders lost in a vicious battle and were forced to withdraw.

Two years later, in 1510, another Ayutthayan invasion fared no better, and the skirmishing persisted for five years until the army of Lan Na attacked Sukhothai and Kamphaeng Phet. King Ramathibodi

II and his two sons mounted a strong offensive, evicting enemy troops and pushing them back into Lan Na as far as the Wang River, near Lampang; there King Ramathibodi II was victorious in battle. The king of Ayutthaya looted Lampang and carried away both the people and the crystal Buddha statue taken from Chiang Mai by his son in 1492.

Following his victory over Lan Na, King Ramathibodi II was honored by the ceremony of Indraphisek or "Churning the Ocean." The ceremony was one of the most prestigious, lasting twenty-one days and involving the entire community, and it was rarely held due to its extravagance. The deeply symbolic ceremony drew on the joint heritage of Hinduism and Buddhism. It culminated in a reenactment of the cosmic tug-of-war that took place at the creation of the world, with the devatas, or gods, pulling on the tail of a great naga while asuras (demons) pulled it by the head. This struggle led to the churning of the ocean of milk—an action that gave rise to the foundation of the world.

☙

To the south the sultanate of Malacca had expanded rapidly, dominating trade and spreading Islam across the region. It had extended its control to encompass much of the Indonesian archipelago.

With the acquisition of Tenasserim and Tavoy on the west coast of the Malay Peninsula, Ayutthaya found itself more embroiled with Malacca. The influence of the sultanate was being felt northward along the Malay Peninsula as it gradually moved toward the states that paid homage to Ayutthaya.

"I have questioned Abdel Nour, the Muslim leader in Ayutthaya, as you have requested," said Chao Banmai, the king's first minister.

"And what have you discovered?" asked King Ramathibodi II.

"It seems what we think is true. Their faith tells them to travel from their lands and convert others to their religion. More than that, if people do not willingly convert their lives are considered forfeit and they can be killed."

"My tutors taught me of the Muslims in the times of the Mongol emperors. How they attacked Buddhist temples. It was only when the great khan invaded their lands and exacted retribution that the threat from them receded."

"They have turned Malacca from a Buddhist city into a Muslim sultanate in only a short period. As we have taken Tenasserim and Tavoy they have become more active along the periphery of our territory. Kelantan was recently attacked, although Governor Putamata turned them back."

"Our claim on Malacca is strong, dating back to the reign of King Ram Khamhaeng the Great. We attacked them in the reign of King Borommaracha II, only to be defeated. My father continued the attack but the wars with Lan Na forced him to look north. My brother strengthened our navy as their pirates have increasingly raided our coast. When they had something to gain in the way of trade they left us alone. Now that we have two cities with access to the Indian Ocean and our need for them is reduced, they look to invade us—if not now then sometime in the future."

"I think it is more than that. The more strident among them see a country they can convert to their faith. They have conquered the Majapahit kingdom and have converted that country to Islam. The tales told by our returning sailors from that land are dreadful."

"And they increasingly look at us."

"I fear they do. They look at taking first the peninsula and then using that as a base to enter our country. With Aceh and Riau under their remit they will soon have all of Sumatra from which to mount an attack."

"Then we war against them by sea and by land," said the king. "We have no choice."

The Siamese fleet launched against Malacca only to be met by a superior force. Malacca was a seafaring nation and had built its navy up accordingly. The Siamese navy could not compete.

The battle on land developed into a war of attrition that continued for many years. The city of Pahang fell to Malacca, and despite considerable efforts the Ayutthayan army was unable to wrest the city back. The thick jungle and monsoon climate of the peninsula made the war difficult for both sides. The Malaccan army gained Pattani when the Thai prince accepted Malaccan suzerainty and converted to Islam. Following this the governor of Kedah on the neck of the Malay Peninsula rejected Ayutthayan overlordship and switched sides. Gradually a stalemate developed whereby Ayutthaya could only exert its overlordship over the most northerly of the states on the Malay Peninsula, but there was a sense that the sultanate of Malacca was slowly winning the battle.

After the subduing of much of the Indonesian archipelago and the conversion of most of the inhabitants to Islam, the sultans of Malacca along with their Arab allies concentrated on the conquest of Ayutthaya with the aim of converting the Siamese to Islam. Many worried they would succeed and Ayutthaya would be forced to convert. The war dragged on for nearly twenty years; then in the year 1511 everything changed.

In 1509, the Portuguese had been the first Europeans in Southeast Asia when they reached Malacca. In 1511, they succeeded in conquering the sultanate. For Ayutthaya, the coming of the Portuguese gave them a respite from what had been a costly and prolonged war, and one that threatened their dominance of the region and their religion.

The Portuguese learned quickly. As Malacca had been claimed as part of the kingdom of Ayutthaya since the reign of King Ram Khamhaeng, Portugal decided to dispatch an ambassador, Duarte Fernandes, to Ayutthaya. Fernandes returned to Malacca accompanied by a Siamese envoy bearing a letter to the king of Portugal together with presents for Viceroy d'Albuquerque, the leader of the conquering fleet. The letter and the gifts from the Siamese monarch were sent back to Lisbon on the ill-fated *Flor de la Mar*, which sank in a storm off Sumatra with much of the wealth looted from Malacca, together with many artisans and weavers who were being sent to teach the Portuguese their craft.

*

"We have observed the Portuguese over these past five years," said the king. "What is your opinion of them?"

"My first opinion was mixed. Their arrival stopped the war on the Malay Peninsula, a war that was of great concern to all of us. They are very different from us," replied his chief minister.

"Their appearance was at first frightening. They are so tall and their beards make them look fearsome. Their smell is off-putting. It seems they rarely bathe, and they smell of milk," said the king. "But there is more to them than that. My concern was that they were looking for conquest, but that does not seem to be the case. They have secured Malacca but use it only as a trading base. Some of their monks have learned to speak *rachasap*, and we can now converse fluently with them. Like the Muslims they want to spread their religion. From talking with them I understand their religion is one of peace, but I feel—much like the Muslim faith—it has been interpreted differently. I will allow them to stay and build their churches in much the same way that the Muslims, the Cham, and the Chinese have done, but they will be confined within their compound," continued the king.

"We have exempted them from attending most court ceremonies as they frequently cause disturbances. As you know yourself it has been hard to teach them to speak only when given permission."

"Malacca seems to be a wonderful city, one that has grown in magnificence to rival Ayutthaya by all accounts. There are many benefits to trade, but many issues arising from it. We need to ensure our spies are well placed within both the Malaccan and the Portuguese camps."

"That is underway. Their religious are already teaching their language to some of our people."

"Language can hide deceit, but for now we trust them," said the king.

The Portuguese were the first of the Westerners to establish a relationship with Ayutthaya. They brought with them the technology for manufacturing high-quality cannons and constructing fortresses. The introduction of Western guns and ammunition gradually changed the face of Southeast Asian warfare. Within a few short decades the era of the "gunpowder kings" had arrived, marked by the widespread use of modern military weapons and tactics. The face of warfare in Southeast Asia would be changed forever.

The reign of King Ramathibodi II saw a flowering in Ayutthayan craftsmanship and creativity. The relative peace and the introduction of new ideas and processes from overseas invigorated the Thai economy.

One introduction that became popular with royalty and the nobles during this period was the giant swing. The first swing was brought to the country by two Brahmin priests during the reign of King Ramathibodi II—according to legend it was on behalf of an Indian king who wanted to make peace with Siam.

Thai literature and poetry also flourished in the reign of King Ramathibodi II. A prominent example is the epic poem *Khun Chang Khun Phaen*, which became a staple of Thai literature and folklore.

The Tale of *Khun Chang Khun Phaen*

Khun Phaen, Khun Chang, and Nang Phim were childhood friends. Khun Phaen was handsome, clever, brave—but poor. He ordained as a novice monk to gain an education and excelled at martial arts. Khun Chang was his opposite: bald, ugly, and crass, but very rich. Nang Phim was the most beautiful girl in the village. She met Khun Phaen at the temple during the Songkran festival, and they had a passionate courtship. Khun Chang also tried to win her love through his wealth, but Khun Phaen and Nang Phim were married.

Only two days after their marriage Khun Phaen was called to lead a campaign in the north. As Phim pined for her husband, Khun Chang spread a rumor that Khun Phaen had died in battle. He tempted Phim's mother with his wealth. Phim resisted at first but soon came to enjoy a comfortable life with her new husband.

Khun Phaen won victory in the north and returned with both fame and a new wife, Laothong. On hearing of his marriage, Phim quarreled with Laothong, after which Khun Phaen departed. After Khun Chang told the king tales of Khun Phaen missing royal service, Khun Phaen was stripped of his rank, received one hundred lashes, and had his property seized. Khun Chang was told to take Laothong away from Khun Phaen and to never allow them to see each other again.

Having fled to the forest, Khun Phaen desired to regain what he had lost. He equipped himself with the three requisite things: an enchanted sword, a trusty steed, and a powerful spirit baby, Kuman Thong. He returned to Khun Chang's house and kidnapped Phim, making himself a wanted man. When she became pregnant he turned himself in.

At the trial he cleared his name and asked to have his second wife. This demand angered the king, who threw Khun Phaen in jail. Khun Chang kidnapped Phim, who gave birth to Phlai Ngam, the son of Khun Phaen. When Phlai Ngam was thirteen, Khun Chang beat him and left him to die in the forest. The spirit Kuman Thong found the boy, who recovered. Phim sent her son to live with his grandmother. Khun Phaen, who had languished in jail for many years, was called out of his imprisonment to again lead an army in conquest. The young Phlai Ngam joined him on the campaign and, following the example set by his father, won the hand of the beautiful Simala. Khun Phaen was victorious, and the favor of the king returned. At the wedding of Phlai Ngam and Simala a drunken quarrel erupted between Phlai Ngam and Khun Chang, resulting in a court case. Khun Chang lost the case, but Phlai Ngam petitioned for him to be freed.

Khun Chang then asked the king for the return of his wife, Phim. The king declared that Phim could not have two husbands and would have to choose one or the other. But she loved them both—for different reasons—and could not make a choice. The king grew frustrated with her indecision and sentenced her to death. Khun Phaen lodged an appeal, which was granted, but before the news was delivered, the execution was carried out.

꧁ꦮ

The war with Lan Na continued throughout the reign of King Ramathibodi II; however, the constant warfare proved too much for Lan Na. The Shan territories to the west, which at that time were under the suzerainty of Lan Na, broke away, and a 1523 battle effectively ended the stability of the Lan Na kingdom for decades to come.

Ayutthaya received crucial Portuguese support by way of guns and training, and by the time of King Ramathibodi II's death in 1529 the forces of Lan Na had been ousted from Ayutthayan soil.

In 1526, Prince No Phutthangkun, was appointed upparat of Phitsanulok, which designated him as the next king of Ayutthaya. King Ramathibodi II died in 1529, during which a great comet appeared, as recorded in the chronicles:

> In 891, a year of the ox, an omen was seen in the sky in the form of Indra's Bow crossing from the southwest to the northwest and colored white. On Monday, the eighth day of the waxing moon of the twelfth month, King Ramathibodi II passed on.

13

KING BOROMMARACHA IV 1529–33
KING RATSADA 1533–34
KING CHAIRACHA 1534–46

PRINCE NO PHUTTHANGKUN SUCCEEDED his father as king of Ayutthaya at the age of twenty-seven, taking the title King Borommaracha IV. The new king did not put the title "Phra" in his name, thinking only monks and divine beings should carry the title. This showed he did not see himself as a divine being. The new king was different from his predecessors in many ways. He loved the arts—in particular *nang yai*, where leather puppets are brought to life by the puppeteers against a blank screen, supported by the grand *pi phat* orchestra.

His first act following his coronation was to return the crystal Buddha, originally stolen by his brother and later reappropriated by his father. By this act he gained much merit among both his own people and those of Lan Na. The crystal Buddha was returned to its original abode at Wat Chiang Man.

The young King Borommaracha IV was also himself creative, and he was trusting of those around him. It was this trust that would cause issues within the court. Gradually the officials in his court looked more to their own self-interests than to serving the king. As their excesses were exposed his leading ministers were dismissed, or worse, and the king took greater responsibility himself and started to rule his kingdom with a firm hand.

The king sent ministers to Chiang Mai to negotiate a treaty with Lan Na and continued to make Ayutthaya accessible to foreign traders. He commenced work on the *khlong lat* (shortcut canal) in the southern section of the Chao Phraya River and had plans drawn up that would aid navigation around the city.

As with all Ayutthayan kings he had a keen interest in the military, particularly as things were changing so fast following the arrival of the Portuguese. He encouraged the Portuguese to train his soldiers and to supply arms and munitions. The king above all could see how European weapons would change the nature of war in southeast Asia. He moved to put down an insurrection in the town of Choulok toward the western frontier with Hanthawaddy (Burma). It was here, after reigning for only five years, that he contracted smallpox and died, leaving five-year-old Prince Ratsada the twelfth king of Ayutthaya.

As a rule, children who inherited the throne of Ayutthaya met violent ends; this was the case with the young Prince Ratsada. Disputes over how to govern the country while he reached maturity came to a head one night when Prince Chairacha, governor of Phitsanulok and a half-brother of King Borommaracha IV, launched a coup. The young king was taken, placed in a velvet sack, and executed. His body was never found. King Chairacha purged government officials to ensure Ayutthaya was loyal to him. This bloodletting completed, he settled down to rule.

The early years of the king's reign were peaceful. The digging of the first *khlong lat* on the Chao Phraya River was completed in 1538, bypassing a bend in the river with a more direct transit. The city of Ayutthaya was being transformed as increasing numbers of overseas traders sought to make a living within their designated compounds.

The influence of the Portuguese took an insidious turn when in 1536 the king introduced an unexpected piece of legislation, the Law for Trial by Ordeal. To a nation where the divine justice of the king ruled, the acceptance of the outcome of these trials fit in well with the thinking of the time.

> The Law for Trial by Ordeal provides for several kinds of ordeal. One method consisted in walking over red-hot charcoal; the party whose feet were burnt was adjudged the loser. Another system was by diving under the water; the man who stayed under the longer won the case. Sometimes the parties were made to

swim a race across the river; sometimes they lit candles of equal size, and the man whose candle went out first was the loser. The Law lays down most minute regulations as to the procedure to be followed for every kind of ordeal, and provides long prayers to be read out by the Clerk of the Court, begging for the intervention of the heavenly powers to secure justice.

℮⁓

King Chairacha appointed his brother Prince Thianracha upparat of Phitsanulok but did not grant him the title of king of Sukhothai. His intention was to reduce the power base of Sukhothai royalty, the seat of which was now firmly in Phitsanulok.

By 1538, King Chairacha had a personal bodyguard Portuguese soldiers, and he encouraged the settlement of Ayutthaya by all foreign nationalities as his predecessors had done. This brought not only wealth to the growing city but also life, color, and new ideas.

Since the fall of the Bagan empire many centuries before, Ayutthaya's neighbors to the west had been riddled with internecine conflict. Slowly the country rebuilt itself—the Confederation of Shan States to the north, Toungoo to the center, Prome to the east, and Hanthawaddy to the south. It would take a great king to unite Burma, and that great king came in the person of King Tabinshwehti.

The second monarch of the Toungoo dynasty, King Tabinshwehti commenced his military campaign to unite Burma under his control in 1535, heading south into the rich, fertile lands of the Irrawaddy delta. With no more than seven thousand soldiers, limited weaponry, and intrigue he first took the city of Bassein and after four years finally captured Pegu, the capital city of the region.

The strength of King Tabinshwehti's army came partly from the ruthless Portuguese mercenaries he employed, coupled with hard-bitten mercenaries from Java and India. The king was a realist. The fighting skills, tactics, and weaponry of the Portuguese in particular enabled him to subdue his enemies and build his empire. He was the first of the "gunpowder kings."

Both Hanthawaddy and Ayutthaya held claims on territory along the coast of the Andaman Sea. Tavoy and Tenasserim now lay in Ayutthayan hands, but it was the cities of Martaban and Moulmein that became the target of King Tabinshwehti as part of his drive to subdue the Mon territory farther along the coast. It was here that the kingdoms of Ayutthaya and Hanthawaddy would first collide.

"Martaban has fallen," said General Taoklam.

"Then he will redouble his efforts to secure Moulmein," said King Chairacha. "The army is ready?"

The general nodded.

"Then we march to protect our interests. We cannot afford to show weakness to this king of Hanthawaddy."

By the time the Ayutthayan army arrived the city of Moulmein was under heavy siege. The town of Chiang Kran was inland from Moulmein and was subject to Siam. Within its earthen walls the army of Hanthawaddy had made camp.

"Send a message to their commander. Make it plain that he is to leave our territory immediately," said the king. "They are to be gone by dawn."

The following morning as the sun rose over the mountains to the east, the Ayutthayan army attacked. The Portuguese bodyguard of King Chairacha led the attack and surged forward, their skill and muskets overwhelming the Burman army and causing them to flee after only an hour's fighting. The fighting fury of the Portuguese mercenaries became legendary, and the king honored them by allowing a church to be built near the Takhian Canal and by extending their trading privileges in Ayutthaya.

Later that day a message from King Tabinshwehti arrived apologizing for encroaching on Ayutthayan territory and asking forgiveness.

"This King Tabinshwehti likes to play games," said King Chairacha. "He knew it was our territory. He was testing us. He knows it and I know it."

"I think it unlikely he will risk a conflict with us," said General Taoklam. "He still has his own country to subdue first."

"He will get around to us," said King Chairacha. "And we must be prepared."

To the north, Lan Na underwent a turbulent period as the Mangrai dynasty started to crumble. In the year 1538, King Ket Chettharat was ousted by his own son, who in turn was later deposed due to his bad governance, and his father retook the throne. The restored king saw himself as a wheel-turning universal monarch whose righteousness and might make all the world turn around him—the wheel representing the *dharma* of the Buddha's teachings and its eradication of obstacles and false beliefs. He was judged insane and after further subterfuge, the last king of the Mangrai line was murdered.

In July of 1545, the Shan attacked Chiang Mai in an attempt to restore order. As he attacked an earthquake rocked the region. Undeterred, for a month the attackers poured dirt into the city moat and tried to cross it with bamboo bridges, but the city stood firm.

The Shan then sought help from King Chairacha, who was happy to lend his forces to the cause. But in the meantime a group of disgruntled nobles in Chiang Mai got the word out to Luang Prabang that they needed help. The king of Luang Prabang took the city of Chiang Mai by force and then appointed the daughter of King Ket Chettharat as Princess Regent Chiraprapha of Chiang Mai. When King Chairacha arrived at Chiang Mai, there was no battle waiting for him—only the new princess regent and her loyal subjects.

"As you can see our recent problems have been resolved," she said. "The usurper is dead and our people are united."

"It appears that my army sitting patiently outside your gates is no longer needed," replied King Chairacha.

"That would appear to be the case. However, I appreciate your support in coming to the aid of Lan Na in this time of crisis."

"Then, my honored sister, we have accomplished part of what was understood."

"We have accomplished the very thing we set out to accomplish. You have my sincere gratitude for coming to my aid. Our countries can put the enmity of the past behind us."

"Our agreement was for Lan Na to accept Ayutthaya's suzerainty in return for my help."

"As you realize your help was not needed. The matter was settled by the time you arrived. You have come to pay your respects to my late father," said the princess regent, changing the subject. She clapped and a plethora of court attendants arrived with presents for the king.

"Tomorrow we will honor my father. I intend to build a temple in his memory and would like you to attend as the ground is consecrated," she continued.

"Yes," said a confused King Chairacha.

"Good that is settled," said the princess regent.

My army was at their gates. She had indicated they would accept the suzerainty of Ayutthaya, and I walk away with a handful of gifts and her goodwill? Not only that, she got me to give five thousand pieces of silver to help build the temple for her father, thought King Chairacha wryly, shaking his head in disbelief as he and his army headed back to Ayutthaya.

Two years later the Shan again launched an attack on Chiang Mai. Their armies were driven away by Princess Regent Chiraprapha. With the army of the princess regent fighting in the west of her country, an army from Luang Prabang arrived outside Chiang Mai with the objective of securing the throne for Prince Setta, the eldest son of the king of Luang Prabang. King Chairacha set out again to Chiang Mai.

The king's son Prince Thianracha attacked from Phitsanulok. He attacked Lamphun and burned down much of the city. King Chairacha advanced on Chiang Mai, but the city had been further fortified since his last visit and he was unable to break down the walls. The Ayutthayan army looted the surrounding area as they retreated.

The army from Luang Prabang pursued King Chairacha and his army, defeating them in battle at Wat Chiang Krung. As King Chairacha and his battered troops continued their retreat, additional troops from the northern regions again pursued and attacked. The Siamese forces retreated further and continued to draw attacks. In this disorderly retreat, Ayutthaya lost two city governors, three generals, and entire divisions of their army.

Prince Setta was crowned King Setthathirat shortly afterward, and the battered and bruised army of King Chairacha returned to Ayutthaya. The king was greeted with the news that the Burmese had taken Tavoy on the Andaman coast. He immediately dispatched an army to regain the valued port.

At the sight of the Ayutthayan army the governor of Tavoy fled. Angered by the meek submission of his governor and perhaps wishing to test the resolve of the Ayutthayan forces, King Tabinshwehti of Hanthawaddy sent naval and land forces to expel the Siamese from Tavoy. The Burmese two-pronged attack trapped the Siamese in Tavoy, and a bitter battle finally ended with the Ayutthayan army fighting their way through the Burmese lines as they sought to retreat. Tavoy was lost. King Tabinshwehti and his army had gained their first success over Siam.

This series of disasters weighed on King Chairacha, who died shortly afterward. After his death, stories began surfacing that he was poisoned by a consort called Lady Si Suda Chan.

The Portuguese explorer Fernão Mendes Pinto wrote of King Chairacha:

> This prince had lived in the reputation of being charitable to the poor, liberall in his benefits and recompences, pitifull and gentle towards every one, and above all incorrupt in doing of justice, and chastising the wicked; his subjects spake so amply thereof in their lamentations, as if all that they said of it was true; we are to believe that there was never was a better king than he; either amongst these Pagans, or in all the countries of the world.

14

KING YOT FA
1547–48

KING WORAWONGSTHIRAT
1548

HER NAME FROM CHILDHOOD is lost to the historical record. She was of the house of Lopburi, grounded in the stories of her city, and classically beautiful. Her name as one of the senior nonroyal consorts of the king was Lady Si Suda Chan.

Lady Si Suda Chan harbored an ambition—that she would become the first queen of Ayutthaya. She bore the king two sons, Prince Yot Fa and Prince Si Sin. With her sons in line for the throne her status in the palace was assured. It was said that she killed King Chairacha by poison. Time would tell that she was certainly capable of such an act.

Before the king died Lady Si Suda Chan had brought into the royal palace many eyes and ears from Lopburi. They were placed in key positions at all levels of the palace hierarchy. Her actions were planned down to minutest detail. She had discussed them with no one. She knew better than to be reliant on others. The goals were hers, and no one would be allowed to stand in her way.

As the king's body was being cremated, the king's council met to discuss the succession. It had passed almost without notice that an increasing number of council members owed their loyalty to Lopburi—to Lady Si Suda Chan.

"Our young King Yot Fa will shortly be crowned," said Phraya Mahasena, the minister of defense and the most respected general in the land. "He is but a boy. It is our duty to appoint a regent to rule in his stead."

A noise was heard outside and the door to the chamber swung open.

"Has the kings' council commenced without me?" asked Lady Si Suda Chan, immaculately attired, and looking directly at Phraya Mahasena.

This is a meeting of the king's council," responded Phraya Mahasena. "Women are not allowed."

"By whose orders, Phraya Mahasena?"

"It is the way it has always been."

"Then it is time to change. If a lady can rule as princess regent in Chiang Mai then surely Ayutthaya can have no objection to my presence in this meeting. I am the mother of King Yot Fa and of the second in line, Prince Si Sin. They are both my boys, and I intend to speak on their behalf."

"Your presence here has not been requested," responded a frustrated Phraya Mahasena.

"Lady Si Suda Chan has made a good point. Let her stay," said a voice from Lopburi.

"Yes. She has that right," said another.

Murmurs passed around the table. It was clear to Phraya Mahasena that the Lady Si Suda Chan had carefully engineered this appearance. It was equally clear that he had no choice but to let her stay.

"As I was saying, King Yot Fa will shortly be crowned. A regent must be appointed to rule in his stead until he comes of age," Phraya Mahasena repeated.

"Khun Intharathep is the boy's uncle. He would seem an excellent choice," said a voice from Suphanburi.

"Prince Thianracha is the king's brother. Should he not be given precedence?" asked another from Suphanburi.

"Is Prince Thianracha willing to accept the position? He is young and pious. Is he suited for such a role?" asked a voice from Lopburi.

"He has royal blood and a direct line to the throne. Should not that be enough?" volunteered another voice from Suphanburi.

"You are not taking into account the interests of the two young princes. They should be represented by the regent most suitable to look after their needs," said Lady Si Suda Chan.

"You are only their mother," said a voice from Suphanburi.

Lady Si Suda Chan responded only with a look of total disdain.

You are marked for death, she thought to herself.

A voice from Lopburi, interjected, "Then a joint regency of Prince Tianracha, if he is willing to accept, and the Lady Si Suda Chan."

"They can act together in the best interest of the king," said an enthusiastic voice from Lopburi. "It is only five years until King Yot Fa comes of age. It is an excellent solution."

"But what of Prince Intharathep?" asked Phraya Mahasena vainly. But the argument had been lost.

Over the coming months two of the ministers in attendance at the council meeting would meet unexplained deaths. Within the palace there was a constant aura of being watched as Lady Si Suda Chan inexorably placed her followers, sycophants, and retainers in key positions. Prince Thianracha, a gentle man, felt increasingly isolated. He could not gain admittance to see the young King Yot Fa. A myriad of excuses stood in his way.

Around him Lady Si Suda Chan took over the pending Loi Krathong celebrations, involving the young king at every step. She sat with King Yot Fa on her right and Prince Si Sin lounging on a cushion on the tiled floor.

"The festival began in the Sukhothai kingdom in the time of King Ram Khamhaeng the Great," she said as her sons listened with interest. "The great king welcomed Brahmins from India into his court. They told of showing their respect to the Ganges River by floating reed boats with flowers and offerings. Lady Nopphamat, a noble in the court, wanted to follow suit. She made the first *krathong* of banana leaves and flowers and set it afloat on the river."

"I like the festival," said the young King Yot Fa. "It is a happy time."

As the festival started Lady Si Suda Chan sat with her sons as dusk fell and as the full moon began to rise. They looked out as the people released thousands of krathongs into the gentle river currents, their candlelight flickering in the wind, illuminating the waters surrounding the city of Ayutthaya.

Princess Suriyothai looked on as Lady Si Suda Chan plotted and schemed. She was not fooled. Unlike many others she could see where this was leading. Or perhaps others could see too but chose not to acknowledge it. Her concern was for Prince Thianracha, her husband

and the joint regent. She feared for his safety. The princess could see that eventually he would stand in the way of Lady Si Suda Chan, and it did not pay to do that.

She walked alone through the palace gardens as the sun rose. It was the best time of the day. The air was clear and cool; the oppressive heat of midday had yet to arrive. Khun Intharathep, her husband's best friend since childhood, was waiting in the trees at the far end of the garden. He had slept there overnight to avoid being seen.

"Thank you for meeting me," said an anxious Princess Suriyothai.

"You were not followed?" responded Khun Intharathep.

"I don't think so,"

"Good. What is it you ask?"

"I fear for the life of my husband. Lady Si Suda Chan seeks the regency for herself, and I fear that is just the beginning. I need you to help him see the danger he is in. We have spoken but he does not see. You have known him for many years. He sees the best in people, and Lady Si Suda Chan charms him and flatters him."

"I fear you are right. She smiles to your face while plotting behind your back. What is it you have in mind?"

"I want you to bring these concerns to him as if they were concerns of yours. Suggest to him that for his own survival he should enter the monkhood at Wat Ratchapraditsathan, where he will have sanctuary and where I have placed monks who can protect him."

"I will do that willingly. From today you are to walk here every day. If I need to talk with you I will wait in this stand of trees. Most days I will not be here, so the spies of Lady Si Suda Chan will just see you taking your usual early-morning walk. Now be gone before they suspect," said Khun Intharathep, still looking a little bedraggled after sleeping in the open overnight.

"My darling, I am with child," said Lady Si Suda Chan with joy.

Her lover, Phan But Si Thep, was a captain in the palace guards but was of Lopburi and had distant royal blood from U-thong, although many generations had passed. He was flattered when the Lady Si Suda

Chan first approached him, and she was so mesmerizingly beautiful. They made love while the old king lived, the subterfuge heightening their passionate lovemaking. Now she carried his child and he was concerned.

"I will make you king," she said excitedly. "And I will be queen alongside you."

And then it will be your turn to die, she thought to herself.

Word of Lady Si Suda Chan's pregnancy blazed through the palace. An anxious Princes Suriyothai walked in the fresh morning air.

"He has agreed," came a voice from the bushes. "He will tell you himself today."

"I will still walk every day. Thank you," said the princess not catching sight of Khun Intharathep hidden in the stand of trees.

The Lady Si Suda Chan called a meeting of the council of ministers.

"I am to be married," she announced.

"We have already heard that you were pregnant and that the father is the commoner Phan But Si Thep," said an increasingly exasperated Phraya Mahasena.

"As you know full well, Phraya Mahasena, Phan But Si Thep is keeper of the inner chapel. King Yot Fa has graciously elevated his status further—he is now to be referred to as Khun Worawongsthirat, and he has been appointed to handle conscription affairs."

"But that is part of my remit," said Phraya Mahasena the annoyance showing in his face.

"Then your workload has just been eased," said the Lady Si Suda Chan with a smile. "Furthermore, the king has ordered that a new residence be built next to the Conscription Pavilion, inside the palace walls. The site under the white mulberry tree has been deemed auspicious. The king has further ordered that a royal seat is to be placed in his office for him to sit on.

"What has Prince Thianracha to say on the matter?" asked a red-faced Phraya Mahasena. "And why is the prince not here?"

"Have you not heard?" said a triumphant Lady Si Suda Chan. "Prince Thianracha has taken vows. He entered Wat Ratchapraditsathan this morning. I am to rule as sole regent until his monkhood ends."

"But nothing has been agreed," said Phraya Mahasena, but his voice was not heard as those from Lopburi cheered the announcement.

Exactly one week later, Phraya Mahasena was found dead in his bed.

"I have spoken to the doctor. He says that Phraya Mahesena's lips had a blue tinge. He suspects poison but will not say this out loud," said Princess Suriyothai. "I have also heard that she proposes to bring her lover into the palace and make him king."

"No, that we cannot allow. The young king still lives. Visit with your husband. Explain this to him and express both of our concerns. Ask—no, tell him to put his troops under my command," said Khun Intharathep. "I have spoken to Khun Phirenthrathep in Phitsanulok. He commands the army of Sukhothai. They will move on my orders."

Lady Si Suda Chan gave birth to a daughter by her lover Khun Worawongsthirat. She was disappointed it was not a boy. A boy would have been able to claim a clear lineage to the house of U-thong, the house of Lopburi. The descendants of the usurper king Intharacha would finally have been thwarted.

King Yot Fa was not yet a man, but he came to understand what was going on around him. He was heard talking with boys of his age from Suphanburi. When the spies reported back, their conversation had become a plot to overthrow Lady Si Suda Chan. Khun Worawongsthirat moved quickly. The young King Yot Fa was seized in the dark of night, placed in a velvet sack, and beaten to death in the customary manner for royalty.

No one dared object as the second son of King Chairacha and the Lady Si Suda Chan was declared the rightful king. There was no debate at the council of ministers as the Lady Si Suda Chan declared that as Prince Si Sin was only seven years of age she and Khun Worawongsthirat would act as joint regents.

The coup was completed only one month after when Lady Si Suda Chan ordered that the palace hold a royal elephant procession to honor her husband as the rightful king. King Worawongsthirat was crowned with all the pomp and ceremony that befitted a monarch of Ayutthaya. The house of Lopburi ruled again.

Princess Suriyothai had expected much of Lady Si Suda Chan, but even she was amazed at the speed and ferocity of her rise to power. However, the house of Suphanburi was not dead. The princess passed messages between Khun Intharathep and her husband, Prince Thianracha, still under the protection of holy orders. She knew that their planned revolt would have to happen soon. To finally secure her power Lady Si Suda Chan needed to have the brother of the old king gone. He was the only existing threat to her reign.

Khun Phirenthrathep, Khun Intharathep, and the other conspirators knew they had to act. To take the throne was no small matter. Together they consulted an oracle in the recitation hall of the Pa Kaeo Monastery. They swore oaths to one another and uttered incantations to obtain victory. The oracle ruled in favor of Prince Thianracha.

Those loyal to Suphanburi opened a side gate into the palace and the forces of Khun Intharathep and Khun Phirenthrathep stealthily made their way through the palace compound before being spotted. The soldiers of Lopburi and the joint forces of Suphanburi, Sukhothai, and their allies fought valiantly against each other. It was the common soldiers, those who had been loyal to the old king, King Chairacha, that swayed the battle as they gradually defied orders and fought alongside the men of Suphanburi and Sukhothai.

The battle was lost. King Worawongsthirat, who had reigned for only forty-two days, and Lady Si Suda Chan took their young daughter and fled to the royal barge to make their escape, but they were caught by a group of soldiers before they could board the barge. The usurper king, Lady Si Suda Chan, their baby daughter, and many others from the House of Lopburi were killed. The usurper king and his would-be queen had their heads cut off to be displayed in the city.

"They are dead," said Khun Intharathep triumphantly.

"The young Prince Si Sin still lives. My men have just caught him trying to make good his escape," replied Khun Phirenthrathep.

"Then we must kill him now. End the line of U-thong for ever."

"No. That I cannot allow. He is of royal blood. He carries the blood of U-thong in his veins. If we allow him to live it shows goodwill toward Lopburi and to the memory of U-thong."

"And sets up a future succession dispute."

"I cannot countenance the death of another with a rightful claim to the throne," said Khun Phirenthrathep.

"Be warned—I do not support this idea, but it is only thanks to your men that we were able to rid Ayutthaya of this usurper king and his Lopburi whore," said Khun Intharathep, the blood of battle still coursing through his veins.

Khun Intharathep and Khun Phirenthrathep left their men as they cleared the palace of the dead and wounded and together walked purposefully over to Wat Ratchapraditsathan where a relieved Prince Thianracha and Princess Suriyothai were waiting.

"It is over," said Khun Phirenthrathep, supplicating himself before his future king.

Prince Thianracha left the monkhood, and a vast procession accompanied him as he was transported from Wat Ratchapraditsathan to the royal palace on the royal barge *Chai Suphannahong*. He was crowned King Maha Chakkrapat; on the same day the new king adopted Prince Si Sin, the son of King Chairacha and Lady Si Suda Chan.

The new king bestowed honors on Khun Phirenthrathep and Khun Intharathep and others who had supported the overthrow of the usurper king. Khun Phirenthrathep was given the ancient Sukhothai title of Maha Thammaracha, the governorship of Phitsanulok, and the hand of the king's eldest daughter, Princess Wisut Kasattri. Khun Intharathep accepted the regency of the southern city of Nakhon Si Thammarat, the title Chao Phraya, and the ministerial insignia of office. Others supportive of the coup were awarded similar honors.

The death of King Worawongsthirat spelled the end of the pretensions of Lopburi to the throne of Ayutthaya. In the reign of King Maha Chakkraphat, the threat would come from the west.

@m~

One of the difficulties in accurately dating and depicting the history of Ayutthaya is the scarcity of written records. This was worsened by King Worawongsthirat (Khun Chinnarat):

When Khun Chinnarat became king, he had the old chronicles burnt or thrown into the water. On this account, parts of the old chronicles were missing from that time onward.

15

KING MAHA CHAKKRAPHAT
1548–69

THE REIGN OF KING MAHA CHAKKRAPHAT commenced with only good omens. Two white elephants were captured and brought to the king. They were the first of seven white elephants that would bless his reign. The internal strife of the succession upheavals in Ayutthaya did not pass without notice. King Ang Chan and his Khmer army attacked the town of Prachinburi and successfully took away its inhabitants. It was here that King Ang Chan heard the news that the succession dispute in Ayutthaya had been settled, so he did not advance any further.

"King Ang Chan has raided Prachinburi. He will pay heavily for this," said King Maha Chakkraphat angrily. "You will pursue him as he retreats. Let him be made aware that the king of Ayutthaya requests that he send back the people he has taken and that he send a white elephant in restitution and respect."

The king's second son, Prince Ong, the governor of Sawankhalok, set out toward Cambodia in pursuit of the retreating Khmer. King Ang Chan launched a counterattack and shot Prince Ong, who was mounted on his elephant, dead. The Siamese army was routed and nearly ten thousand soldiers were killed or captured.

"My son is dead, and his army lost! I will lead an army into Khmer territory. King Ang Chan will pay heavily for what he has done," raged King Maha Chakkraphat only one year into his reign.

As he spoke a messenger arrived from the garrison at the Three Pagodas Pass, one of only two practical passes for armies moving from Hanthawaddy into Ayutthaya. With him he carried a sealed letter from the commander of the garrison.

"What does it say?" asked the king anxiously.

"It is from Commander Nantawa. It reports that King Tabinshwehti has brushed the garrison aside and is heading toward Ayutthaya with a huge army bent on conquest," said Chayakon Seekom, his first minister.

The king reflected.

"King Tabinshwehti will head south to Sai Yok and Kanchanaburi. Does the letter give any more detail?

"The governor states that the army numbers about twelve thousand with many elephants, boats, and mercenaries. He has retreated to Sai Yok where he will gather the forces available to him and await your instructions."

"This was not foreseen. King Tabinshwehti has taken advantage of our internal dispute as King Ang Chan did. King Ang Chan is fortunate that we can no longer pursue him. Our battle now is with King Tabinshwehti. He represents a far greater threat. I will have to avenge my son after we have rid ourselves of the king of Hanthawaddy. Send messengers to the provinces. Tell them to assemble their armies and come to the aid of Ayutthaya. I will send Prince Ramesuan to Sai Yok to assess the threat. In the meantime we need to get Ayutthaya ready for a siege."

Prince Ramesuan set out with an army numbering no more than three thousand men. His task was to assess the threat and, if it was as serious as it appeared, retreat with as many men as he could.

The threat was indeed as serious as it appeared. King Tabinshwehti had taken personal command of his army. Gathering his forces at Martaban he organized his invasion force into three main armies. The vanguard was led by Bayinnaung, his childhood friend and now the crown prince. The main army was led by King Tabinshwehti and his personal bodyguard of four hundred mercenaries armed with morions and arquebuses. The rearguard army was led by Thado Dhamma Yaza. Each had a retinue of four thousand men, eight hundred horses, and forty war elephants.

The army of King Tabinshwehti had been constantly at war since he ascended the throne of Toungoo in 1534, and its grandeur struck feat into the enemies of the king. However, the army's movement was also hampered by its imposing size.

The pace of the advance allowed Prince Ramesuan time to assess the situation. The army was too large for him to mount a battle against it. He would follow his father's instructions: slow the advance, and retreat with as many people as possible, instructing the others to retreat to the forests, destroying their crops and poisoning the water. When the Burmese army reached the walled town of Kanchanaburi they found it deserted. The advance slowed as King Tabinshwehti closed in on Suphanburi. The towns of Don Rakhang, U-thong, and Ban Thuan fell quickly, and the three Burmese columns converged on Suphanburi. After putting up a stout defense, the Siamese forces withdrew to Ayutthaya. The path to the capital city lay open.

King Tabinshwehti made his camp north of the city on the Lumpli Plain and placed his commanders on the other sides of the city. Ayutthaya sat enclosed on three sides by the wide Lopburi River. With its natural and man-made defenses the city was well protected. The wet season would start toward the end of June. King Tabinshwehti had five months in which to take the city before the floods—so crucial for rice production—came.

"Do we stay behind the walls and sit out the siege?" asked King Maha Chakkraphat, looking out over the Lopburi River—which by now had a number of canals leading from and feeding into it. The river was usually teeming with life as boatmen, wearing the tattoos that told their life story, plied their trade up and down the river. Today the river lay silent and barely moving as the dry season continued.

"Their first attempts at bombardment have proven unsuccessful. No doubt, with the help of their mercenaries they will improve. The waters around the city ensure they have to fire from distance. To take the city they will have to cross the in numbers and scale the walls. We have ensured there is little ground outside our walls where they can build siege towers. We are safe within these walls at present, although we must be watchful of traitors," replied Prince Ramesuan.

"To sit here presents us to the king of Hanthawaddy as cowards, unwilling or unable to fight."

"Our strength lies behind these walls. I too long to lead my men against these invaders."

"We will test their strength," said the king. "Ready the army and the mercenaries. We will leave by the northern gate and meet them on the Lumpli Plain."

"The battle will not be decisive. We need to leave sufficient men with the city to guard the walls and we need to secure our line of retreat. If our army is cut off from the city then they could surround us."

The two armies faced each other on the Lumpli Plain. The Burmese were caught by surprise as the Ayutthayan army emerged but quickly organized. There was a stillness in the air as captains rode up and down their lines motivating their men. Prince Ramesuan donned his magnificent royal decorations and was seated on his royal elephant Mongkhon Chakkrapat. Queen Suriyothai and Princess Boromdhilok, seated together on one war elephant, followed dressed as men. They were as eager to fight as the king and Prince Ramesuan. Alongside them were men carrying long-handled elephant hooks; the soldiers would fight to the front, to the rear, and guarding each foot of the elephant.

Mahouts sat at their posts to the rear of the beast. Following came a line of foot soldiers carrying swords, shields, javelins, great spears, paired spears, tasseled lances, and banners. The foot soldiers crowded together, and the sound of marching soldiers and elephants shook the earth.

King Tabinshwehti on seeing the advancing forces put on his battle cuirass, covered for protection with occult spells and Buddhist charms. He took his seat on Mongkhon Prap Thawip, his war elephant, also clad in leather armor and bedecked with charms.

The army of Ayutthaya, led by King Maha Chakkraphat on his war elephant, charged, scattering the infantry of King Tabinshwehti. The Ayutthayan army held the advantage in the number of war elephants. Trained and controlled by Mon warriors as mahouts, from the very regions recently viciously subdued by King Tabinshwehti, they were eager to exact revenge against this invader from Toungoo.

The mercenaries fired, but this was a battle dominated by elephants. Prince Ramesuan, his trademark long hair blowing in the wind, rode alongside his father as the two sides clashed. King Maha Chakkraphat, seated on his war howdah, saw the viceroy of Prome and rode to fight him, leaving Prince Ramesuan engaged in his own battle. The king's elephant engaged the viceroy's. Honored soldiers stood at the four feet of the elephant, with a lead warrior protecting the king. The two men and their foot soldiers engaged in battle. For no apparent reason the elephant of King Maha Chakkraphat was startled and fled into the Burmese ranks.

The viceroy of Prome, sensing a crucial victory, chased after the Ayutthayan king and drew alongside the elephant of King Maha Chakkraphat. The viceroy had the advantage in that his own elephant was fully controlled. Queen Suriyothai, dressed in male attire, saw the situation and rode in pursuit of her husband. As the viceroy of Prome was closing in on the elephant of King Maha Chakkraphat, the queen and the princess placed their elephant in between and engaged the viceroy.

As the battle between them raged the elephant of the viceroy placed its shoulder under Queen Suriyothai's and lifted it into the air. The queen's elephant swung its head up and lost its position. At that moment the viceroy reached down and slashed with his war scythe, striking Queen Suriyothai on the shoulder and down to her breast, her daughter dying alongside her. It was only when her helmet fell off, revealing the queen's long hair, that the viceroy realized he had been fighting a woman.

Prince Mahin, the king's eldest son, forced his elephant to intervene, but it was too late to save his mother. His soldiers retreated carrying the bodies of the dead queen and princess. King Maha Chakkraphat, unaware at that time of what had happened, regained control of his elephant and signaled for the Ayutthayan forces to withdraw as planned. Many Ayutthayan soldiers died as the Burmese routed the retreating Siamese. It was only when he returned to Ayutthaya that the king heard the news of his wife's and daughter's deaths.

The two bodies were taken to the area called Suan Luang. It was not until the war had ended that King Maha Chakkraphat held the full funeral rites. A temple bearing the name Wat Sop Sawan was built in their honor on the north bank of the Chang Maha Chai Canal.

The Burmese continued with their bombardment and probing attacks through March and April but could find no way past the city walls. King Tabinshwehti attempted to bribe Galeote Pereira, the captain of the mercenaries employed by King Maha Chakkraphat, who promptly told his king. On hearing this the king had the city gates opened and invited the king of Hanthawaddy to deliver the money to him in person.

The months dragged on, and the Burmese could still see no way of getting into the city. The burning summer sun was taking its toll as dysentery and other illnesses passed among his troops. The rainy season loomed. King Maha Chakkraphat had a giant culverin secured on a royal barge rowed along the river to fire on the Burmese. It inflicted much damage and caused panic among the Burmese.

King Maha Thammaracha, king of the ancient kingdom of Sukhothai and governor of Phitsanulok, formed an army with the governor of Sawankhalok at the request of King Maha Chakkraphat and set out to attack the rear of the Burmese forces. The Burmese king heard of the troops coming from the north and considered the state of his army—hungry and with disease spreading through their ranks. He knew the rain due in July would flood the area around Ayutthaya, and when news reached him that the Mons in his southern provinces had rebelled in his absence, King Tabinshwehti decided to withdraw.

The fleeing Burmese retreated to the north, besieging Kamphaeng Phet on the way, but the "Wall of Diamonds" was too well protected for them to enter. Prince Ramesuan and King Maha Thammaracha were sent to harry the retreating Burmese. After sustaining considerable losses, King Tabinshwehti turned and fought. He and his forces hid on both sides of the road and ambushed the pursuers, capturing both the prince and King Maha Thammaracha. King Maha Chakkraphat was forced to negotiate for their return.

The negotiations were acrimonious, and in order to secure the release of the two princes together with many other prisoners, the king of Ayutthaya paid a ransom of two white elephants together with an annual gift of thirty elephants, a token sum of money, and the surrender of the city of Tavoy.

The two elephants caused so much trouble that the Burmese sent them back. Years later it was said the death of King Tabinshwehti started the day he returned the elephants. He conquered many lands and had built an empire but was undone by the loss of his elephants, his attempt to subdue Ayutthaya, and his acquired taste of Portuguese wine. He would eventually be killed by his own bodyguards working on behalf of a Mon leader.

Fearing a further attack from Hanthawaddy, King Maha Chakkraphat prepared for another war. Good relations were maintained with Lan Na and Lan Xang, but occasional raids from the Khmer continued. The king heavily fortified the city of Ayutthaya while reducing the defensive capabilities of Suphanburi, Lopburi, and Nakhon Nayok to prevent the Burmese from taking them as bases. A census was taken to assess all available manpower and mandatory weapons training was introduced.

The king instigated a series of elephant hunts to ensure his superiority over the Burmese, and the number of war elephants gradually increased. During the king's reign he would gain a total of seven white elephants, attaining the title "King of the White Elephants," but it was the war elephants with their leg chains flailing that could win battles.

It would be fourteen years before the Burmese returned under their new king, King Bayinnaung, the Conqueror of Ten Directions.

Prince Si Sin, the son of King Chairacha and Lady Si Suda Chan who was adopted by King Maha Chakkraphat, had grown up feeling that the crown was his by right. He argued with his adoptive father and railed that he should be king. King Maha Chakkraphat had him ordained as a Buddhist monk and put him in a temple where he could be watched.

The move did not work. The young pretender escaped with the help of his supporters and launched a surprise attack on the city.

Prince Si Sin on his war elephant struck down one of King Maha Chakkraphat's generals. Seeing their commander lying injured on the ground, the guards panicked. Many left their posts. Those who remained were heavily outnumbered and either died or were forced to retreat as enemy troops surged through the gate and the heavy fighting moved inside.

King Maha Chakkraphat fled Ayutthaya, escaping on the royal barge and retreating to Maha Phram Island, formed by a canal that had been dug to connect the waters of the Chao Phraya River to those of the Lopburi River. There he waited for his sons Prince Ramesuan and Prince Mahin to ready their troops for a counterattack.

The counterattack was launched on the second afternoon. Those loyal to the king were still not subdued by the rebels and were emboldened by the sight of the two princes as they advanced on the city. They forced a gate open, allowing the troops to enter. By early evening it was all over. Prince Mahin killed Prince Si Sin in combat, and the enemy troops were either killed or captured.

The nobles who had supported the upstart prince—including the supreme patriarch of the Buddhist forest-monk sect—were all killed on the spot, and King Maha Chakkraphat reentered the city.

When Bayinnaung became king of the Burmese, his first wish was to attack Ayutthaya, but his ministers and generals convinced him that he needed to secure Hanthawaddy first. Over the following years then he consolidated his control of the empire. The diverse and independent Shan states to the north fell to a concerted effort from King Bayinnaung in 1557 before he launched an attack on the neighboring kingdom of Lan Na. It was here he first came into contact with King Setthathirath of Lan Xang. The two would fight many times in the coming years.

King Maha Chakkraphat could only look on with concern.

With the northern regions secure King Bayinnaung could now advance on Ayutthaya. King Bayinnaung sent a request to King Maha Chakkraphat for one of the four white elephants he held at the time.

The message was more than a request—in the language of the period it was a prelude to war. If King Maha Chakkraphat sent the white elephant to King Bayinnaung it would signal Ayutthaya's submission to Hanthawaddy. If the elephant was not sent it would mean war. The white elephant was not sent.

King Bayinnaung left Pegu with one hundred sixty thousand men in six battalions—the cream of his troops. He would call on soldiers from all the states owing him allegiance. He advanced through the northern Mae Lao Pass, capturing the cities of Tak, Sawankhalok, Kamphaeng Phet, and Sukhothai before moving into the heartland of Ayutthaya. He paused outside Phitsanulok, the first major obstacle in his path.

King Maha Thammaracha, the governor of Phitsanulok and one of the men who had given the kingship to King Maha Chakkraphat, stared out over the parapets of his town, his son the young Prince Naresuan by his side. As King Maha Chakkraphat had been preparing, so had the governor of Phitsanulok, but in a different way. He knew that Phitsanulok could not halt the Burmese advance and that defeat was inevitable. His friend, King Maha Chakkraphat, had not allowed him to abandon the city and withdraw to Ayutthaya, as rulers of other towns and cities had been allowed to do. His king was prepared to sacrifice him.

"King Bayinnaung disdains those who do not stand up to his army," said King Maha Thammaracha.

"Are we to fight?" asked his son.

"We will hold him at bay for five days and then surrender. Defeat is inevitable."

King Maha Thammaracha and Prince Naresuan gazed down together as the magnificent and seemingly endless army of King Bayinnaung gathered to the south. Tents were raised, elephants corralled, and horses ridden. Trumpets blared and banners blew in the wind.

"So many men, so many men," said King Maha Thammaracha to himself.

So it was that after a five-day siege the governor of Phitsanulok requested terms of surrender. King Bayinnaung and King Maha

Thammaracha knew each other from many years before, from when King Tabinshwehti had captured King Maha Thammaracha and Prince Ramesuan on his retreat from Ayutthaya.

King Bayinnaung, General Kyawhtin Nawrahta, and the Mon commander entered the palace in Phitsanulok. King Maha Thammaracha sat on his throne, Queen Wisut beside him. The king and queen moved to stand as the king of Hanthawaddy entered, but the king bade them to remain seated. Those in the chamber knew that a favorable surrender had been concluded.

King Bayinnaung was often willing to work with the kings whose domains he conquered. Those who swore loyalty to him as a *chakravartin*, or universal ruler, were permitted to keep their ministers and high officials and remain in power, paying tribute to their overlord. King Bayinnaung took their kin hostage as guarantors of their continuing allegiance. This policy was held together not by formal institutions but by traditional personal relationships between King Bayinnaung and each ruler who submitted to his overlordship.

After King Bayinnaung left, King Maha Thammaracha gathered his family around him.

"I have sworn allegiance to King Bayinnaung," he said. He could see the disappointment in his son's young face.

"We were facing overwhelming odds and King Maha Chakkraphat offered no support."

"But to surrender . . ." said Prince Naresuan.

"To surrender is to survive. For me and for my family. You will understand in time."

"And the price?" asked Queen Wisut Kasattri, daughter of King Maha Chakkraphat.

"Our sons, Prince Naresuan and Prince Ekathotsarot, will be taken as hostages to Pegu, where they will receive some of the finest schooling in military and administrative affairs. Khru Muay Outtaphon has agreed to accompany them and to train them in the warrior skills of Muay Thai."

Queen Wisut gasped and pulled her younger son, Prince Ekathotsarot, to her. He was only five years old and did not understand. Prince Naresuan stood alone jutting his chin out.

"We will both make you proud, Father," he said.

"And what of me, Father?" asked his daughter, Princess Suphankanlaya.

"After much discussion King Bayinnaung agreed you will stay here. Do not argue. It was a long and protracted fight to achieve this."

"My army now fights for King Bayinnaung. Ayutthaya will fall—of that I am sure. My decision has been made."

❦

The army of King Bayinnaung headed south. They met the army of Prince Ramesuan outside Chainat, where the Ayutthaya prince won the best of the battle.

"It is only a battle, not the war," said King Maha Chakkraphat.

"His army is vast, and I understand other soldiers are coming from Lan Na and the north," said Prince Ramesuan.

"Our supporters are also coming to our aid. The news that King Maha Thammaracha has sided with him is worrying. He has been my friend of many years. For him to turn against us is concerning."

"He is a traitor," said Prince Ramesuan. "He traded his loyalty. That is unforgivable."

"What may be unforgivable is that I sought to sacrifice him and Phitsanulok. I did not aid him, nor did I give him the option of sanctuary in Ayutthaya.

"He had the temerity to negotiate terms of surrender on our behalf."

"Perhaps he thought we would not hold out and he was acting on our behalf."

"The terms are onerous and would destroy our kingdom," said Prince Ramesuan.

King Maha Chakkraphat had rebuilt the walls of Ayutthaya following the last visit by the Burmese in 1548. Now those walls would be tested. It was February 1564. The rains were not due for many months and the river and and canals were low. The Burmese had time, better cannons, better mercenaries, and far greater numbers. The Siamese forces retreated behind the walls as Ayutthaya awaited its fate.

With the help of his Portuguese mercenaries, King Bayinnaung was able to bombard the city with cannon fire and flaming projectiles day and night. The mood inside Ayutthaya changed from tacit support for Prince Ramesuan and his war party to one that blamed the prince for not accepting the surrender terms detailed by King Maha Thammaracha.

The change was gradual, but as the siege continued the voices for surrender became louder. The walls remained firm, yet with the war council inexorably losing credibility and facing many months more bombardment, King Maha Chakkraphat was pressed to come to terms with the Burmese invaders. The demands of those nobles who had first favored the surrender of the two white elephants grew louder, and the king finally acquiesced. Now was the time to sue for peace.

King Maha Chakkraphat ordered the erection of a royal building between Wat Phra Meru Rachikaram and Wat Hatdawat. Enclosed within were two identical golden thrones equal in height and design. These sat below a jeweled throne with a golden image of a seated Buddha looking down over the two kings. King Maha Chakkraphat was well aware of King Bayinnaung's commitment to the Buddha.

King Bayinnaung and his entourage entered. The carefully prepared royal building did not mellow King Bayinnaung's harsh terms. He upped his demand to four white elephants and the payment of an annual tribute. In addition, Prince Ramesuan and the other leaders of the war party were to be delivered up as hostages. King Maha Chakkraphat had to acquiesce.

King Bayinnaung would also take one hundred thousand people as slaves, including all the leading artisans and many of King Maha Chakkraphat's soldiers. Ayutthaya would be left dangerously vulnerable to attack. As the negotiations drew to close, news of a rebellion at home prompted King Bayinnaung to return earlier than he would have liked. He had little time to enjoy his victory or to reflect on the fact that he had now built the largest empire Southeast Asia had ever seen.

As King Bayinnaung led his army from Ayutthaya others were preparing to follow. The king of Ayutthaya watched as his eldest son, Prince Ramesuan, left on foot with his former commanders. The prince had refused to travel by horse. His men were to travel on foot and so too would he.

Maha Thammaracha and his remaining troops were to return to Phitsanulok. Both of his sons were to travel to Pegu, where they would remain as hostages to the Burmese king. He and King Maha Chakkraphat were now sworn enemies.

16

KING MAHA CHAKKRAPHAT
1548–69

KING MAHINTHRATHIRAT
1569

KING MAHA CHAKKRAPHAT was soon to follow his eldest son to Pegu. As part of his agreement with "black tongue," as the Siamese disparagingly called King Bayinnaung because of his habit of chewing betel, he was to travel to the capital of Burma to swear the oath to the chakravartin and then remain there as King Bayinnaung's hostage. With Prince Ramesuan already in Pegu, the king's eldest son, Prince Mahin, would rule in his stead.

It was only one month later that Ayutthaya faced another war. Soon, the raja of Pattani and his navy arrived. Their original purpose was to support Ayutthaya against the king of Hanthawaddy, but as it was too late for that, he reassessed the situation. The city was weak and had only just started to recover from the bombardment and defeat by the Burmese. He launched his own attack to take Ayutthaya.

When the army from Pattani attacked, King Maha Chakkraphat fled the city for a second time, leaving the indolent Prince Mahin to lead the defense of Ayutthaya. It was fortunate that King Bayinnaung had left one of the leaders of the war party of Prince Ramesuan behind. Prince Mahin, the purported slayer of Prince Si Sin all those years before, was no leader of men. General Phraya Ram took control of the city's defenses.

The raja of Pattani had surrounded the city and was setting up for a prolonged siege. He and his men were caught completely by surprise when shortly before the sun rose the cavalry of General Phraya Ram charged through their camp followed by his infantry, their blood lust at its height following their recent capitulation by the Burmese. It felt good to get revenge on someone, even if it wasn't the Burmese.

As the raja of Pattani fled, the soldiers of Ayutthaya—totally demoralized only a few days before—had a new-found confidence. General Phraya Ram was urged to take the crown. The king had fled, his son was seen as little more than a playboy, and Ayutthaya needed a strong leader. All the soldiers knew that it would only be a question of time before others, most likely the Khmer sensing Ayutthaya's weakness, would come to conquer as well. The general quelled the argument. He brought King Maha Chakkraphat back into the city.

King Maha Chakkraphat left to make his oath in the court of King Bayinnaung. He would remain in Pegu for two years, entering the monkhood and planning for the future. He caused King Bayinnaung no trouble, and when he asked to return to Ayutthaya on pilgrimage the Burmese king agreed.

"The question is, how can we free ourselves from the yoke of King Bayinnaung," asked Prince Mahin, "and dispose of King Maha Thammaracha? He is a threat to us now."

"I have given both those questions considerable thought during my time in Pegu," said King Maha Chakkraphat. We need to form an alliance. Clearly the Khmer cannot be trusted."

"When can you ever trust them? They are as bad as that fool Soon of Pattani," interrupted Prince Mahin.

"Lan Na is now a weak tributary of Hanthawaddy, but King Setthathirath of Lan Xang is a different matter. He knows he needs to take the war to King Bayinnaung before he is attacked. I feel we can make an arrangement with him," said King Maha Chakkraphat.

"We need an alliance, and we have a bargaining chip in Princess Thep Kasattri," said Prince Mahin as his eyes narrowed.

"She is as beautiful a girl as any, but young. Too young in her ways. I fear she will not like being married off to a king renowned for his cruelty to his people and to his enemies," King Maha Chakkraphat replied. "But as you say she is a bargaining chip."

"Her needs are not important," said Prince Mahin. "It is the future of Ayutthaya that is important. She will do as you tell her."

King Maha Chakkraphat sent emissaries to Lan Xang. King Setthathirath was told the story of the heroic Queen Suriyothai, who had fought bravely in the elephant battle against the Burmese only to die helping her husband escape. He was also told of the beauty of her daughter, Princess Thep Kasattri. Both kings saw the advantage of an alliance against the Burmese, and King Setthathirath agreed to the marriage and the military alliance.

When the news of the arranged marriage was broken to Princess Thep Kasattri, she was distraught. Next to King Bayinnaung, there was no one she would less like to marry. King Setthathirath's reputation for cruelty matched that of King Bayinnaung.

"I will not go!" she screamed, slamming the door behind her.

"It is for the future of Ayutthaya," pleaded her father.

"I will not go! I want to marry a prince, not an old man," she sobbed.

She had no desire to be sent to an aging king she had heard of only by reputation, and not a very flattering reputation at that. As the departure neared she was—conveniently for her—taken ill and was in no condition to go. King Chakkraphat decided to send another of his daughters, the less attractive Princess Kaeo Fa, in her place.

On seeing Princess Kaeo Fa, King Setthathirath rejected her and demanded his original bride, but he kept Princess Kaeo Fa, as he felt was his right.

❦

King Bayinnaung was famed for his patience, but today it was being tested. His Buddhist faith taught him to remain calm, but when he read the letter from King Maha Thammaracha telling of the proposed arranged marriage and the alliance between King Maha Chakkraphat and King Setthathirath his anger flared. He readied his troops for departure. Before they left, additional news arrived informing him that King Mekuti of Chiang Mai was plotting to regain his independence only a few years after swearing allegiance. His famed patience was at a breaking point.

Fortunately for King Bayinnaung, the two kings were on the same planned northern route out of Burma. He could deal with King Mekuti before moving on to address this unexpected alliance between King Maha Chakkraphat and King Setthathirath. He took with him his new general, Prince Ramesuan, who had so impressed him as his adversary at the Battle of Chainat.

King Bayinnaung knew the need to enforce the oath of the chakravartin. The swearing of allegiance held together the Toungoo empire. If one leader was allowed to renege then others would follow. The declaration of independence by King Mekuti needed to be met with force. An example needed to be made to the empire.

The Burmese king marched his troops through the now familiar Mae Lao Pass and headed directly to Chiang Mai. The city fell easily. King Mekuti was captured to be brought back to Pegu. Before leaving King Bayinnaung named Princess Thewi as regent for the second time. Many of the king's confederates left, fleeing to Vientiane and to King Setthathirath. King Bayinnaung thought this very convenient. He now had the perfect excuse to attack the kingdom of Lan Xang.

The Burmese attacked Vientiane with a force numbering upward of one hundred thousand men, supplemented by soldiers conscripted from the army of Chiang Mai. They gradually closed in on the capital of Lan Xang, and King Bayinnaung began to see that in his adversary, King Setthathirath, he had a worthy opponent. Surprise attacks, hit-and-run tactics, and specialist teams harrying his men were all well employed by the Lan Xang king. No matter what King Bayinnaung tried, he could not draw his adversary into a pitched battle.

But the fate of Vientiane was inevitable, and eventually the Lao king fled the city, leaving it at the mercy of the Burmese troops. Among the spoils, the Burmese also captured his young son, his brother, and all his wives, who were duly taken back to Burma. They also captured the unfortunate Princess Kaeo Fa, daughter of King Maha Chakkraphat, who met the same fate. Prince Ramesuan was a casualty of war and failed to return.

King Setthathirath lured the Burmese into the unfamiliar terrain of the Lan Xang jungle, where their losses mounted. Finally King

Bayinnaung withdrew, leaving only a garrison to hold the city. He took with him, however, many prisoners and valuables.

News of the defeat of his ally reached King Maha Chakkraphat in Ayutthaya. The plan he had developed with his son had unraveled in the worst possible way. The Burmese stood to the north, his ally King Setthathirath had run from the oncoming Burmese, his two youngest daughters were either dead or taken prisoner, and his brother-in-law, King Maha Thammaracha, whom he had left without support, had even greater reason to despise him.

This time the gates to Ayutthaya were opened and the Burmese army led by King Bayinnaung entered unopposed. King Maha Chakkraphat had broken his oath to the chakravartin, and he as well as other members of the royal family were to be taken to Pegu.

The Burmese king called upon King Maha Thammaracha in Phitsanulok for his counsel.

"You did well in advising me of the intended marriage between King Setthathirath and Princess Thep Kasattri. My men were able to intercept the princess as she traveled to Vientiane," said King Bayinnaung.

"It was a hard decision as she is a cousin to Queen Wisut. But I have sworn the oath of the chakravartin. It is a shame she took her own life while on the way to Pegu."

"I am considering placing Prince Mahin as regent," said King Bayinnaung.

"He is a playboy. He is not kingly in his manner or his ways," King Maha Thammaracha replied.

"He will not pose a threat then," King Bayinnaung said.

"He is easily led. That could cause trouble."

"I would like you to watch over him. I will make it clear to our playboy prince that you must approve all decisions. Will you do that?" asked King Bayinnaung.

"I have little time for the prince, and he has little for me. I think it could be a task I might quite enjoy. If it is your wish then I will undertake it, but in order to do so I will move to Ayutthaya. You set me a task that I cannot carry out from Phitsanulok," said King Maha Thammaracha.

"Good. We need to talk of your visit to Pegu. Your sons have settled well. Prince Ekathotsarot is very clever, but Prince Naresuan—he is a future king. One I need to look out for," King Bayinnaung said, smiling broadly.

The task of being regent proved difficult. Prince Mahin was a man of considerable vanity and of limited ability. He found himself incapable of dealing with the difficult problems that faced him. King Maha Thammaracha watched him closely and would question or interfere in almost all decisions. King Maha Thammaracha was working on behalf of the Burmese, and he opposed every measure that did not favor the interests of the king of Burma. This drew the enmity of those who longed to be free of their Burmese overlords.

General Phraya Ram, the former governor of Kamphaeng Phet who had been forced to capitulate before the Burmese, was now the chief adviser to Prince Mahin. He was strongly anti-Burmese, and his views were being heeded by a sympathetic Prince Mahin.

As the arguments intensified between King Maha Thammaracha and Prince Mahin, it was Phraya Ram who conceived a plan to regain control of Ayutthaya and the northern provinces. King Maha Thammaracha was soon to travel to Pegu to pledge his allegiance to King Bayinnaung. His absence offered many opportunities.

General Phraya Ram contacted King Setthathirath of Lan Xang and invited him to attack Phitsanulok in the absence of King Maha Thammaracha. There was an abiding hatred between King Setthathirath and King Maha Thammaracha following the interception of King Setthathirath's bride by the Burmese. The Lao king had surmised, quite correctly, that the governor of Phitsanulok was behind the kidnapping. As soon as King Maha Thammaracha had departed the plan swung into action. King Setthathirath advanced on Phitsanulok at the head of a large army and laid siege to the town. Prince Mahin marched north from Ayutthaya, supported by a fleet of boats traveling upstream along the Nan River. The prince purported to be coming to the aid of Phitsanulok, but no one in the city believed him.

The prince was refused admittance and the siege continued. Phitsanulok was well prepared to withstand a prolonged siege, and the city hunkered down behind its defenses and waited. It was two weeks later that a messenger arrived in Pegu with the news that Phitsanulok was under siege. King Bayinnaung felt betrayed again. He was normally a calm man, but this time he vowed to crush this rebellion. He would then crush Ayutthaya. An example had to be made.

The Burmese king dispatched an army under the command of Saopha Song Khae to relieve the siege of Phitsanulok, and as King Maha Thammaracha set out to accompany him he said his farewells to his sons. The Shan general led the Burmese army northward. In the meantime, King Bayinnaung was planning his third and final invasion of Ayutthaya, one that would ensure no further trouble.

Unaware that the Burmese were on their way, King Maha Chakkraphat ordered a second attack on Phitsanulok, finally breaking through the walls and entering the city. Prince Mahin moved to take Kamphaeng Phet, but the defenses of the "Wall of Diamonds" proved too strong. When he returned from his failure Prince Mahin was declared king of Phitsanulok by King Maha Chakkraphat. His reign was short-lived as news of the approaching Burmese forces reached the Ayutthayan king. King Maha Chakkraphat, Prince Mahin, and General Phraya Ram retreated, but not until after the forces of Phitsanulok had sent burning rafts into their fleet, destroying it.

Upon hearing the news of the approaching Burmese forces, King Setthathirath withdrew. He was pursued but engineered a counterattack on his way back to Vientiane, killing five Burmese generals in the process.

"His time will come," said King Bayinnaung to himself when he heard the news.

With the Burmese army nearing Phitsanulok, King Maha Chakkraphat and Prince Mahin headed ignominiously back to Ayutthaya to prepare for the city's defense. With them they took Queen Wisut (also King Maha Chakkraphat's daughter) and Suphankanlaya, daughter of King Maha Thammaracha. The debacle plus the earlier loss of his daughters seemed to have broken the spirit of King Maha Chakkraphat. Upon his return in July of 1567, he abdicated and entered a monastery. With due ceremony, Prince Mahin was crowned king of Ayutthaya.

For a time the new king tried to manage the administration of the kingdom and deal with the ceaseless demands of King Maha Thammaracha, but he was overwhelmed. Finally, he successfully persuaded the increasingly fragile King Maha Chakkraphat to return in April 1568. All knew it was now only a matter of time until King Bayinnaung would come again.

By the later months of 1568, King Bayinnaung led his army of elephants, horses, cannon, and soldiers through the packed streets of Pegu and northward to the Mae Lao Pass. Drums beat out a slow, monotonous rhythm as the king passed. All fell to the ground and supplicated themselves in front of their lord, not daring to raise their eyes until he had passed.

The procession leaving Pegu contained troops from Lan Na as well as Mon, Shan, Lu, and soldiers of the many others territories that made up the Toungoo empire. Each unit flew its respective colors. Three hundred thousand men, twelve thousand horses, and five thousand elephants marched to the drums as Ayutthaya waited, fearing their arrival.

King Bayinnaung knew the importance of gaining the respect of his enemies. His army grew as it was joined by more Shan forces from the north, and together they made their way by the northern route out of Burma and past the cities of Tak and Kamphaeng Phet. The people in those cities breathed a sigh of relief as the mighty Toungoo army passed them by. The invaders set up camp outside the still-damaged walls of the city of Phitsanulok.

King Bayinnaung had demanded that Princess Thewi of Chiang Mai send additional troops, and the bulk of the army waited outside Phitsanulok until all was in place before moving toward Ayutthaya. The Burmese king summoned King Maha Thammaracha to the royal pavilion. The governor of Phitsanulok entered and bowed to his overlord before sitting cross-legged on the floor next to King Bayinnaung, with the Shan general Saopha Song Khae alongside them. A cooling December breeze whistled through the royal pavilion.

"King Setthathirath is regrouping and preparing to fight," said General Saopha Song Khae. "He is allied with Ayutthaya and has developed a strong dislike of the King of Phitsanulok here, whom he blames for the death of his bride-to-be."

"He is likely to send troops for the defense of Ayutthaya then?" asked King Bayinnaung.

"Yes, I think so. This raises the question of how many. We forced him to flee his capital a few years ago. He will remember that and hold many of his men back," said the general.

"He will have to send his troops through the valley at Phetchabun. The alternative route via Phitsanulok is not an option for him," King Maha Thammaracha said.

"As you know, my captain is in pursuit of him now," the general replied. "With your permission, King Bayinnaung, I would like to take extra men and ride to do battle with him. I will take your advice, King of Phitsanulok, and seek out a suitable battlefield near Phetchabun where we can meet his troops when they head that way to Ayutthaya."

"You will leave first thing in the morning," King Bayinnaung ordered.

"From what I understand Ayutthaya remains ill prepared for the siege ahead," continued General Saopha Song Khae. "Prince Mahin is hapless in his efforts, and it is his younger brother who appears to be organizing the city's defenses. King Maha Chakkraphat has left the monastery but I fear the last few years have sapped his resolve. According to my spies he spends a lot of time in his chamber being looked after by your wife, Queen Wisut."

King Maha Thammaracha looked at King Bayinnaung. Over time these two men had grown to have a mutual respect for each other. They both understood the duties and obligations that came with kingship and could talk openly to each other without fear. To be included in this meeting was a great honor, and one that King Maha Thammaracha fully appreciated.

"I can take Ayutthaya, but I fear it will cost many of my men," said King Bayinnaung, sipping a deep red wine that he had brought with him from Pegu.

"Then you must be considering other options," King Maha Thammaracha replied. "I tried to entice General Phraya Ram with the offer of the governorship of Phichit some time ago, but unsurprisingly he did not accept. Without him Ayutthaya would be severely weakened."

"The question is how we can get him," King Bayinnaung replied. "He is not susceptible to bribery and is ardently loyal to Ayutthaya. He has, however, not always acted with the prudence he might, as his siege on Phitsanulok proved."

"Then we need to entice him out some other way," replied King Maha Thammaracha.

"Not entice him. Force them to surrender him," said King Bayinnaung, a smile escaping from his lips. "Your wife is loyal to you, is she not?" he continued.

"We have talked about her loyalty. Although King Maha Chakkraphat is her father she sees him as weak, particularly in a war situation. She is loyal to me."

"Good. Send her a letter. Put in it that I see General Phraya Ram as both the author and instigator of the war, and if he were handed over terms could be arranged. You will do that for me, will you not?" asked King Bayinnaung.

"Of course," said King Maha Thammaracha, wondering what plans King Bayinnaung really had.

"Without Phraya Ram they are reliant on King Maha Chakkraphat. And without him that wastrel, the self-proclaimed King Mahin, would rule. It seems unlikely the people of Ayutthaya would rally to him," added King Maha Thammaracha. "It is only the fear of your retribution on the city that holds them loyal."

"The Mongol emperor Kublai Khan merely sent a mandarin with a letter to the cities he intended to capture. Fear of him coming was usually enough," King Bayinnaung replied.

"Even Sukhothai paid homage, though he never came," remarked King Maha Thammaracha.

"If I recall my history, he came to Burma," King Bayinnaung said with some bitterness. "I have a plan for King Maha Chakkraphat," he added. "I feel his end is near."

Upon receipt of the letter, King Maha Chakkraphat and Prince Mahin sought the advice of the faction opposed to Phraya Ram and, hoping to appease the Burmese, delivered their most successful general to them. The king and the prince of Ayutthaya learned another lesson in dealing with King Bayinnaung when the Burmese king reneged on his assurances of discussing a truce. The general would return to Pegu in chains.

King Setthathirath and the army of Lan Xang regrouped after the failure to take Phitsanulok. Following the invasion of his country by Burmese forces three years earlier and recalling his ignominious retreat from his capital, Vientiane, the king of Lan Xang knew that it was not in his best interest to sit idly by while Ayutthaya was attacked. His ally was facing defeat, but to do nothing was not an option he considered. His hard-won moniker "the chieftain who never knelt before the king of kings" possibly describes him best. To King Setthathirath attack was the best form of defense, although in his case the attack was often surreptitious.

The Burmese forces had anticipated that King Setthathirath would send troops to the aid of Ayutthaya and were waiting for them. In a two-day battle at the Pa Sak valley near Phetchabun, the forces of Lan Xang prevailed over the Burmese, driving them from the battlefield. The forces of Lan Xang then split in two, with one army heading to reinforce Ayutthaya and the other returning to Vientiane. The Burmese, under the command of General Saopha Song Khae, rallied, attacked, and defeated the forces destined for Ayutthaya before they could reach the city. There would be no help arriving from King Setthathirath.

The Burmese forces were now redirected to hold the forces of Lan Xang at bay but not to engage them unless absolutely necessary. King Bayinnaung knew he could not war on two fronts. In December 1568, the forces of King Bayinnaung, supported by those of King Maha Thammaracha commenced their advance on Ayutthaya. Their conquest of Ayutthaya gave King Setthathirath time to plan and recover.

King Bayinnaung was an acknowledged expert in all aspects of warfare. He had also mastered the skills of winning wars by means other than fighting, be they fear, intimidation, bribery, or assassination. Many had surrendered rather than fight and face his wrath. In January 1569 King Maha Chakkraphat died. His death was opportune for King Bayinnaung, and so speculation over his death followed. Whatever the cause, his death left the ineffective King Mahin in his place, a king who had handed over his best general and supporter over only a few short months earlier.

Within the city of Ayutthaya panic started to spread. King Mahin was out of his depth. He became moody and drank heavily. He grew paranoid and ordered the execution of his younger brother, Prince Si Saowarat, who was only fourteen years of age. Prince Si Saowarat had taken upon himself the role of the strengthening of the walls and ensuring that the troops of Ayutthaya were battle-ready. King Mahin accused the young prince of taking too much responsibility.

The order to execute his brother turned the people of Ayutthaya against him. It was only then, with the army of King Bayinnaung days away, that he started to act as a king. He gathered and organized his troops, then watched as the army of King Bayinnaung came into view.

The forces of King Bayinnaung came with drums pounding, banners waving, and elephants trumpeting their arrival. King Bayinnaung had learned from his previous visit and dug trenches around the moat to form a tight siege ring. The army and naval forces established their camp at Wat Maheyong. When the siege ring was completed, King Bayinnaung issued orders for all of his forces to lay siege. Siege towers were prepared, and his Greek engineer had trebuchets built to spread terror within the walls.

Many armies under Burmese control were deployed around the city. The attack commenced. Nanda Bayin, heir to the throne of the Toungoo empire and son of King Bayinnaung, made it clear to King Maha Thammaracha, who had been commanded to fight alongside him, that he would lead the attack on the front ramparts. King Maha Thammaracha had little choice but to agree. Nanda Bayin had sound military schooling—that much was clear—but it was his cruelty to both his men and those taken captive that King Maha Thammaracha found unsettling. Deserters were tortured before being put to a painful death, and captives would have every last vestige of information extracted before often being burned alive. King Maha Thammaracha was not a squeamish man, but his introduction to the heir to the Toungoo throne concerned him greatly.

In a style of warfare made famous in earlier years by the Roman emperor Julius Caesar, King Bayinnaung ordered three causeways built across the Lopburi River to the southeast of the city. The northern, western, and southern walls of the city were well protected by the waters that flowed past Ayutthaya as natural barriers. This left the eastern flank more susceptible to attack, but it was difficult to access. When a breakthrough was finally made, the Greek engineer made siege towers that could be placed against the walls, but with the river and canals running alongside them this was a difficult proposition. The river needed to be diverted before a siege engine could be of any use, but slowly, inexorably, the forces of King Bayinnaung closed in.

"He may be a playboy king, but he is putting up an obstinate defense," said King Bayinnaung as the siege dragged into its sixth month.

"If I may suggest a different approach?" King Maha Thammaracha offered.

"That sounds as if you have something underhanded in mind," King Bayinnaung mused.

"Very underhanded. We have with us Prince Ramesuan's general Phraya Chakri, whom you took to Pegu as a hostage and who accompanied you here. I spoke with him yesterday, giving nothing away, of course. He no longer has the zeal and idealism he had under the prince. I feel that with the right offer he may be able to provide another way to enter Ayutthaya."

General Phraya Chakri, still confined in chains, was found the following morning before one of Ayutthaya's forts. He claimed to have slipped away and made his way through King Bayinnaung's troops. He was welcomed back by Prince Mahin, who badly needed a proven general to revitalize his defense. General Phraya Chakri was promptly given command of the city's defenses.

After assessing the situation, General Phraya Chakri placed his less-trained troops at key locations along the defensive wall. This information was relayed to the Burmese, who then stormed into

Ayutthaya. The city was taken and the looting and destruction began. King Bayinnaung would now exact a high price for the king of Ayutthaya breaking his chakravartin vow.

Nanda Bayin and King Maha Thammaracha proceeded triumphantly into the city on their royal elephants, stopping in front of the royal palace. King Mahin left his palace in his royal palanquin, escorted by King Maha Thammaracha, who took much pleasure in this victory. King Mahin was escorted out of his former city and presented to King Bayinnaung in his pavilion near Wat Maheyong.

The looting, raping, and pillaging ran its course, unimpeded by either King Bayinnaung or King Maha Thammaracha. King Bayinnaung had the city walls demolished, making the city defenseless and easy prey to neighboring armies—in particular to Ayutthaya's sworn enemy, the Khmer. The people of Ayutthaya thought that things could not get worse. Their city, ravaged, had fallen and lay exposed. King Bayinnaung took huge numbers of the population with him as slaves, leaving only fifteen thousand people in a city that was once home to nearly half a million.

King Bayinnaung left Ayutthaya and made his way back to Pegu. He took with him most of the people, war elephants, weaponry and cannons, horses, and—most prized of all—two white elephants. As the Burmese withdrew they scourged the land and took the people. They left behind a ravaged countryside of once-rich rice lands that returned to scrub and forest. Hope had deserted the people of Siam.

King Mahin, together with many members of the royal family, was taken back to Burma. He died on the journey. Whether by illness or assassination, his death, however it happened, spelled the end of the Suphannaphum dynasty.

Sukhothai Dynasty

17

KING MAHA THAMMARACHA
1569–90

IN AYUTTHAYA, King Bayinnaung waited to witness the coronation of his vassal, King Maha Thammaracha, who was given the title King Sanphet. King Maha Thammaracha had proven his loyalty to King Bayinnaung. He was also, by virtue of his descent, a suitable occupant for the throne of Ayutthaya, with a direct line from his father, a descendent of the kings of Sukhothai.

After his coronation he went to visit King Bayinnaung.

"You have left me little with which to defend the city," he said.

"Ayutthaya is of little consequence to me now," King Bayinnaung replied. "I have demonstrated to the Toungoo empire what it means to break the chakravartin oath. I leave it in your hands. I leave you, your own troops, and the city of Phitsanulok intact. Its people will not be harmed," he added. "I have enjoyed our time together. You are a clever man, a devious man—I like that."

"I have a request," said King Maha Thammaracha. "I would like you to release my sons. In return, my daughter Princess Suphankanlaya will go with you to Pegu as your secondary wife."

"She does this willingly?" asked the Burmese king.

"She herself suggested the exchange to me," said King Maha Thammaracha.

"Then it is agreed, although I will miss Prince Naresuan in particular. Your sons will be returned. I feel you will need them as you seek to rebuild Ayutthaya," said King Bayinnaung. "Keep Prince Naresuan close. He will make a fine warrior someday. Do not let him cross me though," he warned.

King Maha Thammaracha was a puppet king from the northern provinces of Ayutthaya. His association with King Bayinnaung was connected in the minds of his people with the defeat of their country. He faced an uphill struggle to rebuild his new kingdom, but he had no thoughts of not accepting the challenge. He was king, and he intended to remain so.

"Ayutthaya has been all but destroyed," said Queen Wisut, now reunited with her husband.

"It falls to us to rebuild not only the city but the kingdom," replied King Maha Thammaracha.

"I fear we have a monumental task," Queen Wisut replied. "The people will not take kindly to a king imposed on them by King Bayinnaung."

"The Burmese administrators will allow us to do little. They are to take over all offices of state and religion, and clearly want me to be a ruler in name only."

"Then we must thwart them," Queen Wisut said.

"What do you have in mind?"

"Royal protocol needs to be vigorously enforced. It is the position of king that commands respect, and that respect must be seen to be given. Even by our Burmese masters. They are to prostrate themselves at your feet in the manner expected by our people. Both the people of Ayutthaya and the Burmese must see that you are king. Our people must act in the same way," Queen Wisut explained. "They must see that you are not a king to be trifled with."

"King Bayinnaung took a great many people with him as slaves," King Maha Thammaracha replied. "He has decimated the countryside on his route back to Burma. Those who fled will be making their way down from the mountains and the forests. We face two immediate threats, famine and the Khmer. We need to bring those who have survived to Ayutthaya and plant enough rice for them to live on. Many fields and villages will have to be abandoned."

"People will not like being forced to leave their land," Queen Wisut remarked.

"We will not give them a choice. I will issue a royal decree. They will come to Ayutthaya on pain of death. Our people are our future. In time, they will see what we are doing."

"We still have our troops from Phitsanulok," said the queen.

"And small contingents in Kamphaeng Phet and Sukhothai," the king agreed. "After sacrificing so many in the first attack, our losses were thankfully quite small. We need to ensure that the sick and wounded soldiers recover as soon as possible. We will need all the troops at our disposal when the Khmer attack, as they most certainly will."

"King Bayinnaung has forbidden us from rebuilding the walls. How do we defend the city?" asked Queen Wisut.

"We use the water that flows around Ayutthaya. We defend the city with the Lopburi River and expand our network of canals to act as barriers."

"The people are still exhausted after the siege," commented Queen Wisut.

"They already hate their puppet king. Let them hate me more. If we can avoid famine and if we can keep the Khmer from sacking Ayutthaya during the first two years, then we can start to rebuild our kingdom," said King Maha Thammaracha.

Dealing with the Burmese administrators proved difficult. They had moved from conquered city to conquered city, putting in place the administrative systems that ensured control could be maintained and revenues raised. King Maha Thammaracha thought back to only a few years before, when he was doing the same with Prince Mahin.

The king sent his soldiers into the hinterland. People left their villages either willingly or unwillingly and came to Ayutthaya. The rice crop was planted, famine was averted, and the population of Ayutthaya grew quickly to fifty thousand. It was just in time, as news came that the army of King Satta of the Khmer was on its way. Those to the east of Ayutthaya fled to the city, leaving nothing for the invading army. King Maha Thammaracha had prepared well in advance.

King Maha Thammaracha ordered three thousand soldiers to the front. The advance of King Setta's army was halted at Wat Sam

Philan with brutal hand-to-hand combat. The Khmer brought thirty elephants and a further four thousand soldiers to attack Wat Phra Meru Rachikaram. They launched five boats to cross the river, but many were killed as they landed. King Maha Thammaracha ordered that his few remaining cannons should be fired across the river at the Khmer elephants on the opposite bank. The war elephants panicked and bolted, causing the Khmer to retreat in disarray, leaving many of their elephants and much of their weaponry behind.

As the Khmer retreated they hunted for captives to take home. Many of the inhabitants of Chanthaburi, Rayong, and Chachoengsao were taken as slaves. King Satta had been told of the low numbers remaining in the city and the destruction of the walls of Ayutthaya, but the city was better populated and more secure than he had been led to believe. He saw that in King Maha Thammaracha he had a worthy adversary. He would not be so complacent when he returned.

Those who had heeded the call of their king and returned to Ayutthaya began to understand that their new king was more than just a Burmese puppet. The attack was also used by the king in another way. The Burmese administrators had been frightened by the Khmer attack and realized that the city could have fallen—and them with it. Under pressure from King Maha Thammaracha, they authorized the rebuilding of some of the walls as well as the purchase of cannons and arms to defend it. It was a minor concession, but one that the new king would exploit to its fullest.

The following month Prince Naresuan and Prince Ekathotsarot arrived back in Ayutthaya. Queen Wisut was told of their coming and waited expectantly as the small group made its way through the demolished outer walls and through the main gate into the city. The repairs to the damage to the Wang Luang Palace sustained in the Burmese invasion were nearing completion, and the queen stood on the steps as her two boys came into view.

Prince Naresuan was now fifteen. He sat upright in the saddle, his hair cropped straight across and shaved at the sides. Prince Ekathotsarot, at twelve years of age with his topknot still in place, leapt from the saddle and ran to the welcoming arms of his mother.

Prince Naresuan rode alongside his mother and dismounted. He then bowed to his mother.

"It is good to be home," he said, speaking for both of them.

They met their father after they had refreshed themselves from their journey.

"My sons, apologies for not greeting you. These Burmese continue to make demands that we simply cannot meet," he said. "You have grown into fine young men by the look of it, but much has changed since you left. We bow to the Burmese now."

His eyes met those of Prince Naresuan. Father and son were of one mind.

The following morning as Prince Naresuan was lifting wooden logs above his head, his father studied his boy. He was tall with a rugged face. He was muscular. His hands were calloused and his shins hardened from his years of training with Khru Muay Outtaphon, who had accompanied the prince on his journey. It was his arms that drew the attention of his father though. They were broader than many men's thighs.

The prince's instructor stopped when he saw the king.

"You have done a fine job, Khru Muay, while my sons were away in Pegu, and have prepared my sons well," said the king. "Go to your family. They have missed you as much as I have missed my sons."

"Thank you. It was an honor to work with the two princes," Khru Muay Outtaphon replied, bowing to his king.

"We will talk later. Go to your family," the king bade him.

Prince Naresuan stopped his exercise and sat next to his father on a low wall.

"You said yesterday that we bow to the Burmese. That will not always be the way," said Prince Naresuan.

"What happened was inevitable. The Burmese are too strong. We brought about our own downfall. I foresaw what was happening and made a choice to side with the enemy. That is my personal legacy, and it is how I will be judged by history. Now I try to rebuild Ayutthaya. It will take many years, but with you and Prince Ekathotsarot alongside me, I have hope."

"Father, before I left you told me that a ruler must think beyond today and see how his actions will influence the future." This is what you have done. Others may not see it, but I do," Prince Naresuan replied.

"We have much to discuss. I need to hear of your years in Pegu and you need to know how we arrived where we are today. Go and get your brother and join me and your mother in the palace. Today is a day your mother and I have looked forward to for many years," said the king. "Getting to know our sons again."

King Maha Thammaracha knew the problems that could develop if the succession was not clear. He commenced the building of the palace of the front (*wang na*) as the residence of the prince who was next in the line of succession, Prince Naresuan. In doing this, King Maha Thammaracha made a statement to his people. Ayutthaya, as the capital city became the symbol of the kingdom. The royal palace represented its capital, and the palaces of the princes surrounded it as though they were the provincial towns. The most important of all these princes was the upparat, the heir who occupied the palace of the front.

The king also understood the importance of tradition and ceremony. He ordered the preparation of a new ceremonial ground to the northeast of the city. It replaced the old elephant kraal and was overlooked by the Ko Chawet Maha Prasat Pavilion, where the king and his entourage could watch processions as they passed by. Roads were widened and ditches dug. The roads would enable troops to be moved quickly in defense of the city, and the ditches redirected water to the moats around the city. The Burmese administrators did not understand, but slowly the people of Ayutthaya did.

Both Prince Naresuan and Prince Ekathotsarot studied official affairs under the guidance of their father. It was a time that proved frustrating for Prince Naresuan but interesting for Prince Ekathotsarot. The differences in the two brothers seemed to bring them closer together, and there was a seemingly unbreakable bond between them. Over the years they had had many disagreements and, on occasion, fights. The older and bigger Prince Naresuan would win, but his younger brother did not let that deter him. Like many brothers, fighting bonded them. It helped them understand each other.

Prince Naresuan's understanding of administration, particularly that required by their Burmese overlords, brought another aspect to his education. King Maha Thammaracha wanted the northern cities in particular to be made stronger. The Burmese were less concerned with Phitsanulok, and his son could recruit soldiers and develop their skills without the Burmese becoming too suspicious.

Phitsanulok was well positioned. It was protected from the west and the north by the Burmese empire controlling Lan Na and from the south by Ayutthaya; the only threats came from the kingdom of Lan Xang to the northeast and from the east, where the Khmer empire was awaiting an opportunity for revenge. It was a fortress town that, as King Maha Thammaracha had ruled for many years, had been spared the worst excesses of King Bayinnaung.

The king appointed his sixteen-year-old son upparat of Phitsanulok. The two men rode side by side through the streets of Phitsanulok, their subjects prostrating themselves as they passed. Those lining the streets to welcome the royal party showed respect to both the king and his son. All supplicated themselves as the royal party passed through the city on the way to the palace. It was just as King Maha Thammaracha and Queen Wisut had wanted.

"This is our hometown and we are welcome here," said King Maha Thammaracha. "But remember, never let down your guard and always maintain a distance between yourself and your people. They need to respect you, and they need to respect your position."

"I will ensure they respect both," said Prince Naresuan, upparat of Phitsanulok.

It was a few years later that a command from King Bayinnaung arrived. King Maha Thammaracha and Prince Naresuan, together with their armies, were to accompany the Burmese forces as they invaded the realm of King Sumangkhala, the "royal grandfather" and disputed successor to King Setthathirath in Lan Xang. King Maha Thammaracha and his sons feared a further attack from the Khmer after they had left Ayutthaya, but they could not refuse King Bayinnaung. Prince Naresuan drafted some of his best men from

Phitsanulok into the area surrounding Ayutthaya should they be needed, and left the city in the hands of Prince Ekathotsarot.

The victory over King Sumangkhala proved to be hard won. Despite superior numbers, many of the smaller towns and principalities put up a strong defence. Somehow the royal grandfather had united his people in the face of the Burmese invasion. Gradually the forces of King Bayinnaung wore them down, and the Burmese king meticulously consolidated his victory. It was Prince Naresuan, however, that gained the plaudits. A series of daring raids and well-planned victories raised his profile, making him the hero of King Bayinnaung's army. He was developing into a general of the highest caliber.

"Father, we cannot allow Prince Naresuan to humiliate us in such a fashion," said the Burmese upparat Nanda Bayin. He wins victory after victory. And as he does so his fame passes among the troops."

"He always showed the traits of becoming a fine general," King Bayinnaung remarked. "He excelled in the military school in Pegu and humiliated your son on more than one occasion, or so I am led to understand."

"I want him gone," Nanda Bayin demanded. "He is a threat to us and he will not stop there. He will champion a resurgent Ayutthaya if given the chance."

"I like the boy," King Bayinnaung commented. "I always have, but maybe you are right. Maybe it is best that he dies young and is forgotten. I will leave it you, but be subtle. An accident or death in battle would be best. Nothing that can be traced back to me. Do you understand?" said King Bayinnaung forcibly.

King Sumangkhala retreated to the jungle in the same way King Setthathirath had only a few short years before. The difference now was that he did not have the support of the people, and many of his troops deserted him. King Bayinnaung easily entered Lan Xang and placed one of King Setthathirath's hostage brothers on the throne. Despite the involvement and continued presence of the Burmese, the internal squabbles within Lan Xang would continue for many years, which suited King Bayinnaung.

Shortly before the victorious King Bayinnaung entered Vientiane, Ayutthaya was hit by two major blows. The first was that the Khmer, realizing that the Siamese army was away in Lan Xang had decided to launch an attack on the city; the second was Prince Naresuan falling ill with smallpox.

"The Siamese want to return to Ayutthaya," said Nanda Bayin. "They claim Prince Naresuan has contracted smallpox. I think he fears for his life."

"Has word got out that we plan to kill him?" asked King Bayinnaung.

"I cannot see how. I have told only my elite guard, and they are completely loyal. We may have been overheard, but we were careful when we discussed killing him."

"Then I will let them leave. We have all but accomplished our goal here. Maybe the smallpox will kill him for us."

"I, for one, do not believe this story, but as long as he is held in isolation we cannot check. It is a clever ruse, if in fact it is a ruse," said Nanda Bayin.

"You will have plenty more chances to kill him—of that I have no doubt," said King Bayinnaung.

The Khmer had fought the forces of Ayutthaya or their predecessor states over many hundreds of years. For centuries it was the Khmer who were in the ascendant, exercising control over the entire region. Finally, their ancient capital of Angkor had been sacked. They were defeated as their enemies worked together against them, and they had been forced to pay tribute to Ayutthaya for many generations. Now that Ayutthaya was weak, the Khmer could sense the opportunity for revenge.

While Ayutthaya had been struggling, the Khmer had been rebuilding. A new capital had been built at Lovek, to the north of Phnom Phen, and in King Satta they had an able leader. King Satta had learned much from his earlier foray attacking Ayutthaya and set out to right the many wrongs inflicted on their nation. He strengthened defenses and built forts in the east, securing peace with their eastern neighbors. With Lan Xang now under attack from Burma and with his northern and eastern frontiers secure, King Satta prepared for his long-awaited assault on Ayutthaya.

King Satta recruited Chinese migrants to form an army of ten thousand and then added a further ten thousand Khmer soldiers. These troops were to move into the disputed land and secure it. King Satta led his Khmer army directly to Ayutthaya.

The Khmer arrived outside the city and encamped in the vicinity of Krathum Village. An elephant stockade was set up at Wat Sam Wihan, and a further thirty elephants were also housed at Wat Na Phra Meru, accompanied by five thousand men. The Khmer forces suffered an early blow when their general was shot while on the back of his elephant.

The Khmer set up camp, unaware that the Ayutthayan troops they thought were fighting in Lan Xang had already been allowed to return home by King Bayinnaung. The Khmer king commenced his offensive by sending a letter demanding the return of territory ceded to Ayutthaya after earlier battles:

> The Kingdom of Kamboja has never committed any fault against Ayudhya or the Siam country. On the contrary, Ayudhya has sent troops to attack the Khmer Kingdom many times. Now we, as your younger brother, have brought up an army (against you). If the elder brother agrees to delegate the province of Nokorrajasima at the west from Bachin until the sea that was a part of Khmer territory wrested by Siam in the past, your younger brother would return his troops back right away.

King Maha Thammaracha replied citing the influence of the Burmese:

> The request of the younger brother about the western province could not be granted because of the suzerainty set by the king of Hamsavati.

The scene was set for war. King Satta sent a message to King Maha Thammaracha.

Now we, the son of Prah Chan Raja and the younger brother of Prah Dharmaraja, the king of Siam, have brought an army here to your palace. We invite the elder brother to come out and fight with us. If you choose not to, we request that you hand over control of Bachinpuri, of Chandapuri and of Nokorrajasima provinces back to the Kamboja Kingdom.

With the forces of King Maha Thammaracha withdrawn behind the rivers, canals, and partially rebuilt walls of Ayutthaya, the political wrangling continued. Finally, the armies of King Satta and Prince Naresuan met at Phaneng Xong, where Prince Naresuan halted the larger Khmer army. Despite this, his father, hearing of another combined Khmer and Chinese army on the way, concluded a treaty.

We, the elder brother, received your message and acknowledged your request about the control of Bachinpuri, of Chandapuri, and of Nokorrajasima provinces to be handed back to Kamboja Kingdom in accord to the border set by Prah Botumsuryavang in the past. We agree to your proposition and wish to form an alliance of brotherhood between the two countries.

King Maha Thammaracha had secured peace with the Khmer, but at a price. The disputed regions were returned to the Khmer, and the agreement formed an alliance between the Khmer and Ayutthaya where each was expected to join forces with the other against any external intervention. As the Khmer army returned, both King Satta and King Maha Thammaracha fully intended to honor the agreement and form an alliance. Prince Naresuan, in his first major show of defiance against his father, had no intention of honoring the agreement.

"Why did you make such an agreement?" said an angry Prince Naresuan. "It benefits us in no way."

"That is where you are wrong. It benefits us in many ways," replied King Maha Thammaracha.

"I cannot see any!" exclaimed the prince, his chin jutting forward.

"Come and sit, my son. I see the Burmese were not wholly effective in teaching you politics. Yes, we have ceded land to the Khmer. They are happy and will bother us no further. They have their victory. The land is of little consequence. It is far from Ayutthaya and we cannot spare the troops to defend it. At least not for now. And we have secured our eastern territory. The Khmer have promised to send us troops if we are attacked. Think beyond today, as I never tire of telling you. Think ten or twenty years ahead. While I am king, I will honor the agreement that I have made with King Satta. When I am gone you have a wrong that needs righting. We are not the force we once were. We need time and we need peace in which to rebuild. Both I and King Satta are kings of the old school. We understand each other. He knows I will keep my word, and I know he will keep his. Times change and leaders change. The Khmer are not our enemy at the moment—the Burmese are," said King Maha Thammaracha firmly to his son.

18

PRINCE NARESUAN

PART 1

"so king bayinnaung is dead," said Prince Naresuan upon receiving the news.

"Nanda Bayin is his nominated successor," Prince Ekathotsarot replied.

"I fought alongside him during the last siege of Ayutthaya," King Maha Thammaracha commented. "He lacks the diplomatic skills of his father. To my mind he was a bully, and a sadistic one at that. I cannot see him holding the Toungoo empire together. He is a man who makes enemies too easily."

"And Mingyi Swa is his son," said Prince Naresuan.

"The prince with whom you had the cockfight?" asked King Maha Thammaracha.

"We have been enemies since that day," replied Prince Naresuan.

※

It was many years before, when Prince Naresuan was a hostage in Pegu. The prince struck up a friendship with Bayinnaung's grandson, Mingyi Swa, and two Mon princes, Ram and Kiat. The four of them fought, played, and enjoyed many adventures over the years. Twice a week they would attend the cockfights that were held outside the temple grounds. All the boys would bet among themselves. They knew all the birds and their owners. They understood the nuances, whether the bird attacked fast and decisively or whether the bird studied his opponent before moving in. It was only natural that they started to keep and breed birds themselves.

The site of the fight was unspectacular: a mere patch of dirt worn smooth by the feet of generations. Three bleached, aged wooden tables stood around the edge. Two skinny trees cast a dappled shade. Hens and their chicks pecked at the dirt for food, and two dogs lay prostrate in the shade.

The fight had been three years in the making, though some would say it had been hundreds of years. The boys were in their early teens now, and with many years of watching cockfights and breeding birds behind them a challenge had been made. Tonight the cockerel of King Bayinnaung's grandson, Mingyi Swa, would fight the cockerel of Prince Naresuan.

The boys had been schooled together since the age of eleven. As they matured there was an increasing recognition of their differences. Mingyi Swa may inherit the throne of the Toungoo empire, and Prince Naresuan may be king of the backwater of Phitsanulok, part of the tributary state of Ayutthaya.

Prince Ekathotsarot had bred generations of gamecocks over the past three years, and the best fighters were bred again and again. Prince Ekathotsarot was very good at breeding fighting cocks, as had been proven in numerous fights. Mingyi Swa had bragged about his fine fighting cockerel too many times. In the minds of the boys this was not just a fight about finding the best cockerel. It was Siam against the mighty Toungoo empire.

Prince Naresuan and Prince Ekathotsarot would fight with the colorful and nimble *lung hang kho* strain of white-tailed gamecocks popular in Siam, while Prince Mingyi Swa had chosen to breed and fight the *pama* strain favored in Burma. There was a small bet on the outcome, but the money was inconsequential. To all those involved it was the winning that was important. Mingyi Swa wanted to put the upstart Naresuan in his place, while Prince Naresuan wanted to make a bigger statement.

"If our cock wins then Ayutthaya is free," declared Prince Naresuan.

Prince Mingyi Swa grinned confidently. "We shall see," he said.

Prince Ekathotsarot was adept at preparing the gamecocks for fights. His technique was similar to that used by those practicing "the art of the eight limbs." He would wrap the cockerel's feet in order for the birds to spar with each other. He would remove some of their feathers and tie them down in the sun to toughen up their skin. With the help and knowledge of Khru Muay Outtaphon, the prince had developed a mix of ginseng and local herbs that he gave daily to the birds to keep them in prime condition.

Prince Ekathotsarot held the fighting gamecock between his legs using a damp cloth to massage the bird. Avoiding the wings he slowly washed the bird, working his way down the head, neck, chest, stomach, back, and feet. He then used a warm cloth to rub the cockerel's muscles in a circular motion. He tucked his prize bird under his shirt and took him out to meet the champion Burmese cockerel. The fate of a nation was at stake, or at least that was how the fight appeared to the two princes from Ayutthaya.

More than forty boys were gathered as Prince Ekathotsarot brought his fighting cock into the "arena" where Mingyi Swa was waiting.

"About time! My cock wants to get back to his hens. He is in a hurry," said Prince Mingyi Swa.

"Well, let us hold him up no longer," Prince Naresuan replied.

Talons and spurs had been sharpened. This was a fight to the death. The gamecocks moved forward. To the untrained eye it was just a flurry of activity, but to the trained eye the birds were gauging the fitness and strength of their opponent. As the other boys bet among themselves, it was the two princes from Ayutthaya and Prince Mingyi Swa who knew the real importance of the contest.

Heads stretched forward, the cockerels gauged each other. Both birds raised their feathers in the dominant fighting position, a show of strength. Then the attack came with hard blows, caution creeping in as they gauged their opponent and fought: brute strength to overwhelm the opponent, retreat, then renewed attack. Then, after a slashing blow and two pecks to the head, the gamecock of Mingyi Swa lay dead.

"The impudence of that Ayutthayan bird!" exclaimed Prince Mingyi Swa. "Ayutthaya is and will remain a slave kingdom," he added in his anger.

"Be warned—this fighting cock can not only fight for money, it can fight for kingdoms too!" replied Prince Naresuan defiantly.

The haughty Prince Mingyi Swa threw some coins at the feet of Prince Naresuan and then turned on his heels and left. They were friends no more.

⊛

"I will have to prepare and travel to Pegu," said King Maha Thammaracha.

"No, Father. I would like to go in your stead. We can say you were too ill to make the journey."

"Why?" asked Prince Ekathotsarot.

"The balance of power has shifted," Prince Naresuan explained. "The chakravartin ideal rests on homage to one man, and that man is dead. Others who look to escape the Burmese yoke will be considering the same thing. It is an opportunity to sound out others, to see what they are thinking even if they do not voice their thoughts."

"You will visit with our sister while in Pegu?" asked Prince Ekathotsarot.

"I will, and I will send your best wishes," Prince Naresuan replied. "She was a second wife to King Bayinnaung. I am concerned what will become of her now following his death."

"Let us hope that King Nanda Bayin does not take her as his concubine. He does not treat his women well, by all accounts," said Prince Ekathotsarot.

"Your life will be in danger if you go," said King Maha Thammaracha.

"My life is in danger every day. King Bayinnaung plotted to kill me. Do you think his son desires less?" Prince Naresuan asked. "But I don't think now is the time. Our new king will face many challenges closer to home. I have no doubt he will get around to me eventually."

"Not to mention the new crown prince, Mingyi Swa, who would dearly love you dead," added Prince Ekathotsarot.

"I will take an army of three thousand men and General Penprapha and Phraya Si Sai Narong with me to show due respect."

"And to protect yourself," added Prince Ekathotsarot.

"And to protect myself. There is little likelihood of trouble while this change is taking place. My brother, will you take command of Phitsanulok in my absence?" asked Prince Naresuan of Prince Ekathotsarot.

"Only if you promise not to cause trouble or start a war," said Prince Ekathotsarot with a wry smile.

Prince Naresuan arrived in Pegu in the February of 1582. He was welcomed like a brother by King Nanda Bayin, although it was all an act. The new king wanted as little trouble from his vassal states as possible. Ayutthaya, in particular.

"Prince Naresuan, thank you for coming to honor the chakravartin oath, said King Nanda Bayin.

"My father sends his apologies. He is unwell and unable to sit on a horse. He asked that I serve in his stead," Prince Naresuan replied.

"I am told you have brought an army with you."

"Only a small one. I felt you might be in need of support in these difficult times," said Prince Naresuan, though both knew why the army was truly there.

"You will perform the oath as your father did all those years ago," said King Nanda Bayin. "You will enter the Shwemawdaw Paya to pledge your allegiance in front of the image of Buddha, as well as to myself, my ministers, and my generals?"

The prince of Ayutthaya nodded affirmatively.

"I would like to visit with my sister, if that could be arranged?" asked Prince Naresuan.

"Of course. My courtiers will arrange the time and place and let you know."

The following day Prince Naresuan met with his sister Princess Suphankanlaya for what would prove to be the final time.

"My sister, all is well I hope?" asked Prince Naresuan.

"It has been many years, but yes, all is well," said Princess Suphankanlaya. But the sadness in her eyes showed it was not the case.

"Father and mother send you their deepest love, as does Prince Ekathotsarot."

"Send my love and affection to them all. Tell them I miss them so. Walk with me," she said taking Prince Naresuan by the arm.

"They said you had smallpox. I see no scars."

Prince Naresuan looked back at her.

"We live in troubled times," he said.

"You fear those times will worsen?" asked Princess Suphankanlaya.

"I fear so."

"My life is forfeit. You are to take the best course of action for our family and for Ayutthaya," said Princess Suphankanlaya. "I am now King Nanda Bayin's concubine. Fortunately there are many like me, so he rarely visits me. You must forget me when you make any decisions. Do not be influenced by my being held hostage here. Promise me that."

"Your bravery makes me proud. In time there may be changes, but for now I will play the game."

They walked for nearly an hour with Princess Suphankanlaya's ladies-in-waiting who had traveled with her from Ayutthaya. Finally they said their farewells, not knowing if they would ever meet again.

The following day Prince Naresuan supplicated himself in front of the Buddha image in the Shwemawdaw Paya and pledged the allegiance of Ayutthaya to King Nanda Bayin. By May of 1582, all the vassal rulers had sworn allegiance and sent tribute, with the exception of two: the prince of Mueang Khang and Thado Minsaw, the viceroy of Ava. King Nanda Bayin had to make an example. He could not allow weakness or tolerance to be shown; if he did the entire empire might unravel.

The new king dispatched three forces: two Burmese under the command of Prince Mingyi Swa and Prince Natchinnaung, and one Thai under the command of Prince Naresuan. They rode to the citadel of Mueang Khang.

"This should prove an interesting outing," remarked Prince Naresuan. "There is bad blood between the new crown prince and myself. I think that our new king may have put us with the Burmese for reasons other than quelling a mutiny in Mueang Khang."

"I don't trust these Burmese," said General Penprapha, as he and Prince Naresuan rode at the head of their men out of Pegu toward the Shan province of Mueang Khang. "They would kill you as soon as look at you."

"King Bayinnaung tried it once, as you know. Their new king Nanda Bayin makes his father look a pleasant man," Prince Naresuan said scathingly.

"They see you as a threat."

"Good," said Prince Naresuan, as he turned his horse and rode back down the line of his men.

The Siamese forces walked behind two armies, one Mon and one from Prome. At their head the new heir apparent, Prince Mingyi Swa, rode on his royal elephant. The former childhood friend now held nothing but enmity toward Prince Naresuan, as the prince did toward him. After they broke camp the following morning the crown prince rode on his white Javanese stallion into the Siamese camp, accompanied by twenty of his men.

"I have no idea why King Nanda Bayin saddled me with your army. I can see no reason apart from you eating our dust. Stay behind and keep out the way. Do you understand me?" asked Prince Mingyi Swa.

"I look forward to seeing your men die," replied Prince Naresuan.

With that the crown prince snarled, wheeled his horse, and rode back to his men.

"They are goading me," said Prince Naresuan to Phraya Si Sai Narong, with a touch of irony.

Ten days later the armies entered the mountainous northern Shan province of Mueang Khang.

"It appears there was a local rebellion and Saopha Thaik had to stay behind to quell it," said Phraya Si Sai Narong.

"The Shan have a long history of rebellion. He will still pay the price though. Whatever the reason, King Nanda Bayin will see him dead. He needs to show the entire Toungoo empire that he is not a man to be trifled with," said Prince Naresuan.

"Saopha Thaik is an able general. He will not submit lightly. Not to mention he is ensconced in his mountaintop fortress, which is famed as impenetrable."

"I have heard of the fortress at Mueang Khang," the prince replied. "The old saffron-robed monk would often talk of it in classes. He too said it was impenetrable. We will sit back and watch the Burmese, as requested."

The following day the armies looked up at the fortress of Mueang Khang, sitting proudly on the edge of a precipice with high walls to three sides.

"That is a true defensive position," said Prince Naresuan, marveling at the mountaintop citadel.

Prince Naresuan and his army camped near the base of the mountain. They looked on as the armies were repeatedly repelled by Saopha Thaik and his defending army.

"Shall we go and help?" asked Phraya Si Sai Narong.

"Let's give them another day. Then we will take the fortress," said Prince Naresuan.

The forces of the crown prince of Burma and the other army, commanded by Prince Natchinnaung, were heavily reduced in numbers and nearing exhaustion as Prince Naresuan rode into their camp.

"Prince, we are tired of eating your dust. May we try, as you seem to be meeting with little success?" asked Prince Naresuan.

"You arrogant vassal!" exclaimed the crown prince. "Go ahead and be damned!"

"May we use your drums?" asked Prince Naresuan.

"What? Why do you need them?" asked the crown prince, puzzled.

"All in good time. All in good time," said Prince Naresuan with a look of contempt.

The Siamese army stood two deep in a line facing the front walls of the citadel. Drums played. Horses rode up and down the lines. The army marched two steps forward and two steps back shouting at their enemy at the top of their voices. Then they would mount a mock charge only to retreat over and over again.

"What are they doing?" asked the crown prince incredulously.

Unseen, Prince Naresuan and his men were clambering up the steep path that led to the sheer rock face lying under the overhang of the precipice. With ropes already prepared and the Shan army looking outward expecting a frontal attack at any moment, the Siamese troops scaled the cliff and made their way over the precipice. Those who slipped on the climb knew that their last duty was to die in silence as they plummeted to the earth below. Slowly and quietly, led by Prince Naresuan, they started to enter the city.

The Siamese army brought forward five cannon, aiming them directly at the front gates.

"About time they did something," said Prince Natchinnaung.

"We tried that yesterday. Is this the best they can do?" asked Prince Mingyi Swa.

By the time those inside knew what was happening, it was all over. Saopha Thaik lay down his sword. Prince Naresuan took it in both hands and while the Saopha was held down, he cut off his head.

"Better this way. I think his death would have been far more painful if he'd been returned to King Nanda Bayin," said Prince Naresuan.

As the crown prince and Prince Natchinnaung watched from outside they could see soldiers coming down from the walls inside the citadel. The Siamese army stopped their noisemaking and watched in silence as the front gates of the citadel were opened. A mighty cheer went up as Prince Naresuan emerged from within. In his hand he held the severed head of Saopha Thaik. He walked slowly to the crown prince and threw the head at his feet.

"He was to be captured alive," said the crown prince.

"He might well have been if you could have taken the city!" said Prince Naresuan scathingly. He turned and walked to his cheering troops.

"That man must die," stated a vengeful Prince Mingyi Swa.

Prince Naresuan and his army regrouped at the bottom of the hill. As they did so the troops of the crown prince and Prince Natchinnaung charged down the hill and into their midst. The ground opened and many impaled themselves on the stakes that lay hidden under matting. Prince Naresuan had foreseen this eventuality and had planned accordingly.

After twenty minutes of close combat, the troops of the two Burmese princes were forced to withdraw. The Siamese forces were too strong and well prepared.

"You are a dead man!" yelled Prince Mingyi Swa to Prince Naresuan as the Siamese army left to return to Ayutthaya.

"Not today though!" shouted back Prince Naresuan as he waved cheerily at the crown prince from a distance.

The crown prince and Prince Natchinnaung returned south to Pegu, wary of their welcome.

"What do you mean you failed to take the city, and that Prince Naresuan took it!" roared King Nanda Bayin, pacing up and down in a fit of rage. "Are you trying to make me look a fool in front of the entire empire?"

"But Mueang Khang was taken," stuttered Prince Natchinnaung.

"You fools! Do you not realize that being out-thought and out-generaled by this Ayutthayan upstart makes us all, particularly *me*, look ineffective? If you were not the heir apparent, and if you were not my brother's son, your heads would sit on a stick outside the Shwemawdaw Paya. Be gone from my sight!"

The many wars under King Bayinnaung had seen a huge loss of life. Southeast Asia now faced a manpower crisis, and the days of the legendary million-man army of King Bayinnaung had passed. In order to tackle the threat from Ava, King Nanda Bayin ordered troops from Prome, Toungoo, Lan Na, Lan Xang, and Ayutthaya to accompany him. The combined armies, minus that of Ayutthaya, converged on Ava in March 1584.

King Nanda Bayin could wait no longer wait for the missing army. Prince Naresuan had slowed his march—of that he was certain. The Burmese king had a plan that would rid him of the prince from Ayutthaya once and for all.

The armies of King Nanda Bayin and Thado Minsaw, the viceroy of Ava, met in yuddhahatthi, the elephant battle, in which King Nanda Bayin drove his outnumbered adversary from the field. Thado Minsaw, badly injured, died during his retreat into the mountains. With that victory King Nanda Bayin sent a message to all those looking for signs of weakness. Prince Naresuan chose not to listen.

While King Nanda Bayin was still securing Ava, Prince Naresuan marched his troops to the city of Khraeng to the south, where they established camp on the banks of the Sittaung River near the monastery of their former teacher, the old, saffron-robed monk Mahathen Kanchong. As they rested, Prince Naresuan was unaware that the Burmese king had put in place a plan for his army to be attacked from the rear. Prince Mingyi Swa had ordered their mutual childhood friends, Phraya Kiat and Phraya Ram, to lead the attack.

Phraya Kiat and Phraya Ram had been placed in an impossible position by the crown prince—either show disloyalty to their king or to their lifelong friend. They talked at length before seeking out the advice of Mahathen Kanchong, who had returned to his homeland after twenty years in Pegu, where he had schooled the young Prince Naresuan.

The prince was sitting outside his pavilion with his general, Phraya Si Sai Narong, when he saw the old monk pass through his guards and walk toward him with two men he knew from his childhood captivity in Pegu. The prince and the general prostrated themselves at the feet of the monk.

"Stand up, my fiery prince. I have urgent news," said the old saffron-robed monk. "A plot has been hatched by the crown prince, on the orders of King Nanda Bayin, to attack your troops and have you killed. The king was annoyed that you took so long to arrive with your army to help him fight in Ava. He saw it as a deliberate act."

"He was right in his assumption," said Prince Naresuan candidly. Prince Naresuan had had two relatively peaceful years in Ayutthaya, apart from incursions by the Khmer. In two years he had built an army. It was not obvious to Ayutthaya's Burmese overlords, with their heads buried in religious change and finance, but under their very eyes Ayutthaya was far stronger than they ever would have imagined.

"The crown prince has charged your old friends Phraya Kiat and Phraya Ram with leading the attack. They came to ask my advice. My advice was to come to you," the old saffron-robed monk replied.

"Phraya Kiat, Phraya Ram, what have you to say?" asked Prince Naresuan.

"Our orders came directly from Prince Mingyi Swa—at the behest of his father, I feel," said Phraya Ram. "He is not only trying to have you killed, he is also testing our loyalty."

"He is much the same as he was in our schooldays. Devious," added Phraya Kiat.

"We are Mon. Like you, we pay homage to the king of Burma. We no longer wish to," said Phraya Ram. "We would like to join with you if it is your intention is to wage war against this unjust king."

It was in the town of Mueang Khraeng on May 3, 1584, in front of his army, officials, and the gathered townspeople, that Prince Naresuan at the age of twenty-nine declared independence from Hanthawaddy and announced the restoration of the kingdom of Ayutthaya. He asked the old monk Mahathen Kanchong to provide holy water. He poured the water from the cup onto the ground with these words:

> Since the king of Pegu does not observe the traditional norm of interstate alliance, violates the law of unity, and behaves dishonestly by planning to assassinate me... Ayudhya and Pegu no longer share the same golden land, and our alliance comes to an end and will never be reinstituted.

Prince Naresuan moved swiftly. After declaring Ayutthaya's independence his thoughts were on how to secure that sovereignty. The prince levied the Mons to join his campaigns under the leadership of Phraya Kiat and Phraya Ram. He marched on Pegu but failed to enter. King Nanda Bayin had had the foresight to leave a substantial army under the command of the crown prince. However, before King Nanda Bayin could return from Ava, Prince Naresuan freed many of the Thai people who had been held hostage. He set off for Ayutthaya with over ten thousand former Siamese captives, the monk Mahathen Kanchong, Phraya Kiat, Phraya Ram, and many Mon people, together with those who had been taken as captives.

On hearing that King Nanda Bayin had defeated and killed Viceroy Thado Minsaw in an honorable elephant duel, Prince Naresuan regrouped before setting out to return to Ayutthaya and fight to regain the independence of Siam. The army of the Burmese crown prince left Pegu in pursuit of his returning army. The gap was too large, and Prince Naresuan and those with him had just finished crossing the Sittaung River when the crown prince's forces arrived on the far bank.

Prince Naresuan looked back to see General Surakamma of the crown prince's army sitting on his war elephant on the other side of the river. The prince ordered his long musket to be prepared. Lying prone on the ground, the muzzle of the gun supported, he carefully took aim. The wind from the west, the distance, the trajectory all needed to be considered. He fired what has become known as "the royal shot across the Sittaung River" and watched as the Burmese general slumped to one side and then fell from his war elephant. On seeing this, the crown prince ordered his troops to stop. They turned and retreated to Pegu, allowing Prince Naresuan free passage back to Ayutthaya.

As the army of Prince Naresuan made the journey back, their numbers grew. News of Prince Naresuan's break with Hanthawaddy spread quickly, and people of the many nations held captive under the Burmese left to join his journey. As they neared Ayutthaya thirty thousand people followed him, many of whom were returning to their homeland while many others simply hoped for a better future.

☙

"You have broken with Hanthawaddy," said King Maha Thammaracha, sitting cross-legged on the floor in the company of his queen and his two sons. "Then we had best prepare for war."

"You are not angry?" asked Prince Naresuan.

"The break was inevitable. It was not possible in the time of King Bayinnaung, but the empire he left behind after his death is in trouble. I had hoped you would wait longer, but that was not to be. You did what you had to do, and I support you fully. Now we need to prepare for the onslaught that will follow."

He looked over at his ever-impatient son.

"Prince Naresuan, you will control military affairs, and I will handle the politics. To your brother I give the most difficult job: to serve as intermediary and peacemaker between us. I fear it will not always be an easy job," he added.

Prince Ekathotsarot sighed deeply.

"I have planned our strategy over many years," Prince Naresuan explained. "As Sun Tzu said, 'Victorious warriors win first and then go to war, while defeated warriors go to war first and then seek to win.'

Following the declaration of our independence, many have flocked to join us. I have the foundation of a strong army in Phitsanulok—one that has been many years in the making. But we still need more people in order to defeat the men of Hanthawaddy."

"What do you propose?" asked Prince Ekathotsarot.

"The border with the Burmese is now Kamphaeng Phet. The Burmese are ensconced there. We bring our people from Sukhothai and Phitsanulok—in fact any direction where the Burmese will come from—to Ayutthaya. We leave nothing behind to provide succor to the enemy. No livestock, no food, and no safe drinking water. We poison the rivers with dead livestock. Working alongside General Penprapha we have trained a guerrilla army of the highest order," said Prince Naresuan.

"We will rebuild the walls of Ayutthaya starting today," said Prince Ekathotsarot.

"The Mon people whom you brought back with you are renowned for their skills with elephants," said Prince Ekathotsarot. "People are one factor, elephants are another. We will organize a hunt, as King Maha Chakkraphat did all those years ago."

"And weaponry," the king added. "We have the funds that the Hanthawaddy administrators were to send to Pegu. The administrators are no more, but we have a good supply of gold that they thought to steal from us."

"Then so be it," said Prince Naresuan. "I and Phraya Si Sai Narong will begin to clear the countryside and have people come to Ayutthaya. Prince Ekathotsarot, you will organize the elephant hunt. Father, will you organize the rebuilding of the walls and the purchase of military equipment from the Portuguese, together with some mercenaries, who I am sure will be available for a hefty price."

His mother interrupted him as he was about to leave.

"I ask that you recreate the moment where you poured the holy water on the ground here, in Ayutthaya," Queen Wisut said. "It is a moment that will remain with our people for centuries."

"I would be honored," Prince Naresuan replied. "It is important that those fighting understand what they are fighting for."

"It is important for those who stay behind also," the queen remarked.

"Of course, I focus on the war and nothing else. That is my failing— it has always been. You are right to chastise me for my oversight."

The following day Prince Naresuan reenacted his declaration of Siamese independence from Hanthawaddy. Sitting on a low stool with the court gathered around him, he poured the holy water on the ground, the symbolism understood by all. The prince added to his initial declaration that his action had the full support of his father, King Maha Thammaracha. The prince further directed that a Siamese-style chedi was to be built to commemorate Ayutthaya's newly declared independence.

19

PRINCE NARESUAN

PART 2

A MESSENGER UNDER THE BURMESE FLAG came into Ayutthaya carrying a message from King Nanda Bayin. In it he demanded the return of the ten thousand Shan people who had left their homeland to join with Prince Naresuan. It was a thinly veiled declaration of war. To send the Shan back would be seen as a sign of capitulation. King Maha Thammaracha passed the letter to his son, asking him to reply. For the reply to be written by a mere prince would annoy King Nanda Bayin in itself. The curt reply penned by Prince Naresuan that emphasized the Ayutthayan declaration of independence from Hanthawaddy only served to inflame King Nanda Bayin's fury further.

King Nanda Bayin fumed at Prince Naresuan's response and he flew into another of his famed rages.

"We attack them now!" King Nanda Bayin declared.

Prince Mingyi Swa led an expeditionary force through the Three Pagodas Pass and along the Khwae Noi River to Sai Yok. King Nanda Bayin was to raise another army and follow. Prince Mingyi Swa left with a force of four thousand men, four hundred horses, and forty elephants and proceeded to take the deserted city of Kanchanaburi, where he waited for the army of the king of Hanthawaddy to arrive. King Nanda Bayin arrived over a month later. His hastily planned invasion had none of the hallmarks of those of King Tabinshwehti or King Bayinnaung. A revolt at home meant he could only arrive with a force of seven thousand men, five hundred horses, and fifty war elephants.

"King Nanda Bayin has joined the crown prince in Kanchanaburi," said Prince Ekathotsarot. "By all accounts he has between ten and twelve thousand men at his command."

"That number is too low," Prince Naresuan replied. "Surely he realizes we can put three or four times that in the field. Maybe he is sending another army from the north?"

"Not according to General Penprapha. He has captured and interrogated a number of prisoners and none of them speak of another army," said Prince Ekathotsarot.

"And General Penprapha is very thorough in his methods."

"The timing is wrong. To get to Ayutthaya he will have to cross first the Chao Phraya River to our west and then the Lopburi River at our gates. The rainy season is almost upon us, and the river will flood. Even if he brought canoes with him it will prove difficult for him to keep his troops together."

"I don't see it either. It is as if his temper got the better of him. This is no well-thought-out battle plan," Prince Ekathotsarot remarked.

"Then let us go and meet him."

Prince Naresuan and Prince Ekathotsarot left at the head of an army of twenty-five thousand men with four hundred horses and fifty war elephants. Additionally they traveled with three thousand canoes, plus the tools to make more when they reached the rivers that would soon be in flood.

The Burmese were in disarray before the Siamese forces even arrived. The rain poured down in torrents and the rivers soon burst their banks. Unprepared and without adequate canoes, King Nanda Bayin realized the futility of the attack and ordered the retreat. The Siamese forces pursed them through the Three Pagodas Pass and as far as Martaban before returning with over one thousand captives, horses, and twenty war elephants. The first Burmese invasion had been hastily planned and ill-conceived. King Nanda Bayin would now take a more measured course.

Prince Naresuan with his generals and troops returned to Phitsanulok, where the prince ordered the town be emptied and its people moved to Ayutthaya. A small garrison was left there but the people with their belongings embarked on the trip south to Ayutthaya.

The prince proceeded ahead to Sukhothai, where his father was king, as he would be one day.

In a ceremony the officials and the people of Sukhothai swore their allegiance to Prince Naresuan by drinking sacred water. His father was a descendant of the Phra Ruang dynasty of Sukhothai, and what he was asking—that the city and the surrounding area be emptied and that the people move to Ayutthaya—was his right as their prince.

It was agreed that only the monks would stay with their sacred ground. They placed their faith in the fact that the Buddhist army of the King of Hanthawaddy would leave them and the temple complex alone. The old, golden-robed monk Mahathen Kanchong had traveled to Sukhothai with Prince Naresuan. He had determined to stay. He was greatly revered, and now was the time to use that respect.

"You have undertaken something that will change everything, young prince," said the monk.

"It is a war long in the making," Prince Naresuan replied.

"The time of Kings Tabinshwehti and Bayinnaung cost many lives. Too many lives. The future will see many more people die. War has driven us throughout my life. I am tired of seeing those I have known reduced to corpses. I am a man of peace. I feel only our religion will save the people. I long for peace. Bring it to us."

"Your words always resonate with me," said Prince Naresuan. "Perhaps when Ayutthaya is free, peace will reign as in the golden age of Sukhothai."

"The people demand it. They have seen so much death,"

"Thank you for everything you have taught me, Mahathen Kanchong," said Prince Naresuan, using the old monk's name for the first time in their long friendship.

The prince and his army removed many people from the areas south of Kamphaeng Phet and Sukhothai, either willingly or by force. His army spread far to the south, bringing back as many people and their livestock as possible. The towns of Sawankhalok and Phichai were taken back from the Burmese and their people returned to Ayutthaya.

In December of 1584, a Burmese army estimated at thirty thousand men invaded the kingdom of Ayutthaya via the southern

Three Pagodas Pass. The Burmese garrison at Kamphaeng Phet was reenforced in preparation for invasion, and the army of Lan Na was readied. The Burmese plan was to split the Ayutthayan forces with a two-pronged attack and to converge on Ayutthaya, where the armies would lay siege.

The southern army was led by the prince of Bassein, an experienced campaigner and an uncle of King Nanda Bayin. Nawrahta Minsaw, son of King Bayinnaung, was now ensconced as the king of Chiang Mai. He would head a far larger army, gathered from all the northern provinces of the Toungoo empire.

After his third and final conquest of Ayutthaya, King Bayinnaung had taken most of the population of this part of Siam as captives to Burma. Rice fields had turned to scrub. Trees and plants had encroached on the roads and trails, making progress difficult. To maximize the difficulty to the invading troops the water had been poisoned in advance by the forces of Ayutthaya, and any food taken or burned as the advancing Burmese army drew close. As the army advanced in full state, elephants to the fore, they watched the black smoke rise ahead of them as anything that would sustain them was burned by the forces of Ayutthaya.

It was the horses that suffered the most. The elephants could strip the trees, but the burning left little for the horses to eat. The soldiers started to go hungry as well, and the army was forced to forage over an increasingly wide area in order to survive. As they did so they met the guerrilla forces of Prince Naresuan, the Wild Tigers, lying in wait.

The prince had studied the campaign waged by King Setthathirath against King Bayinnaung: harrying the enemy, never letting them sleep, poisoning their water, depriving them of food, and killing them where they felt safe. His fighters formed elite teams of experts in hand-to-hand combat, survival techniques, and killing in silence. As the Burmese army slowly advanced, fear filled their ranks. Stories of "Siamese devils" and "the ghosts of the removed" spread among their men.

It was General Penprapha, one of the few ever to defeat Prince Naresuan in hand-to-hand combat, who led these men. They were highly trained killers who wanted to take down as many of the

Burmese invaders as they could. They showed no mercy and expected none in return. They were simply carrying out the wishes of their king and their prince as they had been trained to do. They were the elite of Prince Naresuan's forces, and their lives were considered forfeit the moment they joined.

News of the plan for the northern troops to move south reached King Maha Thammaracha. The troops were coming from the Shan territories, Lan Na, Lan Xang, and other tributary states. They were gathering in Chiang Mai before their direct advance on Ayutthaya. The spies of King Maha Thammaracha put their number at one hundred thousand, although the actual number was considerably lower. Their plan was to march southward via Phetchabun directly to Ayutthaya, bypassing Phitsanulok. Here they would meet up with the troops of the prince of Bassein and mount a joint siege on Ayutthaya.

King Maha Thammaracha redoubled his efforts in rebuilding and strengthening the city.

"We can raise only fifty thousand men to combat this joint attack," said Prince Ekathotsarot.

"The Khmer have promised an army of ten thousand men under the treaty agreed between us," King Maha Thammaracha replied.

"I don't trust the Khmer," Prince Naresuan said. "At least you know where you stand with the Burmese. We have little choice. I will lead the army to the north with the governor of Sukhothai in support. Prince Ekathotsarot, you will face the prince of Bassein. He is a soldier of the old school, and he intends to lay siege to Ayutthaya. He will be vulnerable on the march. Only engage in small battles where you feel the ground works in your favor. Slow him further. He is a man of short temper and is likely to make rash decisions if pushed. Stop him before he gets here, or make him pay a high price before he arrives. Take the Mon leader Phra Racha Manu and his men. They are battle-hardened and familiar with the Burmese style of fighting. They will serve you well."

Prince Ekathotsarot marched his troops toward the advancing prince of Bassein. The prince also ordered an increase in guerrilla attacks. The Burmese foraging parties were continually attacked and were in constant fear. One nighttime raid released over half the Burmese horses.

Slowly the confident prince of Bassein was losing patience. Recognizing his keenness to give battle, Prince Ekathotsarot drew his troops up in full battle regalia blocking his path. The prince of Bassein, eager to fight, charged the Siamese forces, his elephants leading the attack. The army of Prince Ekathotsarot melted away into the forest on either side only to attack the Burmese flanks and melt away again. The prince of Bassein wanted a full battle, but Prince Ekathotsarot was not going to give him that satisfaction. He reached the now-deserted town of Suphanburi and sent messengers to find out the progress of the army from Chiang Mai. To his dismay, he learned they were late in leaving Chiang Mai and their progress had been equally slow under constant guerrilla attacks. The plan was starting to unravel.

Prince Ekathotsarot held the prince of Bassein in Suphanburi for five days. Unable to escape and with food and water running low, the prince of Bassein started to consider his situation. Forcing his hand further, many of his troops had started to desert. The penalty was death, often an unpleasant one, but many of his men were losing heart or siding with the enemy. The prince reflected back on the days of King Bayinnaung, the days when men rarely deserted.

The armies finally met outside the town on a battlefield of Prince Ekathotsarot's choosing. The prince of Bassein was defeated and fled the field with his remaining troops. Pursued by Prince Ekathotsarot, the fleeing army regrouped only to suffer a further defeat. The prince of Bassein was harried all the way back to the Three Pagodas Pass by the guerrilla fighters under the command of General Penprapha. Prince Ekathotsarot had no need of his elder brother's support.

Prince Naresuan used these same tactics, and the constant guerrilla attacks slowly sapped the resolve of the army of King Nawrahta Minsaw. Hearing that the prince of Bassein had retreated, King Nawrahta Minsaw was uncertain whether to proceed further. The forces of the king of Lan Na continued on to Kamphaeng Phet, where there was a reasonably defensible position. With the army of Prince Ekathotsarot moving northward to Kamphaeng Phet, and being chased by the forces of Prince Naresuan, Nawrahta Minsaw saw the futility of continuing and ordered a retreat.

King Nawrahta Minsaw saw the danger of his position. He was unlikely to get his troops to the relative safety of Chiang Mai before the forces of Prince Naresuan caught up with him, and it would be better to make a stand before the two Ayutthayan armies combined. He found suitable ground on which to give battle, and turned to face the oncoming army of Prince Naresuan.

The prince rode on horseback, reconnoitering the army that blocked his path. The high ground King Nawrahta Minsaw had chosen favored his army. The soldiers of Prince Naresuan would have to fight against the slope, as well as attack the defensive position of the king of Lan Na. He thought back to his days in Pegu and his lessons in battle tactics. The Battle of Hastings, where the Norman forces of King William the Conqueror had defeated King Harold, came to mind: a charge up the hill, giving battle, mock retreat in disarray, and then regrouping as the enemy gives chase, their momentum driving them onto the waiting swords.

Had the current king of Lan Na been in the same lesson? Had he been paying attention? wondered Prince Naresuan, looking up the hill at his old classmate. The battle went exactly as Prince Naresuan had planned. The king of Lan Na had either missed the lesson or had not been concentrating. The army of Lan Na was routed, and vast quantities of armaments were captured along with twenty war elephants. The king of Lan Na barely escaped, leaving all his personal goods on the battlefield.

In 1587, three more Burmese armies advanced on Ayutthaya from the north, the west, and the east. The three-pronged invasion was launched with troops from Hanthawaddy, the Shan states, Lan Na, and Lan Xang. They were to meet at Ayutthaya. The army headed by King Nanda Bayin left Pegu in a royal splendor that both King Tabinshwehti and King Bayinnaung would have been proud of.

Trumpets were blown as the king rode his war elephant, looking down as his subjects supplicated themselves before him. Fifty war elephants, resplendent in polished leather armor and with religious reliquaries dangling from their necks, wound their way through the streets of Pegu, followed by the cavalry riding side by side. The infantry, fully armed, marched with both pride and concern. Many had been mere farmers only one month before. Now they marched to an unknown and uncertain future to fight for a king who ruled by fear.

As the three armies entered the land of Ayutthaya, they were met by the Wild Tigers, the guerrilla force of Prince Naresuan. With faces covered in white paint they would appear as ghosts in the night as they caught the soldiers of King Nanda Bayin unawares. They concentrated on the foraging parties scouring the barren land looking for food or livestock. They killed quickly and efficiently without compassion, usually leaving one man alive to return with fearful tales that played on the superstitions of many of the farmers.

The Wild Tigers could not halt the inexorable advance of the Burmese army, but they could cause fear and panic. King Nanda Bayin, as his father had before him, surrounded himself with a bodyguard of Portuguese mercenaries. Five of these mercenaries died at the hands of the Wild Tigers, but the elite forces of Prince Naresuan were unable to kill the Burmese king. As the other armies advanced Prince Naresuan ensured they were given the same welcome.

Villages, towns, and cities were found deserted by the Burmese. Prince Naresuan had decided that they would prove indefensible against the superior numbers of the attacking army and ordered the inhabitants to Ayutthaya. As the Burmese army marched through a barren land, it was only the saffron-robed monks of Sukhothai who greeted them.

As the vanguard of King Nanda Bayin's army neared Sukhothai, an old monk stood alone in the middle of the road. A soldier rode back to fetch the king and his son.

"Well," said King Nanda Bayin. "I never thought to find my old teacher and that of my son so far from home."

"The temples of Sukhothai have been left in my hands," said the monk Mahathen Kanchong. "They are not part of this war."

"Do not worry. I have no desire to cause harm," King Nanda Bayin replied. "In fact, come and join me and my son. My men would also enjoy the chance to give their thanks and make merit," said King Nanda Bayin.

They passed the temples by. King Nanda Bayin was a devout Buddhist, as his father was before him. Sukhothai was not his target. He would bide his time until Ayutthaya.

Ayutthaya was well prepared. Crops were gathered, and people fled to the safety of the city. King Maha Thammaracha had rebuilt many of the walls, and the rivers and canals flowed. The rainy season lay five months distant, and King Nanda Bayin knew he had those months in which to take the city. King Maha Thammaracha knew he had to hold out until then.

King Maha Thammaracha, Prince Naresuan, and Prince Ekathotsarot watched as the Burmese trumpeted their arrival. This time there was none of the courtesy that had marked previous invasions. There were no requests for white elephants, and there were no letters of communication. The first communications from King Nanda Bayin were cannon balls.

"He is an impatient man, this son of King Bayinnaung," said King Maha Thammaracha. "My forces were alongside him when King Bayinnaung captured the city. I wonder if he has the patience that this siege will need."

"He is a man who drives his troops by fear. He does not value the lives of his soldiers. I feel he will make many reckless decisions but also many unexpected ones. We must remain vigilant," said Prince Ekathotsarot.

"We must also unsettle him," said Prince Naresuan. My Wild Tigers have returned. We will go among his troops at night."

"You will fight alongside them?" asked Prince Ekathotsarot.

"Of course. I understand your concern, but I lead my men from the front. I will not change now."

"And you enjoy it, do you not?" asked King Maha Thammaracha.

"That I cannot deny," said Prince Naresuan giving a rare smile. "The Burmese will bring food down the river and overland from Lan

Na. I have men waiting to disrupt their supplies. Without food they cannot last for long."

Prince Ekathotsarot escaped death only a few days later when a bullet crashed into the wall behind him, missing his head by inches. The story, as it spread, served as a warning to all of those within the city.

King Maha Thammaracha had learned much from the fall of Ayutthaya to King Bayinnaung. The roads leading to the city were dug up and the spoil used to reinforce the walls. There was going to be no easy way to get close to the walls of Ayutthaya.

King Nanda Bayin set up his cannon and sent his troops against the walls of Ayutthaya. Protected by rivers, canals, and the partially rebuilt walls, Ayutthaya would prove a difficult city to take. He concentrated on the still-incomplete northeast corner, where continual bombardments slowly weakened the walls. As the corner of the wall started to crumble, he sent his soldiers to make a concerted attack. Inside the city, soldiers, well trained and disciplined, stayed at their posts until called for. The Burmese surged over the water on rafts and boats and by swimming. Oil was poured onto the water and then set alight. Their screams were followed by the unmistakable smell of charred bodies.

As King Nanda Bayin watched from afar he could see Prince Naresuan, dressed in his customary black leather armor, moving through his men as they charged over the wall. He was using the *krabi-krabong*, the combination of a straight longsword and a cudgel, and the sight of it coming toward any soldiers was usually enough to make them retreat. As limbs flew and blood spurted from the Burmese troops, their attack began to falter.

I hate that bastard! King Nanda Bayin thought, but he also marveled at the prince's fighting ability.

It takes enormous strength to wield the krabi-krabong. The secret, as the prince knew, was to get into a rhythm so the sword and the cudgel flowed as one. It looked at one point as though the Burmese would get sufficient numbers over the wall, but Prince Naresuan inspired his troops and together they pushed back the invaders.

The driving back of the Burmese forces marked a fundamental shift in the battle for Ayutthaya. The weak point in the wall was slowly reinforced despite the remorseless cannon fire, and within a matter of days a stalemate prevailed. The Burmese troops were already short of food, and sickness was passing among the troops. With no food left by the Siamese in the area surrounding Ayutthaya, the attacking troops were totally reliant on food brought in from Lan Na. The food was slow to arrive, and supplies were often disrupted and of poor quality.

The organizational skills of Nawrahta Minsaw, king of Lan Na, in delivering the food were not helping the Burmese king. With the constant attacks by Prince Naresuan's guerrilla fighters, it was becoming increasingly difficult for food even to get through. King Maha Thammaracha had already contaminated much of the water surrounding Ayutthaya before the siege began, and he ensured that dead animals and rotting corpses were regularly put into the rivers that flowed through Ayutthaya.

As March turned to April, the weather turned and the relentless heat of summer beat down on the Burmese troops. King Nanda Bayin became increasingly frustrated, ordering futile attacks. If any officer disobeyed or hesitated, their life was considered forfeit. The men feared King Nanda Bayin more than they feared the Siamese. Their king became even more short-tempered and vindictive than before. He would have deserters burned alive in front of his men, forcing them to watch. As they slowly starved, illness spread through their ranks.

By the beginning of May, four months into the siege, it was apparent that the Burmese troops could no longer sustain their attack. Prince Naresuan could sense the change and increased the frequency of his forays, particularly at night. The cannon bombardment from the Burmese continued as their attacks lessened. As Prince Naresuan became aware of his enemy's vulnerability he mounted attacks on the wooden forts the Burmese had constructed to protect themselves.

It was one of these occasions where Prince Naresuan and two of his men were caught and surrounded by a group of Burmese soldiers. Rather than surrender Prince Naresuan attacked against overwhelming odds using two swords and slashed the leader of the

Burmese group to death with the sword in his right hand. He then escaped back to Ayutthaya in the night.

Another time, the prince decided to attack the camp of King Nanda Bayin. With a sword clamped firmly between his teeth, he led his men as they scaled the walls. They were discovered and the Burmese put up fierce resistance, forcing them to retreat.

It was not until the end of May that the king of Hanthawaddy ordered the retreat. One morning, as the sun rose, the people of Ayutthaya looked out over the detritus the Burmese army had left behind. Prince Naresuan would dearly have loved to send his army to harry the Burmese as they made their way back, but news had been coming in throughout the siege of the Khmer taking territory along the border and the southern coast.

"The Burmese fled in the night. King Nanda Bayin is king here no more," said Prince Ekathotsarot.

"He never was our king. However, now is not the time to savor our victory," Prince Naresuan replied. "The Khmer are in our territory and for all we know could be coming to renew the siege."

"King Satta is not set on conquest," replied King Maha Thammaracha. "He is a cunning man. If I were him I would have expected Ayutthaya to fall. His intention was to capture as much land as possible and then negotiate with the Burmese. At least that is what I would have done in his place."

"So you are saying you do not fear an attack from the Khmer?"

"They would have been at the gates already. No, they expected us to lose. That was their mistake. King Satta will be far from pleased when he hears the news of our victory."

"We will pursue them now that there is no threat from the Burmese. King Nanda Bayin is not finished with us, but we can use this time to destroy the Khmer threat," said Prince Naresuan.

One month later, an army of twenty-five thousand men left Ayutthaya heading for Prachinburi. At its head were Prince Naresuan and Prince Ekathotsarot. The army of the Khmer Prince Srisuphanma, an ally-turned-adversary of Prince Naresuan, made battle on a flat plain, bounded by a river to one side and marshland to the other. Prince Naresuan led an elephant charge that broke through the Khmer lines. Prince Ekathotsarot led the Siamese cavalry into the gap, and the Khmer soldiers broke and ran, leaving four thousand of their dead on the battlefield.

Princes Naresuan and Ekathotsarot relentlessly pushed the Khmer forces back. Prince Srisuphanma made two more stands during the retreat, but within six weeks the army of Ayutthaya sat outside the walls of Lovek.

"Prince Ramesuan would have been proud of your cavalry action at Prachinburi," said Prince Naresuan.

"They were caught by surprise," Prince Ekathotsarot replied. "They expected a flanking maneuver from the cavalry, not a direct charge."

"Surprise as well as strength can win battles."

"And now?" asked Prince Ekathotsarot.

"And now we return home. Our supply lines are not established for a long siege. The Khmer will be more cautious from this day forward. I will write to King Satta telling him that the provinces of Prachinburi, Chanthaburi, and Nakhon Ratchasima are now rightfully returned to Siam, and he is to withdraw his men. We need not wait for his reply."

KING NARESUAN THE GREAT
1590–1605

The king has his court in the city of Ayutthaya, which is encircled
by brick walls and surrounded by two very broad and deep rivers.
It is situated on the bank of a branch of the Ganges, some 40
leguas inland, and even the largest of baxeles can enter and the
anchor right beside the city's walls. The medium-sized vessels
can enter into the city since it is criss-crossed by rivers, where
there are innumerable and very large crocodiles.

Jacques de Coutre

In June of 1590, King Maha Thammaracha—the kingmaker who had
become king—died. He left behind a country still fighting to survive,
but one no longer under the thrall of Burmese domination. His legacy
was to be seen as a puppet king, but he can also be viewed as a king
of his time. He needed all his political skills and wiles to survive,
and it was how he dealt with first King Tabinshwehti and then King
Bayinnaung that formed the foundation for the rebirth of Ayutthaya.
He left behind a wife and two sons who would continue to fight for
the independence of Ayutthaya in his stead.

The king was cremated with all the pomp and ceremony due to
a revered monarch. The king's ashes were collected to be placed
within a chedi and the bony relics would be returned to Sukhothai,
the ancestral home of King Maha Thammaracha. The family, gathered
together, all thought of Princess Suphankanlaya and how she should
have been here for this occasion above all others. That evening saw a
huge feast with dancers, tumblers, and many other entertainments.

Food and drink was distributed throughout the city in order that all could pass their best wishes on to the deceased king.

"My brother, I fear being king," Prince Naresuan confessed.

"I have known you all your life and I have never seen you show fear. You are to be crowned. You will be known as King Sanphet II. There can be no greater honor. What is there to fear?" asked Prince Ekathotsarot.

"I am a soldier, not a king. My entire life has been fighting. I have no time for the niceties of the royal court. My role is to safeguard the realm. The Burmese will be back, and the Khmer are only biding their time. If my duties as king conflict with my duties as a soldier then I fear I may end up as king of nothing. Our father spent his life to pass us this legacy of a revived Ayutthaya. He endured much for the sake of the kingdom. I fear tainting his legacy.

"I have given what I am about to say much thought. People respect me—they fear me, but they do not like me. I am a soldier. I enforce strict discipline and do not hesitate to take the lives of those who fail me. This is the way of a warrior. It is not the way of a king.

"I want you to rule alongside me. I want you as upparat with honor equal to myself. I ask you to act in my stead as king. You understand the court, the diplomacy, and the intrigues. You understand the need for the empire to grow. Father told me that two major changes are being felt: the Europeans and the need for wealth. The Europeans bring weapons—better weapons than the Indians and the Persians—and they bring more trade. With more trade comes more wealth. You understand these issues. While I fight, I will leave it to you to build our country," said Prince Naresuan. "What say you?"

Prince Ekathotsarot paused to consider.

"I need ports with which to trade," he said finally, clapping his brother on the back.

There would be not one crowning but two. King Naresuan, at the age of thrty-five, held the title Sanphet II and would ensure the security of the realm while Prince Ekathotsarot would ensure the future of Ayutthaya.

Within a matter of weeks news came of another imminent Burmese attack. King Nanda Bayin had not given up on his quest to regain Ayutthaya. Under the command of his son Prince Mingyi Swa, the Burmese launched a further invasion of Siam in November of 1590. King Nanda Bayin had thought to offer support to his son, but his plans changed when the northern Shan states of Mohnyin and Mogaung refused to send troops but sent a message instead:

> If we go with the king, we will die in a strange place. If we refuse to go with him he will certainly send an army to kill us. We choose to defy him and die in our own native place.

It was a sentiment that King Nanda Bayin could not let grow. He diverted the troops of Thado Dhamma Yaza III and Prince Natchinnaung to fight the Shan rebels, leaving only thirty thousand men under the command of Prince Mingyi Swa to invade Ayutthaya.

Prince Mingyi Swa led an army through Three Pagodas Pass and into Kanchanaburi. His plan was to lay siege to Ayutthaya until the city fell. As his army neared the small town of Ban Khoi, they were totally unprepared to see King Naresuan and his army blocking their progress. King Naresuan's spies had advised him of the Burmese crown prince's movements.

Before they had the chance to form battle lines, the Burmese were pushed steadily into an open area, bounded to the rear by a river. King Naresuan had carefully chosen the site of the battle and had planned how the battle was to be fought. Prince Mingyi Swa realized he was in trouble within minutes. His attempts to rally his army and charge the enemy failed. Prince Naresuan, in choosing the battleground, had also secured the victory.

After fierce hand-to-hand combat and with his army being pushed back to the banks of the river, the Burmese crown prince sounded the retreat. The Burmese fled the field of battle, leaving many elephants, horses, arms and ammunition as well as the dead and the dying. Prince Mingyi Swa had again been bested by King Naresuan. Neither he nor his father could allow this to continue. The losses of men and of prestige hung heavy over the declining Toungoo empire.

With his army scattered, the Burmese crown prince fled back to Hanthawaddy. As the victory was gained and the enemy fled, news came of another incursion by the Khmer. King Naresuan left some his men to chase the Burmese while the rest of his army gathered and made the trek back to Ayutthaya. The fourth attempt to regain Ayutthaya by the Burmese had failed.

℘〜

It was late in 1592 when what would prove to be the final Burmese invasion into Siamese territory would take place. All previous attempts had failed, and King Nanda Bayin could not allow this invasion to fail too. Prince Mingyi Swa, along with the viceroy of Prome and Prince Natchinnaung, led the Burmese armies into Siam while King Nanda Bayin marched his army north out of Hanthawaddy, past Lampang, and on to Chiang Mai before the planned move south and the assault on Ayutthaya.

News of the two-pronged invasion took King Naresuan partly by surprise. He responded by sending a force under General Phichai north to Lan Na, while his main force headed west to meet Prince Mingyi Swa and his army.

His success of the previous two years had taught the new king of Ayutthaya the fragility of the Burmese. They were fighting for a dying cause, while his own men were fighting for an ideal. Under the pressure of battle this meant everything.

Ayutthaya was readied for another siege. King Naresuan and Prince Ekathotsarot rode out at the head of their troops, knowing that this could be the final battle. As they neared Suphanburi, the king roused his men. He told them of the coming battle, he reminded them of the sacrifices of their fallen comrades, and he spoke of a Siam independent of the hated men of Hanthawaddy. He may not have been effective at talking within the court at Ayutthaya, but here on the battlefield he could embolden his men like no other leader.

As King Naresuan surveyed the opposition forces, he could see that his numbers were inferior. He wondered to himself how the Burmese were still able to put so many men on the field; however, he remained confident that he could out-general his Burmese opposition. He had proven it many times. He had humiliated his childhood friend Prince Mingyi Swa and Prince Natchinnaung at Mueang Khang, and before that he had humiliated Prince Mingyi Swa in the cockfight. Now was the time to fight for kingdoms!

The armies met outside Suphanburi at Nong Sarai, near the Thakhoi River. Thousands of men stood poised for battle. King Naresuan sent a small force forward under Phraya Si Sai Narong to assess and report back. The following morning when the Ayutthayan forces were readying themselves for battle, shots were heard. Contrary to orders, Phraya Si Sai Narong and his men had fired on the Burmese. In a rare show of humor, King Naresuan sent a message to Phraya Si Sai Narong saying that he should expect no reinforcements. On receiving it Phraya Si Sai Narong and his men retreated. The Burmese pursued them, possibly thinking the entire Siamese army was in retreat. The Burmese advanced toward them, their elephants at the center making ready to charge. The soldiers of King Naresuan turned to retreat, and the elephants of the Burmese, perhaps excited by the noise, smells, and color before the battle or just by the enthusiasm of their mahouts, chased after them.

It was a ruse. As the Burmese charged the Siamese forces turned, as they had been drilled to do, and let the elephants pass before moving in on them from the sides. The battle then started in earnest as the two infantries clashed head-on. With the Burmese elephants out of position, the Ayutthayan elephants crashed into the Burmese infantry unopposed, opening a gaping wound for the Ayutthayan cavalry to exploit.

Slowly, the larger numbers of the Burmese began to tell, and, inexorably, they regained position and their elephants gained the center of the battlefield. The Burmese elephants held the advantage in height and weight. The many victories of King Bayinnaung had meant that the finest elephants from his conquered dominions had been returned to Hanthawaddy. Trained by the Mon people, these elephants were now war elephants of the highest order. Once they regained position, they began to inflict carnage among the Siamese troops.

It appeared the tide of battle was turning in favor of the men of Hanthawaddy. King Naresuan slashed at the body of a young Burmese nobleman. As his arm separated from his body, a gush of bright crimson blood covered the king's elephant. His elephant, Phlai Phukhao Thong (Golden Mountain), readied slightly, and as he did so King Naresuan noticed the decorations on the chest of Prince Mingyi Swa, who was sitting high on his elephant near a jujube tree not far away.

King Naresuan pointed out the Burmese crown prince to Nai Mahanuphap, his mahout. He did not move alone—five nobles stood guard around his elephant.

The king signaled to his brother with his sword, and together they advanced into the fray, away from the body of their men, to do battle with the crown prince of Hanthawaddy. One of the Burmese generals near his crown prince rode an elephant in musth, the elephant's eyes bandaged so he would not see other male elephants. The general saw King Naresuan coming and removed the bandage from his elephant's eyes. The elephant, instead of attacking King Naresuan, attacked the elephant of the Burmese crown prince before running amok on the battlefield. Another Burmese elephant moved alongside Prince Mingyi Swa to offer protection. King Naresuan drew his elephant alongside the crown prince's larger animal while Prince Ekathotsarot moved to do battle with the protecting elephant.

King Naresuan called out to the Burmese crown prince.

> "Whatever is our royal older brother doing standing in the shade of a tree? Come forth and let us fight an elephant duel for the honor of our kingdoms!"

The Burmese crown prince slashed with his sword, narrowly missing King Naresuan and knocking his hat off as he sliced through its brim. As he cursed at King Naresuan, he landed another blow, slightly cutting the Siamese king's right arm. The larger Burmese elephant started to overpower the Siamese elephant. Phlai Phukhao Thong, King Naresuan's elephant, pushed back against the larger Burmese elephant but gradually was forced to concede ground. The elephant of King Naresuan set its legs against a hillock next to the jujube tree, laden with ripe fruit. The elephant lowered its head and gored the elephant of Mingyi Swa, causing it to squeal and stumble. The fight was so vicious that all the surrounding soldiers had stopped to watch this epic encounter. As Prince Mingyi Swa's elephant stumbled, King Naresuan cleaved his halberd down on the Burmese crown prince, splitting him from the shoulder down to his hip. He fell from his elephant, dead.

The body of Nai Mahanuphap, King Naresuan's mahout, had fallen too, shot toward the end of the fight. A Mon soldier, bloodied during the battle, calmed Phlai Phukhao Thong and mounted him, taking the place of King Naresuan's long-serving mahout.

King Naresuan felt a satisfaction that he had never felt with any other kill. The heir-apparent to the throne of the Toungoo empire lay dead at his feet. The cockerel had won the day. He looked for his brother who was fighting elephant-against-elephant to his right.

As they battled, the Burmese general Prince Ekathotsarot was fighting began to tire. The younger and more athletic Ayutthayan prince finally saw an opening and impaled the Burmese general with his krabi-krabong. The general remained still on his elephant as blood trickled from his mouth.

By the time most of the Siamese soldiers had fought through to the site of the elephant battle, it was over. A lull settled over the battlefield as the Burmese realized that two of their own leaders were dead. The will to fight ebbed away from the Burmese. The battle was over. King Naresuan looked back, angry at his generals who had not ridden to support him.

The Burmese troops fell into disarray and started to flee the battlefield. King Naresuan ordered them to be brought back or to be killed should they resist.

King Naresuan ordered,

> "Because he lost in a cockfight and spoke to shame me in Hanthawaddy we fought this fight as good men do. Do not take any prisoners."

Prince Ekathotsarot dismounted from the elephant. Blood covered his tunic as he faced his brother after this epic battle. On hearing of the order not to take prisoners, he confronted his elder brother.

"You are wrong to order these deaths," he said, head to head with his brother. "We have our victory and it is truly a magnificent victory. Do not spoil it by massacring those who simply followed their king."

"We must rid Siamese soil of these men of Hanthawaddy. We must let them know they are not welcome in my realm," said King Naresuan. Despite the satisfaction of killing the hated Mingyi Swa, he still had the hot blood of battle coursing through his veins.

"Father said I was to moderate your excesses. You said I was to counsel you as an equal. This time I do not ask you to show clemency—I demand it," said Prince Ekathotsarot forcefully. "I will not be party to a massacre. The soldiers may be fighting for the Burmese, but you and I know they have little choice."

King Naresuan took a step back and took a deep breath.

"I will do as you ask," he said. "But my generals must pay for not coming to our aid."

℘

King Naresuan ordered the captured Burmese to build a chedi on the site of the battle as a victory monument before the prisoners were moved onward.

"You have won a famous victory. I ask you to show clemency to those generals who have offended you," said the abbot as they sat within the walls of the recently completed Chankasem Palace in Ayutthaya.

"When I charged Prince Mingyi Swa, they did not follow," said King Naresuan. Within him was an anger that would not dissipate. Maybe it was the satisfaction at the death of the Mingyi Swa, or maybe it was the generals' failure.

"They were engaged in the heat of battle. They did not see what you had done," responded Somdet Phra Wannarat.

"My generals know only too well the price of not supporting me. My brother saw what was happening and rode to my aid, defeating one of their generals single-handedly."

He looked at his brother. Suddenly, it was as if the heat had gone.

"Bring the generals to me," ordered King Naresuan.

The two generals entered and supplicated themselves at the feet of their king. They feared the worst. They had served with King Naresuan for many years and knew he did not tolerate what he perceived as failure. Failure drew only one penalty.

"The bhikkhu Somdet Phra Wannarat has begged me to spare your lives. What he said has merit, and I am minded to agree with him. You have both served me well over many years. That is also in your favor. You will redeem yourselves by leading the conquest of the southern Burmese territories of Tenasserim and Tavoy. We take our war to the Burmese. We will attack them in their own lands. When you succeed, your failure at Nong Sarai will be forgotten," King Naresuan ordered. "If you fail, do not return home."

The generals bowed as they backed out of the chamber. The relief they felt was evident to all in the room. Months later, the cities of Tavoy and Tenneraserim would fall to the Ayutthayan forces in both land and sea battles. With the west coast secure it would be possible to advance into Burmese soil.

"You have made a wise decision," said Prince Ekathotsarot. "One worthy of a king." As he said it a messenger arrived.

"King Nanda Bayin has retreated. General Phichai did not engage him in battle," said King Naresuan after removing the seal. "The news of the death of his son has reached him. His retreat signals the end of his aspirations on Ayutthaya. I believe he will no longer be able to raise an army of sufficient size to attack us again," said King Naresuan, as a flood of relief coursed through him.

"More than that, his failure to conquer us will leave him vulnerable at home. I feel the tide has changed," said Prince Ekathotsarot. "The vultures will be looking to peck at his corpse."

"He has attacked us five times and failed with each attempt. He can have only a limited number of troops to call on. Do you think he has returned to Hanthawaddy because of the death of his son? He is not that noble. He has returned to keep his army intact. He knows he will need as many troops as possible when he returns to Pegu."

"I would prefer to fight the Burmese on their soil and the Khmer on theirs. That is what we are going to do, and we start with ports you wanted—Tavoy and Tenasserim. They are Mon cities that would dearly love to shake off the yoke of the Burmese, and they lie on our side of the Three Pagodas Pass. Even if King Nanda Bayin decides to defend them they will be a heavy drain on his resources," said King Naresuan.

"Do not write him off too soon. He will regroup and fight to the bitter end. King Nanda Bayin is not a man to give up his kingdom lightly," responded his brother.

"This is something I have wanted for so long, to fight the Burmese on their own soil. That, and lose a hated foe. I have killed the son—now what remains is to kill the father. With the Toungoo empire defeated it will be the time of Ayutthaya," said King Naresuan.

☙

Phlai Phukhao Thong died two years after the battle of Nong Sarai.

> The day the animal died [the king] was extremely upset, saying that his father had died. He ordered the people and all the leading figures of his kingdom to go and worship the elephant. To this end they took the elephant outside the city to the other side of the river and they placed it before a temple. They erected a very large canopy made of blue damask over the elephant and cut open the animal's abdomen. After they had removed its intestines they embalmed it with ointments and placed a large quantity of flowers and roses on top of the animal. They inserted some golden poles into the animal in order to keep its stomach open and four talapois, who are their priests, sat inside the cavity. The priests were dressed in yellow and held some beads in their hands, which they call gantra and there were lit wax candles around them. . . . The elephant already stank for more than half a league around. Subsequently, all the leading figures and

gentlement came. . . . Everyone worshipped the animal on their knees. This barbarity went on for eight days, during which dances were continuously held and infernal music could be heard day and night, consisting of rattles, drums, and gongs and other instruments like tambourines. . . . At the end of the eight days the talapois covered the elephant with large and small pieces of wood. The king then came and walked around the elephant three times and set the pyre ablaze. After the elephant's carcass had been burnt he ordered the ashes to be collected and put into some golden urns, and they put the urns in the same place as the ashes of his parents and ancestors. After the urns had been gathered two men came to the king who were carers or mahouts of the elephant. They said that since the elephant, their master, was dead they wished to go and serve the animal in its next life. After thanking them profusely for their gesture the king drew out his sword that he was wearing around his waist; he ordered them to be cut in half and then burnt with many honours. . . . The barbaric festivities for the elephant were concluded in this fashion.

In the time of King Bayinnaung the heir to the throne of Lan Xang was the young Prince Koumane, the son of King Setthathirath. He was taken hostage and spent his childhood in Pegu, much as Prince Naresuan had done all those years earlier. He became accomplished in the military strategy and tactics taught by the Burmese and European teachers but remained a captive until the age of twenty. Lan Xang, the "land of a million elephants," had endured much as a vassal of the Burmese. The ministers of Lan Xang petitioned King Nanda Bayin for the prince's return, but it was only after a delegation was sent to Pegu and Prince Koumane had come of age in 1590 that he was allowed to return home. No doubt inspired by the actions of King Naresuan, King Koumane declared independence from Burma in 1593. The Toungoo empire was starting to fracture.

In Lan Na, the Burmese king Nawrahta Minsaw soon found himself under attack from Lan Xang. King Nanda Bayin was feeling the pressure of trying to hold the empire together and could spare no further troops. King Nawrahta Minsaw now found himself in a position of great danger. He petitioned King Naresuan for help, which King Naresuan gave over the coming years—but at the price of Lan Na accepting Ayutthaya's suzerainty.

To the west of Ayutthaya the city of Moulmein fell to Ayutthayan forces, and in December 1594 the combined Siamese forces of twelve thousand troops, six hundred horses, and sixty elephants besieged the capital of the Toungoo empire. Finally, Burmese armies arrived to relieve the siege in April of 1595, and King Naresuan was forced to retreat.

Although unsuccessful, the siege of Pegu drove wide divisions in the fast-fracturing Toungoo empire. Internal divisions became increasingly apparent. It was during the Siamese siege of Pegu that Mingyi Hnaung, viceroy of Prome, openly revolted against his father, King Nanda Bayin. It had a domino effect as vassal kings from Toungoo to Chiang Mai to the Shan provinces revolted as well. The pressure mounted on the increasingly isolated king of the Toungoo empire.

Before long King Nanda Bayin's once-mighty empire was reduced to a strip of coastal land that included Pegu, the port of Syriam, and the Irrawaddy delta. His former vassals had now effectively turned from their king, viewing each other as rivals. As King Naresuan had predicted, it appeared as if Burma was reverting to a country of warring city-states.

Prince Natchinnaung, son of King Minye Thihathu of Toungoo led a land attack on Pegu supported by the navy of King Razagyi Gyi, king of Arakan. King Nanda Bayin surrendered and was taken away to Toungoo in chains. The victors pillaged the city, looting all the gold, silver, and other valuables that had been collected during the reigns of King Tabinshwehti and King Bayinnaung. When they left, Pegu was destroyed.

King Naresuan was called on by the kings of Toungoo and Arakan to help them in the siege of Pegu, but when he arrived it was too late. The city had fallen and its riches had been pillaged. There was no one he could ask about the fate of his beloved sister, Princess Suphankanlaya. That others had taken advantage of the moment he had worked so hard for angered him, but that he would never know what had become of his sister angered him more. King Naresuan turned his army toward Toungoo in order to have King Nanda Bayin surrendered to him, but his siege failed, and after sustaining heavy losses he returned to Ayutthaya.

Peace, of a sort, had reigned over the city of Ayutthaya in the years since King Naresuan had taken the war to his neighbors. It was a period of rebuilding and renewal as the wars of the past fifty years began to slip into memory and folklore.

It was while King Naresuan and Prince Ekathotsarot were quelling a rebellion in Lan Na that a visitor from his school days in Pegu came to visit.

"King Naresuan, Prince Ekathotsarot, I come seeking your help," said Sopha Noi. "Our people are under threat so soon after the death of King Nanda Bayin."

"The power vacuum is being filled. It is King Nyaungyan, no doubt. He is the power in Burma now," said Prince Ekathotsarot.

"He demands tribute from us, as does the emperor in Beijing. I feel the emperor is unlikely to attack this far south, but what King Nyaugyan asks is far deeper than mere tribute. King Nyaugyan needs people for his armies as the Toungoo empire did before him. We have seen so many of our sons taken, never to return. King Nyaungyan has made overtures of friendship to us but we, the Shan, hold that Ava should be ruled by Shan kings or those of Shan blood," Sopha Noi responded. "The successive reigns of King Tabinshwehti, King Bayinnaung, and King Nanda Bayin have taught us that we do not want to be ruled by a king of Burmese descent again. Our people have common cause in this and are united in their desire to drive King Nyaungyan from Ava. Already rebellions have broken out. But King

Nyaungyan has a son, Anaukpetlun, who is a fearsome warrior and, from what we have seen of him so far, an excellent general."

"You offer a challenge you know I cannot refuse," said King Naresuan. "You know me all too well from our school days. You already tempt me to meet this Anaukpetlun on the battlefield."

"You will help us?" asked Sopha Noi.

King Naresuan looked at Prince Ekathotsarot, who nodded in agreement.

The help that Sopha Noi, waited for never arrived. King Naresuan set his camp on the eastern bank of the Nam Hang River. While there, he fell ill with an infection. The poison spread throughout his body, and as his condition worsened, couriers were sent to bring his brother Ekathotsarot, the upparat and heir to the throne of Ayutthaya. With his brother by his side, King Naresuan died at the age of forty-nine. On Monday, April 25, 1605, his fifteen-year reign drew to a close.

The spot where he died is thought to be situated to the northeast of Hui Auw, on the eastern bank of the Nam Hang River. The corpse was cremated ahead of the place where King Naresuan had fallen, meaning that he did not retreat but marched forward, even after death.

21

KING EKATHOTSAROT

1605–10

KING SI SAOWAPHAK

1610–11

AFTER CALLING OFF THE CAMPAIGN and returning to Ayutthaya with the remains of his brother, King Ekathotsarot organized one of the grandest royal funerals Ayutthaya had ever known. The new king ordered the building of a temple, thought to be Wat Worachetharam, as its chedi is in the style used during the reign of King Naresuan and sits close to the royal palace where the remains of other great kings were placed.

King Ekathotsarot ordered three golden and two silver images of the Buddha made as a tribute to his brother. To celebrate his brother's life he sponsored a royal boat-race ceremony, followed by a procession of royal boats that conveyed the newly created images of the Buddha around the city for seven days.

Boat racing was a favorite of both King Naresuan and King Ekathotsarot. King Naresuan believed, in much the same way as King Ram Khamhaeng did centuries before, that racing was the best way to train his oarsmen for war.

@﹋

King Ekathotsarot had served as joint ruler of Ayutthaya alongside King Naresuan. With King Naresuan relentlessly on campaign, often absent for years at a time, it fell to then Prince Ekathotsarot to both rebuild the city of Ayutthaya and to develop the trade that was so important to the city's future; with Ayutthaya now militarily secure King Ekathotsarot could focus his energies on the nation's finances and trade. The warring had also forced King Naresuan and Prince Ekathotsarot to transform their kingdom from one that was largely fragmented, with princes and governors only owing their allegiance, to one that was more centralized and controlled from Ayutthaya.

"We need to move forward with our plans for centralization," said Chief Minister Phothong.

"Yes. They have been put on hold since the death of my brother, but if we wait then the old system will reestablish itself," replied the king.

"We have the opportunity to build on the work started by King Trailok and extend the control of Ayutthaya firmly throughout the realm."

"You know my views on the matter. I will not allow things to go back to how they were before the war. To allow Ayutthaya to flourish we need to command the entire country, not just the capital and the surrounding area. We have placed governors in the major cities. They are not to be in their positions for more than three years before they arc moved. The cities are of the kingdom of Ayutthaya and will remain so," said the king. "Those governors in Lopburi, Phitsanulok, Nakhon Nayok, and Sawankhalok have been in place for one year. Now is the time to show them our teeth."

"They will shortly be visited by my men. I have told them to be rigorous, to go through the city's finances and listen to the complaints of the people. As you know I already have men in place watching the governors—it may be that they can be bought, though I have taken great care to install only men of the highest integrity."

"Rigorous. A good word. If we find evidence of corruption it will be dealt with harshly. You have explained that to your men?" asked the king.

"Yes, Your Majesty. In these early years they are to return with the governor to Ayutthaya if corruption is found or suspected. Here in Ayutthaya we can find out the truth of any wrongdoing. We need to set an example,"

"The governors should return here during their second year with a full report on their management of the city. Your men should investigate all complaints made against any governor and report to you. I want you to know as much as possible about the governance of the city and the feeling of the populace before the governors report. I do not want their return to Ayutthaya to be easy. If they have done wrong they will be openly punished. If they have done well then another city beckons.

"Their loyalty should be assured. They are to drink the water of allegiance. They all know the commitment they are making. We have governors in our major cities. Now is the time to ensure control of our second-tier towns and cities," concluded the king.

"Yes, Your Majesty," said Chief Minister Phothong.

It is said that in the latter years of King Ekathotsarot's reign a governor of Phitsanulok was beheaded in front of two ministers after he had been found to be corrupt.

☙

King Ekathotsarot's reign saw an influx of foreigners—particularly traders and mercenaries. The king established volunteer regiments of foreign soldiers and weapons specialists. He developed close relations with Japan under the shogun Tokugawa Ieyasu. The new and burgeoning port of Songkhla was one of the first ports in the region visited by the Japanese; it was not long before they starting coming to Ayutthaya as well.

"We have one of the Japanese shogun's 'red seal ships' being readied for departure. The final consignment of hides is being loaded today," said Chief Minister Phothong.

"Excellent. We need to maintain a good relationship with the shogun. I cannot imagine how life here would be bearable without the silks and other luxuries we gain from trade with the Japanese," said the king.

"The Japanese have established their village, Ban Yipun, to the south of Ayutthaya as we agreed," said Chief Minister Phothong.

"Their presence is welcome. They are not only good traders but their skills as fighters are legendary. Their samurai tradition places them apart from others, and we need to make use of their abilities," responded the king.

Besides the Japanese, the kingdom had long been in contact with the Portuguese and had employed many Portuguese mercenary soldiers to assist in defense. The Portuguese were now established at Malacca and throughout Southeast Asia. Emissaries had been exchanged with the court of Ayutthaya. The status quo was threatened when new traders arrived from Europe around 1600: the Dutch.

Following the destructive war with Burma, Ayutthaya was going through a period of reconstruction. Many traders had abandoned Ayutthaya, and King Ekathotsarot actively sought the return of the Portuguese. The Dutch arrived, followed by the English about ten years later, and both were welcomed. The increased income was needed not only to rebuild the kingdom but also to strengthen the navy and the merchant fleet—not to mention to fund the elaborate court. Ayutthaya's openness to trade and its religious freedom attracted many foreigners to the city during this period.

King Ekathotsarot's accession to the throne in 1605 saw the founding of the city of Songkhla, a port in the deep south, to the north of Pattani. It had been an inconsequential fishing village until a Persian Muslim named Dato Mogol approached the king with a proposal to develop this natural port on the burgeoning trade area of the Gulf of Siam. The port's natural harbor was able to handle eighty vessels, and it was also well situated for the development of tin and gem mining. Dato Mogol became the sultan of Songkhla and accepted Siamese suzerainty, paying tribute to the king of Ayutthaya. The Ayutthayan king now had wider access to the South China Sea. Traders from Siam journeyed to Penang, to Singapore, to Aceh, and onward, encouraged by their king.

"The Portuguese call them bandits and pirates, enemies of the faith, and men without a king," said Chief Minister Phothong.

"That is not surprising. They threaten Portuguese trade," replied the king.

"They acted well on their visit with us in the final year of King Naresuan's reign. The Dutch are keen to establish trading relations with China and Japan as well as us."

"We supported their embassy to the emperor. You say they are looking to send an embassy to us to establish trade relations?" asked the king.

"I have received a written request from their trading station in Pattani."

"They would provide a new source of revenue and they have powerful weapons that they are happy to trade. More than that they may provide a balance to the Portuguese. It is dangerous to become reliant on one country, and it is clear these nations are enemies. Perhaps we can use that to our advantage. We will welcome their embassy, but we need to go further," said the king. "My brother always doubted his mercenaries. He said he used them as he had no choice. They were unreliable, particularly when faced with danger. It was King Naresuan's wish that we form our own elite troops who can fire the arms and cannon we acquire from the West. The Dutch will arrange for that if they want a concession to trade here."

"May I suggest a further strategy?" ventured the chief minister.

The king nodded.

"We now have ready access to the southeast from Ayutthaya and Songkhla. It is Tenasserim on the west coast that concerns me. The area is riddled with pirates—particularly the Burmese and the Arakanese. We have permitted the Portuguese a trading post there. I fear they will become emboldened when they are established in the city. They may threaten the overland route between Ayutthaya and Tenasserim—or worse, seek to claim Tenasserim for themselves."

"The Portuguese are a threat as well as an ally. You are right to be concerned. If we had a Dutch presence along that coast or in the city itself, it would act as a deterrent. The two nations may war between themselves, or balance each other out. It may aid us in avoiding a costly war. Nothing is certain. Invite them. We will make them welcome," concluded King Ekathotsarot.

King Naresuan had left Lan Na in the dry season of 1604–5 to go to the aid of his friend Sopha Noi. The country of Lan Na had accepted the suzerainty of Ayutthaya some years earlier, but the Burmese king had spent considerable effort in trying to placate both his Burmese and his Ayutthayan masters. The Burmese chronicles indicate that King Naresuan was married to King Nawrahta Minsaw's daughter, and that her son Prince Tu Luang, the heir apparent to the throne of Lan Na, lived in Ayutthaya. Following King Nawrahta Minsaw's death in 1608, King Ekathotsarot led his troops northward to place Prince Tu Luang on the throne.

Meanwhile the younger son of the dead king moved quickly to secure the throne. The country had fluctuated between Burmese and Ayutthayan overlordship during the Ayutthayan-Burmese wars with many claimants to the throne from cities such as Chiang Saen, Nan, and Chiang Rai, and even from the neighboring country of Lan Xang.

"You have been invited by the court to take the throne of Chiang Mai," said King Ekathotsarot.

"I have been invited by the Burmese faction, whose grasp on power is tenuous following the death of King Nawrahta Minsaw. It is my understanding that most local nobles are putting forward Minye Deibbe as king," replied Prince Tu Luang.

"You are the son of King Naresuan, and Lan Na is under our suzerainty. The throne is yours by right. King Nawrahta Minsaw remained in power only at our behest."

"That may be, but his son sits safely behind the walls of Chiang Mai. It may prove difficult to pry him out."

"Time will tell," said King Ekathotsarot as he rode on his horse alongside Prince Tu Luang. Behind him came an army of over twenty thousand men, five hundred elephants, and the pick of his Portuguese mercenaries.

"It feels different not to have my brother alongside me," the king mused.

"You fought many battles alongside my father. Both your exploits are legendary," replied Prince Tu Luang.

One reason the old king, Nawrahta Minsaw, had defied the odds and remained in power for decades was the sturdy defensive walls he placed around the city of Chiang Mai. The walls stood no higher than the defenses that surrounded Ayutthaya, but they were of greater thickness and able to withstand a concerted cannon bombardment—as King Ekathotsarot and Prince Tu Luang were to find out. Their bombardment of the city continued unabated for thirteen months until a ball fired from a musket ended Prince Tu Luang's life. King Ekathotsarot lifted the siege and returned to Ayutthaya. It would have to be up to a future king to secure Lan Na for Ayutthaya.

In 1608, the Dutch Verenigde Oost-Indische Compagnie (VOC) opened a factory—a trading post led by a "factor"—in Ayutthaya, and in 1610 King Ekathotsarot offered the VOC the opportunity to build a fort at Mergui, the port adjacent to Tenasserim on the west coast. The VOC quickly became the principal Western traders in the kingdom.

The king sent the first Siamese diplomatic mission to the Netherlands in 1608, where they were received in audience by Prince Maurice. When the embassy arrived in Holland, the members were taken to pay respect to the prince of Orange in the Hague. With them they carried a range of exquisite gifts from King Ekathotsarot for the Dutch prince, along with a letter from the king of Ayutthaya, engraved on a sheet of gold.

The Siamese ambassadors told of Ayutthaya and the power of its king.

> The King of Siam wished to send another person, who, having disobeyed, he had roasted in a heated cauldron in which he languished a month until he expired. . . . He is a very powerful monarch, having under him four or five vassal kings. He can send into the field three hundred thousand men and two thousand war elephants, and has active links with the King of China who is the most powerful of all.

The Dutch were impressed by the manner of the Siamese. They hoped that through King Ekathotsarot and the kingdom of Ayutthaya they would be able to make overtures to China, and the embassy was well received by the prince of Orange. They introduced King

Ekathotsarot to the recently invented telescope, which became the wonder of the court in Ayutthaya. The king, however, made sure to balance his sending of an embassy to Holland by also sending one to Portuguese Goa.

In 1608, the Englishman William Keeling had under his command three vessels of the East India Company: the *Dragon,* the *Hector,* and the *Consent.* After dropping anchor in Bantam he met with a Siamese ambassador of the king of Siam, whom he invited to dine with him aboard the *Dragon.* Keeling steered the conversation toward trade and the Siamese markets. That night Keeling wrote that the ambassador assured him "a million lengths of red stuff [i.e., cloth] would sell in his country in two days, and in great quantities each year, because they use it to adorn their elephants and horses." He further said the king of Siam would be willing to trade with the illustrious king of England, to whom "the King of Holland could not be compared."

"So you were invited aboard the English ship?" asked the king.

"They made me very welcome," said Phraya Kongtan. "They like to drink."

"I have heard that from the Portuguese," said the king.

"Their ships are quite small compared to the Portuguese, but their cannon are far more numerous. Their captain, William Keeling, is a huge, bearded man. Quite fearsome. Not a man to cross in a fight," said Phraya Kongtan.

"It does seem that the other foreigners fear them."

"Their captain told me that their navy defeated the Spanish in the time of their old queen 'Good Queen Bess,' and from that time on their navy has struck fear into all the other foreigners."

"They are clearly a warlike people."

"Yes, but they can drink and laugh like no other people I have met. They told tales and stories to amaze. They were keen to trade and showed me some excellent samples of their wares. They also told me that the Dutch had no king,"

"No king!" exclaimed the king.

"Indeed, Your Majesty. They are ruled by a prince."

"No king, no king!" said the king as he burst out into a fit of uncontrollable laughter. "All these years dealing with them, and they have no king!"

꒰ꜜꜜ

King Ekathotsarot fathered two sons, Prince Si Saowaphak and Prince Suthat. Prince Si Saowaphak was stricken with boils, a potentially deadly disease at the time. Although doctors saved his life, he lost his sight in one eye. In a time when kings were considered divine it was not appropriate to put an heir on the throne who carried a deformity. The king's second son, Prince Suthat, was elevated to be upparat. Prince Suthat died only four months after becoming upparat. There are reports he killed himself by drinking poison after offending his father, but the circumstances of his death have remained a royal mystery.

King Ekathotsarot gradually went mad after the death of his son. The king himself died in 1610 after a reign of five years. Although his father had never made him upparat, Prince Si Saowaphak seized the throne, despite his deformity, and became King Si Saowaphak.

King Si Saowaphak had reigned for one year and two months when Phra Intharacha, a famous Buddhist monk and son of King Ekathotsarot, fomented a rebellion and deposed the king. The devout Phra Intharacha was given the title "the pious" and crowned King Songtham.

KING SONGTHAM 1611–28
KING CHETTHATHIRAT 1628–29
KING ATHITTAYAWONG 1629

ON NOVEMBER 16, 1611, a group of Japanese traders and mercenaries, upset at the way the changes had affected them, caused a great commotion at the Ayutthayan court. Over five hundred Japanese stormed the palace. King Songtham was not there at the time.

Phra Maha Ammatya was able to gather support from monks and attacked the Japanese, who were defeated and fled. Phra Maha Ammatya invited the king to return to his palace. The king appointed Phra Maha Ammatya as Chao Phraya Kalahom Suriyavansa as a mark of his favor. The Japanese fled in disarray to Phetchaburi, taking with them the supreme patriarch of Ayutthaya as a hostage. Ayutthayan troops pursued, eventually allowing them to board a ship in return for freeing the supreme patriarch.

It was an unsettling start to his reign but one that did not greatly upset the king. Relations with Japan would be stronger under King Songtham than under any other Ayutthayan monarch.

Elsewhere, war loomed. In 1596, King Nawrahta Minsaw of Lan Na and King Naresuan had jointly appointed a child, Voravongsa, as ruler of Lan Xang. The country of Lan Xang had been stripped of many of its people in Ayutthaya's wars with the Burmese, and the nation was left severely weakened. Voravongsa was a compromise candidate and was chosen to stop the country from fragmenting. His father, Vorapita, would act as regent until the young king came of age in the year 1610.

Hearing the tales as he grew, the young Voravongsa wanted revenge against both Ayutthaya and Burma for the excesses carried out against his people during the war. A nephew of King Setthathirath, he had the same fighting spirit, and as a generation came of age new soldiers wanted to avenge the perceived wrongs of the past. Voravongsa, ruling from Luang Prabang, fought a bitter civil war with his father, finally defeating and killing him.

He entered Ayutthayan territory, using horsemen and mercenaries to lead the attack—the same tactics he employed in his battle to secure the joint throne of Vientiane and Luang Prabang. The bulk of these foot soldiers and his elephants followed, consolidating the ground he had taken. He stormed into the territories of Ayutthaya from the northeast, through the Chao Phraya valley, and captured Phetchabun before the Siamese were aware of the attack. He took people from the lands he passed through and sent them back to Lan Xang as captives. His army cut a swathe through the countryside, encamping outside Lopburi, only seventy kilometers from Ayutthaya.

"How has he gotten as far as Lopburi?" fumed the king. "Why were we not told about his advance? What has happened to our spies?"

"He is attacking like the Mongols. Swift attacks on horseback. King Voravongsa is encamped outside Lopburi, but the bulk of his army has yet to catch up," said Chao Phraya Kalahom Suriyavansa.

"Lopburi is poorly defended. King Maha Thammaracha had the walls taken down so they would not provide cover for the Burmese. They have only been partially rebuilt."

"Governor Pengnum in Phitsanulok has sent troops from the north. Our army is ready to move on your orders."

"We leave immediately. I will lead the army," said the king.

Although not a warrior-king, King Songtham rode in magnificence as his army, elephants, horses, and mercenaries made the short journey to Lopburi. When they arrived the young king of Lan Xang was not in the city. The army of King Songtham camped to the south of Lopburi and sent out scouts.

"What does he want from us? He is in no position to conquer Ayutthaya. He must know that?" wondered the king.

"I have learned from the sangha that he would motivate his men with the righting of the wrongs of the past when both we and the

Burmese took so many of their people in the time of King Naresuan," replied Chao Phraya Kalahom Suriyavansa.

"The Burmese took far more from Lan Xang that we did. It was King Bayinnaung's theater of war, not ours. Besides, King Setthathirath cost him many lives as he fought in the deep jungles of Lan Xang."

"But he paid the price eventually. The tales of the march to Burma, when nearly half of those taken died, are known to all of us."

"Then why attack us?"

"Glory, booty, or revenge for our support of his father."

"That support was King Ekathotsarot's policy, and one that has clearly failed. We will see what this young king wants before engaging him in battle. We have made the mistake of watching as King Anaukpetlun of Ava rebuilds the kingdom of Hanthawaddy, not realizing what was going on in Lan Xang. That is my error, and one I intend to put right with as little bloodshed as possible," said King Songtham.

The entrance to the war tent of King Songtham opened and four soldiers entered accompanied by a tall, thin man in Chinese silk.

"Their king has retreated to Phetchabun. He has left an ambassador here to discuss terms," said the captain smartly.

"Indeed. Let us see what the king of Lan Xang wants of us," said the king.

The ambassador, an elderly man, was brought before the king. He prostrated himself on the ground. After a moment the king told him to stand.

"You have wronged us greatly in the past," said the aging Chao Oun. "Our king rides against you to right those wrongs."

"You have taken our people. They are to be returned," said the king more curtly than he meant to.

"We took them as you took our people. King Voravongsa has ordered their release and his army is returning to Lan Xang."

"Why?"

"News has reached us that the Viet are marching in support of the dead king."

"Your king cannot expect us to merely walk away from your invasion of our territory."

"King Voravongsa has made his point. He is young and will learn. He is angered at your support of his father, which caused our civil war to go on far longer than it should have."

"That was the policy of King Ekathotsarot."

"It is not your policy?"

"I seek only peace and stability with our neighbor. Neither of us stands to gain anything in a protracted war."

"That is good news, and I will convey your sentiment to my king. King Voravongsa asks that you accept three white elephants as a gesture of peace—not submission—and hopes that matters will be righted between us."

"It seems that your king has overextended himself. We will send an embassy to Luang Prabang to discuss matters further, and we will accept the white elephants as evidence of your desire for peace," said the king.

"Our king asks that you look to your west. Our spies tell us that Ava covets Tavoy and Tenasserim and is planning an attack. He asks me to tell you this as a sign of our good faith," said Chao Oun.

"Then we wish you good fortune as you war with the Viet while we look west and war with the Burmese," said the king.

In 1613, King Anaukpetlun of Ava attacked Tavoy and Tenasserim in response to an alleged attack made by the Siamese governor of Tavoy on a town under Burmese control. One of the princes of King Anaukpetlun was captured and taken to Ayutthaya. In response the King of Ava immediately attacked with a small force of four thousand soldiers, one hundred horses, and only ten elephants. In December of 1613 his army defeated the Ayutthaya forces at Tavoy before continuing the attack on Tenasserim by land and sea.

King Anaukpetlun had learned from the mistakes of King Tabinshwehti, King Bayinnaung, and King Nanda Bayin. He had no intention of attacking the city of Ayutthaya, but the ports on the west coast of the Malay Peninsula had long been disputed, and he wanted them back under his remit.

The Burmese continued down the coast to Tenasserim but were driven back with the help of four galleys manned by the Portuguese.

The forces of King Anaukpetlun were driven off, and in January of 1614 Tavoy was retaken by the Siamese.

King Anaukpetlun simply switched the theater of war from the west coast of the Malay Peninsula to another area of interest to Ayutthaya, Lan Na. He had earlier installed his brother in Chiang Saen. He then sent in two armies totaling seventeen thousand soldiers. King Thado Kyaw of Chiang Mai sought support from Ayutthaya, but King Songtham decided to let the war run its course and not interfere.

The Burmese forces finally encircled the combined forces of Lan Na and Lan Xang in the Chiang Mai and Lamphun basin in December of 1614. The city of Chiang Mai surrendered to the Burmese.

"What does he really want?" asked King Songtham.

"He has no intention of trying to invade Ayutthaya," replied Chao Phraya Kalahom Suriyavansa. "And to make war on two fronts stretches his resources too far. His army is simply too small. The wars with us cost us many people but, in the end, decimated the men of Hanthawaddy."

"It is as if he is goading us to attack him."

"No, I think not. He understands that our business with Burma is done. Our people would not support another war after what they went through, and I think it is the last thing he wants."

"So he wants either the ports or Lan Na, but not both."

"He knows we regard Lan Na as part of our remit. We have fought many years for Tavoy and Tenasserim, but the Burmese have long regarded them as part of their sphere of influence."

"Then he wants to trade. Is that what you are saying?"

"He is a clever man. He knows we could take Lan Na if we really wanted to. The kingdom is divided and a shadow of what it was under King Mangrai. He wants the ports. I am more certain than ever," said Chao Phraya Kalahom Suriyavansa.

"But first he will want Martaban," said the king.

Martaban was ruled by Binnya Dala. Ostensibly it was a tributary state of Ayutthaya and had been since the time of King Naresuan. In reality Binnya Dala ruled the strategically important city as a king. This suited the best interests of King Songtham as the city was a buffer between Ayutthaya and a resurgent Burma.

Time proved King Songtham and Chao Phraya Kalahom Suriyavansa right. King Anaukpetlun moved his army quickly, leaving Chiang Mai and marching on Martaban, the city that controlled the northern entrance to the Three Pagodas Pass. When news reached Ayutthaya, reinforcements were sent to Ye, a small town to the south of Martaban, to halt any further incursion into Ayutthayan territory. No attempt was made to retake Martaban. The stalemate was ended by diplomacy in 1615 when the Burmese ceded sovereignty of Chiang Mai to Ayutthaya in return for Martaban. Both sides knew that eventually the Burmese would move again on Tavoy and Tenasserim, but now was not the time.

No sooner had the peace been agreed than news came of a massacre of Siamese troops stationed in the Khmer kingdom since the time of King Naresuan. King Songtham readied his troops and the navy to launch an attack. The king asked both the Portuguese and the Dutch to support him, but no help was forthcoming. Both nations were in Southeast Asia for trade, and they traded with both countries. They had no desire to become embroiled in a local war. The first Siamese army was led into an ambush, where they suffered a heavy defeat, while the Siamese navy saw no action and returned. This war would continue until 1622 when a tentative peace was agreed.

Around this time a delegation of monks traveled to Sri Lanka on a pilgrimage to the Buddha's footprint there. When they arrived, the Sri Lankan monks were puzzled.

"Why would you come here to see the Buddha's footprint?" they asked. "We have been taught that your own kingdom has just such a footprint."

When the pilgrims reported what they had been told. King Songtham ordered that a hunt for it should be carried out across his realm.

In Saraburi, a hunter named Bun was chasing a deer he had wounded. It disappeared into some brush and then emerged unscathed. Bun then crawled through and found a hole full of water. Bun then cleared the area, uncovering the footprint of Buddha. Bun reported his find to the governor, who in turn reported it to the king. The king set out to visit the footprint. Led by Bun the hunter, King Songtham saw the holy footprint and drank from the water in it. He dedicated the land surrounding the footprint to be the site for a temple, and from then on visiting the footprint of the Buddha was an annual pilgrimage for the kings of Ayutthaya, a tradition that would last until the end of the city.

The emperor or king of Siam is surrounded by as much magnificence and such splendid ceremonial as any other king in all the Indies. His foot never touches earth; wherever he wishes to go, he is carried on a golden throne, and he shows himself once a day to the lords and nobles of his court with a display of ostentation which exceeds that of any Christian king. This magnificence and grandeur cannot be imagined or believed by those who have not seen it, and though I have often observed these at the court and elsewhere, and have been invited to pay my respects to His Majesty, I am unable to describe adequately the scene.

Some years before this Dutch trader's description of the court of King Songtham, the British East India Company ship the *Globe* reconnoitered the Gulf of Siam in 1612. Its merchants set up a factory at Pattani and went to Ayutthaya to deliver a letter from King James I. The English were received cordially by King Songtham and received permission to set up a factory in Ayutthaya.

In the year 1616 King Songtham sent the first of a number of missions to the Tokugawa shogunate. The Japanese shogun had promoted cordial relations with the Thai kingdom since the reign of King Ekathotsarot. During King Songtham's rule, ties between Japan and Thailand grew even stronger. Thailand dispatched several envoys to Japan, and the shogun always responded to Thai letters, such as one requesting that Japan refrain from involvement in any actions taken by Thailand to keep Cambodia in line. The shogun replied that it was an internal matter and added that the Japanese in Thailand were traders who should not become involved in domestic affairs. Therefore, if ever they interfered in internal politics, Thai rulers were free to punish them. King Songtham communicated regularly with the shogun and, during his reign, the relationship between the two countries reached its peak. In one such friendly exchange of letters, King Songtham wrote,

> The existence of a sea separating [Siam] and Japan has made contact between our two nations difficult. However, merchant ships of both nations now ply regularly between our two countries, causing relations to become even closer. It is now apparent that you (the Shogun) have sincere affection for us, an affection even stronger than that of our immediate kin."

The shogun replied,

> The cordial relations between our two countries cannot be destroyed. Since we both have mutual trust, the existence of a sea between us is not of any significance.

Yamada Nagamasa was a Japanese adventurer and trader who came to Ayutthaya in 1612. Over time he gained the ear of King Songtham and rose through the ranks of Thai nobility. He became the head of the Japanese village known as Ban Yipun and in this position supported King Songtham's military campaigns at the head of a Japanese army flying the Japanese flag.

Ban Yipun was home to around one thousand Japanese inhabitants. Christian converts, attracted by Ayutthaya's welcoming of all religions, came in increasing numbers to the city following the persecution by the Japanese shoguns. Ronin, unemployed Samurai who had been on the losing side of some battles in Japan, also came. But the mainstay of Ban Yipun was the traders who worked to extend their influence at court, usually at the expense of the Dutch.

Yamada Nagamasa traveled to Japan in 1624 on behalf of King Songtham and again in 1629. He was rewarded for his efforts by King Songtham and was finally named governor of Nakhon Si Thammarat, where he was accompanied by three hundred samurai.

Both the Dutch and the English closed their "godowns" (warehouses) in 1622. With the incursion into their business by the Japanese, there were more profitable markets to develop.

@ww

King Songtham had appointed his brother Prince Si Sin as upparat. Late in his reign the king decided that his son Prince Chetthathirat was rightfully entitled to be king, and when King Songtham died in 1628 Prince Chetthathirat ascended the throne.

Prince Si Sin had taken the precaution of entering the monkhood. The Japanese trader-turned-Thai-noble Yamada Nagamasa lured the prince away from his sanctuary by offering the support of his Japanese troops. The prince left his sanctuary only to be seized. The supporters of Prince Si Sin were purged, and the prince was thrown into a pit and left to die.

Luang Mongkhon, a supporter of the prince, rescued him by tunneling to where the prince was being held prisoner. A dead slave was brought into the pit and the prince exchange clothes with the corpse. Then the real prince escaped. In the morning, the guards saw the dead "prince," filled in the pit, and notified Okya Suriyawong, now minister of defense under King Chetthathirat, that the prince had died.

Prince Si Sin organized a rebellion and marched on Ayutthaya, to no avail. Prince Si Sin was captured, returned to Ayutthaya, and executed in the customary manner on the orders of King Chetthathirat.

Luang Mongkhon, the rescuer of Prince Si Sin, was captured in a failed attempt to kill Okya Suriyawong. After being sentenced to death, he was chained and put into position for his execution. Wih his great strength, however, he snapped the chains and charged forward before he was tackled and finally subdued. He was then told he would be spared if he agreed to end his rebellious ways and serve the king. He stared back.

"How can I do so? The King is dead."

King Chetthathirat now ruled unopposed, and honors were heaped on Okya Suriyawong. Within a year it was clear that Okya Suriyawong was accumulating so much power that he was rivaling the king's authority.

The mother of Okya Suriyawong died, and he held an extravagant cremation ceremony that lasted for several days. Every government official was obliged to attend. The king became annoyed that he was unable to conduct business, and issued threats against Okya Suriyawong. But Okya Suriyawong moved first. He insisted his life was in danger and ordered his soldiers to enter the royal palace and capture King Chetthathirat, who was summarily executed. Okya Suriyawong replaced him with his eleven-year-old half-brother, Prince Athittayawong. Okya Suriyawong became regent and declared himself upparat. But this last coup had cost him. His ambition was now clear for all to see.

Okya Suriyawong again moved quickly, removing threats to his power. Yamada Nagamasa went back to Nakhon Si Thammarat, far away from Ayutthaya. Thirty-eight days after being crowned, King Athittayawong, described as "too childish," was deposed and executed. Okya Suriyawong took the regnal name of King Prasat Thong. With the death of King Athittayawong the royal line of Sukhothai came to an end.

Within a year Yamada Nagamasa, leader of the Japanese community and friend to King Songtham, was dead, poisoned by an assassin.

Prasat Thong Dynasty

23

KING PRASAT THONG 1629–56
KING CHAI 1656
KING SUTHAMMARACHA 1656

THE DUTCH MERCHANT JEREMIAS VAN VLIET tells that King Prasat Thong, born in the year 1600, was the illegitimate son of King Ekathotsarot. His story relates that King Ekathotsarot was shipwrecked on Bang Pa-In Island near Ayutthaya and while there was befriended by a local woman; the result of their liaison was the future king.

Many, however, claimed he was just a scheming noble who had already had a checkered career before his rumored hand in the death of King Songtham and his certain involvement in the death of the two princes. They regarded him as a usurper who held no hereditary claim to the throne, and he would have a troubled reign.

On news that the usurper had taken the throne of Ayutthaya, the northern province of Lan Na, which had been ceded to Ayutthaya during the reign of King Songtham, declared independence. King Prasat Thong responded by heading an army to retake Lan Na and its capital city of Chiang Mai in a ruthless campaign. In order to terrorize the population the king promised that he would put to death the first four women he met. This he did, smearing their blood on the deck of his boat as it lay moored in the Ping River. However, the campaign proved unsuccessful and the king withdrew. King Tado Tammaraja of Ava captured Chiang Mai in 1632, and the Lan Na prince was deposed. The Burmese installed Phaya Luang Thipphanet as king, leaving Chiang Mai under direct Burmese control for the next century.

Cambodia also refused to accept the usurper as their king and rebelled, declaring independence from Ayutthaya. On hearing that the Khmer king had aligned himself with the Japanese expelled from Ayutthaya and that they were planning an invasion of Ayutthaya, the king dispatched an army that returned with trophies and examples of Cambodian architecture but little else. The king realized that the resources of the kingdom and the changing face of warfare would not allow for a repetition of King Naresuan's wars, and although plans were drawn up for an attack on the Khmer they were abandoned.

☙

"Both Yamada Nagamasa and his son are dead, but I remain unconvinced of the loyalty of the Japanese in Ban Yipun, the Japanese village," said Okya Sangiamyu.

"I agree. They blame me for the death of Yamada," said King Prasat Thong.

His son, Oin Yamada, fought bravely defending Nakhon Si Thammarat against my army. When he left he set half the city ablaze. Do they blame me for his death also?" asked the king.

"He was killed by our troops after he joined with the Khmer. It would not surprise me if they blame you for his death."

"Then you question their loyalty?"

"It is more than that. They regard themselves highly. They have an arrogance toward others that upsets many of our people. They regard their enclave as their domain, not allowing others to enter or leave without permission."

"They are important to our economy. Their ships bring us exquisite goods and the silk we rely on so much in the heat of summer," said the king.

"In the reign of King Songtham the Japanese stormed the royal palace. They are excellent fighters and craftsmen of the highest order, but I feel their loyalty is questionable."

"Let us surprise them with a visit," said King Prasat Thong. "Bring twenty of our best men and our interpreters. I would like to judge the Japanese for myself."

The king and his entourage headed through the open wooden gates of Ban Yipun. Those at the gates fell to the ground in supplication.

To the king's left three men appeared out of an ornate wooden house. They were dressed in samurai clothing and carrying their *daisho,* the long and short swords of the samurai. King Prasat Thong's soldiers immediately drew their weapons. The samurai were standing and carrying weapons in the presence of the king. Both were reasons for death.

The king indicated for his men to sheathe their weapons. The shorter of the men, bald with broad shoulders, spoke to the king in the language of the court.

"King Prasat Thong, you honor us with your visit," said Iwakura Heimon, the headman of the Ban Yipun.

The king waited for fully one minute before speaking.

"You stand in my presence, and you carry weapons. Do you not understand our laws and customs?" asked the king.

"I understand. In our land it would not be proper to greet a person of your rank without wearing the proper dress."

"And the weapons?"

"These swords are made of the finest Edo steel. To not wear them in your presence would not only be an insult to Your Majesty but would also be an insult to the swords."

"You think our laws do not apply to you?"

"We respect your laws, but as a samurai I respect the laws, culture, and traditions of Japan."

"But you are ronin. You have no master. You are not samurai."

The three Japanese placed their hands on the hilt of their swords but did not draw them.

"We are samurai. I can trace my ancestry back through twenty generations."

"You and your people cause me concern," said the king staring directly at the Japanese headman.

"We are samurai. We are not afraid. It is not our wish to cause offense."

"And if you were to cause offense?"

"We are prepared to accept the consequences."

The king returned to the royal palace and turned to Okya Sangiamyu.

"So they are willing to die for their beliefs," he said.

"It would appear so. To stand in your presence, and to do so armed, shows no respect."

"But in their eyes it does show respect."

"I have doubts. The samurai seem to welcome death. An honorable death. Perhaps their headman was goading you. Perhaps he feels you will give him the honorable death he seeks?"

"Then let us honor his request," said the king after a few moments reflection.

The following day the king sent thousands of troops to attack the Japanese village and burn it down. Iwakura Heimon took a heavy toll of King Prasat Thong's men before dying honorably in battle. Those who succeeded in escaping with their lives, mainly the craftsmen and artisans, were unable to return to Japan under the edict of the Japanese shogun, so the majority fled to Cambodia.

From the year 1634, the Tokugawa shogun, informed of the troubles that had taken place in Ayutthaya and for what he perceived to be attacks on his authority, refused to acknowledge the rule of King Prasat Thong, branding him a usurper. The shogun refused to issue any further shipments to Siam. In an attempt to regain the favor of the shogun, King Prasat Thong sent an embassy and a trading ship to Japan in 1636, but the embassy was refused.

A number of Japanese returned to Ayutthaya after being granted amnesty by the king, but the once-thriving community of Ban Yipun was vastly reduced.

The war against Spain—and against Portugal, its partner in the Iberian Union—continued into the reign of King Prasat Thong. The king looked to the Dutch to counter the impact of Ayutthaya's European aggressors.

The Dutch were eager to increase their involvement with Ayutthaya. They were charmed by the canals that allowed people to paddle throughout the city, and they saw it was bustling with people buying and selling their goods.

A VOC ambassador arrived in Ayutthaya in September of 1633. With King Songtham dead, now was the time to forge a new alliance with King Prasat Thong. The ambassador breached protocol by taking the letter and the gifts to the VOC compound himself, and the Dutch had to surreptitiously return the letter and the gifts to the ship without the knowledge of the Siamese.

The returned letter was duly collected by Siamese officials and transferred to the royal barge to be taken to the king. During the transport of the letter the Dutch again showed their lack of cultural understanding by firing a cannon, meant as a salute to the king. The ambassador was forced to explain that in his country the firing of the cannon was regarded as a tribute.

The king gave a length of cloth "of low value and with weird pattern" to the ambassador, who in turn felt this was patronizing to the Dutch because it implied the Dutch required money and commodities. Nonetheless, the Dutch ambassador and his party were well received by the court. There were thousands of people alongside ranks of ornately adorned elephants. The ambassador approached, body bent and hands folded, crawling on his hands and knees and performing the required gesture of respect to the place where the king was shielded behind curtains. The ambassador was allowed to enter and to speak with the king, whose grandiose costume and glittering crown impressed the ambassador. The ambassador was told later that the king had never before held such a long conversation with a foreigner.

The letter from Prince Frederick Henry was placed in "the most splendid spot of [the king's] throne under a ceiling decorated with gold and precious stones where the gold statues of the late kings also stood, and beside two other missives"—one from the shogun of Japan and one from the emperor of China. Cultural misunderstanding aside, the visit cemented Siamese-Dutch relations.

However, within two years relations were again strained. On December 10, 1636, a party of Dutchmen spent a day carousing on the Lopburi River. They drank heavily and behaved badly. They intruded on the monks and worshipers at Wat Worachet and even attacked the house of the king's brother.

"They have desecrated temples, attacked my house, and abused people. They must be punished!" said the king's brother angrily.

"I agree, brother. This behavior cannot be tolerated," replied the king, sharing his brother's anger.

"They have been arrested and sit in the palace in the cells."

King Prasat Thong sentenced two of their leaders to be tied to a post and left in the baking sun before being trampled to death by elephants. The king in his anger also placed restrictions on all the trading activities of the VOC.

Jeremias van Vliet was acting director of the VOC. It fell to him to resolve the situation. After six weeks of negotiations and giving presents to the king and his principal officials, van Vliet was granted an audience. He crawled in like one of the king's subjects. By signing an undertaking stating that all the Dutch in the kingdom pledged themselves to absolutely obey the orders of the king, he was able to obtain their release, but not before they were bound in chains and displayed for the public in the center of Ayutthaya.

King Prasat Thong told van Vliet,

> You will henceforth carry the weight of your men. I shall hold you personally responsible. Since you are their head, it is just that you look after your members and you assume responsibility for them.

Perhaps more telling, van Vliet also recorded that the king himself was frequently drunk:

> This drunkenness (which occurs very often and often reaches a dangerous limit) has caused many evils during his reign and is frequently the reason why innocent blood has been shed.

The matter was not ended. Van Vliet was severely reprimanded by his superiors for having allowed himself to be humiliated and for signing on behalf of the VOC an agreement that tarnished the company's esteem. In 1638, the governor-general in Batavia expressed his outrage in a letter to King Prasat Thong, who reacted angrily at being written to in this manner by "a mandarin of the Dutch king" and said that not even his enemies treated him with such disrespect. In time the anger of the king mellowed. He weighed the importance of the Dutch to Ayutthaya and made a calculated decision—perhaps not one he was comfortable with, but one that served his kingdom's best interest. For the sake of his long friendship with the Dutch, the king chose to formally receive the Dutch letter and its bearer, van Vliet, as part of the ceremony of the oath of allegiance. No foreign dignitary had ever received this honor previously.

In 1642, shortly after Jeremias van Vliet left Ayutthaya, Sultan Sulaiman of Songkhla declared independence, triggering decades of conflict. King Prasat Thong sent an expedition to subdue the colony. The Dutch in Batavia gave orders that some vessels were to be sent to aid the Siamese fleet, but due to a dispute with England the Dutch ships never arrived. Westerwolt, the successor to van Vliet, was treated with great indignity when he returned to Siam, and was informed that any attempt to interfere in Siamese affairs again would result in his being trampled to death by elephants, together with all his compatriots.

The tempestuous relationship continued throughout King Prasat Thong's reign; however, the unpredictable king is reported to have sent to Batavia an impressive array of goods including a gold crown and twelve elephants in the year 1650, six years before his death.

King Prasat Thong was a deeply disturbed man, and unhappy throughout his reign. He was constantly seeing threats to the throne and to his life. The king increasingly trusted no one. His advisers came and went. Still regarded by many as a usurper of the throne, he lived in constant fear of assassination. The king had earlier ordered three infant princes executed, together with a blind prince whom he suspected of being disloyal.

March of 1638 was also the start of the year 1000 of the Chulasakarat calendar. King Songtham feared that a calamity would occur and determined to avoid it by changing the name of the year. He changed the number of the year and renamed it as the year of the pig. He sent word urging King Tado Tammaraja of Ava to do the same. However, the Burmese king had already ordained one thousand monks to avoid any danger and dismissed the idea. On hearing this King Prasat Thong flew into a rage, and the Burmese ambassador who had delivered this news fled in fear.

In the year 1635, one of the king's daughters died. Following the cremation, part of her body remained unburned. The king took it as a sign that his daughter had been poisoned. Mad in his suspicions, he had all the women who had been in attendance placed under guard, and tried to extort by torture information about the imaginary crime. The entire court endured punishments, but not even this could appease the cruelty of the king. The nobles of the kingdom were summoned, and he had trenches dug and filled with hot coals so as to put them to the ordeal by fire. The torture began by scraping the soles of the feet with a sharp piece of iron before they were made to walk over the coals. Those whose feet were injured were held to be guilty.

The king falsely accused the eldest daughter of the late king of "having given an exhibition of unholy glee" at the cremation of his daughter. She was condemned to the ordeal by fire, together with all her ladies. The pain was such that she confessed to the charge. The executioner was ordered to cut off part of her flesh and make her eat it. At this she cried out to the king,

> "Vile tyrant! You can rend my body, but remember that my spirit is not under your command. You will observe that the fixity of my purpose renders me superior to your tortures. Learn also that your crimes will not go unpunished and that my blood shall be a seed from which shall arise the avengers of my family and country."

The king was a great patron and supporter of the sangha. He built many new temples and renovated old ones, not only in Ayutthaya but throughout the country. It was important to make merit, particularly after the manner in which he acquired the throne. It was also important that the sangha portray him in the right light to the general populace.

After reigning for twenty-seven years, King Prasat Thong died in August 1656 without clearly appointing an heir. In consequence the throne of Ayutthaya was claimed by three factions: the brother of King Prasat Thong, Prince Chai (his son who had been born before his enthronement), and finally Phra Narai (who was born of a queen who was a daughter of King Songtham.)

Prince Chai seized the royal palace immediately after his father's death and claimed the throne as King Chai. The king's brother and Phra Narai combined their forces and overthrew him on his first day. King Prasat Thong's brother took the throne as King Suthammaracha. Friction between King Suthammaracha and Phra Narai was kindled by Okya Chakri, who is thought to have been motivated by his own desire to succeed King Suthammaracha, who had no male heir. Phra Narai's men were assaulted, sent out of the capital, and some murdered. On October 26, Phra Narai did not appear in the court on the day he was expected. King Suthammaracha took this to be a rebellious act and issued an edict condemning him.

Despite the king's edict Phra Narai gained widespread support. His sister had been the recipient of unwelcome advances by King Suthammaracha and had to be spirited out of the palace in a cabinet. He secured the favor of his younger brothers and then gained support in the unlikely guise of Okya Chakri, whose brother had been beheaded at the behest of King Suthammaracha. Phra Narai also recruited support from the foreign communities in Ayutthaya. Meeting only limited defense, Phra Narai's attack on the royal palace quickly succeeded. King Suthammaracha was captured and taken to Wat Khok Phraya, where he met the customary end after a reign of only three months.

24

KING NARAI THE GREAT

1656–88

PART 1

In that year [1633], the princess consort gave birth to a son. When the royal family glanced at the infant, they saw the baby had four arms before having two arms as normal. Upon learning this, the king thought it was a miracle. Therefore he named his son "Narai" [another name for Vishnu, who is usually shown with four arms].

Royal Chronicles of Siam

The King is below the average height, but very straight and well set up. His demeanour is attractive, and his manners full of gentleness and kindness. He is lively and active and an enemy to sloth. He is always either in the forest hunting elephants, or in his palace, attending to State affairs. He is not fond of war, but when forced to take up the sword, no Eastern monarch has a stronger passion for glory.

Father Tachard

KING NARAI SUCCEEDED TO THE THRONE of Siam in 1656 at the age of twenty-four. His realm stretched south to the kingdoms of Pattani, Ligor (Nakhon Si Thammarat), Phatthalung, and Songkhla; to the east, where the Khmer had acknowledged Ayutthaya's suzerainty; and to the west, where the port of Tenasserim lay under Siamese control.

When he acceded to the throne King Narai immediately challenged tradition by not moving into the king's palace after his coronation.

In time he took to spending a large part of the year in Lopburi, fifty kilometers to the north of Ayutthaya, distancing himself from the royal capital, the symbolic center of his power. In many ways during King Narai's reign it was Lopburi that was the true center of power.

The violent deaths of two monarchs within three months had unsettled the country, and initially King Narai did not feel very secure upon his throne. He had not been king for long when two of his younger brothers were accused of plotting against him. They were both executed.

In the mid-seventeenth century the Chinese empire, now under the Manchus, attacked Burma over who could claim tribute from the Shan territories. Prince Saenluang of Chiang Mai was concerned. What if the Chinese turned in his direction? He begged King Narai for help. King Narai sent the first of his armies north in November of 1660, sensing the opportunity to regain control of the Burmese-dominated region of Lan Na.

His fears proved unfounded as news reached Chiang Mai that the Chinese had returned to their homeland. Prince Saenluang now faced other issues. He had requested the help of Ayutthaya, which was preparing to come to his aid, and if his Burmese overlords knew of his request for help from King Narai he would be viewed as disloyal.

The Ayutthayan king sent his army as requested but was angered when he received news that his presence was no longer required. King Narai set out to take Chiang Mai. His force proved inadequate, but he resolved to return the following year with a larger and better-equipped force.

The army that set out to take Chiang Mai, led by Chao Phraya Kosa, first seized Lampang and Lamphun, capturing a great deal of weaponry, elephants, horses, and the local Yuan people. The Siamese army faced strong resistance but relentlessly fought their way through the barricades and obstacles that the defenders had placed around the city of Chiang Mai.

Chao Phraya Kosa erected a stockade to the south of the city and, confident of victory, sent a report to King Narai in Ayutthaya. The king was pleased. He readied his own substantial army and commanded Chao Phraya Kosa not to take the city until he arrived.

Inside the city fear spread as the king arrived in force. The defenders of Chiang Mai readied containers holding gravel, sand, and lime powder, and placed logs along the walls to push down on the invaders below.

King Narai rested for two days before ordering the assault. His soldiers, dressed in leather for protection, readied over one thousand ladders for the attack. The elephants and horses, armored in leather and protected by amulets and reliquaries, steadied themselves as loud explosions sounded the attack.

The king sat on his favorite war elephant, Subduer of Ten Directions, and had lit a firework as a signal of attack. As he did so the cannon were fired at the city walls and his men advanced. The Siamese soldiers clambered over the damaged walls and with surprisingly few losses charged into the city, killing soldiers and civilians alike. The king of Chiang Mai was captured together with all his wives and children. The Burmese later launched a counterattack to regain the city but were repelled.

King Narai remained in Chiang Mai for fifteen days. To cement the new relationship he married a princess of Chiang Mai. On his departure King Narai took as a trophy of his victory the famous Phra Sing Buddha image to Ayutthaya, as King Trailok had done many centuries before. Eventually, however, the territory was slowly won back by the Burmese, and in 1664 Chiang Mai rebelled, evicted King Narai's troops, and restored Burmese rule.

By the start of King Narai's reign in 1656, Ayutthaya had a population of perhaps a million people. The first French Catholic missionary arrived in Ayutthaya in 1662 and was joined by others two years later. King Narai was curious about both religion and science, and the missionaries were given land on which to build churches and establish schools. Very quickly they established themselves and became an important force in relations between the two countries.

In 1659, the kingdom of the Khmer erupted into civil war over which of two brothers was to assume the throne. Taking full advantage of the upheaval, the Nguyen lords to the southeast attacked. A number of English traders there fled to Ayutthaya, where they eventually reopened a factory for the East India Company.

The return of the English did not sit well with the Dutch, who had received small concessions during the reign of King Prasat Thong. They wanted more from the new king. When the king refused they sent ships to blockade the Chao Phraya River. The Siamese fleet was no match for the Dutch fleet. King Narai reluctantly backed down and granted many of the Dutch demands, including a stipulation that Siam stop employing Chinese and Japanese people on their ships—a major blow to Ayutthaya's ability to carry out its trade with China.

One provision of the treaty harked back to problems during the reign of King Prasat Thong:

> In case (which God forbid) any of the Company's residents should commit a serious crime in Siam, the King and the Judges shall not have the right to judge him, but he must be handed over to the Company's Chief, to be punished according to the Netherlands laws.

"The Dutch have humiliated us," stormed the king. "They set terms and dismiss our laws."

"We have given them our trust and they have abused us," replied Chao Phraya Kosa, echoing the anger of the king.

"They dare to dictate terms of trade to us. They are useful, but there is a limit to their usefulness."

"They are afraid of the English, who seem to have a fearsome reputation among all the foreigners. But the English seem to want only to trade. They have no interest in our domestic politics."

"We need to find a way to reduce our reliance on the Dutch. The Portuguese have not proven their worth, and the Spanish seem little more than pirates. The French missionaries have been requesting

an audience for some time. Perhaps it is time to listen to what they
have to say."

℮ww

It was in the year 1660 that the first French bishops and priests
left France under the banner of a new missionary order established
by Pope Alexander VII. Bishop Pierre Lambert de la Motte, the first
apostolic vicar of Cochin, accompanied by Fathers de Bourges and
Deydier traveled to Asia on donkeys, on camels, or by foot, as the
Catholic Church was not allowed to move them by sea.

They arrived in Tenasserim, the city that lay on the west coast of
the kingdom of Ayutthaya, after a journey of over twenty months.
There they visited a Buddhist monk. Father Jacques de Bourges wrote
of the encounter:

> The whole region of Tenasserim professes paganism and idolatry,
> and lives in total ignorance of God and eternal salvation. . . .
> We found the poor man full of darkness, contradictions and
> absurdities. . . . However, he made it clear to us that he valued
> Christian people and thought well of their religion, without
> rejecting his own, and that the higher esteem the sanctity of
> Christian religion is held in, is the only reason why they tolerate
> those who profess it. And in fact, religious freedom could not
> be greater.

The mission finally arrived in Ayutthaya in 1662, and was followed
by another in 1664. The French priests clashed with the Portuguese
Jesuits and Dominicans already established in Ayutthaya, but
gradually they gained the ear of the king. Bishop Pierre Lambert de
la Motte was invited to an audience with King Narai.

"Bishop Lambert, your religion is of great interest to me," said the
king. "I will think more on it. In the meantime a request."

"Anything, Your Majesty," said Bishop Lambert, perhaps a little
too keenly.

"You talk of your God performing miracles, of him being able to cure the sick and the lame," said the king.

"Yes, Your Majesty," said the French bishop, concerned with direction the conversation was taking.

"Prince Aphaithot, my half-brother, is stricken with paralysis. It is my request that you ask your God to intervene and cure him of this illness," said the king.

"Of course, Your Majesty," blustered the French Bishop. "But as I have said during our talks I can offer no guarantee as to whether the Lord will intervene."

"Where the body of one so young is involved, and where his actions could result in many more souls for his church, why would he not intervene?" asked the king.

The recently constructed church, bedecked in flowers to welcome the king, gleamed under a new coat of white paint. The king's seven-year-old half-brother was carried into the church by two bearers. The bearers placed the young prince at the foot of the altar and stepped back. Bishop Pierre Lambert prayed, as did the others in the mission. The recently formed choir sang hymns to glorify God, prayers were said, but nothing happened. The young prince was carried out by his bearers past the king.

"You are to see me tomorrow. My officials will make the arrangements," said the king.

It was with trepidation that Bishop Lambert and Bishop Laneau prostrated themselves before the king the following day.

"I would like to thank you for Father Thomas," began the king. "His skills in the design and the building of our new forts at Bangkok, Ayutthaya, and Nonthaburi have been most welcome."

"Thank you, Your Majesty," said a very relieved Bishop Lambert. "Consider him in your service."

"I am to rebuild Lopburi and would value his skills. That is, if you can spare him?"

"Of course, Your Majesty," replied Bishop Lambert.

"Good. Now, to business," said the king. Both French bishops steeled themselves, but when it came it was not what they expected.

"Bishop Lambert, Bishop Laneau," translated the French priest Bénigne Vachet. "You have requested me on a number of occasions to send an embassy to your king in Versailles. I would like that to be arranged."

"Yes, Your Majesty," said Bishop Lambert. As the two French bishops backed out of the audience hall the king allowed himself a slight smile. King Narai could see the French as a counterweight to the Dutch.

It would take many years to organize the embassy of Bishop Pierre Lambert and his fellow clerics to return to Europe. Bishop Laneau remained behind, starting a seminary and slowly gaining converts. Bishop Lambert returned to Europe where he regaled Pope Alexander VII and King Louis XIV of France with wondrous accounts of Siam, the city of Ayutthaya, and its king—a king he claimed was on the verge of converting to Christianity. The pope promised his full support of the bishop's endeavors in Siam, and King Louis XIV, on hearing how the work of Father Thomas had been so highly appreciated, sent engineers and architects to help the Siamese king.

In 1685 a Persian embassy made its way upriver to Ayutthaya in order to meet King Narai and "guide him into the fold of Islam."

The Persians were welcomed by King Narai in much the same way as the French had been some years earlier. There was already a strong Muslim presence in Ayutthaya, but this embassy was different. Although the Persians arrived with gifts their main interest was not trade but the conversion of the king and the nation of Ayutthaya to the Islamic faith.

King Narai viewed the Persians as another possible counterweight to the Dutch, who continued to irritate the king immensely. In a similar manner to hearing about the Catholic faith from the bishops, the king listened and questioned intently as Shah Sulaimān explained his religion. The Persians did not think highly of Siamese ways, even after a royal banquet in their honor:

> The food of the Siamese in no way resembles normal, proper foods, and the natives are not familiar with intelligent methods of preparing meals. In fact no one in Siam really knows how to

cook and eat, or even how to sit correctly at a table. The Siamese
have only recently arrived from the world of bestiality to the
realm of humanity.

The French missionaries were greatly perturbed by the Muslim
embassy. Their fears were not necessary. King Narai was not impressed
by the merits of the religion. Later in his reign the king said that "if
he were ever to change his religion he would certainly never become
a Mohammedan."

The letters were duly presented, but the gifts had been left behind
at Bantam. The presents never arrived. A Siamese vessel that was sent
to bring them was captured by the Dutch after it left the port, and
the gifts were confiscated.

In 1680, King Narai sent the first Siamese embassy to France.
Astrologers, who were held in high esteem within the Siamese court,
foretold disaster should Siamese officials board the foreign ship.
Nevertheless, they boarded the *Soleil d'Orient*, a French merchant
ship. Along with valuable cargo including gifts for the king, they took
with them a letter to the king of France, written on a sheet of gold
that offered to cede Songkhla to France as a gesture of good faith. The
vessel never arrived, and it is thought to have been lost somewhere
between Madagascar and the Cape of Good Hope. It was years before
the news to arrived in Ayutthaya.

KING NARAI THE GREAT
1656–88
PART 2

Although the prince devotes himself assiduously to affairs of state and to the good government of the kingdom, he also allows some time for his diversions. His favourite pastime is hunting tigers and elephants and this he does all the time that he is at Louveau [Lopburi], that is to say from November to the end of July or the beginning of August. Never has there been a prince more skillful or fortunate than he. Never a year passes during which he fails to take more than three hundred elephants. He reserves the most beautiful for his own use and presents those who are less so to the mandarins who are in favor or who have rendered him the greatest services. The rest he sells to foreigners, who send them to the Mogul and to neighbouring kingdoms. But the enjoyment which the king derives from this hunting is dearly paid for by the thirty thousand men who are usually employed for it. Many of them die of exhaustion, some being obliged to run night and day in the forests to discover and take by force the strongholds where these animals take refuge, while others are ceaselessly occupied in constructing terraces and palisades to prevent them from escaping.

Nicolas Gervaise

IN 1675 the *Phoenix,* an East India Company ship under the command of Captain George White docked at Ayutthaya. Captain White's factor on that ship was Constantine Phaulkon—his original surname, Gerakis, meant "falcon." Born on the Greek island of Cephalonia around the year 1648, the young Phaulkon ran away from home at the age of ten and joined an English ship. After cruss-crossing the Mediterranean, Phaulkon headed to Asia, finally settling in Ayutthaya. It was not long before he was one of the most prominent foreigners in the city. When even King Narai took a liking to him, Phaulkon was placed in charge of foreign trade and given the title Luang Wichayen.

The appointment of Phaulkon was considered an affront by the East India Company. He had left their employ. To the East India Company he was an "interloper," an English merchant who traded independently of the company. Phaulkon encouraged other interlopers—perhaps to get back at his old employers—but the simmering ill-feeling between him and the East India Company tended to turn his favor, over time, more toward the French.

Over time Phaulkon created many jealousies from both foreign merchants and the Siamese nobility, who could not understand why their king was so influenced by this foreigner.

> He was one of those in the world who have the most wit, liberality, magnificence, intrepidity, and was full of great projects, but perhaps he only wanted to have French troops in order to try and make himself king after the death of his master, which he saw as imminent. He was proud, cruel, pitiless, and with inordinate ambition. He supported the Christian religion because it could support him; but I would never have trusted him in things in which his advancement was not involved.

By the time news of the ill-fated *Soleil d'Orient* reached Ayutthaya the brilliant career of Phaulkon was underway. Privy to the king's thoughts, he urged the king to send another embassy to France. This time only two high-ranking officials departed for France in January of 1684, reaching Paris safely by the end of the year. The two envoys showed no interest in following French court protocol or customs. When brought before King Louis XIV in the Hall of Mirrors in

Versailles, they crawled forward as they would if approaching King Narai.

With the help of their interpreter, Béninge Vachet, they successfully convinced the king's ministers that it would be in the interest of France to send an impressive embassy to Siam. Vachet also implied that King Narai might convert to Christianity. This exaggeration on his part would lead to future conflicts and misunderstandings.

The Sun King had Alexandre de Chaumont lead the embassy and made Abbé de Choisy second-in-command. A number of priests accompanied them, including Father Guy Tachard. After stopping in Cape Town and Batavia, the two ships of the embassy arrived safely at Ayutthaya in September of 1685.

This first official French embassy was welcomed with great fanfare, but what would have the most impact was the quiet dealing, particularly between Phaulkon and Father Tachard. Phaulkon hoped he could rely on the French to protect him against his detractors in Ayutthaya. He wanted a French military presence in Siam. The two ambassadors refused to talk of the idea; however, Father Tachard promised to secure this if Phaulkon would offer two "keys of the kingdom," the port fortresses of Bangkok and Mergui, to the French.

Meanwhile, the king asked Chaumont what had led the king of France into thinking he might become a Christian.

> I regret that the King of France sets me so difficult a choice. I would be rash to embrace a religion of which I know nothing. I wish for no other judge than this wise and virtuous prince. A sudden change might cause a revolution, and I do not intend to forsake lightly a religion received and practised without interruption in my kingdom for the last 2229 years. Besides this I am greatly surprised at the eagerness with which this King upholds the cause of heaven, it seems that God himself takes no interest whatever in the matter, and that He has left the mode of worship which is due to Him to our own discretion. For could not this true God who has created heaven and earth and all the dwellers therein and has endued them with diverse characters, in granting souls and bodies to mankind, have inspired mankind

with similar ideas on the religion they ought to follow, and have indicated to them the mode of worship most agreeable to Him and to have submitted all nations to a uniform law.

As he has not done so we ought to conclude that he has not wished it to be so. This ordered unity of worship depends entirely upon a divine Providence that could have introduced it into the world just as easily as the diversity of sects that are established. It is then natural to believe that the True God takes as much pleasure in being worshipped in different ways as by being glorified by a vast number of creatures who praise Him after one fashion.

Would the diversified beauty which we so admire in the physical, be less admirable in the ethical world, or less worthy of the Divine Wisdom? Whatever may happen, since God is the absolute ruler and director of the world I resign myself and my kingdom entirely to His good provenance and with all my heart I trust that His eternal wisdom will so order them according to his good pleasure.

King Narai authorized another high-level embassy to be sent to France. Chao Phraya Kosa, the king's childhood friend and most successful general, was to head the embassy. This embassy prepared with great care, learning French court etiquette and manners, learning the names of French dishes, and mastering polite French introductions. Paris went overboard for their Siamese guests. They were featured in all the French papers, and their style and clothing influenced both fashion and the French court.

The king's brother hosted a splendid entertainment at St. Cloud at which the objects of art drew their attention. The French were astonished to find such good taste and appreciation of beauty coming from strangers from so distant a country. The prince of Condé invited them to Chantilly, and the most distinguished people vied with one another for their company during their two-month stay.

Behind the scenes Father Tachard spun his web. The king and his navy secretary would send an army of six hundred under the command of General Desfarges. Two envoys, Simon de la Loubère and Claude Céberet, were appointed, but with strict instructions to do nothing without Father Tachard's approval. When Chao Phraya Kosa heard of Phaulkon's promise to hand over Bangkok and Mergui he was understandably angry. The instructions given to the embassy were to offer only Songkhla as a trading port to the French. There had been no discussions of a military nature.

The return journey was not as smooth as the outward leg. The relations between the envoys and Tachard were fraught. Icy, violent storms damaged the vessels, and scurvy and dysentery took about two hundred of the soldiers and sailors.

On arrival Father Tachard hurried off the ship and met with Phaulkon before Chao Phraya Kosa could warn the king not to surrender Bangkok and Mergui. Phaulkon asked King Narai to put the two forts under French control. An official named Phra Phetracha, together with the king's half-sister, were the only dissenting voices. The proposal was approved by the king. Those who were jealous or skeptical of Phaulkon declared that he had invited the French only for the furtherance of his schemes, and to place himself on the throne, as that was the summit of his ambition.

Phaulkon himself oversaw the transfer of the fortresses to the French. He had the crews swear an oath of obedience to him, in the presence of both General Desfarges and Father Tachard. The embassy discussed only minor religious and commercial treaties of little significance. The troops, however, would prove more contentious.

While Phaulkon worked to ensure the prosperity of the kingdom and his own position, many nobles were concerned about him and the direction the kingdom was taking. Phra Phetracha along with Princess Si Suphan, the king's half sister, looked for allies to stop Phaulkon and curb the French.

The sangha considered themselves without royal favor. The king would attend the necessary rites and rituals, but King Narai was more open-minded to differing religions than his predecessors. The sangha viewed Phaulkon, a foreigner, as a man who held their religion in contempt. They, however, remained a powerful voice with the nobles and with the common people.

Phra Phetracha had grown up with King Narai, his first cousin, and they were childhood friends. The relationship between the two men was strong, built on the mutual respect and understanding that comes only over time. The daughter of Phra Phetracha attracted the attention of the king and become his concubine. While there she became embroiled in a passionate affair with one of the king's half-brothers. She was found out and put to death.

Phra Phetracha pretended not to be concerned. The king then placed him in charge of punishing the king's half-brother Prince Noi. The punishment, delivered by Phra Phetracha himself, left the king's brother scarred for life. As for Prince Aphaithot, his lifelong deformity—the one that was not healed by the sought-after miracle—meant that subjects who expected a divine king would never accept him as their sovereign. King Narai was now in bad health, and there was no obvious natural successor.

Phra Phetracha was a small man with piercing eyes. He was fifty-six years and popular. He was a frank and eloquent speaker, even to the king, and several times voiced his concerns over the actions of Phaulkon and the surrender of the garrisons of Bangkok and Mergui.

Despite his past transgressions, Prince Noi was given considerable license by King Narai and loaded with honors. Those in the court were thus wondering if Prince Noi might be a future successor after all.

Phra Phetracha ensnared Prince Noi in his scheme—the elder statesman to the young pretender, only one step removed from becoming king. Phra Phetracha fooled many, but the ever-watchful eye of Phaulkon suspected his deception. As the king was weakening, Phaulkon put his faith in the French and another favorite of the king, his adopted son, the Catholic Prince Mom Pi.

Phaulkon found out that Phra Phetracha had forged the king's seal in order to carry out his plan. When confronted, Phra Phetracha tried to persuade Phaulkon to trust him:

> "It is unfortunate for you and for the State, that being a foreigner, you are not eligible for the throne, as otherwise you would rule

as King, an Empire that you administer to-day in your official capacity. The King, who is well aware of the capacities of his brothers would always have a scruple against giving us such masters. If by some unlucky chance they came to power they would use it against the favorites and officials whom they hate as the authors of the punishments they have had to bear. Believe me, let us anticipate their revenge and as soon as the King is dead, let us take possession of the palace. I would see you were conducted to Bangkok by my friends and there you could bid defiance to any who might wish to supplant you. . . . Our safety is dependent on our union, but for my own part I have resolved to bury myself in solitude and to consecrate the rest of my life to the worship of our gods whom it is quite impossible to serve amid the stress of state affairs."

Phaulkon was far from convinced. In reply Phaulkon said that he was loyal to the king and would never form the alliance Phra Phetracha suggested. He did not, however, reveal the conversation to the dying king.

As the king's condition worsened, Phaulkon and Phra Phetracha acted as joint regents. Phra Phetracha worked zealously, and even Phaulkon believed that Phra Phetracha was genuine in the sentiments he had expressed. A friend even warned him of the danger facing him should the king die and Phra Phetracha prove false, but Phaulkon brushed off the concerns.

❦

"It is only a matter of time before the king passes," said Phra Phetracha.

"What am I to do?" asked Prince Noi.

"You are to be married. Your adoptive father, the king, cannot be there, but I will represent him at your wedding if that is acceptable to your family and you," replied Phra Phetracha. "After your wedding I will hold a reception for you at the palace in Lopburi. It will be an opportunity for you to show off your new bride to the king and the guests. I will ensure it will be a memorable affair," said Phra Phetracha before returning to his rooms in the palace at Lopburi. His son was waiting for him.

"It is done," said Phra Phetracha. "Prince Noi will attend the reception in honor of himself and his new bride. He could not have timed his wedding better. I will invite Prince Mom Pi and his father, Okya Kraisitthisak—he would not miss any chance to advance himself and his son."

Phaulkon finally realized the state of affairs, but he was surrounded by Siamese nobles who offered little support to a foreigner, particularly the favorite of a dying king. His only hope was the French. He sent instructions for them to assemble at Lopburi and told them that their presence was necessary to the mutual interests of the allied monarchs.

"I have invited Prince Aphaithot. He still needs to be carried everywhere due to his affliction, but I feel confident he will appear, although he is maintaining a careful distance. He still blames me for questioning his loyalty to the king. If the day turns out as we have planned you can deal with him later," said Phra Phetracha.

"My spy in Phaulkon's camp, the obsequious Okphra Chula—a Moor—tells me that Paumard, the priest-doctor, has assured Phaulkon that the king will recover," said Luang Sorasak, Phra Phetracha's son.

"And Phaulkon believes this?" asked Phra Phetracha.

"Okphra Chula believes he does, but Phaulkon is far too shrewd to trust the priest-doctor entirely. The Moor tells me that he has sent a message to General Desfarges in Bangkok. Although Okphra Chula did not read the message and was not privy to its contents, he was certain it was a request for troops to come to his aid in Lopburi."

"That would make sense," commented Phra Phetracha. "You are to position our men on the road from Bangkok to Lopburi. I need you to stay here as we may have the kind of work you enjoy. Ensure the men stop the French from arriving here, whatever the cost.

"Now I must go and see the king and tell him of the reception we are to hold for Prince Noi. If nothing else the thought of a reception for the young prince should ensure we see some response from Prince Mom Pi. It will be interesting to see how adept he is at playing the game," continued Phra Phetracha.

As Phra Phetracha entered the king's bedchamber, the three doctors in attendance left the room. Remaining next to the king's bed was Prince Mom Pi.

"My king," said Phra Phetracha, "how are you faring today?"

"My friend, Paumard tells me I am recovering but I have no faith in their medicine or their skills," said the king. "Prince Mom Pi tells me you have arranged a reception for Prince Noi."

"Yes. I came here to tell you myself, but it appears I have been preempted," replied Phra Phetracha.

"News travels fast," said Prince Mom Pi. "Particularly these days."

"I am to attend Prince Noi's wedding in your stead. It is his wish that you meet his new bride, but as you cannot go to him I thought it would be worthwhile if he and his bride were to come here," said Phra Phetracha. "A thoughtful act," said the king. "Prince Mom Pi, please leave us. There are matters I would like to discuss with Phra Phetracha."

Prince Mom Pi left, but not willingly.

"Paumard thinks I will recover, but I think not," said the king. "The succession taxes me. On one hand we have Prince Noi. Popular among the court and an affable young man, but is he up to the task of ruling Ayutthaya? He is your man. What say you?"

"My king, the choice is yours. He has the right lineage and is qualified to rule. He needs help and guidance and it is my wish that I be allowed to provide that for him," replied Phra Phetracha.

"And he is a Buddhist," said the king.

"That is in his favor also," said Phra Phetracha.

"And Prince Mom Pi?" asked the king.

"He is also your adopted son and as such has a claim to the throne. He is of low birth, but my main concern is that he is Catholic. I speak to you directly in saying that Ayutthaya may not stand for a Catholic king," said Phra Phetracha.

"You never were one to take peoples sensibilities into account," said the king. "With your support of Prince Noi and Phaulkon's support for Prince Mom Pi, I am placed in a difficult position. My regents sit in two different camps."

The reception for Prince Noi and his new bride took place during the early afternoon. Following their wedding the prince and his bride entered the palace at Lopburi as guests of honor. The palace had been richly decorated, and a sumptuous feast greeted the guests.

"You have outdone yourself, Phra Phetracha," said Okya Kraisitthisak, father of Prince Mom Pi.

"I felt that the king should have the opportunity to enjoy the wedding of his half-brother," said Phra Phetracha.

"I wonder if you would have extended the same courtesy to my son—the king's adopted son," asked Okya Kraisitthisak.

"He appears to be blessed with two fathers," said Phra Phetracha, ignoring the insinuation. "I have always been puzzled why you agreed to the king adopting your only son."

"Ambition, as you know only too well, Phra Phetracha," replied Okya Kraisitthisak.

"At least you are honest about it," said Phra Phetracha.

"And you disapprove?" asked Okya Kraisitthisak.

"I disapprove of a Catholic becoming king of Ayutthaya, but that you know already. I must leave you. It is time to introduce the prince's new bride to the king."

"May I interrupt?" asked Okphra Chula to Phra Phetracha. "I have news. Somewhere more private if that is acceptable.

"Last night Phaulkon met with Prince Mom Pi. They were not as circumspect as they might have been and their conversation was overheard by Okya Kerewatnan, two royal concubines, and me. We were in the adjoining room. We listened as they colluded together to take the throne by force following the death of the king. The army of Okya Kraisitthisak would link up with the French army and secure the palace until the king dies. Prince Mom Pi would then be declared king," he whispered.

"And you would be prepared to repeat this in the presence of His Majesty?" asked Phra Phetracha.

"Both Okya Kerewatnan and I are willing to tell the king of this treasonous act," replied Okphra Chula.

"Then we will go to the king directly," said Phra Phetracha. He pulled his son aside. "Kill Mom Pi!" he said. "He is not of royal blood," he added, thereby ensuring that Luang Sorasak would not allow him the royal privilege of being placed in a velvet sack and being clubbed to death.

Phaulkon heard the news that his allies the French were being held outside Lopburi, though not that his conversation with Prince Mom Pi had been overheard. He finally realized the threat posed by Phra Phetracha and went to see the king.

> "Sire, the time for repining and speech is over. We must act, and that silently. Decisive measures must be taken against the impending evils, and a half hearted policy will only favour the progress of their designs. If [Phetracha] is arrested, the conspiracy will come to naught. Remember the greatest secrecy is absolutely necessary to the success of this enterprise, and, to be successful we must dissemble our feelings."

The king's anger at hearing of the conspiracy reached the ears of Phra Phetracha, who reacted by having the palace surrounded by his men. The king, loyal to Phaulkon, railed against Phra Phetracha. He was no longer fooled. He saw too late that Phra Phetracha had planned the succession all along.

Prince Mom Pi was resting in his quarters in the palace. Luang Sorasak and his men overpowered and killed his two guards. The prince jumped to his feet. Without a word Luang Sorasak plunged a dagger into his heart. The prince died instantly. The sound of the palace guards echoed as they ran along the corridor to the chambers of Prince Mom Pi.

"We came to arrest him but he and his men fought. There was no option but to kill him," said Luang Sorasak.

"I dare say you have given him a better fate than the king would have given him," said the captain of the guard.

"And Phaulkon?" asked Luang Sorasak.

"He is coming from his house to see the king," replied the captain of the guard.

"That I will not allow," said Luang Sorasak.

In his weakened state, and faced with incontrovertible evidence that his favorite was plotting a coup and that the French were advancing, the king was induced, at the request of his leading officials, to appoint Phra Phetracha to act as sole regent during his illness. Phra Phetracha assumed control over the palace guards; he had all those in the palace in his power. He had planned to wait patiently for the death of the king and then take the necessary action to be proclaimed as his successor, but with the news that an armed force was advancing to press the claim of Prince Noi he had to bring forward his plans.

"I have been told that an army is marching on the palace to support your claim to the throne," said Phra Phetracha to Prince Noi.

"It is my uncle's doing. He said I was wrong to trust you."

"Maybe he was right," said Phra Phetracha as two of Luang Sorasak's men grabbed him from behind before tying his hands and placing his struggling body into a crimson velvet sack.

॰

General Desfarges led his men in support of Phaulkon. His soldiers fought their way through a far larger force of Siamese loyal to Phra Phetracha waiting to stop his advance. As he neared Lopburi a rumor that the king was dead reached him. General Desfarges was beset by doubt. He sought sanctuary in a seminary, but the missionaries told him that his being there was a risk to them all. After a crucial delay, the general realized his only hope was with Phaulkon. He still sent one of his officers ahead to assess the situation. His emissary returned, convinced that the king was dead. General Desfarges heard this and ordered a retreat, and they returned to Bangkok.

Phaulkon was left to the mercy of his enemies. He lamented,

> "Alas they do not consider that they themselves will be involved in my downfall. I was wrong to trust to human aid, I wait for God only."

Phaulkon found the treatment of the king by Phra Phetracha unacceptable. Accompanied by a number of French officers and

Portuguese and Englishmen in his employ, he decided to go see the king and said to his young wife,

> "Farewell for ever madame. The King is a prisoner, and I am going to die at his feet."

He had hoped to enter the room of King Narai but as soon as he entered the courtyard he was surrounded. His guards slipped away, with the exception of the French officers, whom he told to disarm. Phaulkon was arrested and thrown in the deepest dungeon.

> Soon after his Silver Chair, wherein he was usually carried, came back empty, a bad omen to his friends and domesticks, who could not but prepare themselves to partake in their master's misfortune.

As he had with Prince Noi, Luang Sorasak arranged the death of Prince Aphaithot by having him arrested and clubbed in the customary manner, in a crimson velvet sack.

Two days later, on July 11, 1688, King Narai died in his beloved city of Lopburi at the age of fifty-one. Phra Phetracha was proclaimed king. On his deathbed the king cursed Phra Phetracha. He had realized too late that Phra Phetracha had wanted the throne for himself all along.

> H. M. King Narai was dressed in a high top hat, which is similar to French hats, but the width of the rim is not wider then one inch, and there is a hat strap made of silk under his chin. His Majesty's clothes are golden, with a blaze of color, and there is a very beautiful Kris on his belt, and valuable rings on his fingers. H.M. King Narai is about fifty years old, with a thin build, no mustache, but a big mole on the left side of his chin with two long hairs.

Ayutthaya under the rule of King Narai the Great was known as "Golden Ayutthaya," a tribute to its wealth and to the gold that adorned the city, the temples, and the images of the Buddha. Contact and trade with neighboring nations, such as the Malays and the Japanese, enhanced the kingdom's prestige. This, together with the trade that came from the European nations, brought wealth and recognition as never before. King Narai walked a tightrope between the pressures from outside his kingdom and the pressures from within; hence his well-earned sobriquet of "the Great."

One story early in the reign of King Narai illustrates the man behind the king. A proud abbot once dared to tell the king that he was ruling too harshily. The king said nothing, but days later sent the abbot a monkey and told him to care for it well and allow it freedom to play.

The monkey caused great mischief, running about and breaking the abbot's belongings. When he could take it no longer the abbot begged the king to free him of this task. Then the king replied,

"Well, can you not put up with the petty annoyances of an animal for two days; and yet you wish that I should endure, for the rest of my life, the insults of a people one thousand times worse mannered than all the monkeys in the forests! Learn then, that even if I punish wickedness, still more will I reward virtue and merit."

Ban Phlu Luang Dynasty

26

KING PHETRACHA
1688–1703

KING PHETRACHA HELD THE CROWN. In common with others before him who had seized the throne, he was viewed by many as a "usurper." With the death of the popular Prince Noi and rumors that he might have poisoned King Narai, the new king needed to secure his position—and secure it quickly. King Phetracha, however, had a common cause with the people: the overwhelming desire to see the foreigners gone. This was his strength. He knew he would still have to fight for the throne. Internal dissent could be dealt with. He saw the French as his main obstacle in gaining power. With them gone he could consolidate his realm.

The sangha, now in the ascendant again following the reign of King Narai, praised the new king. With the change of king the nation seemed to unite against foreigners, particularly those from the West. King Phetracha's mind was set on the removal of the French, and the sangha were only too willing to pass the view of their new king to the people.

The French were a daunting proposition, ensconced as they were in the two strongest defensive positions in the country. The new king sent for a representative of the French in Siam and gave him an ultimatum:

"It is with the greatest disgust that I learn that the French troops who come to Siam to serve the King, refuse to obey his commands. I order you to write to their commander to enforce their obedience. Should he persist in the contumacious behavior you shall suffer for it. I will give your Seminary and Church over to pillage, all the French will be blown from the cannon's mouth, and every Christian shall be put to death."

The revolution that ended the Prasat Thong dynasty and ushered in the Ban Phlu Luang dynasty was carried out so smoothly that things seemed relatively peaceful to the outside world. This was far from the truth. With Phaulkon gone and the French confined to their forts, King Phetracha was crowned in Lopburi before returning the court to Ayutthaya, where he was acclaimed by the multitude. The new king replaced those in senior positions with those whose loyalty he could count on. He married King Narai's daughter, Princess Yothathep, and proclaimed her queen. She had her own territories, together with officers and soldiers who reported to her only. As queen she would hold regular audiences; those in attendance would crouch in front of her just as they would in front of the king.

Queen Yothathep loathed the new king, as he had killed her father's brothers, but she had little choice in the matter of the marriage. Her territories and men were not large enough to mount a challenge against the new king, and she understood that King Phetracha could not leave her as a possible focus for dissent. The marriage was purely political, although they had a son, Phra Khwan, and it removed much of the lingering doubt about King Phetracha as a usurper. Her marriage placed a "seal of approval" on King Petracha taking the throne.

King Phetracha continued his prolonged negotiations with the French, readying his army while impressing his authority on those who had demanded immediate war. In an apparent attempt to defuse the situation King Phetracha invited General Desfarges and his son to Lopburi, away from the prying eyes of Ayutthaya.

"General Desfarges. Thank you for coming," said the king.

"A summons from the king is not one to be disobeyed," said the French general.

"Your bishops seem to hold a different opinion on that."

"They are men of the church, not men of war."

"Then let us talk. We face a worsening situation. The people seek you gone, but I still see possibilities in our relationship," said the king. "King Narai was right in wanting the French here as a counterweight to the Dutch. Despite all that has happened I was of one mind with him on that."

"That is good to hear."

"I have a proposition. The early days of my reign have been beset by minor rebellions in the Lan Xang states and among the Khmer. I would like you, as a sign of good faith, to send troops alongside mine as we battle these insurgencies. In return I will offer your son a noble rank."

"That is indeed an honor, Your Majesty, and one worthy of discussion with my son," said General Desfarges.

"I ask only that you leave your son to enjoy our hospitality," said King Phetracha. The general knew this was not a request. He also understood that King Phetracha wanted the French to leave the forts in order that they could be slaughtered.

General Desfarges left promising to send the troops requested by King Phetracha. At no time in their meeting was the name Phaulkon mentioned, and that day King Phetracha left the fate of King Narai's counselor in the hands of his son.

Phaulkon was punished for bringing in foreigners, whom he had used for his own self-aggrandizement rather than for the good of the nation. Phra Phetracha did not inflict an easy death on Phaulkon. While in prison he endured two weeks of torture, much of it at the hands of Luang Sorasak and his men as they sought both retribution and the secrets of where his wealth was located. When he could learn no more, Luang Sorasak arranged for Phaulkon's execution. The severed head of Prince Mom Pi was placed on a chain around his neck.

"See, there is your king!" said Luang Sorasak, a man feared by many, with low morals and no qualms about killing.

The Greek bowed his head and prayed. The soldiers who surrounded him were uneasy at witnessing the killing of one once so powerful. He addressed his final words to Luang Sorasak.

"I am about to die. Remember that even if I am guilty, I leave a wife and child who are innocent. For them I ask neither rank nor wealth, but at least let them enjoy freedom and life."

With that Luang Sorasak delivered the telling blow. Phaulkon's final wish was not to come true. Luang Sorasak would ensure that it didn't.

That same day King Phetracha held a council of war with his officers where he outlined his agreement with General Desfarges. A council decision was made not to obey King Phetracha but to mount an attack against the fortresses in Mergui and against the twin forts that straddled the Chao Phraya River in Thonburi and Bangkok. The king, still at the start of his reign, purged the council of those who stood against him.

On June 24, 1688, the fort at Mergui was abandoned after relentless Siamese pressure. Many of the French escaped under fire and managed to capture a Siamese warship. They did not get far and ran aground.

King Phetracha led a huge army to attack the French fortress in Bangkok. The Dutch supported the Siamese attack by blockading the port—an act that would see the VOC rewarded with trading privileges when the siege was over.

☙

In Ayutthaya, Phaulkon's Catholic Japanese-Portuguese wife was arrested and beaten about the arms. The soldiers beat any of her family and servants who complained. She was thrown into a dungeon, where she languished for some time. She was an attractive woman of noble disposition, only twenty-four years of age. Finally the jailers brought her young son to her.

When she was told of Phaulkon's death she asked,

"Well, why is he dead? What was his crime that he should have been treated like a felon?"

An officer nearby took pity on her and whispered, "His only crimes were that he was loved by the king and that he was a man of great ability.
She was finally freed from the dungeon to serve as a slave. During the initial weeks she had to endure the unwanted attention of Luang Sorasak, and even turned down a marriage proposal from him.

> "Are you unaware who I was and how I have lived? My religion forbids so sinful a marriage. I loved my husband with all my soul, and, faithful to his memory, my heart is closed against any new passion."

Luang Sorasak had her taken to his palace anyway, but soon he worried that this might anger his father. He sent her back and threatened her not to tell anyone what had happened. To ensure her silence, Luang Sorasak accused her of embezzlement. She was sentenced to be given one hundred lashes. The punishment was stopped after fifty, but she was forced to watch as her family received the remainder of the beating.

A French soldier took pity on her and offered to help her escape to the fort in Bangkok. Together with her son and the brave French officer she escaped at night and made her way south. The soldiery in the fort cheered at her coming. The commander did not. He was worried this would invite an attack.

King Phetracha threatened to do just that. He demanded her back saying that he would "abolish the vestiges of the [Christian] religion" if she were not returned. The French soldiery was moved by her plight, but General Desfarges had determined to send her back.

Finally a French officer came for her, finding her draped in the French tricolor, and took her back by river to Ayutthaya. In the end, she was treated better than she had feared. She was sent to work in the palace kitchen, where she oversaw food preparations as well as other functions of the royal household.

Both parties continued their negotiations. The Siamese finally agreed to lend the French ships that would take them to the French garrison in Pondicherry. To ensure the ships were returned, the bishop of Métellopolis, the head of the French trading company, agreed to stay along with two hostages, while King Phetracha sent two of his sons to the French commander as hostages. All the officers arrested during the "revolution" in Lopburi were released. As they returned they brought with them stories of seminaries being looted, Christian girls being raped, and priests being put in stocks and pilloried, or killed.

On November 13 the French finally left Bangkok. Of the French hostages who were supposed to stay in Siam until the Siamese ships returned, only the Bishop of Métellopolis remained. The other two managed to flee with the departing ships. General Desfarges feared a Siamese attack and hurried to set sail, accidentally leaving some French soldiers and priests behind in his haste.

With the French gone, the remaining Christians were persecuted with impunity. The bishop of Métellopolis was the first to suffer. He was dragged off the ship where he had taken sanctuary, and was beaten. Some French officers were fettered after being beaten; others were simply hacked to pieces. The bishop was taken to Bangkok and put in the care of a Christian woman, who nursed him back to health. When he had recovered he was taken back to Ayutthaya and jailed there.

Throughout the country foreigners were vilified. Soldiers raided seminaries and carried off priests, students, and servants. They were abused and left in the hands of jailers who thought it was their duty to ensure the suffering of the foreigners. The lucky ones were allowed to beg for food in the streets. The mere mention of the word "foreigner" or the showing of the slightest sign of pity was sufficient to arouse hatred and fury.

Eventually, the violent frenzy subsided. General Desfarges sent back the Siamese hostages unharmed, but only the bishop of Métellopolis was released in return. The remaining priests and missionaries were taken to a fetid island where they slowly perished. The French, however, were gone.

The Chinese had returned to international trade after 1684 following the lifting of the imperial ban. On his accession to the throne King Phetracha rewarded his Chinese supporters with properties and positions. He encouraged the Chinese to reestablish themselves in Ayutthaya and allowed the Chinese to dominate many areas of trade.

Despite the hostility to foreigners that had gripped the country, King Phetracha understood that Ayutthaya needed foreign trade to survive. The Dutch had helped him covertly when the French were driven out and were rewarded with new commercial concessions. The Dutch VOC needed very large profit margins to cover its costs operating in such a far-flung region of the world, and with the French gone that again became a possibility.

The optimism that surrounded this start to the reign of the new king was short-lived. King Phetracha appointed a new phrakhlang (minister of the treasury), Kosa Pan, King Narai's former ambassador to France on the 1686 embassy. It was another of the king's Chinese favorites, Okya Sombatthiban, who rose to such power that the requests of all foreign traders had to be submitted to him for approval. Kosa Pan dared not act on any foreigner's behalf without the approval of Okya Sombatthiban.

> The noblemen, who are extremely self-seeking people, will never fail to swindle part of the gain for themselves. It occurred so even when they knew that the King would punish them for it and arrest them as a result of it. [That is] because the Siamese have such a nature that, [even if] one has by now seen his predecessor beheaded today, one [still] would commit the same offense tomorrow, like we have seen enough in Siam at court—that is within the King's sight. And if they do so in court, one can easily assess what they are supposed to do in remote places.

The VOC began to encounter payment problems from the Siamese royal court; the phrakhlang intentionally hampered the payments, even if authorized through the courts. Word reached the king and he summoned his phrakhlang before him.

Kosa Pan fell on his knees before his monarch.

"I am not blind to the excesses of your office," said the king.

"But Your Majesty, you always get your share as you know well," replied the phrakhlang.

"You have been jailed many times, but you do not learn," said the king.

"And I have been reinstated on all occasions," replied the phrakhlang boldly.

"Your previous service to your country holds you in good stead," said the king." We owe the Dutch a considerable sum. The courts have authorized payment but I am told no settlement has been made,

"The sum is indeed considerable. The amount is beyond our ability to pay at the moment," replied the phrakhlang still speaking to the dust beneath the king's feet.

"Rise," said King Prasat Thong. "One of your rank should not prostrate himself before me. The situation must be resolved."

"I will work toward that," said the phrakhlang."But I ask you to consider this, Your Majesty—if the Dutch are unable to make a profit in Siam why are they still here?

The answer was one not only of trade considerations. The VOC feared that others—notably the English but also the French—would rush in to fill the void. As the English expanded their empire they were increasingly locking horns with the Dutch in Southeast Asia, and the Dutch wanted them kept out.

The general increase in Chinese shipping—and renewed trade with the Japanese—could not prevent a slowing of trade. Siam was troubled by rebellions in the south and east, an epidemic swept through the northern provinces of Siam, causing the death of animals and livestock.

Trade throughout Southeast Asia declined in these years, and in 1700 a French missionary wrote,

> The traders are reduced to great misery, foreigners no longer come. One has seen here this year only three or four Chinese junks with not much merchandise.

With the loss of revenues from international trade, Ayutthaya gradually started to lose its ability to control its manpower, which in turn led to weakness and factionalism at its center. Almost imperceptibly the real power began to shift away from the king and toward the nobility.

꧁

After the French had departed the reign of King Phetracha was much troubled by unrest, not only throughout the country but also in those states that owed allegiance to Ayutthaya.

In 1690 the king failed to receive tribute from Pattani and sent an expedition to ensure the payment was made. To not do so would be seen as a sign of weakness from other states under the suzerainty of Ayutthaya. The expedition consisted of ten thousand men and over one hundred boats. It was heavily defeated, with over six thousand Siamese troops killed. No new expedition was launched, and Pattani declared itself independent of Ayutthaya. A stalemate remained throughout the reign of the king.

In 1693 the sultan of Kedah, emboldened by Pattani's example, refused to send tribute and imprisoned the Ayutthayan envoys sent to negotiate. These were bold moves. It was only a decade before that the Siamese navy of King Narai had taken the rebellious city of Songkhla on the Malay Peninsula and burned it to the ground, later offering its charred remains to the French.

In the city of Mergui, on the Andaman Sea, at Siam's distant west coast, a monk and close companion to King Narai's dead half-brother Prince Aphaithot was determined to avenge the killing of the prince and place himself on the throne of Ayutthaya.

Thammathian spoke of a legend, one that would be echoed later in the reign of King Phetracha, of a *phu mi bun*, a Buddhist man of merit who would bring peace and fairness to his people. Many embraced his message. He spoke in a soft voice and people would gather around; many would fall prostrate at his feet. He spoke not of war but of peace, the peace that would follow after the usurper king, King Phetracha, had been removed from the throne by the people of Siam.

King Narai was much loved, and with the tales surrounding his death and of the murder of Prince Aphaithot and Prince Noi still fresh in the people's minds, the march of Thammathian attracted many who felt loyalty to the memory of King Narai or who could see no future under the rule of King Phetracha.

The governor of Nakhon Si Thammarat was among the first to lend his troops. Word of the coming of the holy man and his goodness went ahead of him, and others joined his ranks.

The city of Ayutthaya was in festive mood. The temples were opened and people took the opportunity of an extended holiday to visit friends and relatives and to pay homage at their temples. As the early April sun beat down on the city the people enjoyed themselves as the army of Thammathian moved closer.

A few days earlier an advance party of twenty men had been captured and vigorously interrogated. They knew little, but their capture indicated that the army of Thammathian was near. Ayutthaya stood in readiness.

Luang Sorasak decided to visit Wat Chedi Daeng, a temple endowed by his father in the years before he became king. He and his compatriots, ten in all, walked toward the elephant kraal to the north of the city. Normally as they were visiting a temple they would be unarmed, but with the threat of Thammathian they openly carried their weapons.

As they turned a corner they came face to face with Thammathian, clad in his saffron robe, sitting on his war elephant and surrounded by at least fifty of his men.

"It must be him. Look at the monk's robes," said Chun Yommarat.

There was no time to plan. The soldiers of Thammathian drew their weapons and advanced as one. These were no ordinary soldiers; these were the elite of Thammathian's army, his personal bodyguard. In Luang Sorasak and his men he would be fighting some of the most highly trained warriors in Ayutthaya, but the odds favored Thammathian.

"Move back around the bend," ordered Luang Sorasak. "If we stay here they can force us directly back toward the Pa Sak River. They backed up facing the oncoming enemy. Outnumbered they grouped together facing outwards as the soldiers of Thammathian clashed steel with them. There was little time for thought, only for survival. The overwhelming odds forced them gradually backward. Chun Yommarat fell to the ground to the left of Luang Sorasak. He would be the only one, other than Luang Sorasak, who would survive this battle.

It is only a matter of time before they kill us, thought Luang Sorasak. He charged forward and his men followed. Luang Sorasak threw one man who stood in his way over his shoulder as though he weighed nothing. He grabbed a short spear that the man was holding and, sword failing, advanced on Thammathian, who was sitting high on his elephant. When in striking range he thrust his sword into the right front foreleg of the elephant. The elephant bellowed in pain and reared. At that moment Luang threw the short spear at Thammathian catching him high on the shoulder. Thammathian sat back as the deep red of blood clashed with the saffron of his robes.

For a split second the men of Thammathian froze.

"Retreat," ordered Luang Sorasak. "Warn the king."

The four remaining men ignored the order, allowing Luang Sorasak to pass through their ranks and return to King Phetracha with the news. They died where they stood, but they had bought time for their leader to report to the king. Luang Sorasak returned bloodied and exhausted to the royal palace. From the upper story of his palace, the king saw his son as he staggered toward the royal palace. He ran down to greet his son on the steps

"Father, Thammathian is in the city. I have just fought with him near the elephant kraal," he gasped.

"Fetch Okya Mahamontri," the king commanded of one of his generals.

"I wounded him as he sat high on his elephant. My men allowed me to pass. They gave their lives."

As troops poured onto the streets, panic ensued. The people initially had no idea what was going on; for most their concern was too survive. They hid their valuables or grabbed them and headed to the rivers, where ships large and small jostled with one another to make their way upstream or downstream. Anywhere but in the center of Ayutthaya.

The king enlisted the support of the Portuguese still in Ayutthaya, positioning them at key points around the city to advise his men.

The army of Thammathian was sighted outside the walls, and the king's general led an army out to meet them. The army of Thammathian, which had numbered seven thousand men only hours before, now numbered no more than four thousand. Thammathian had died following the wound inflicted by Luang Sorasak, and on receiving confirmation of his death the army from Nakhon Si Thammarat retreated southward. The four thousand who remained were leaderless and without purpose. They were slaughtered.

The aftermath was bloody. Three elephants were captured together with only three hundred men. Many of Thammathian's army fled into the countryside and would be hunted down with dogs. Many Moors had fought on the side of Thammathian. Their horses were much prized, but the Muslim community of Ayutthaya would pay a heavy price for the actions of others of their faith.

The battle had been won and the city was secure, but stories of the return of the ghost of King Narai and that of Thammathian lingered for many years.

❦

Almost immediately King Phetracha faced another rebellion, this time in Nakhon Ratchasima, in the northeast of his kingdom. The governor revolted, and efforts to reclaim the walled city failed. Finally the Ayutthayan troops managed to set fire to the tinder-dry city with the help of flaming kites that were wafted into the city on the prevailing wind.

In 1699 a further rebellion broke out in Nakhon Ratchasima led by a charasmatic spiritual leader named Bun Kwang, who was also seen by his supporters as a *phu mi bun*. King Phetracha sent an army, but his forces failed to enter the city. The general, Okya Lakhon, a lifelong friend of King Phetracha, returned to Ayutthaya to ask for reinforcements. Despite their friendship the king did not tolerate failure and commanded that he and his generals be caged to await their fate. Fearing the retribution of a king that he knew so well, Okya Lakhon attempted suicide. His attempt failed and the king commanded that his wounds be healed. Okya Lakhon feared that his wounds were being healed only to permit the king to kill him slowly. One night, he, Okya Phonlathep, and his other generals managed to escape and fled to Cambodia.

Bun Kwang led his followers from the city, pursued by the Siamese forces. His peasant army of men, horses, and elephants marched toward Lopburi, where the Siamese counterattacked. The holy man's peasant army vanished into the surrounding forest, and Bun Kwang and twenty-nine of his followers were killed.

Within the court two factions had developed, supporting either Luang Sorasak, the king's eldest son and a man feared throughout the nation, or Queen Yothathep, the mother of Phra Khwan. Both awaited the death of the king. Her son was the king's chosen successor, but as often happened, this was to be disputed. Both Luang Sorasak and Queen Yothathep had their own palaces and respective courts, and both had standing armies, collected separate taxes from their own domains, and operated apart from the king.

Phra Khwan was only fourteen. The king had mentored his son, guiding him through statecraft and ensuring that any contact with his elder brother was always in the presence of armed guards. Luang Sorasak inspired fear. Tales of his excess and rumors of his treatment of women were the whispered talk of the court. He was an experienced general who did not suffer failure, and a major participant in foreign trade, sending his junks as far afield as China, Japan, Batvia, and Coromandel. His reputation, however, went before him and instilled fear.

During the turmoil of 1699–1700, he was rumored to have been the true instigator of the Nakhon Ratchasima uprising. He often kept within his own palace in Ayutthaya and was not seen for long periods of time. At one point rumors spread that he was dead. Luang Sorasak married a princess of Lan Xang in the April of 1702. The Dutch had speculated that during the time he was rumored to be dead, he was actually in Lan Xang. With his hedonistic lifestyle he was often in and out of his father's favor.

He returned to his father's favor after the marriage. The Dutch wondered about this change:

> We believe . . . that the King, while still alive, has no other option [than] that the eldest son take over the kingdom, principally if he [Sorasak] keeps on with his present behaviour, because one now begins to love and glorify him [for] this [which is] completely contrary to his former [behavior]. [He is] everywhere reknowned for his clemency, generosity and just goodness. Yes, even though the local people have been afraid of [him] in the past.

King Phetracha died on the evening of February 5, 1703. The new VOC governor-general at Ayutthaya recorded that King Phetracha had been ill for sometime and had kept his illness secret, but as he neared death this became increasingly difficult. Queen Yothathep became aware and immediately gathered her supporters, including Okya Sombatthiban, the Chinese favorite of the king, in order to secure her son's succession. Word of her actions reached Luang Sorasak, who quickly had the palace surrounded by three thousand of his men. With his death imminent the king, realizing that his chosen successor Phra Khwan would not be allowed to succeed him, the king tried to draw a promise from his eldest son not to harm his brother.

It was not to be.

Wat Khok Phraya had already been the killing ground of many child kings: young Prince Thong Lan, son of King Boromaraja I; the child king King Yot Fa, son of King Chairacha; Prince Si Sin, the younger brother of King Songtham. Once Prince Phra Khwan joined them, the main impediment to Luang Sorasak securing the throne would be removed. Luang Sorasak and Phra Khwan were riding horses together. Phra Khwan was on "the best horse from the king's stables," when a group of his half-brother's most trusted courtiers dragged him down from his mount and executed him in the manner befitting his rank.

One of the last acts of King Phetracha was to nominate a distant nephew, Phra Phichaisurin, as his successor. Once King Phetracha died Phra Pichaisurin quickly offered the throne to Luang Sorasak and retreated to the relative safety of the monastery. The path was now clear for Luang Sorasak to become king.

27

KING SURIYENTHRATHIBODI
1703–9

LUANG SORASAK ASCENDED THE THRONE, taking the title of King Suriyenthrathibodi. He was a brutal man, a violent man, as history would attest. One of his first orders was that the people should refer to him as "Phra Chao Suea," or the Tiger King. The name was referring to the new king's powerful personal features; he was a big, impressive man, but his subjects came to see the "tiger" as bloodthirsty and cruel. As a king he was much maligned even in his own records:

At that time, the King was of vulgar mind, uncivil behavior, savage conduct, cruel habit. He engaged Himself in no charitable business, but in that against the royal traditions. Also, He lacked inhibition, but was consumed by unholy sin. Eternal were anger and ignorance in His mind. And the King habitually drank liquor and pleased Himself with the intercourses with the female children not yet attaining the age of menstruation. In this respect, where any female was able to endure Him, that female would be granted a great amount of rewards, money, gold, silks and other cloth. Should any female be incapable of bearing with Him, He would be enraged and strike at her heart, putting her to death. The caskets were every day seen to be called into the palace to contain the females' dead bodies and to be carried out of there through a royal gate at the end of the royal confinement mansion. That gate thereby gained the name the "Gate of Ghosts" until now.

Furthermore, when His Majesty made a trip to any canal, sea, island or any other place plentiful with sharks, sawfish and other aquatic beings, He always drank liquor. If any concubine, lady, page or official caused His barge shaken, His Majesty would exercise no judgment and express no mercy, but would be enraged and order the person to be dragged with a hook and thrown into water to be consumed by sharks and sawfish.

Moreover, His Majesty never maintained Himself in the five precepts. He gratified Himself by having carnal knowledge of the wives of His public officers. From that time onwards, He was given the name the "Tiger King."

His short reign was relatively peaceful. His father's reign had laid most of the insurrections to rest. He appointed both his sons Prince Phet and Prince Phon to the position of upparat, the elder Prince Phet having precedence, but evidenced little trust in them throughout his reign.

Once, during an elephant hunt the king and his party came to a swamp.

"We cannot take the elephants through that!" said Prince Phet, looking across the low-lying swamp that seemed to go on as far as the eye could see.

"We will move forward" said King Suea. "I am not a man to back down, to anyone or anything, as well you know."

"But Father," implored Prince Phet.

"I will not turn back. You and your brother go and find me a path through the swamp, and do not fail me. Be back in the morning, or you will pay dearly," said the king.

The king watched as his two sons left on foot with a handful of their retainers and moved into the swamp.

"Be careful of the snakes," the king yelled out. "And the tigers," he added quietly.

"Now set the camp and fetch me some of that Portuguese wine," he said to no one in particular.

The royal tent was raised quickly. All knew better than to raise the ire of the king.

The king entered the royal tent with his chief minister and two of his generals. His throne stood on a dais at the far end facing the entrance to the tent. It was thought that this position was unlucky, but the king did not believe in luck. The Portuguese wine had been placed on the low table to his left, and a group of half-naked girls, none over fourteen years of age, prostrated themselves as their king entered.

"Wine," bellowed the king, and the drinking started and would continue well into the night.

⁂

"The ground looks higher over there," said Prince Phon.

"We need to follow that sparse line of trees. They must stand clear of the swamp," said Prince Phet.

The trees stood only slightly higher than the swamp.

"Will this patch carry the weight of an elephant?" asked Prince Phet.

They moved on slowly, leaving markers as they went. It took over four hours. They were often knee-deep in the snake-infested waters before they emerged onto solid ground on the far side of the swamp.

"It will be getting dark soon," said Prince Phon.

"Are you more afraid of the snakes or Father?" asked Prince Phet. "We must get back before sunrise or he will take his anger out on us."

They set off back across the swamp. The sun set quickly, and snakes and mosquitoes could be both seen and heard. It was the tigers that couldn't be heard. The small party, led by an experienced tracker and pathfinder, relied on dry wood torches to light the way for their return journey, but they soon became damp and difficult to keep lit. The moon was nowhere to be seen.

It was early morning when the party returned. Miraculously none of their number had been lost.

"We have been watching your torches," said their father. The two princes knew their father by now. He had been drinking, and laying with his young concubines throughout the night. He had slept little or not at all. He would not be in the best of moods.

"Ready the elephants. We leave as soon as the sun rises," ordered the king.

The royal hunting party left within minutes of the sun rising over the low mountains in the distance. Twenty elephants, one hundred beaters, fifty servants, and nine concubines followed the king as he rode his hunting elephant along the marked track.

Progress was steady. Suddenly the front left leg of the king's elephant sank into soft ground and slipped into the swamp. The elephant reared and the king's mahout struggled to regain the trackway. The hunting party came to a halt. The mahout got control of the king's elephant and they struggled on to higher ground. The mahout made the elephant lower his front legs in order for the king to dismount. As the king dismounted so did the others in the hunting party.

"Are you trying to kill me!" shouted the king. His two sons blanched. The king pulled out a hunting spear and thrust it at Prince Phet. Prince Phon instinctively moved in front of his brother and parried the blow. The two brothers looked at each other, and fled together into the swamp.

"Find them and bring them to me!" ordered the king. Less than an hour later the two princes, wet and muddied, with their hands tied behind their backs, were thrown unceremoniously before the king. He raised their heads and slapped them both across the face with the palm of his hand.

"Take them back to Ayutthaya. I will deal with them there," said the king. "And make them walk. Tie them to the tail of an elephant!"

"You will each receive fifty lashes with the rattan rod," he said to his sons, prostrate before him upon his return to Ayutthaya.

Those in attendance exchanged glances. They knew fifty lashes could kill a man.

It was the intervention of the elderly Princess Dusit that saved the boys from this punishment. Princess Dusit had helped look after King Suea when he was young, and although she was now elderly the king held her in great respect and would usually follow her advice. Now, with his father dead, she was the only one able to curb his excesses.

Back in the reign of King Narai, then Luang Sorasak had been taking part in a training exercise under the tutelage of the palace guards. On this day the king's favorite Constantine Phaulkon happened by.

"May I fight?" asked Phaulkon, as he did on occasion.

The captain of the guards looked to a volunteer and Luang Sorasak rose to his feet immediately.

"This is a friendly exercise," said the captain of the guard.

Phaulkon anticipated the type of fights he had had in the past. This particular fight was far from friendly. Within a minute, the young Luang Sorasak felled Phaulkon with a right uppercut. As the captain of the guard pulled Luang Sorasak back, the dazed Phaulkon spat out two teeth.

King Narai was furious that his esteemed first minister should be treated with such savagery during a friendly boxing match and ordered that the agressive teenager be executed. The boy would have been put to death if not for Phaulkon and Princess Dusit, who asked that the teenage boy's life be spared. And so the boy Luang Sorasak survived to become the Tiger King of Siam.

❦

Okya Sombatthiban, the phrakhlang of King Phetracha, was incarcerated within days of the new king assuming the throne. Despite his support in bringing King Suea to power, his usefulness was over. He was a legacy of the old regime. It was Okya Phetchaburi that the Dutch met with. For many months they had been trying to gain an audience with the king, but to no avail. They finally secured an audience with his new phrakhlang. But the delay tactics by the Siamese did not bode well.

The two Dutchmen entered the audience hall where Okya Phetchaburi stood above them on a raised dais, enclosed on three sides by interwoven bamboo frames. The small, obsequious phrakhlang wore the thin-brimmed tapering top hat favored by top officials.

He remained seated. Two guards pushed the Dutchmen in the back indicating they should kneel in his presence. The 1688 treaty allowed the Dutch to stand in the presence of the king and top officials. "The treaty signed by the old king is now void," said Phrakhlang Okya Phetchaburi without preamble. "You may continue to trade and your monopolies granted under the treaty remain in place. However, your employees will be subject to our laws, not yours, and you will be expected to honor those above you in the manner of the Siamese people. This audience is concluded."

Aarnout Cleur, the incoming governor-general of Batvia, and Opperhoofd Nicolas de Roij backed out of the chamber in the manner the phrakhlang of Ayutthaya required. Aarnout Cleur sailed on the first ship to Batavia to discuss the implications of the audience.

"This is a serious setback," said the outgoing governor-general, Gideon Tant. "The history of our agreement goes back to the infamous 'picnic incident,' where our people were treated badly."

"Their punishments are barbaric. We cannot allow the Siamese to inflict these punishments on us," replied Aarnout Cleur forcefully.

"What choice do we have?" asked Governor-General Tant. "It is not only about trade. We are required to maintain a presence as a deterrent to the French and the English. If we allow the English to establish a meaningful presence in Siam it would threaten our entire interests in the region."

"But to accept their laws, not to mention the bowing and scraping. It is unacceptable. We fought long and hard to establish our rights, and this new phrakhlang takes them away with a wave of his hand. We cannot access the new king. We are stopped by the phrakhlang on every occasion," said Aarnout Cleur.

"I will write to the king," said the outgoing governor-general. He did so, but failed, after all his years of experience, to realize that the translation of the document would be made by the interpreters of the phrakhlang.

The new king, unlike his father, who had used the services of the Dutch when gaining the throne, had no allegiance to them. The legacy of the French remained in the minds of the Siamese. Their country had nearly been lost to those from the West. Ayutthaya would trade but not engage in politics—particularly Western politics.

๑๛

The reign of King Suea was affected by both pests and drought. The rice harvest failed after six months without rain, and people starved. The area around Phitsanulok suffered badly as the drought continued. With poor crops both in Lan Na and in the south of Siam, the people were driven to eat not only the insects that usually formed part of the peasant diet but also hard-to-digest bamboo seeds and coconut husks.

The houses, particularly in the poorest villages, were almost impossible to enter with the stench of decaying bodies. Roads and tracks leading away from the worst-hit areas were strewn with corpses. The price of rice rose steeply, well out of the reach of the poor. The rivers became covered by a pervasive green slime that blocked the sunlight, and many of the fish died. Those fish that survived in the increasingly brackish water were too poisoned to be eaten. Disease spread throughout the nation. The people looked to their king for salvation.

King Suea understood that in his role as king he was "divine" in the eyes of the people, and in this moment of crisis he dare not fail them. Fearing revolt he announced that he had received a divine message that the green slime on the surface of the rivers was a cure for all ills. When the people heard this news they covered their bodies with the green slime, and after that fifteen days of continuous rain fell.

๑๛

King Suea, like most Thai kings, was a lover of hunting. His true passion, however, was fighting in the Muay Thai style.

The Department of Royal Boxing was founded with the responsibility to find and recruit men worthy to fight as entertainment for royalty and to become royal guards. These guards were also given the task of training members of royalty and the court in combat. The king insisted that his two sons master Muay Thai, sword fighting, and wrestling. Muay Thai was referred to as "the art of eight limbs," using eight points of contact to mimic weapons of war. During the reign of King Suea the popularity of Muay Thai became widespread. SEvery village staged prizefights, and heavy betting, often for all or nothing, transformed ordinary bouts into vicious battles. Fighting camps developed and numerous tournaments were held. A new standard set of rules was introduced throughout Siam, and King Suea himself modified some of the techniques.

Many Thai children would strengthen their shins by kicking against a young bamboo plant. Many fighters displayed tattoos that signified their personal history and their allegiance. There were no formal weight divisions or timed rounds, although often a halved coconut shell with a hole in the center would be placed in water. When the coconut shell sank the round would be over.

The king himself even went out in disguise among the people to watch and participate in the fights, and although he often won, he was not afraid to lose. Once when a courtier mentioned that there 'was a temple fair at a nearby village, King Suea decided to make a secret visit. The next day, the king traveled with a party of close attendants. After going partway to the fair by river, they then went the rest of the way on foot and in disguise. When they reached the boxing ground, the king was eager to fight anyone willing to step into the ring with him. Weight and size were of no importance. He defeated three fighters that day.

Late in his short reign, King Suea took to drink and died. In the first smooth transition of power since the reign of King Ekathotsarot, his eldest son succeeded him, taking the regnal name King Phumintharacha. The new king appointed his younger brother, Prince Phon, as the new upparat and heir to the throne of Ayutthaya.

28

KING PHUMINTHARACHA
1709–33

THE NEW KING WAS A KEEN FISHERMAN, spending much of his time in a throne hall next to a royal pond near the back of the royal palace property. His zeal earned him the name King Thai Sa—"King of the Backyard Pond."

Two years into his reign unrest surfaced again in Pattani. A 1688 invasion by the Siamese had left a legacy of decades of unrest where royal power was diminished and lawlessness had spread throughout the country. Raja Dewi, now the queen of Pattani, under pressure from her ministers refused to pay the expected tribute. Pattani was in chaos and had been for over thirty years.

Despite the problems facing Pattani, which he well understood, King Thai Sa had to act. Pattani had been an aggravation for his father and a bother even during the reigns of both King Narai and King Phetracha. Siamese troops were sent with the objective of installing a Thai governor to replace the queen, thus bringing Pattani firmly under the control of Ayutthaya.

The once-powerful queens who had ruled Pattani in former days had given way to powerless figureheads. As one observer wrote,

> It is said that the people of Patani grew tired of obeying kings who ill-treated them and threw off the yoke by dethroning the king who was reigning at the time and putting in his place a princess, to whom they gave the title of queen, without giving her the authority. They chose the most able among them to govern in her name and without her participation, for she is not privy

to any secret affairs of state and has to content herself with the respect and homage which everyone pays her outwardly as their sovereign.

King Thai Sa dispatched ten thousand troops together with ships of his navy to ensure the payment of the tribute. The Siamese troops landed safely but well short of their intended target. Their subsequent trek through the jungle made them easy targets for the Malays. Siamese ships launched a cannonade at Pattani but were made aware of two Dutch merchantmen that lay at anchor. No conclusive battle was fought, and after a meeting with the ministers of the queen Pattani declared its allegiance to Siam and guaranteed payment of the required tribute the following year if their queen remained—a promise that it honored.

Further north on the opposite coast a rebellion broke out under a Mon monk from Tavoy who claimed to be the son of a brother of King Narai. He had taken vows alongside his father to escape the retribution of King Phetracha. His small but growing army attacked Tenasserim and Mergui, successfully capturing the latter. His army contained not only many Mon people, fleeing the increasingly repressive regime in Burma, but many Moors from Persia and Arabia, skilled in armaments and horsemanship.

"It is the name of King Narai that they still flock to," said King Thai Sa.

"There is no evidence that this so-called prince is anything more than an imposter," replied his eldest son, Prince Naren.

"The legacy left by King Narai still overshadows us all."

"But surely you give no credence to this?"

"He also claims lineage from Chao Phraya Chamnan Bhakdi and from the house of Qomi."

"The house of the Arab princess?" asked Prince Naren. "That would account for the Moors that ride with him."

"Then this could spread if not dealt with quickly. No doubt the Moors would inflict their religion on us. They will have to come over the mountains to reach Ayutthaya. One thing Father did well was to leave us an army of very well-trained soldiers. Now is the time to see how effective they are," said the king.

"You will ride with me?" he asked.

"Of course," said his son.

The two armies met at Ratchaburi, where King Suea's Muay Thai fighters proved their worth in battle.

"Kill them all," said King Thai Sa. "The revolt stops here."

@∿

King Thai Sa appointed a Chinese phrakhlang who had been prominent in court toward the end of his father's reign. In the previous king's reign much of the trade that had earlier been controlled by the Dutch had fallen into the hands of private Chinese traders. Both the king and the phrakhlang understood the importance of maintaining trade links with the Dutch. The Dutch were looked on as traders with a network and knowledge unrivaled in Southeast Asia.

The improvement in the relationship between the VOC and Ayutthaya had begun toward the end of King Suea's reign and was affirmed when the new king agreed to a new contract in March 1709. Their previous agreement was restored and the VOC men were granted the honor of attending the tonsure ceremony of the king's eldest son, an important rite of passage marking the cutting of the prince's topknot, which symbolized his coming of age.

The Dutch entered the Sanphet Mahaprasat Palace, built in the time of King Trailok. As the Dutch delegation entered they failed to appreciate the tapering pillars, the sweep of the basement, the elaborate pinnacle ornaments, the lotus moldings, and the pedimented door and carved window frames. The building had long served royal purposes such as receiving ambassadors, holding banquets and other grand occasions. Phra Phetracha and Luang Sorasak were the last kings to receive the tonsure ceremony here, but the legacy of the building swept back over the centuries.

The Dutch looked on as the young prince entered the miniature model of Mount Kailasa, the mythical abode of Shiva. The lower mountain was dressed by stone sculptures of the mythical animals of the Himavanta forest. The prince entered wearing an exquisite golden, gem-encrusted coronet over his topknot. The ceremony lasted five days and involved not only the praying and chanting that underpins these rituals, but a purifying bath using waters from around the nation, culminating in the cutting of the topknot by the chief Brahmin.

The Dutch only recorded the ceremony as "one of the most magnificent and most esteemed feasts."

@‿‿

"A rider from Prea Srey Thomea, king of the Khmer, requests an audience. He has ridden long and hard," said the courtier.

The rider quickly changed into clothes suitable for an audience with the king. The king, as was customary, sat raised above the messenger. The rider, unable to raise his eyes and speak directly to the king, communicated by addressing the "dust beneath the royal feet."

"My king sends greetings and requests your help in his hour of need," he said.

"Tell us," responded the king, his son Prince Naren by his side.

"The former king, Keo Fa, returned to Oudong with a mighty army of Vietnamese. We fought long and hard, but when the Viet were joined by Lao men we could no longer stand our ground. The king retreated to the old capital of Lovek and now has retreated to Siem Reap. The Vietnamese are in pursuit and the king asks you to grant him and his men sanctuary in your country so he can regroup and fight to regain his crown," said the messenger.

"Leave us. I will talk with my son and consider Prea Srey Thomea's request," said the king.

"Is it wise to give the fleeing king sanctuary?" asked Prince Naren, when they were left alone.

"The king of the Khmer has been loyal to us. It befalls us to be loyal to him," replied his father. "But this is not about him. It is about the Nguyen, the Vietnamese."

"You fear they may threaten us?"

"In time, perhaps. They are resurgent and the Khmer are weak. The Khmer provide the buffer between us."

"It has been in our best interest to keep them weak. It has been our policy since the time of King Naresuan."

"And that weakness is now being exploited by the Nguyen."

"Then we must remain firm in the face of this threat."

"Yes, my son. We will offer sanctuary to Prea Srey Thomea, and we will help him regain his throne. We need the Khmer under our suzerainty.

The Khmer king and his army passed by the overgrown ruins of Angkor Wat with barely a thought to its glorious past as they made their way into Siamese territory. A welcoming force under the command of General Wongdon met the Khmer king and escorted him and his troops back to Ayutthaya where they were given sanctuary and land.

"I thank you for allowing myself and my men sanctuary," said Prea Srey Thomea. He was seated opposite the king on a small chair, his head remaining lower than King Thai Sa's.

"You seek our help to regain your throne?"

"It is in both our interests—for me, to regain my rightful position, and for you, to stop the advance of the Nguyen."

"We are both kings and we understand the wider game," said King Thai Sa. "I understand the Nguyen were joined by Lao soldiers?"

"Before I was forced to flee, a Nguyen embassy was sent to Vientiane and Champasak."

"Since Lan Xang finally split into three, there has been peace between us. It is concerning to hear that both Vientiane and Champasak sent troops."

"Did Luang Prabang support the Nguyen?" asked Chaofa Naren.

"No. It was the southern states alone. Luang Prabang is too distant and too prudent to involve itself in a war so far south."

"Return to the land I have allocated for you and your men. Together we will send an expeditionary force next warring season. I want to ascertain their strength and their willingness to fight," said King Thai Sa.

In the year 1715 General Wongdon led a sizable army along the old road built by King Jayavarman the Great of Angkor. They were accompanied by two of the princes of Prea Srey Thomea, but the deposed Khmer king chose to stay in Ayutthaya. Siem Reap fell easily but General Vongdorn could penetrate no further. It was as if the new Viet-backed king had decided that Siem Reap was the new border town.

"An interesting strategy," said King Thai Sa after hearing the report on the mission by General Vongdorn. "It appears they are prepared to let us have the land as far as Siem Reap as long as we go no further."

"Is that acceptable to you?" asked Prince Naren.

"It is a clever move. By showing no aggression as far as Siem Reap they are, by intent, ceding the land to us and hoping we will be satisfied with that.

"And are you satisfied with that, Father?" asked Prince Naren.

"Of course not," replied the king.

The following year General Wongdon, the two princes, and their army marched southeast. They met no resistance until they passed Siem Reap, where a dogged defense was put up by the combined Khmer and Vietnamese forces. The Siamese forces eventually retreated but were not pursued as they left the country.

"Prea Srey Thomea did not accompany his men again. I wonder if he truly wants to regain his crown?" asked the king.

"I think we have made him too comfortable here. He has his royal residence and many concubines.

"Too many concubines, as my steward put it rather succinctly," replied Prince Naren.

"Next year we war as we must. Ready the navy. They will head south into the Gulf of Siam. I will lead the army with General Wongdon beside me. You will lead the navy. ."

In the year 1717 King Thai Sa sent two forces to Cambodia. The king himself led the land force into Cambodia, while the naval force was captained by Prince Naren. The two forces could not have had more different outcomes.

The naval force followed the coastline along the Gulf of Siam until they met a larger force of Cambodian and Vietnamese vessels. These countries were experienced shipbuilders. Few of the ships, however, were ships of war. Ships were built for trade and for defense against enemy or pirate attack. Many were large and slow. The superior numbers, and the tactical skills of the Vietnamese commanders, swung the battle in their favor. The Siamese fleet was scattered and took to the open sea, only to face a storm that wrecked much of the fleet. Only a handful of ships limped home.

The northern Siamese forces drove forward, past Siem Reap and on to the Cambodian capital of Oudong. The combined Khmer, Vietnamese, Vientiane, and Champasak armies were in full retreat under the concerted effort of King Thai Sa. However, in return for his surrender and allegiance to Siam, King Keo Fa was allowed to keep his throne. King Thai Sa was unwilling to support the idle Prea Srey Thomea any longer.

☙

In 1733, King Thai Sa died. On assuming the kingship in 1709 he had appointed his brother, Prince Phon, the heir to the throne, but later in his reign he changed the succession in favor of his second son, Prince Aphai. At the time of his death he had three sons. The eldest, Prince Naren, had entered the monastery, thereby relinquishing his right to the throne. On the news of the king's death a fierce struggle erupted between Prince Phon and the other two of the late king's sons, Prince Aphai and Prince Paramet. The struggle, which lasted nearly a month, saw the forces of the two brothers initially gain ground, but slowly the soldiers and supporters loyal to Prince Phon gained the upper hand. The fighting moved into Ayutthaya and hand-to-hand battles took place in the streets. Gradually the forces of Prince Phon closed in around the royal palace, the last stronghold of Prince Aphai. Prince Aphai's support ebbed away as his soldiers and supporters could sense their imminent defeat. Many of Prince Aphai's supporters switched sides rather than face certain death, something his private retainers could not do.

The two princes fled, allowing Prince Phon to seize the palace and take control of the city. The fleeing princes were pursued into a swamp, where they were captured and killed, presumably in the traditional manner. Prince Phon took the throne as King Borommakot, the thirty-first king of Ayutthaya.

29

KING BOROMMAKOT
1733–58

KING BOROMMAKOT CAME TO THE THRONE in the bloodiest of circumstances. On securing the royal palace many of those loyal to Prince Aphai were slaughtered, including many of those who had changed sides. Prince Naren, the eldest son of King Thai Sa, who had fled to the monastery, eventually being captured and executed. Many of the leading officials who had supported the king's sons— among them the Chinese phrakhlang—were purged. The new king was a man "known for his cruelty to people and animals alike." In many ways he was the son of King Suea. The bloodletting at the start of King Borommakot's reign was in contrast to the largely peaceful reign that followed.

The title "Borommakot" means "golden royal urn." Though it is not a name he took in his life, it is how he has been known since his death. What no one realized at the time it was coined is that this name would be especially fitting—King Borommakot was the last king of Ayutthaya to be cremated in the traditional manner.

At the time of his coronation he was already fifty-three years old and would reign for a further twenty-five years until his death at the age of seventy-eight. As king, he aspired to support Buddhism and the traditional virtues of a good king associated with the faith. His approach to religion was different than King Narai, who despite recognizing the importance of Buddhism to the role of the king and to the kingdom remained open-minded in his approach to all religions. King Narai favored Brahmanism rather than Buddhism and during his reign attended only essential Buddhist services.

King Borommakot, however, was a very strong supporter and advocate of Buddhism. During his reign, splendid temples were built, expanded, or restored, and the skyline of Ayutthaya changed as the king demonstrated his commitment to the faith. He was a Buddhist king who acted as the sangha, the nobles, and the people expected of their king.

In 1751, the king welcomed a delegation of Buddhist monks from Sri Lanka. In their home country their religion was in decline and they sought the assistance of King Borommakot to restore it. King Borommakot later arranged to send two missions to Sri Lanka. Monks took with them golden Buddha statues, sacred scriptures, and a letter from the king of Ayutthaya to the king of Sri Lanka written on gold.

Both voyages were ill-favored. The first ship got stuck in the mud in front of Nakhon Si Thammarat. The monks took eighteen months to reach Sri Lanka, and two thirds of them died on the way. The second mission saw most of the monks rescued after they were shipwrecked off the coast of Sri Lanka. When they finally arrived, however, their missions were a success. They remained for many years and ordained hundreds of new monks. Thai monks helped create the Perahera festival, in which the sacred tooth relic of the Buddha is carried in a grand parade through the streets of Kandy.

Sri Lanka was the spiritual center of Theravada Buddhism, and it was an important recognition for Siam to send these two missions. The order stemming from the monks ordained by the Siamese monks was called Siam Nikaya in tribute.

The monks from Sri Lanka who came to visit Ayutthaya were impressed by "Vat Puthi Suwan" (Wat Phutthai Sawan), where King Borommakot had commanded the Sri Lankan monks to worship.

> Seven days later on Friday, being full moon, two officers came and informed us that the king had given orders for us to go and worship at two vihāras on this day. We accordingly proceeded in boats and worshiped at the vihārē called Vat Puthi Suwan. The following is a description of the place. On the right of the great river there stretches a plain right up to the river bank; here are built long ranges of two-storied halls in the form of a

square, with four gateways on the four sides; on the four walls
were placed two hundred gilt images. Within the eastern gate is
fashioned a likeness of the sacred footprint, with the auspicious
symbol worked in gold. Right in the centre is a great gilt dagaba
[main prang] with four gates. On entering by the eastern gate
there is found a flight of stone steps gilt; right in the womb of
the dagaba are enshrined the holy relics; and it was so built
that it was possible to walk round within the dagaba without
approaching them. There was also within a gilt reproduction of
the Sacred Foot. On either side of this gate were built two five-
headed Nāga Rājas apparently descending to the bank of earth.
To the north of this was a two-storied building with a throne in
the middle of it; on this was seated a gilt figure of the Buddha
twelve cubits high. To the east of this and facing it was a five-
storied building hung with awnings and adorned with paintings
and gilding; the pillars in the middle were covered with plates of
gold, and on a throne in the centre was a life-size image of gold
supported on either side by two similar gilt images of the two
chief disciples Sariyut Mahasāmi and Maha Mugalan Sāmi and
numerous others. Above the gateway from the roof to the lintel
there was pictured in gilt work Buddha in the Sakra world, seated
on the White Throne and preaching his glorious Abhidharma
to the god Mavu [Maha] Déva and to the gods and Brahmas of
unnumbered worlds; and again, when his discourse was ended,
he is depicted as descending by the golden stairs to Sakaspura.
The viharē itself is strongly guarded by walls and gates; round
about are built pleasant halls and priests' houses filled with holy
men, with worshippers of high rank and devotees of either sex.

After securing the throne King Borommakot honored Khun
Chamnan Channarong, whoe had played a crucial role in capturing
the royal palace where the late king's sons were ensconced, and for
the next twenty years Chamnan Channarong was the most powerful
official in the court.

In the face of fierce European competition, Chinese trading activities increased. Thousands of Chinese junks sailed up and down the China coast and to Japan and Southeast Asia. Ever-increasing numbers of Chinese ships carried goods from one Southeast Asian port to another. Ayutthaya's harbors were filled with Chinese junks, and the city provided a home to many Chinese. They ran much of the economy and controlled many areas of trade. It was not only at the top level that the Chinese held influence. They were the traders, shopkeepers, blacksmiths, and pig farmers that drove the economy. The Chinese immigrants' freedom from corvée duty allowed them to work and prosper. Many arrived penniless, but unlike the Thai commoners, or *phrai*, they were not bound to any lords or kings. They gravitated toward their own kind, eating, working, and helping each other enjoy their common culture and religious practices—sometimes even banding together in secret Chinese-only societies. The secret societies controlled many aspects of Chinese trade, but most concerning was their role in the increasing import and distribution of opium in both the city of Ayutthaya and the country as a whole. The king was concerned about opium use by his subjects, especially by the nobility and those of higher rank. In the early years of the Ayutthaya kingdom, King Ramathibodi I had outlawed it:

> Those who smoke, consume or sell opium shall be subjected to severe punishment, confiscation of all their property, three days on public parade on land, three days of public parade by boat, and imprisonment until they can give up opium.

A series of clampdowns on the secret societies led to a major crisis in 1734 when three hundred Chinese residents stormed the royal palace. King Borommakot was away on a hunting expedition in Lopburi, but loyal troops defeated the Chinese. The royal palace was badly damaged and on his return to Ayutthaya, King Borommakot ordered that forty of the instigators be executed. The incident had little lasting impact. The Chinese continued to trade and the Lopburi River was crowded with floating shops and houses, with dozens of markets in the city. The markets in Ayutthaya were controlled by authorities appointed to protect the king's interests in collecting taxes and the customers' interests by maintaining law-abiding transactions. Trade and commerce invigorated the capital.

> The majority of the population is engaged in trade. Some spend all their time trafficking on the river with their wives and children in large boats commonly called myrous, from which they almost never disembark. Others dwell in the towns, remaining in their shops, where they retail the goods that they have bought wholesale off their ships, work at their own trade and sell what they have made.

The long-standing Ayutthayan strategy was to keep states that fell under its suzerainty weak, be it by division of the vested interests in the country or by levying troops to fight in Ayutthayan wars. This made the state more pliant and more reliant on Ayutthaya. In the east, the successor to King Keo Fa of the Khmer was toppled by Vietnamese forces, and the cycle began again.

"News has reached us of the Nguyen taking the Khmer throne," said the king's first minister.

"King Thai Sa fought long and hard to keep the Viet distant. They are no threat today, but we must not allow them to push toward our territory," said the king.

"You wish me to ready the troops?"

"Now is not the time for a major involvement. We are involved in Perak and Terengganu, and it is proving hard won. I am concerned with both Burma and Lan Na. There is much unrest in both domains and I fear their problems may spill across our frontiers. I think it would be best to keep the bulk of our troops in Ayutthaya."

"What do you suggest?"

"Prea Srey Thomea has succumbed to drink and would at best be a figurehead. His three princes are with him in Nakhon Ratchasima. Let us see if there is a leader amongst them."

"We will support them?"

"Only with a limited number of troops. Their regime would have more legitimacy if the relieving army was led by the Khmer themselves. We make it clear to them that we will continue to demand their suzerainty. Go to Nakhon Ratchasima and persuade them. Take their children as hostages should they decide to go," said the king.

The three Cambodian princes returned in 1737 and reinstated their aging father; ten years later his successor was overthrown again by the Vietnamese. With Siamese support, King Ang Snguon took the throne and presided over escalating violence. Internal wars against rival princes plagued the kingdom, and the war against the encroaching Vietnamese was marked by extreme violence on both sides. The Khmer killed or took captive many of the Vietnamese living in the country and sent many to the king of Ayutthaya as partial repayment of its debt. King Borommakot watched events from afar. The Khmer remained destabilized, honoring his suzerainty, and offered no threat. His concern was Burma, resurgent to the west.

After he attained the throne in 1733, killing Prince Aphai to achieve his goal, the new king undertook a number of administrative changes to ensure the security of his throne. His first step was to take away the power of the Ministry of Defense over the south of Siam, which he transferred to the Ports Department. He increased the number of departments handling government affairs and frequently moved personnel between them, reducing the chances that the head of any one department would have enough power to seize the throne.

The king acknowledged that the severe depletion in the corvée laborer ranks was due to the excessive burdens placed upon them. Many failed to honor their service or military obligations to the king by becoming monks, vagabonds, debt-slaves, or avoiding registration by bribing officials. One popular method of avoiding duties was to become a private retainer to a powerful member of the nobility who could protect his dependents against royal demands. The obligations of these retainers were lighter than those imposed by the crown and reduced the king's pool of available men.

These private retainers, however, did not have the right to change lords—these were the ones who had been compelled to fight to the last against the supporters of the future King Borommakot, even when they saw Prince Aphai's cause was doomed. Though they were in the end defeated, the king had seen the dangers of the private retainers firsthand but seemed powerless to make effective changes throughout his reign.

Both the nobles and the sangha stressed that the king should continually prove he was the best man to rule by following the ten royal virtues: munificence, moral living, generosity, justice, compassion, absence of bad ambition, suppression of anger, non-oppressiveness, humility, and upholding the dharma.

A prophecy surfaced during this era predicting that the city would fall if these moral rules were neglected:

> When virtues ten fall deaf on kingly ears,
> So smash the spheres; sixteen disasters smite,
> The moon, the stars, the earth and, yea, the sky,
> Are knocked awry—in every realm the blight . . .
> Though now Ayutthaya in bliss can claim,
> To shame all heaven's joys a myriad-fold,
> Yet here—behold!—are whores and sin foretold.
> Alas! Alas! Count the days 'til it shall come to pass!

In King Borommakot, Ayutthaya had a king who excelled in fulfilling the ten royal virtues. However, late in his reign his resolve was tested. Prince Thammathibet, the much-beloved poet and firstborn of the king, exceeded his authority and had three of the king's officials flogged. In retaliation one of the officials revealed that the prince—the upparat and heir to the throne—had been having an affair with not one but two of the king's concubines.

"My king, I am the bearer of grievous news," said Chao Phraya Sidarak, his first minister.

The king looked at his first minister. His head was deeply bowed, but there was no mistaking the concern he felt in what he was about to say.

"Prince Thammathibet has been accused of having affairs with two of your concubines."

The king stood, stunned by what he had just heard. Eventually he spoke, his voice choked with emotion as the words of his first minister sank in.

"Who accuses him?"

"He had three of your officials flogged. Khun Sikhom, one of those flogged, came to me and told of the affairs."

"The prince has no right to order my officials to be flogged, but that is unimportant for now. What did Khun Sikhom say?"

"He was angry. He felt humiliated and abused. He accused the upparat of many infidelities, but most telling was the accusation of the affairs with your concubines."

"My son is a known lover. He is the highest poet in the land. Women flock to him like bees around the honeypot. Why would he have affairs with two of my concubines? He is well aware of the penalty for such behavior."

"That is for you to ascertain," said the first minister.

"Where is he now?" asked the king.

"He is under guard in the front palace by my orders."

"Bring him to me," commanded the king.

Prince Thammathibet entered and prostrated himself at the feet of the king.

"My son what have you done?" asked the king.

"The accusation is well founded," said Prince Thammathibet.

"You are guilty of these crimes?" asked the king, his voice barely above a whisper.

"Yes, Father," said the upparat.

"Why? You have so many women to choose from."

"I have so many, but there are only two who are close to my heart."

"The ladies have been named. Will you name them also?" asked the king.

"They are Lady Sangwan and Lady Nim."

"You are aware of the penalty for these crimes?" asked the king.

"Yes father," said his son.

"You will return to the front palace. I will talk further with Chao Phraya Sidarak."

He watched as his son submissively backed out the chamber.

You are the future of Ayutthaya, the king thought to himself. *What have you done?*

Chao Phraya Sidarak, who had been permitted to listen from behind a curtain, entered as Prince Thammathibet left the chamber.

The two men sat in silence for many minutes. It was the first minister who spoke first.

"You rule under the ten royal virtues," said Chao Phraya Sidarak. "You have to be seen to dispense justice. Justice being in this case the death of Prince Thammathibet and the adulterous concubines."

"He is upparat and by far the most capable of my sons. He has worked alongside me through my entire reign. I fear for Ayutthaya should he be executed."

"That is not the immediate concern. He has broken the law and must be punished accordingly."

"The succession will fall to Prince Uthumphon. The leper Ekkathat is not fit to rule."

"You accept the death of your son then?"

"There is no choice," said the king, putting his head in his hands.

"He will be executed. How will it be done?" asked Chao Phraya Sidarak. "I ask as tradition demands that the incident that caused the situation be considered."

"You are saying that the traditional death for royalty may not be applied."

"I am much pained to say this but the flogging of the three men should be considered in your judgment on this matter," said Chao Phraya Sidarak. "I will return when you summon me."

With that Chao Phraya Sidarak backed out of the room leaving the king sitting alone on his throne, weeping.

Prince Thammathibet and the two concubines were executed, flogged to death in the manner Prince Thammathibet had punished the officials, while others say Prince Thammathibet's death was carried out in the traditional manner, with a sandalwood club. After his death the king honored his son. Wat Chaiwatthanaram was the royal monastery where the king and his descendants would perform their religious rites. It was the cremation site used for the princes, princesses, and the royal family of his dynasty. When Prince Thammathibet died the king decreed that an area in the Wat be used as the site for his royal cremation.

King Borommakot was in his early seventies. Being forced to have his heir apparent and two of his concubines executed took its toll. When Prince Thammathibet died, the succession planned by King Borommakot died with him.

King Borommakot died in 1758. He was succeeded by his youngest son, Prince Uthumphon.

30

KING UTHUMPHON
1758

KING EKKATHAT
1758–67

KING UTHUMPHON'S FIRST ACT WAS TO EXECUTE three of his half-brothers. Only his elder brother Prince Ekkathat, scarred by leprosy, remained.

"The generals are still waiting for your command to quell the rebellion in Nakhon Si Thammarat. A king needs to be decisive in times like this," said Prince Ekkathat. "And we still need your decision on the site of the coronation."

"I thought to hold the coronation in the old Bencharat Palace of King Narai," responded King Uthumphon. "Father completed the renovations. I thought it would be a tribute to his work."

"You will do no such thing. The Bencharat Palace is far too small for the coronation that I have planned for you. Only the royal palace will suffice."

"But I am king. My wishes must be considered."

"You are my younger brother and you do not even know your own mind yet. The throne is mine by right. My affliction in no way affects my ability to rule. Be assured, younger brother, that I will be by your side throughout your reign. Closely by your side," said Prince Ekkathat.

Seeing the future clearly, King Uthumphon relinquished the crown to the claims of his elder brother, Prince Ekkathat, and ordained. Prince Ekkathat took the throne as King Suriyat Amarin, the thirty-third and last king of Ayutthaya. He was popularly referred to as King Ekkathat. He seemed to many too blemished to compete for the succession of the throne. Some also called him Khun Luang

Khi Ruean, or the "mangy king"—a reference to his battles with leprosy.

King Ekkathat's accession revived the Siamese economy. He donated generously for the building of temples and the restoration of existing ones. He was active in encouraging trade both with the east and the west. The western ports of Mergui and Tenasserim saw an increase in trade. However, this flowering was short-lived.

◉⁓

In 1744 the Burmese governors of Martaban and Tavoy fled from a Mon uprising led by Smim Dhaw, who looked to form an independent Mon state in the region. King Borommakot offered political shelter to the Burmese governors but extended no help to the Mons in their uprising against the weak restored Toungoo king. On hearing of this, the dominant Burmese kingdom of Ava sent a mission to Ayutthaya, establishing the first diplomatic relations between the two nations for over a century. King Borommakot sent gifts in return. Despite the improvement in political relations between the two countries, King Borommakot protected and supported Smim Dhaw, who was ultimately driven from his Mon homeland. King Borommakot refused to hand him over as the Burmese requested.

To the north of Burma a popular local leader, Alaungpaya, rose up and gained control of the area and then widened his territory, conquering the fledgling Mon kingdom and defeating their French allies. Ayutthaya grew alarmed as the Burmese encroached on their territory. King Ekkathat tried to foster new rebellions in response. Thousands of fleeing Mons had taken refuge in Siamese territory. They were formed into fighting units and sent to the frontier, supported by the Siamese. The area became the scene of much fighting and death.

King Alaungpaya was within a few years the dominant power in Burma. He retaliated against the Mon and Ayutthaya by taking the ports of Moulmein, Tavoy, and Tenasserim. Once his conquest was complete, the Mons subdued and the Siamese driven back over the Tenasserim Hills, he sent a message to King Ekkathat that their friendship was ended as they had failed to deliver Smim Dhaw as requested. King Alaungpaya was also incensed that King Ekkathat had refused to give him one of his daughters in marriage, an act which if carried out may have served to stabilize the impending conflict between the two kingdoms.

War was justifiable in the eyes of the Burmese king, but even more compelling was the opportunity for conquest of an old foe and the wealth that came with such a conquest. The message was a prelude to invasion. The Burmese king's generals and ministers cautioned him against war, but to no avail. Court astrologers warned that there were unfavorable signs in the night sky, but the king was determined.

King Alaungpaya took with him his second son, Prince Hsinbyushin. The Burmese king moved his troops eastward over the Tenasserim Hills toward Ayutthaya. He moved south after clearing the mountains, capturing a few coastal towns, thus being able to meet with his navy, which had sailed along the coast with horses, weapons, and provisions. From there he marched his army along the coast and then turned north where a serious clash with the Ayutthayan army took place along the banks of the Mae Klong River. The Siamese incurred heavy losses but fought bravely. King Alaungpaya could now move on to Ayutthaya unopposed.

"Your Majesty, our army has been defeated and is in full retreat," said First Minister Liampricha. "The Burmese will be at our gates in a matter of days!"

"What do you mean by 'full retreat'? We outnumbered King Alaungpaya and are fighting on our terrain. How could General Phuangkongna lose so quickly?"

"Reports are still arriving, but we need to prepare for a siege."

"I will have General Phuangkongna's head for this. The Burmese at our gates. What am I to do? What am I to do?" the king wailed to himself.

"You need to show leadership. Organize the defenses," said First Minister Liampricha.

"I need to show leadership," snapped the king. "All around me are nothing but incompetents. A general who cannot fight and soldiers that run."

"But Your Majesty, the Burmese will be here. We need to prepare."

"Then fetch Prince Uthumphon from the monastery. He always wanted to be a soldier. Now is his time to prove himself," said the king.

Rallying his supporters, Prince Uthumphon organized defenses and put up a stiff resistance against the invaders. Ayutthaya was surrounded and bombarded. Villages around the city were burned, as were many Dutch and Chinese trading ships. Within days bodies choked the canals, cannon balls hit the royal palace, and many buildings were set ablaze.

Under the popular and competent leadership of Prince Uthumphon the people of Ayutthaya defended their capital and made the enemy realize that a long campaign would be unavoidable. Prince Uthumphon refused to talk with his would-be Burmese conquerors and determined to hold out until the rise of the rivers would flood the camp of the besieger. King Alaungpaya, like King Tabinshwehti centuries before him, had not prepared for a long siege.

The Burmese king sent conciliatory messages, declaring that he came as a bodhisattva with only pure, holy intentions. King Ekkathat merely scoffed at his conceit. In the meantime King Alaungpaya was injured when shrapnel from a cannon struck him. He then ordered a retreat, only five days after he had arrived at the city he had meant to conquer.

The Burmese retreated via the steep Three Pagodas Pass, carrying their king in a litter. He died near the city of Martaban and his body was returned to his capital city of Swebo after being ferried upstream from Yangon.

With the retreat of the Burmese and immediate danger passed, King Ekkathat returned to claim the royal palace, and Prince Uthumphon retired once again to the monastery. As a scholarly and intelligent man he had no wish to be involved in the wiles and machinations of his brother. He would never again return to aid his elder brother.

Meanwhile, King Ekkathat turned to the pleasures of the flesh, and Ayutthaya gradually started to lose control over its outlying cities.

King Alaungpaya was succeeded by his son, King Naungaogyi, who died only three years into his reign. The crown then fell to King Hsinbyushin. As a young man he had accompanied his father on the failed expedition to Ayutthaya. He had felt the defeat and had seen firsthand the insults levied at his father. Perhaps more concerning for Ayutthaya, he had inherited his father's energy and his military talent. He reinforced the army at Chiang Mai with twenty thousand men and appointed new officials loyal to him all across his growing kingdom. With Burma secure he set out to avenge the insults to his father and to secure the wealth of Ayutthaya.

The accession of King Hsinbyushin was of great concern to King Ekkathat, who was aware of the offense his comments had caused to the Burmese king's father during the earlier siege of Ayutthaya. He also knew of the growing military reputation of King Hsinbyushin. Realizing that war was inevitable, the king of Ayutthaya continued to destabilize Tavoy by getting the governor to switch sides and to cause instability along the border, but King Ekkathat knew that this would only delay a Burmese invasion.

"Don't look to me to help you again," said an angry Prince Uthumphon to his elder brother. "You wanted to be king. Now learn what it means to be king!"

King Ekkathat made careful preparations to defend his capital. The king of the previous years was becoming more circumspect. City walls were rebuilt and heightened, numerous guns and jingals positioned, moats widened, and new weapons acquired. The city held enough resources to survive for one season. As with many past kings, King Ekkathat was hoping for the rising river to help drive out the Burmese.

In 1764, under the sovereign rule of King Hsinbyushin, the Burmese began to move two great armies toward Ayutthaya under the command of two of their most respected generals, General Ne Myo Thihapate, who would lead the invasion from the north, and General Maha Nawrahta, who would lead the army from the west and the south. To supplement his forces General Ne Myo Thihapate was sent to raise troops from the semiautonomous Shan states. King Hsinbyushin then sent General Ne Myo Thihapate north to subdue the Lao kingdoms of Vientiane and Luang Prabang, two states that might support Ayutthaya in the coming war. Vientiane surrendered without fighting. Luang Prabang proved more difficult to take but by March of 1765 it was under Burmese control. The northern flank was secure.

In 1765, Burmese armies invaded Siam from three directions. After putting down a rebellion in Chiang Mai, King Hsinbyushin invaded Siam with two armies. The southern army under General Maha Nawrahta divided in two. One of his armies followed the traditional invasion route, the Three Pagodas Pass, while the other came north from the Malay Peninsula. The other army, under General Ne Myo Thihapate headed south from Chiang Mai. They killed or enslaved all the inhabitants of any village that resisted. Where King Alaungpaya had failed, his son King Hsinbyushin would prove dreadfully successful.

The Siamese planned their defense. King Ekkathat conscripted all available men into his army. He placed his best units facing the anticipated onslaught from General Maha Nawrahta as he came through the Three Pagodas Pass and up from the south. In the north the defensive line began at Sukhothai, Kamphaeng Phet, and Phitsanulok.

The northern army under General Ne Myo Thihapate gathered in Chiang Mai and began its advance in August 1765, as the rainy season drew to a close. Their progress was slow as a combination of the rains and pockets of resistance stood in their way. Progress was slow, but the Burmese general fought his way down the Ping River, taking the cities of Tak and Kamphaeng Phet by the end of the rainy season. The plan called for the armies to arrive outside Ayutthaya at approximately the same time. The northern army arrived two months behind schedule, a tribute to the defense put up by the Siamese forces.

General Maha Nawrahta opened his campaign on the western and southern fronts in October 1765. He split his army of some thirty thousand in two. One army invaded by the Three Pagodas Pass toward Suphanburi while the other headed further south to Mergui and Tenasserim and crossed the mountains through the Myitta Pass before moving on Kanchanaburi. After Kanchanaburi the Burmese army marched toward Ayutthaya, where they faced a joint land and naval attack by the Siamese forces. An English ship bombarded the Burmese troops, and casualties on both sides were heavy; however, the Burmese defenses proved effective, forcing the Ayutthayan troops to retreat.

The second army of General Maha Nawrahta made their way through the Three Pagodas Pass, meeting a Siamese army, which it defeated convincingly. His two armies united again, only to meet strong resistance at Bang Rachan near Singburi. Around five thousand villagers formed themselves into guerrilla groups, reminiscent of the Wild Tigers in the time of King Naresuan, and severely hampered the Burmese advance. They continued to beleaguer the Burmese until they were beaten down, destroyed, or enslaved. Today they are still remembered for their bravery and tenacity. General Maha Nawrahta arrived to the northwest of Ayutthaya, where he established his position and waited for the army of General Ne Myo Thihapate to arrive.

General Ne Myo Thihapate had taken Sukhothai and Phitsanulok, where he paused briefly to allow his troops to recover. The governors of both towns drank the water of allegiance and were compelled to provide conscripts for the Burmese army. King Ekkathat attacked the force under General Ne Myo Thihapate before the union of the two armies had been effected. The attack failed, and the Siamese troops retreated to Ayutthaya to await the siege. The army of General Ne Myo Thihapate made contact with General Maha Nawatra's army on January 20, 1766.

The two Burmese armies now completely hemmed in the city. The city was too strong and too well defended to be taken by assault, and as time passed and no signs of surrender appeared, the approach of the dreaded rainy season with the rise of the rivers, which more than once in former times had saved the city, caused alarm among the besiegers.

King Hsinbyushin refused to retreat to when the waters came. When the area surrounding Ayutthaya was flooded, the besiegers moved to the temples, which sat on higher ground outside Ayutthaya, and constructed dykes to keep out the water. The Burmese had come prepared with many boats, and now they constructed others. The Siamese launched their boats against the besiegers, and a series of water battles took place between the two sides. The line of entrenchment around the city was for the time rendered useless, but eventually the water subsided.

The Shan, in response to General Ne Myo Thihapate's enforced recruitment campaign in their homelands, had sent emissaries to the Chinese emperor. The Shan paid tribute to China and had done so since the time of King Naresuan. The emperor was under an obligation to help those under his suzerainty. No doubt he also realized the weakness of Burma with its armies currently engaged in Ayutthaya. He sent a token army of six thousand men who laid siege to the garrison city of Kengtung in northern Burma. Despite the Chinese being driven back, King Hsinbyushin recognized he was now fighting on two fronts and that on one of those fronts he faced the largest army in the world.

When the waters receded, the siege recommenced. Earthen embankments grew, in some places even higher than the defending walls. The city of Ayutthaya became weakened by the lack of provisions. An army of Shan, no friends of the Burmese and an ally of Ayutthaya from the time of King Naresuan, attempted to break the siege, but they were driven back.

The Chinese launched a far larger attack directly aimed at the city of Ava in December of 1766. King Hsinbyushin, despite the threat to his homeland, did not recall his troops. He redirected his troops in the north of Burma and the Shan states, where they successfully held off the superior numbers of Chinese troops, buying time to complete the assault on Ayutthaya.

King Ekkathat offered surrender, saying that the great city would become a vassal state to Burma. The Burmese refused the surrender, replying that nothing but the unconditional submission of the entire Siamese army would be considered. Unlike in the time of King's Tabinshwehti and Bayinnaung, this Burmese king did not seek suzerainty over Ayutthaya. He sought revenge and he sought plunder.

General Maha Nawrahta died after a short illness, too late in the campaign to affect the outcome. He was cremated with full honors by royal decree. The Burmese now held command of the entire resources of the country and had successfully prevented food supplies from entering the city. Their earthworks rose and dominated the defensive walls of Ayutthaya, ominously growing higher each day.

The Burmese dug tunnels under the city walls, and on April 7, 1767, several sections of the wall were brought down by mines set off underneath. The Burmese surged forward, and although the Siamese continued to fight bravely they were eventually overwhelmed. Fierce hand-to-hand combat ensued, along with horrendous butchery of the civilian population as men, women, children, monks, and foreign priests were slaughtered without regard. Burmese troops set fire to buildings, raping and plundering as they moved through the inner city streets and canals. Within hours the palaces, temples, and warehouses, along with huge residential sections of the city, were in flames.

The city was sacked mercilessly. Even gold plating on images of the Buddha was removed. The remaining gold on the Buddha images and chedis melted in the intense heat. Ayutthaya's art treasures, the libraries containing its literature, and the archives housing its historical records were looted and almost totally destroyed. The city was left charred and in ruins.

The queen and the entire royal family were taken prisoner. Immense treasures and stores of war materiel were found in the palace and taken by the Burmese. It is estimated that twenty thousand people died during the sack of Ayutthaya and a further ten thousand were taken as captives and led away to Burma.

Some say King Ekkathat succeeded in fleeing by eventually died from starvation. Others report that he was killed during the wanton plundering of the city and his body lay desecrated at the west gate of the city. Prince Uthumphon was taken captive to the Burmese city of Pegu.

Only one week after entering the city, Ne Myo Thihapate received orders to return home, as the Burmese monarchy was once more threatened by a Chinese invasion. Governors and occupying armies were, however, left in the major cities. The siege of Ayutthaya had lasted fourteen months, and when the city fell the Burmese destroyed it completely. The ruins of the capital were never rebuilt.

@‑‑‑

The sacking of Ayutthaya was an event that never faded from the memories of those who witnessed it:

> The sinful Burmese ravaged our villages and cities. A great number of our citizens and many temples were killed and ruined. Our peaceful kingdom was abandoned and turned into forest. The Burmese showed no mercy to the Thai and felt no shame for all the sins they had committed.

An esteemed monk compared the situation following the fall of Ayutthaya with the Buddhist dark age:

> The fall of Ayudhya in 1767 threw the Thai state into chaos, disrupting normal social life, causing economic and material deprivations, and dividing the population into factions which contended with each other for scarce resources. The harsh conditions broke up families, and food was in short supply. Many Buddhist monks, finding that they could not survive in the ordained state, disrobed and went off into lay life to seek their own livelihoods. Buddhism suffered in other ways as well, as disrespectful people committed violence against Buddhist images and scavenged libraries for the cloth and cords that bound the Pali scripts, thus leaving them prey to insects.

A French missionary at the time also witnessed the destruction:

On the 28th April 1767 the town was captured by assault. The treasures of the palace and the temples were nothing but heaps of ruins and ashes. The images of gods were melted down and rage deprived the barbarian conquerors of the spoils that had aroused their greed. To avenge this loss, the Burmese visited their heavy displeasure upon the townsfolk. They burnt the soles of their feet in order to make them reveal where they had concealed their wealth, and raped their weeping daughters before their very eyes.

The priests suspected of having concealed much wealth were pierced through and through with arrows and spears and several were beaten to death with heavy clubs.

The country side as well as the temples were strewn with corpses, and the river was choked with the bodies of the dead, the stench of which attracted swarms of flies causing much annoyance to the retreating army. The chief officers of state and the royal favourites were loaded with chains and condemned to slavery in the galleys. The King, witness of the unhappy fate of his court endeavored to escape, but he was recognized and slain at the gates of the palace.

Ayutthaya had been reduced to rubble, but from the ruins a new hero would emerge and drive the Burmese out of Siam. A half-Chinese, half-Thai general named Phraya Taksin had gained renown when he fought a successful holding action against the Burmese and later when he was put in charge of Ayutthaya's defenses. With the Burmese forces closing in he was unable to launch an effective counterattack, which drew some unfair criticism from King Ekkathat. Unable to make the king listen to reason, and seeing it was only a question of time before the Burmese breached the walls, Phraya Taksin cut his way out of the doomed city with five hundred followers and escaped southward.

Phraya Taksin established a foothold in Rayong, on the lightly occupied eastern shore of the Gulf of Siam, and his name soon became a rallying call to all those resisting the Burmese invasion. In June 1767 he moved his growing army to capture neighboring Chanthaburi. By October his army had grown to ten times its original size, and he felt strong enough to advance against the Burmese. He mounted a naval attack, sailing up the Chao Phraya River and capturing Thonburi, which he made his capital. The Thai governor appointed by the Burmese was executed.

He advanced north and attacked the Burmese at their main camps outside the ruined city of Ayutthaya. The country was reduced to chaos. Provinces were proclaimed independent states. In Nakhon Ratchasima a son of King Borommakot formed a new state. In Phitsanulok a Buddhist monk clad in the reddish robes of the forest sect took command of the city. Nakhon Si Thammarat established itself as an independent state, and Thonburi saw Phraya Taksin crowned king.

King Taksin set out to unify these states into a single country. He turned back a Burmese attempt to recapture Ratchaburi and followed that with an unsuccessful attack on Phitsanulok. King Taksin regrouped and moved on, winning a decisive victory over Nakhon Ratchasima in 1768 and Nakhon Si Thammarat later that year. King Taksin then moved again against Phitsanulok. This time the city fell after a short siege.

King Taksin went on to turn back four further invasion attempts from Burma. In time he succeeded in restoring Thai suzerainty over the Khmer, Chiang Mai, and the Lao territories of Luang Prabang and Vientiane. His victories not only liberated the country but also revitalized the minds of the people of Siam. From the heaviest of defeats they were, within a little over a decade, on their way to again becoming a dominant power in Southeast Asia.

Fifteen years of uninterrupted warfare took its toll on King Taksin, who declared himself a future Buddha and demanded worship. He was judged insane. Meanwhile General Chao Phraya Chakri was increasingly the one leading Siam's army to victory, and in 1781 his force of twenty thousand was away fighting the Khmer. Rebels plotted a coup against the insane king with the aim of placing General Chakri on the throne. They imprisoned King Taksin. General Chakri returned to the capital, eliminated the rebel leaders, executed King Taksin,

and was crowned King Rama I, establishing the Chakri dynasty and moving the capital of Siam to Bangkok.
Ayutthaya was abandoned.

DOCUMENTATION

Author's Comments

Many, but not all, of the records relating to Ayutthaya were destroyed when the Burmese sacked the capital. Many details can be found in the Burmese and Lan Xang chronicles, in centuries-old books, and in the tales—often fanciful—of the early Portuguese mercenaries and others who traveled to the kingdom.

Two areas that were perhaps the most problematic were the size of armies and the dates of kings' reigns. As an example, the Burmese chronicles, as with any work of the type, needed to be evaluated in the light of who was writing the record. The early Portuguese reports seemed to increase the size of an army by a factor of ten, but it's important to remember they also told of a wondrous land that held them in awe. For the reigns of kings I have used the conventional dates, though sometimes historians have called them inaccurate. My biggest problem with this was the reign of King Ekathotsarot. Some give the dates of his reign as 1605–10 (which I have used), while others indicate 1605–20. I settled on the former after looking at the events of his reign and of King Songtham, who followed him after the early demise of King Si Saowaphak.

The characterization of the kings was an interesting aspect of writing this narrative. Toward the end of Ayutthaya there are detailed accounts that helped me when trying to understand the kings as individuals. In the earlier history I was much more reliant on myths, legends, and my own interpretations. Occasionally a tantalizing tidbit of information would help form the character of a king: the unpreparedness of King Borommaracha II for the throne, King Borommaracha IV's love of the arts and refusal of a divine title, and the relationship between King Intharacha and Okya Mahasena. These all helped me in trying understand the kings, their personalities, and their motivations.

I am English and was struck by the similarities between our history and that of Ayutthaya. Dynastic struggles, the murder of princes, cruelties, and rule by divine right are just some of the examples that we share in common. The more I researched the more the story needed to be told. More than that, it needed to be understood.

This book is about more than the kings; through the kings the reader can understand the development of a nation. I have endeavored to write a book that does not just give the history but also gives a flavor of the cultural heritage of a people.

I owe a debt of gratitude to the many researchers and enthusiasts who have spent much time and energy studying Siamese history and have shared their findings. There is much information to sift through—sometimes contradictory, incomplete, or in some cases even mistaken—but by wading into it a picture emerges. The scholars and sources cited below were most helpful to me in my journey toward understanding the story of Ayutthaya.

Notes and Sources

Chapter 1

3 "Afterwards Pho Khun Pha Mu'ang . . ." From a Sukhothai inscription known as the *Nagara Jum*, quoted in G. Cœdès, "The Origins of the Sukhodaya Dynasty," *Journal of the Siam Society 14*, no. 1 (1921), 7.

10 "My father went to fight . . ." Translation from the Ram Khamhaeng Inscription, kept in the National Museum in Bangkok. Barend Jan Terwiel, *The Ram Khamhaeng Inscription: The Fake That Did Not Come True* (Gossenberg, Germany: Ostasien Verlag, 2010), 97. Available at http://www.reihe-gelbe-erde.de/rge/bilder/005.pdf.

Chapter 2

12 "There is fish . . ." From the inscription translated in A. B. Griswold and Prasert na Nagara, "The Inscription of King Rāma Gamhèn: Epigraphic and Historical Studies No. 9," *Journal of the Siam Society 59*, no. 2 (1971): 205–7.

14 Pact between Ram Khamhaeng, Mangrai, and Ngam Mueang. The meeting of these three kings is remembered in the Three Kings Monument situated near the center of the walled city in Chiang Mai.

24–25 The legend of Phra Ruang. Phra Ruang was a hero of Thai legend in the *Phra ratchaphongsawadan nuea*, or the Chronicle of the North. This extract is from the Ramkhamhaeng National Museum in Sukhothai Historical Park.

Chapter 3

30 "Most families have a hundred . . ." Zhou Daguan, *A Record of Cambodia*, trans. Peter Harris (Chiang Mai: Silkworm Books, 2007), 58.

30–31 "He was formerly a farmer . . ." Adapted from the oldest of the Cambodia Chronicles, the Ang Eng fragment, dating from 1796. Tavit Jitsomboon, "Who built Angkor Wat? (ใครสร้างนครวัด)," GotoKnow. org, February 11, 2011, http://www.gotoknow.org/posts/454062.

34–35 "Meanwhile, he received information . . ." From *Van Vliet's Siam* by Chris Baker, Dhiravat Na Pombejra, Alfons van der Kraan, and David K. Wyatt, quoted in Tricky Vandenberg, "Bueng Phra Ram," *Ayutthaya Historical Research*, April 2016, http://www.ayutthaya-history.com/Historical_Sites_BuengPhraRam.html.

36   "In 712, a Year of the Tiger . . ." Richard D. Cushman, trans.,
        The Royal Chronicles of Ayutthaya, quoted in David K. Wyatt,
        Thailand: A Short History (Chiang Mai: Silkworm Books, 2004).

Chapter 4

48   "king was wise, eloquent . . ." Written later by the Dutchman
        Jeremias van Vleet. From *Van Vliet's Siam*, quoted in Tricky
        Vandenberg, "King Borommaracha I (สมเด็จพระบรมราชาธิราชที่
        ๑), *Ayutthaya Historical Research*, September 2011, http://www.
        ayutthaya-history.com/Dynasties_BorommarachaI.html.

Chapter 5

65   "Then the King went out . . ." Cushman, *Royal Chronicles*, quoted
        in Tricky Vandenberg, "Wat Maha That," *Ayutthaya Historical
        Research*, January 2015, http://www.ayutthaya-history.com/
        Temples_Ruins_MahaThat.html.

66   "One evening the King walked . . ." Cushman, *Royal Chronicles
        of Ayutthaya*, quoted in "Grand Palace," *Ayutthaya Historical
        Research*, accessed February 4, 2017, http://www.ayutthaya-history.
        com/Historical_Sites_GrandPalace.html.

Chapter 7

80–81   "I reverently took on . . ." Quoted in Geoff Wade, "The Ming
        shi-lu as a Source for Thai History: Fourteenth to Seventeenth
        Centuries," *Journal of Southeast Asian Studies* 31, no. 2 (2000):
        249–94, http://hub.hku.hk/bitstream/10722/42537/1/56512.pdf.

86   "One curious tradition . . ." George Bacon, *Siam, the Land of the
        White Elephant, As It Was and Is* (New York: Charles Scribner's
        Sons, 1892), 23–24.

Chapter 8

96–97   "From ancient times . . ." *Sejarah Melayu* (*Malay Annals*). Quoted
        in Sabri Zain, "The Thai Nemesis," *Sejarah Melayu: A History of
        the Malay Peninsula*, accessed December 13, 2016, http://www.
        sabrizain.org/malaya/melaka1.htm.

Chapter 9

109   "And after a while the Siamese . . ." *Sejarah Melayu*, quoted in Zain,
        "The Thai Nemesis."

110 "the spiritual prowess of a Sayyid . . ." *Sejarah Melayu* as explained in Abu Talib Ahmad and Tan Liok Ee, eds., New Terrains in Southeast Asian History (Athens, OH: Ohio University Press; Singapore: Singapore University Press, 2003), 206.

Chapter 10
117–18 The Tale of Prince Wetsandon. Adapted from Sombat Chantornvong, "Religious Literature in Thai Political Perspective," in *Essays on Literature and Society in Southeast Asia: Political and Sociological Perspectives*, ed. Tham Seong Chee (Singapore: Singapore University Press, 1981), 190–91.
119–20 "The chief envoy . . ." W. A. R. Wood, *A History of Siam* (London: T. Fisher Unwin, 1926), 91.

Chapter 12
128–29 "Pra Nakorn Sri Ayutthaya is the capital . . ." From Aphivan Saipradist's PhD thesis (Silpakorn University) on heritage management and tourism in Ayutthaya, quoted in Poramet Boonnumsirikij, "Spirit and Place: The Preservation of Religious Values through Buddha Images at World Heritage Sites in Thailand" (PhD thesis, Silpakorn University, 2011), 42, http://doi.nrct.go.th/ListDoi/listDetail?Resolve_DOI=10.14457/SU.the.2011.521.
135–36 The Tale of *Khun Chang Khun Phaen*. Adapted from summary in Richard Barrow, "The Story of Khun Chang Khun Phan," *Thai Blogs*, June 29, 2006, http://www.thai-blogs.com/2006/06/29/the-story-of-khun-chang-khun-phan/.
137 "In 891, a year of the ox . . ." Richard D. Cushman, *The Royal Chronicles of Ayutthaya*, ed. David K. Wyatt (Bangkok: Siam Society, 2000), 19.

Chapter 13
139–40 "The Law for Trial by Ordeal . . ." Wood, *A History of Siam*, 101–2.
144 "This prince had lived in the reputation . . ." Fernão Mendes Pinto, *The Voyages and Adventures of Ferdinand Mendez Pinto, the Portuguese*, trans. Henry Cogan (London: T. Fisher Unwin, 1897), 406.

Chapter 14

153   "When Khun Chinnarat became king . . ." From the *Khamhaikan Chao Krung Kao (The Statement of the Residents of the Old Capital)*, quoted in Piriya Krairiksh, "A Revised Dating of Ayudhya Architecture," *Journal of the Siam Society* 80, no. 1 (1992): 41.

Chapter 15

164   King Bayinnaung's army arriving at Ayutthaya. Some contemporary Portuguese commentators put the size of the army that arrived outside Ayutthaya at as many as one million men. Given the population at the time that figure is unlikely, but estimates of over five hundred thousand men may be accurate.

Chapter 16

177   "the chieftain who never . . ." Recorded in Mayoury Ngaosyvathn and Pheuiphanh Ngaosyvathn, Paths to Conflagration: Fifty Years of Diplomacy and Warfare in Laos, Thailand, and Vietnam, 1778–1828, Southeast Asia Program Publications (Ithaca, NY: Cornell University, 1998), 63.

Chapter 17

192–93   "The Kingdom of Kamboja has never . . ." Exchange recorded in *Akkasar Mahaboros Khmaer (Chronicle of Khmer Heroes)* by Eng Sot, quoted in Lem Chuck Moth, "Nokor Caktomukh," *Khmer History*, July 31, 2015, http://meruheritage.com/NokorCatomukh.html.

Chapter 18

206   "Since the king of Pegu . . ." Recorded by early Bangkok historians in *Phraratchaphongsawadan Krung Sayam*, quoted in Sunait Chutintaranond, "The Image of the Burmese Enemy in Thai Perceptions and Historical Writings," *Journal of the Siam Society* 80, no. 1 (1992): 92.

206–7   Prince Naresuan's shot across the Sittaung. The musket used by Prince Naresuan in this action formed for many years part of the regalia of Siam, and is known as the "musket of the battle of the Sittaung River."

207   "Victorious warriors win first . . ." Sun Tzu, *The Art of War*, quoted in *Wikiquote*, December 23, 2016, https://en.wikiquote.org/wiki/Sun_Tzu.

Chapter 19

221   Prince Naresuan's attack on camp of King Nanda Bayin. The sword used that day by Prince Naresuan became known as the "camp-scaling sword" and formed part of the royal regalia of Ayutthaya for many years.

Chapter 20

223   "The king has his court . . ." Account of King Naresuan's court by Flemish gem trader Jacques de Coutre. His remark about the "Ganges" reflects the then-common belief that the waterways of Southeast Asia were connected to the Ganges River. Peter Borschberg, ed., and Roopanjali Roy, trans. *The Memoirs and Memorials of Jacques de Coutre: Security, Trade and Society in 16th- and 17th-century Southeast Asia* (Singapore: NUS Press), 129.

225   "If we go with the king . . ." From *Mhannan Rajawan* (*The Glass Palace Chronicle*), the first official compilation of Burmese history, commissioned in the 1820s. Quoted in Than Tun, "Ayut'ia Men in the Service of Burmese Kings: 16th and 17th Centuries," *Southeast Asian Studies* 21, no. 4 (1984): 404, https://kyoto-seas. org/pdf/21/4/210403.pdf.

228   "Whatever is our royal older brother . . ." Cushman, *The Royal Chronicles of Ayutthaya*, quoted in Barend Terwiel, "What Happened at Nong Sarai? Comparing Indigenous and European Sources for Late 16th Century Siam," *Journal of the Siam Society* 101 (2013): 21.

229   "Because he lost in a cockfight . . ." Recorded in Tun Aung Chain, trans., *Chronicle of Ayutthaya: A Translation of the Yodaya Yazawin*, quoted in Terwiel, "What Happened at Nong Sarai?" 24.

232–33 "The day the animal died . . ." Borschberg and Roy, *Memoirs of Jacques de Coutre*, 142–44.

Chapter 21

243   "The King of Siam wished . . ." From a brochure of unknown authorship titled *Ambassade du Roi de Siam envoyée à l'Excellence du Prince Maurice, arrivée à La Haye le 10 septembre 1608*, quoted in Dirk van der Cruysse, *Siam and the West, 1500–1700* (Chiang Mai: Silkworm Books, 2002), 47.

244   "a million lengths of red stuff . . ." From the account Keeling gave in *A Journall of the Third Voyage to the East Indies*, quoted in van der Cruysse, *Siam and the West*, 54.

245   Prince Suthat's death. One account has it that Prince Suthat was angry with some nobles and told his father that he wanted to remove their titles. Dismissing nobles was only the prerogative of the king, so King Ekathotsarot chided his son by sarcastically asking him if he was going to ask for the kingship as well. Another report tells that Prince Suthat asked his father to release a prisoner. This angered his father who felt the prince was trying to influence his rule. Yet another report supposes that Prince Suthat was suspected of actually plotting to overthrow his father, and he fled and killed himself when the plot was exposed.

Chapter 22

252   "The emperor or king of Siam . . ." From an account given by the trader Cornelis van Neijenrode, a director of the Dutch trading station at Ayutthaya. Quoted in van der Cruysse, *Siam and the West*, 52.

253   "The existence of a sea . . ." Exchange quoted in Wan Waithayakon (Prince Naradhip Bhongseprabhan), a grandson of King Rama IV, in *A Diplomatic History of Thailand* (Bangkok: Office of the National Culture Commission, 1991), 17.

255   "How can I do so? . . ." Description credited to Jeremias van Vliet, retold in Wood, *A History of Siam*, 174.

Chapter 23

263   "of low value . . . the most splendid . . ." From the ambassador's reminiscences, quoted in Bhawan Ruangsilp, *Dutch East India Company Merchants at the Court of Ayutthaya: Dutch Perceptions of the Thai Kingdom, ca. 1604–1765* (Leiden: Brill, 2007), 63–64.

264   "You will henceforth carry . . ." Recorded by Van Vliet, quoted in van der Cruysse, *Siam and the West*, 65.

—   "This drunkenness (which occurs . . ." Chris Baker, Dhiravat Na Pombejra, Alfons van der Kraan, and David K. Wyatt, *Van Vliet's Siam* (Chiang Mai: Silkworm Books, 2005), 116.

265   "a mandarin of the Dutch king." Bhawan, *Dutch East India Company*, 67.

266   "having given an exhibition . . ." From the account in F. H. Turpin, *History of the Kingdom of Siam and of The Revolutions That Have Caused the Overthrow of the Empire up to A. D. 1770*, trans B. O. Cartwright (Bangkok: American Presbyterian Mission Press, 1908), originally published in French in 1771, 29.

266 "Vile tyrant! You can . . ." Turpin, *History*, 29.

Chapter 24

268 "In that year, . . ." From the *Phraratchaphongsawadan chabap phraratchahatthalekha* [Royal chronicles of Siam: Royal autograph version] (Bangkok: Fine Arts Department, 1991), quoted in "Narai," *Wikipedia*.

— "The King is below . . ." This remark by the Jesuit missionary Guy Tachard is quoted in Wood, *A History of Siam*, 215.

271 "In case (which God forbid) . . ." Quoted in Wood, *A History of Siam*, 195.

272 "The whole region of Tenasserim . . ." From missionary Jacques de Bourges's account, quoted in Dirk van der Cruysse, "Aspects of Siamese-French Relations during the Seventeenth Century," *Journal of the Siam Society* 80, no. 1 (1992): 65.

274 "guide him into . . ." From an account of a Persian mission to Ayutthaya in 1685. Quoted in Bhawan, *Dutch East India Company*, 135.

274–75 "The food of the Siamese . . ." From *The Ship of Sulaimān*, quoted in van der Cruysse, "Aspects of Siamese-French relations," 66.

275 "if he were ever to . . ." Wood, *A History of Siam*, 197.

Chapter 25

276 "Although the prince devotes . . ." Nicolas Gervaise, *The Natural and Political History of the Kingdom of Siam*, trans. John Villiers (Bangkok: White Lotus, 1989; originally published in French in 1688), 209–10.

277 "He was one of those . . ." From Abbé de Choisy's *Mémories pour servir à l'historie de Louis XIV*, quoted in Michael Smithies, ed., *Three Military Accounts of the 1688 "Revolution" in Siam*, Itineria Asiatica (Bangkok: Orchid Press), 12.

278 "keys of the kingdom." From an account based on French sources in van der Cruysse, "Aspects of Siamese-French Relations," 67.

278–79 "I regret that the King . . ." Recorded by Phaulkon, quoted in Turpin, *History*, 45–46.

281–82 "It is unfortunate for you . . ." Turpin, *History*, 69–70.

286 "Sire, the time for repining . . ." Turpin, *History*, 77.

287 "Alas they do not consider . . ." Turpin, *History*, 76.

288 Farewell for ever madame. . . ." Turpin, *History*, 78.

288   "Soon after his silver chair . . ." Recorded in Engelbert, *A Description of the Kingdom of Siam, 1690* (Bangkok: White Orchid Press, 1987; first published in 1727), 32.

—   "H. M. King Narai was dressed . . ." Recorded by Chevalier de Forbang, a member of a mission from the court of Louis XIV to King Narai. Quoted in "The Biography of H.M. King Narai the Great," website of Lopburi Province, trans. Amporn Samboonying, ed. Timothy Noble, accessed December 19, 2016, http://www.lopburi.go.th.

289   "Well, can you not put up . . ." Turpin, *History*, 32.

Chapter 26

293–94   "It is with the greatest disgust . . ." Turpin, *History*, 79.

296   "I am about to die. . . ." Turpin, *History*, 85.

—   "Well, why is he dead? . . ." Turpin, *History*, 87.

297   "Are you unaware who . . ." Turpin, *History*, 90.

—   "abolish the vestiges of . . ." This threat was recorded in Jean Vollant des Verquains's *Histoire de la révolution de Siam, arrivée en l'année 1688*, published in 1691. Quoted in Smithies, *Three Military Accounts*, 50n97; in turn in "Siege of Bangkok," *Wikipedia*.

299   "The noblemen, who are . . ." From a description by resident Dutch merchant Nicolas de Roij, quoted in Bhawan, *Dutch East India Company*, 118.

300   "The traders are reduced to . . ." Quoted in Anthony Reid, "The Crisis of the Seventeenth Century in Southeast Asia," in *The General Crisis of the Seventeenth Century*, 2nd ed., ed. Geoffrey Parker and Lesley M. Smith (New York: Routledge, 1997), 227.

306   "We believe . . . that the King . . ." Bhawan, *Dutch East India Company*, 175.

—   "the best horse from . . ." From a VOC document by Aarnout Cleur, quoted in Dhiravat Na Pombejra, "Javanese Horses for the Court of Ayutthaya," in *Breeds of Empire: The 'Invention' of the Horse in Southeast Asia and Southern Africa 1500–1950*, ed. Greg Bankoff and Sandra Swart (Copenhagen: NIAS, 2007), 70.

Chapter 27

308–9   "At that time, the King . . ." From *The Chronicle of Ayutthaya*, Phra Chanthanumat (Choem) edition. Quoted in "Suriyen-thrathibodi," *Wikipedia*.

Chapter 28

316–17 "It is said that the people . . ." From the 1688 account of French Jesuit missionary Nicolas Gervaise, quoted in Hung-Guk Cho, "Thai-Malay Conflicts in the Sixteenth and Seventeenth Centuries" *International Area Review* 2, no. 2 (1999).

319 "one of the most magnificent . . ." Quoted in Bhawan, *Dutch East India Company*, 182.

Chapter 29

324 "known for his cruelty . . ." As described by Prince Chula Chakrabongse, grandson of King Rama V, in his royal history *Lords of Life: The Paternalistic Monarchy of Bangkok, 1782–1932* (London: Alvin Redman, 1960), 68.

325–26 "Seven days later . . ." P. E. Pieris, trans., *Religious Intercourse between Ceylon and Siam in the Eighteenth Century* (Bangkok: Vajirañāna National Library, 1908), 17–18. Quoted in Piriya Krairiksh, "A Revised Dating of Ayudhya Architecture," *Journal of the Siam Society* 80, no. 1 (1992): 41–43.

327 "Those who smoke, consume, or . . ." Quoted in Kasian Tejapira, "Pigtail: A PreHistory of Chineseness in Siam, in *Alternate Identities: The Chinese of Contemporary Thailand*, ed. Tong Chee Kiong and Chan Kwok-bun (Singapore: Brill; Times Academic Press, 2001), 55.

328 "The majority of the population . . ." Observation by Nicolas Gervaise in his history of Siam, quoted in Warangkana Nibhatsukit, "The Emergence of Proto-Entrepreneurial Groups in the City of Ayutthaya during the 17th–18th Centuries," *Silpakorn University Journal of Social Sciences, Humanities, and Arts* 6, no. 1–2 (2006): 113, http://www.journal.su.ac.th/index.php/suij/article/viewFile/9/7.

330 "When virtues ten fall deaf . . ." The Long Song Prophecy translated by Richard D. Cushman and David K. Wyatt for the *Journal of the Siam Society*, quoted in Chris Baker and Pasuk Phongpaichit, *A History of Thailand* (Cambridge: Cambridge University Press, 2009), 21.

Chapter 30

343 "The sinful Burmese ravaged . . ." Account by Maha Sura Singhanat, the brother of King Rama I and his first upparat, quoted in Victor Lieberman, *Strange Parallels: Southeast Asia in Global Context*,

c. 800–1830, vol. 1, *Integration on the Mainland* (Cambridge: Cambridge University Press, 2003), 327.

343 "The fall of Ayudhya . . ." Written by Somdet Phra Phonnarat in the years following the fall of Ayutthaya, quoted in Sunait, "Image of the Burmese Enemy," 90.

344 "On the 28th April 1767 . . ." Turpin, *History*, 167–68.